THE AVENGERS
OF THE KING

THE AVENGERS
OF THE KING

By
Jean Drault

Translated from the French by
Ryan P. Plummer

LAMBFOUNT
St. Louis, Missouri

Published in 2022 by Lambfount · St. Louis, Missouri
www.lambfount.com

Jean Drault [pseudonym of Alfred Gendrot], *The Avengers of the
King*, translated by Ryan P. Plummer.

Originally published in French under the title *Les vengeurs du
roi,* appearing serially in the Paris-based semiweekly periodical
L'Ouvrier from 3 December 1910 to 4 March 1911 and in its
initial book edition in 1911.

ISBN 978-1-7328734-2-1

Printing and manufacturing information for this book may be
found on the final page.

Contents

Part One:

The Two Faces

Chapter 1

What Reaper? What Harvest?

THEY WERE NUMEROUS in Paris, the houses where on the night of January 20-21, 1793, they prayed for the soul of the king, who was soon to die.

Doors closed and shutters shut, so that the Convention's spies might not see the lights nor hear the whisperings of the prayers for the dying, the noble family in its old mansion, the bourgeois family in its home, the artisan family in its modest lodging, as well as the poor in their hovels, offered up to heaven a myriad of ardent prayers for the soul of Louis XVI, and beseeched God to work a miracle to save the King of France during those final hours separating him from the scaffold.

Despite all the lies amassed by the propagandists of the Revolution, never was Paris or France so royalist as on that night. And this moral atmosphere especially weighed heavy on the executioners. This was evident hours later in the considerable precautions they took to transport the king from Temple Prison to Revolution Square.

If it truly had been about executing a traitor whose death all the people demanded, why were there so many cannons and cavalrymen? And why so many guards marching about or standing in formation?

In an old mansion on quiet Rue de Savoie, parallel to the Seine, on the river's left bank, a family, gathered in the main drawing room with its faded wallpaper and its high windows hermetically hung with old curtains, was kneeling before a crucifix placed on a table.

On the ebony cross, an old ivory Christ with patinated tones stood out plainly and clearly. The holy image reflected the light of two candles on either side, which were planted in heavy candlesticks of chiseled copper.

A priest was there saying the prayers for the dying, and responding to them was a lady in mourning, three men, one of them aged and seemingly the father of the other two, and two young women, one wearing a black silk dress and one of those twilled fichus that would later be called a Charlotte Corday. The other wore a simple dress and white bonnet typical of women laborers of the time.

Everyone, prostrate and pleading before the Man-God, seemed drowned in sorrow. Though they uttered the responses so softly, and though the murmuring of their voices reciting the Latin verses was so discreet, fervor pierced their intonations. The utterances broke through the silence, sonorous and firm. They came from the heart, and a kind of fever made them resound. With each moment, the supplications grew so ardent, and the voices seemed to want to rise so high, as to better reach God and do Him violence, that the priest interrupted to say, "Not so loud, brethren! They might hear us outside! Let us be resigned and hide our hope to see our unfortunate prince saved! Let us remember that nothing happens except by the will of the Almighty, and let us pray for the son of St. Louis as if his destiny had already been fulfilled! May God henceforth have mercy on his soul! He will save him if such is His will. And His will be done!"

He resumed reciting the office of the dead. And the voices responded to him, as though appeased.

The individuals who prayed thus in the old ancestral mansion almost all belonged to the de Lézardière family.

The lady in mourning was Baroness de Lézardière. She halfway hid her black locks, barely streaked with some white hairs, beneath a widow's bonnet. The aged man was the baron. He was dressed in a black velvet suit and wore a powdered peruke, the queue of which was tied with a black ribbon.

The two young men were their sons, Paul and Sylvestre de Lézardière.

The young girl in the black silk dress and Charlotte Corday fichu was Mademoiselle de Sainte-Pazanne, one of their cousins, aged seventeen, and the only survivor of a family that six months earlier had provided the first victims to the Revolution's so-called "excesses," for one absolved the Revolution of everything! Its normal practices and policies of stealing and bloodshed were simply termed "excesses."

The Count and Countess de Sainte-Pazanne had been besieged in their château in the outskirts of Nantes by some of the city's sans-culottes. An area poacher, who had previously run into some trouble with one of the de Sainte-Pazannes' gamekeepers, led them there. The guardsmen and servants had offered resistance and were massacred.

The count had stood his ground and, shutting himself inside a tower, used up all his ammunition against the assailants. He was ultimately taken and speared to death in front of his wife, who, half-mad, perished in turn in the burning château. Around the château, the assassins, after having inebriated themselves, danced a diabolical saraband, as around a bonfire, driving back into the inferno all those who had escaped the massacre.

Adèle de Sainte-Pazanne was then in Paris at the home of her mother's elder sister, Baroness de Lézardière, who herself driven away with her husband and sons from her château in the outskirts of La Roche-sur-Yon, by the threats of sans-culottes, had come to take refuge in the old Parisian mansion that one of her uncles had bequeathed to her long ago.

The young girl had only found the strength to survive the horrible event that orphaned her in the care and consolation of her uncle and aunt, and let us say right away, in a more tender sentiment she experienced for the elder of her cousins, Paul de Lézardière, a sentiment she believed mutual.

This had started out as one of those holiday flings, as sometimes takes shape between cousins. A lasting affection followed from it. The parents had allowed it to develop. Though no promises had been made by either, they were considered engaged.

Tall, slender, and blonde, Adèle de Sainte-Pazanne, beneath her somewhat haughty exterior, possessed a soul that was loyal, spontaneous, kind, and good. A prodigious energy could be perceived beneath her elegant, refined, socialite exterior and her sweetest blue eyes.

The other young woman was named Cécile Renault. She was a humble day-laboring seamstress whose name history would one day record.

She was at this moment aged nineteen, of rather insignificant appearance, nice rather than pretty, and her comportment manifesting an evident tendency to coquetry. Daughter of a small-scale papermaker named Antoine Renault, whose shop was situated at the corner of Rue de la Lanterne and Rue des Marmousets, a stone's throw from the Palais de Justice, Cécile had lost her mother when she was very little. There remained as family, besides her father, three brothers and one aunt.

One of the brothers, Jacques, tended to the modest papermaking business. The two others had been soldiers for two years. The aunt of Cécile, who was her father's elder sister, was a nun living in seclusion on Rue de Babylone.

The Renaults were taciturn, quiet, orderly, and frugal people, devoid of ambition. They were present for most of the drama of the Revolution, not understanding much of it, like almost all Parisians, and firmly resolved not to get themselves mixed up in all the trouble. We are speaking for the two men, for Cécile was to get mixed up in it, and drag them in behind her. They missed the old regime, during which the atmosphere was peaceful, one was happy, business went well, and one could go to Mass without being looked upon with suspicion. But they kept this sentiment to themselves, without manifesting it in a way that was inopportune or threatening to their safety.

They were fairly well-off. While his son tended to the paper business, the Renault father, as the principal tenant of the building in which he lived, showed apartments, gave and received leave notices, declined repairs, or discussed with people in the building whether it was necessary to redo a fireplace or to rehang wallpaper.

Cécile could have lived without working. If she was a day-laboring seamstress, it was out of a need for change, to see new faces, and to replenish her personal nest egg which was always tapped into for outfits, trinkets, fineries, and so-called "frivolities." It was also, as we shall see, for a more serious motive.

It remains for us to say who the priest was. He was Father Edgeworth de Firmont, a friend of the de Lézardière family, the very one who, a few hours later, was to accompany Louis XVI to his death and help him complete his Calvary.

The room's gilded clock tolled two in the morning. In the fireplace, a half-consumed firebrand rolled out of place. Cécile placed it back over the dying fire with the tongs.

Outside, the January north wind was blowing, cutting and nasty, chilling both soul and bone, shaking the windows, and descending through the chimney to redden the embers and scatter the ashes.

Everyone was quiet, lost in their thoughts, in dismay at the hour that was approaching.

Cadenced steps sounded from afar on the pavement, disrupting the street's tragic silence. They came nearer.

The baroness raised her head, placed her hand on her heart, and her features, so pure and so beautiful, became marred by a kind of nervous tension.

The baron went to cautiously lift the corner of one of the curtains that was sealing off the windows.

"Patrolmen!" he whispered. "They are passing by."

"They are crisscrossing all over Paris!" said Sylvestre de Lézardière.

The baroness had sat down. Adèle de Sainte-Pazanne offered her a glass of mint water, saying, "Drink, Aunt. It will go away."

"Thank you," she said, pushing away the glass. "It's passed. But this accursed heart will no longer allow me any rest. At the least noise, it leaps in my breast and pounds on it... I will die from it!... It's been this way ever since the horrible death of my poor little priest, at Les Carmes."

The eldest son of Baron and Baroness de Lézardière, a deacon at the seminary of Saint-Sulpice, had, in fact, been massacred at Les Carmes Prison the preceding September. His mother had nearly died from the trauma. She had contracted a heart illness that the emotions of this terrible period did not help mitigate.

Father de Firmont, after a large sign of the cross, stood up. He said, "Madame, you are overexerting yourself, as sick as you are! Take a little bit of rest, at least. I must go to the Temple to say the last Mass that His Majesty will hear, and I must remain fasting. But you, my friends: Drink! Eat! Strengthen yourselves!"

In a hushed voice, addressing the baron, he added: "If my duty is to be painful, your own work will be very hard!"

"For my two sons, yes!" said the baron. "For me, no!" He then added with a certain bitterness, "*He* has not deigned to summon me!"

"*He* only wants young people, who are supple, deft, intrepid!" answered the priest. "*He* is perhaps reserving for you other tasks for which not only courage is required, but also the prudence and judgment of ripe age!"

"Perhaps!"

Cécile opened a door connecting to the baroness's room. The baroness, leaning on the laborer's arm, withdrew. Adèle opened another door connecting to the mansion's dining room.

In this latter room, on a table lit with two candles, were bottles, carafes, and leftovers from a roasted chicken served at the previous evening's supper, next to a stack of plates. An old servant, who was not in livery, was setting the table in summary fashion.

Adèle, having gone to help Cécile put the baroness to bed, returned to the drawing room, then drew her cousin Paul with her to the far end of the dining room before any of the others had yet entered. Her blue eyes projected strange gleams, and her beautiful face appeared animated with extraordinary emotion. It seemed the face of a queen in fury.

Paul, a young cavalryman, nicely dressed in his formal suit, his hair unpowdered according to the new fashion, and his face young and fresh, accented with a thin, nascent mustache, seemed at this moment like a schoolboy caught out by his teacher.

But before elaborating on what took place between these two young people whom their family considered engaged, we must return to the baroness's room, where the outside noises were more muffled than in the drawing room, where the windows were draughtproofed by taffeta curtains of faded crimson hues, where the wood fire burning in the fireplace only emitted subdued light, owing to a screen of coated wood decorated with a taffeta sheet of the same shade, which obscured the brightness of the crackling fire.

A single candlestick holding a wax candle stood on a tiny antique three-legged table, close to a large white-lacquered Louis XVI bed. The small flame was reflected from afar in the trumeau mirror above the fireplace. This discreet light was enough for Cécile to assist the sick one, who was sitting up, to take in a cup of warm bouillon.

In a low voice, the baroness told her, "They are going to worry about you at home for not being back yet, my little one."

"No, Madame Baroness. My father and brother know that I am with you; they aren't worried. I couldn't have left you today! And on Rue de la Lanterne, I wouldn't have slept a wink! Staying awake here to keep watch, as much as... Unless I am bothering you?"

"Poor Cécile! Bothering us?... I love you like one of my own children! And what is more, I don't know why!... You radiate sympathy."

"Madame Baroness is very kind!... I also have much affection for Madame Baroness... And I would die for her, as I would be happy to die this morning for the king, if I were a man!"

She became excited as she spoke. The insignificant grisette had gradually transformed into a kind of inspired being. As if she had been ashamed to expose her interior sentiments, always hidden beneath her little cover of indifference and frivolity, she quickly smiled and said, "But Madame Baroness will find that I don't carry myself in a way that is appropriate for my condition?"

"What are you saying, my child?" replied Madame de Lézardière. "On the contrary, you just betrayed and revealed sentiments that unite us and have created for us, without our realizing it, a common atmosphere. But something surprises me..." She hesitated, and then said in a lower voice, "You know then that they are to attempt something to save the king?"

"I know it, yes, Madame!"

"And how do you know it? Is it a secret that you overheard by chance, in which case I would worry for my husband, my sons, and my friends, as that would mean this secret has been poorly kept... Or rather, *are you involved in it?*"

"I *am*, Madame! And this secret is well-kept. One thing will tell you everything: I often go on workdays to the home of Marie Grandmaison, on Rue Ménars, the housekeeper of..."

"Shh!" said the baroness, placing her finger over her lips.

"Of the one whose name we must not even mention among us, for fear a strange ear might hear it. I know this also, Madame... What is more, if you had wanted to know sooner what I am going to tell you, you needed only to have let casually escape from your lips, without even looking at me, this question that is no doubt of quite little importance: 'Will the reaper come?'"

"Indeed!" said the baroness intently. "And how would you then answer?"

"If I didn't answer, you would say, 'She isn't in on it.' But you would immediately be edified if I were to answer, 'When the harvest is ripe!'"

"Oh, dear little one!" said the baroness, pulling her close to her heart. "This man, this friend of the king's, has known then how to draw so many hearts to him, even among the people!"

"Especially among the people, Madame! And you will see so!"

"Then I have confidence! Oh, if it pleases God to permit his rescue! Leave me to pray, my little one! To pray for the king, for him, for this man of courage and sacrifice, for my two sons who will perhaps be slain alongside him in a little while... Oh, good

God, have mercy! Have mercy on us all! One of my sons has already died for remaining faithful to Your law! May his death ransom us all! May his blood prevent the shedding of other innocent blood! Have mercy! Have mercy!"

"Amen!" said Cécile quietly.

And leaving the baroness to her ardent prayer which softly continued, the young seamstress left the room, whose door she silently closed, and found herself in the dining room without Paul de Lézardière or his cousin hearing her enter. The old servant had withdrawn. The two young people believed themselves alone.

Chapter 2

The Police Officer

CÉCILE'S SITUATION WAS very awkward. Without seeking it, her eyes and ears became witnesses to a stormy and intimate argument that certainly would not have continued if her presence had been suspected.

Paul and Mademoiselle de Sainte-Pazanne were so immersed in their argument that they failed to notice they were no longer alone.

On the other hand, the discreet way Cécile had parted from the sick one might make one think she had slipped in there to listen. This thought initially prevented her from signaling her presence by moving a chair or letting out a cough, thereby furthering the wrong impression.

She thus had to hear a part of the conversation already in progress.

Mademoiselle de Sainte-Pazanne was very emotional, and it was with a half-sorrowful and half-indignant tone that she said to Paul, "Stop floundering!... It is over, completely over, this romance begun in the country, in more peaceful times and under clearer skies!... You no longer love me!"

"Why do you say that?" answered Paul. "What gives you the right to say such a thing?... There are oaths between us! You are my fiancée! Still my fiancée!... And never has a Lézardière broken his vow..."

"Let me respond to that, dear cousin... You are rationalizing—you are defending yourself like an old lawyer, in a matter where the least cry of the heart would be far more

12

eloquent!... This cry, you would have uttered it in times past, back when you used to write me those sweet letters, whose secret you have forgotten..."

"I no longer need to write you! You live with us!"

"Let me finish!" she said impatiently. "This cry of your indignant heart, I was waiting for it!... And it did not at all spring forth when I told you at the beginning, 'Paul, you no longer love me!' You remained dazed, without saying anything, probably because you had nothing to say!"

"Oh..."

"Excuse me," she said, imperiously cutting him off to resume her indictment. "You told me you would keep your oath. But I do not want you to keep your oath, Monsieur, if it is just because you have made it!... I don't want to be married out of heroism!... Am I ugly? Am I a freak?... No, no!... I would want to be married because I was loved, it is as simple as that! You no longer love me!... Goodbye!... I release you from your oath..."

"But I don't want to be released from it! It is not at all difficult for me to keep this oath, I swear to you!"

"It was just a pretend oath anyhow," she added without listening to him, "the kind of oath you make when you are fourteen years old. We played little husband and wife... That is all it was!"

"Adèle," Paul resumed after a brief silence, "you are hurting me infinitely! And why would it be that I no longer love you?"

"Because you love another!" she said impetuously, as if this accusation soothed her.

"Me?"

"Yes, you!"

"Then, in heaven's name, who is it?"

"Well, do I actually know this?... I feel this! I sense it! My intuition tells me! This noble conspiracy you are a part of, it has flung you outside of yourself, far away from my heart... Who knows in what milieus it obliges you to go?... Oh, this blasted Revolution has not yet had me shed enough tears!... It took from me my dear father and my saintly mother... It is now taking my fiancé!"

Mademoiselle de Sainte-Pazanne, as though no longer capable of holding back her tears and preserving her dignity on command, let her head fall into her hands and sobbed in desperation.

Very gently, Paul sought to spread apart her pretty, pearly-nailed fingers, between which large, warm tears were flowing. Then, in a serious tone, he said, "I saw you cry like this before, two years ago, on the day we went back, at the end of vacation, you to your convent school, and I to my regiment. But you were only fifteen years old, and it was not on a night like this, a few hours before some business in which I might lose my life in the king's service..."

She stood up straight, pale white, her big beautiful eyes open and dilated from the horror of the future she caught sight of. She saw before her something like an abyss in which all her happiness might be swallowed up. She then took a spontaneous and charming turn: "Paul, you are right!... I am a criminal and a fool right now, for having put my little chagrins before this great sorrow that is enveloping us all, which is now like the air we breathe. But it is so intermingled with my own!... It is a bout of fever that has taken hold of me... I saw you dying, and it was a name other than my own that you pronounced." And muzzling with her pretty hand her fiancé's mouth, which opened to again protest this doggedly persistent accusation, she added, "Oh, accuse only my imagination! And forgive me! I have been very bad! Very, very bad! You are about to involve yourself in some dreadful business! And here I am scolding you, getting on your nerves! I blame myself!"

She was smiling now, through her tears. Paul gave her a prolonged kiss on the hand and said to her with infinite tenderness, "Pray that I escape from danger and come back to you. Only death could separate me from you!"

And he rejoined in the drawing room his father, his brother, and Father de Firmont, who were speaking in hushed voices.

Was there in this new pledge Paul de Lézardière made to his fiancée, who perhaps seems to the reader a little too young to play one of the great abandoned women from the tragedies of old, an insufficiently convincing tone? Behind this pledge, did Mademoiselle de Sainte-Pazanne's female intuition detect more of a policy of appeasement rather than fervent enthusiasm?

Silently, she started to cry again, until a tenderly mocking voice near her uttered, "Come now, come now, what's the matter?"

It was Cécile Renault who intervened, with both superiority of age and the familiarity allowed her in a home where one sensed, according to the baroness's expression, sympathy radiating from this honest, upright plebeian's pure and ingenuous soul.

"You were here!" said Adèle, in a kind of fright.

"I was here despite myself, yes!"

"And you overheard?"

"Everything!"

"Oh well, it's just as well that you did!... I so much need to confide in someone!... Oh, my poor Cécile, how miserable I am!... He does not love me anymore!... I am no fool... He is trying to delude himself!... But I can see it clearly. He would not be spending entire days outside! What is drawing him out there?"

"But you know very well!... At the very least, you have an idea!"

"And then... how sad he is, he is so pensive!... No, no, I am no longer the one whose presence is enough to make his face light up with a smile... I was that one... Another has taken my place in his heart..."

"Keep repeating that to him and you'll end up convincing him of that!" said Cécile, smiling. "So, he supposedly found a siren on his path?... And this siren supposedly made him forget the big blue eyes, the blonde hair, and all of this pretty person in front of me drowning in tears?... Come on!... This siren does not exist! In any case, if you would be sensible and if you would stop crying, I could perhaps promise to try to get you a definite answer about this matter!"

"Really?"

"Really!... But look at how illogical you're being!... Because if she were to exist, this siren, it's very disappointing news I would be giving you... However, at just the thought of knowing, look at how happy you've become!"

"Tell me, do you know where he goes? And what people he associates with?"

"He goes where he is told to go! He associates with the people he is assigned to associate with! He and his brother, like your uncle, you know, are involved in some serious business!"

"I know they are conspiring. They hide things from me. But why? I am not a little girl anymore!"

"You yourself would be willing to conspire as well?"

"Why not? I would be happy and proud to risk my life like them!... There are moments when I so much want to die... My death, at least, could be useful for the cause of religion and king... And besides, what a powerful way to get my mind off my sorrows! I'll go where he goes..."

"And you would know where he goes! Oh, you don't miss a trick!" exclaimed Cécile, who could not stop from laughing. "When Mademoiselle gets an idea in her head, she doesn't let go of it!"

"But," asked Mademoiselle de Sainte-Pazanne, "you yourself are also conspiring then?"

After some hesitation, Cécile Renault answered with much seriousness: "Yes, I am conspiring!... I hate the Republic and the impious people who have made it!... I can't fight like a man, but everyone in their own sphere can do useful work and contribute to the common plan."

"Everyone in their own sphere? Except me, in mine!" said Mademoiselle de Sainte-Pazanne sadly.

"And why would that be?"

"Of what use could I be, kept here as I am with my aunt and reduced strictly to the role of sharing in her anguish?"

"There is still time for you to have a role to play... The man who started the party against the Revolution is building around it a vast network, like an enormous web."

"You know this man?"

Cécile signaled yes, slowly and seriously. She was not at all joking.

"What is his name? My aunt, uncle, and cousins never speak of him in front of me!"

She politely gestured that one was not allowed to speak his name. She then said aloud, "The person you see in front of you is but one mesh in this vast net he has woven, just one little mesh. This man has the right, I have given it to him, to dispose of my life, to throw into the battle he is waging the lives of all his confederates as if they were nothing. When the fisherman casts his net, what does it matter if some meshes are torn, so long as the fish caught is worth the trouble. We are all meshes of his net. Our individual lives don't matter."

"And his own life, does it matter to him?"

"He risks it every day. He is going to risk it again this morning… But he always escapes. It is as though he is marked with the seal of God!"

"Oh, how I would like to offer him my own life!" exclaimed Adèle de Sainte-Pazanne. "Can I not also become one of these little meshes in this great net?"

"You can!" said Cécile, almost softly, as if she were scared to be heard by others.

She seemed to have directed the conversation for the purpose of getting to this point. She added, in a lighter tone, as if she wanted to change the subject, when she was continuing with her original purpose, "Has anyone ever told you that you have something of the queen in your eyes, in your hair, your gait, your height, and in the majesty of your overall bearing?"

"Yes! I have been told that… But why are you asking?"

"Oh, nothing!… This resemblance to the Temple's captive crossed my mind. And I was thinking that in this moment there are in her eyes tears just as in yours! May God want the resemblance to stop there, and that your fiancé not have, this very morning, the same fate as her husband!"

Adèle's hand tightly clutched that of Cécile's. "You don't believe then in the success of what they're undertaking?"

"I know that they will try to do the impossible!... But is the harvest ripe?"

"What harvest?"

"I will tell you, Mademoiselle, when you are one of us and our password can be confided to you... It won't take long..."

"Thank you, thank you!" the young girl said joyfully.

"Don't thank me!... It's one more life that I am risking!... It's one more life that I am bringing to the great leader... But what is one life, if the Counter-Revolution triumphs?"

"I gladly offer mine!" exclaimed Mademoiselle de Sainte-Pazanne. "I now have a goal in life!... I am going to risk my life alongside my fiancé!"

Her eyes scintillated with joy. She breathed the air with greater vigor and seemed a young warhorse eager to rush into battle.

"Contain yourself!" Cécile said. "And don't let your uncle, aunt, or cousins suspect a thing!... They wanted to keep you out of danger... And I am betraying their trust by bringing you into the bloody melee. But they will forgive me—it is for the cause."

"Was it right," said Adèle, "that I was the only one from my family not able to bring my efforts to the service of the king and religion?"

"Shh!"

The priest, the baron, and his two sons entered the dining room.

"I will relay His Majesty's last wishes concerning the queen!" said the priest, concluding the long conversation he had had with the baron.

The baron sat down at the table. The old servant entered and presented a dish to his master. Cécile and Mademoiselle de Sainte-Pazanne poured drinks.

So many thoughts weighed heavy on the minds of those present, at the sight of the priest who was going to witness the death of the King of France, that they only spoke softly, and the servant and two young women walked on tiptoe.

But Paul and Sylvestre, despite the emotions hovering in the air, could not help showing a certain feverish enthusiasm. They felt an immense pride at being involved in this dangerous plot; their warrior blood was clamoring inside them in anticipation of battle.

The two showed each other the mysterious summons they each received the prior evening from a confederate. On a common blue paper were written these simple words: *7 a.m., the Cléry terreplein.*

Four o'clock tolled from the drawing room clock when the two young men who were hungrily eating suddenly looked at each other. The knocker at the mansion's entrance door had sounded.

"Who could that be at this hour?" said the priest.

"I have an idea!" responded Paul de Lézardière. "It must be Citizen Sévignon."

"Who is this Citizen Sévignon?" asked the baron.

Sylvestre, the youngest of Monsieur de Lézardière's sons, satisfied his father's curiosity with these words: "It's the Marquis de La Guiche. He's hiding under the name of Sévignon, like we ourselves are hiding under the name of Robert. He is living at... But by the way, Cécile Renault must know him—he lives in the building where the Renault father is the principal tenant, at the corner of Rue de la Lanterne and Rue des Marmousets."

"I do indeed know Citizen Sévignon!" said Cécile. "But for the last eight days, it is not only his name he has been hiding; he has also been hiding himself! We have not seen him since, not my father, my brother, or myself."

"As for ourselves," said Sylvestre, "it was about eight days ago that we became acquainted with him. Right, Paul?"

"Yes!" said Paul. "At the Palais-Royal."

"At the home of whom?" asked Adèle de Sainte-Pazanne.

Paul's entire face blushed and he did not answer, and his fiancée noted it well. But his brother responded in his place: "In a gambling house where interesting things are heard about what is going on with the enemy."

"Was Citizen Sévignon summoned?" asked the baron in a low voice.

"Yes!" said Paul. "I saw his summons yesterday evening. And he asked if he could stop by to take us this morning."

The old servant showed in the porter, who explained, "It is a certain Citizen Sévignon who is waiting down below for Messieurs Robert."

"It is him!" said Paul. "Tell him we will be down right away."

"You are leaving already?" asked the father.

"We are! It's better that we do. And Citizen Sévignon might have reasons for coming to get us so early—three hours before the rendezvous!"

"Come now, my sons," said the baron, his voice trembling with emotion, "give me a hug!"

They silently embraced.

"Your mother is sleeping!" added Monsieur de Lézardière. "Don't wake her. Go!"

"Cousin," said Mademoiselle de Sainte-Pazanne as she approached Paul, "kiss me and forgive me!"

She appeared radiant with hope, and her heart, which started to race, rushed an influx of blood to her cheeks and temples, rendering her exquisitely beautiful.

She offered Paul her forehead, on which he planted a long and tender kiss.

Then the two young men took their swords; they each loaded their belts with a pair of pistols, threw large coats over their shoulders, and left the drawing room.

Cécile lighted their path on the stairway, but while taking care to hide her face with a scarf, as if she feared a draft of cold air.

Down below waiting for them was a man in a gray coat, with a felt hat pulled down over his eyes. Cécile, without being seen by this man, positioned herself to get a good look at him, but was unable to do so right away, for he so carefully hid himself as if he were suspicious of something.

"Good morning, Citizen Sévignon!" said Paul.

"Good morning, Citizens Robert!" answered Sévignon. "I am here early!... It had to be this way! They say the police are trying to stop a large number of us. We are anticipating them..."

All three exited, and the heavy door slammed shut in the darkness with a lugubrious thud.

"Good heavens!" Cécile said to herself in a hushed voice.

As she went back up, she passed Father de Firmont in the stairway. Having taken off his cassock, he was now clothed in an old frock coat and black cloak and was on his way to the Temple, the final prison of the royal family.

For a second time the door echoed as it shut, when Cécile Renault, breathless and a look of terror on her face, approached the baron, who was back alone in the drawing room, poking the fire and plagued by somber thoughts.

"Monsieur Baron!"

"What is it?"

"Something terrible..."

"What?" he said, standing up, overtaken by worry.

"The man who came to get your sons is not Citizen Sévignon, not the Marquis de La Guiche!"

"It isn't your father's tenant?"

"It's another tenant, but not Citizen Sévignon... The man with whom they left is Sénar, an employee of the revolutionary committees!"

"Good heavens! He has gained the trust of my sons!"

"By passing himself for Citizen Sévignon who has disappeared, been arrested or killed perhaps... And it was impossible to warn them. He concealed himself, and I didn't recognize him until he went out the door and it closed behind him!"

"And this man has a summons?"

"Citizen Sévignon's was passed on to him, no doubt!"

"Everything is ruined!... There is a traitor in the conspiracy!"

"Also," said Cécile, "these summonses should not have been passed on without saying the password!"

"You know it then?" he asked, gripping her arms tightly.

Then, looking at her intently, he uttered in a low voice, "Will the reaper come?"

"When the harvest is ripe!" answered Cécile, looking intently at him in turn.

"Oh, my dear child!" he said. "You did not tell us!"

"The reaper wants us to be discreet, even among ourselves!"

"That is true!"

He reached out his hand towards a bell. She stopped his hand.

"What are you doing, Monsieur Baron?"

"I am calling Joseph to get my coat, then running to the Cléry terreplein, denouncing the traitor, stabbing him if necessary, and preventing disaster!"

"No! Stay!... I am going there!"

"You?"

"You have not been summoned, so it is here that he wants you to stay!"

"Nevertheless!"

"I am going to try to catch up with your sons and warn them. Then, from there, I will run to Rue Ménars to report to the leader what is happening. He will know better than anyone what needs to be done, and a woman like myself can pass through anywhere that a man having the bearing of a former officer like yourself would be noticed."

She ran to the anteroom, threw a mantle over her clothing, darted down the stairway, and then, once out on the street, spiritedly flung herself onto the trail of the two brothers and their dangerous companion.

Chapter 3

The Cléry Terreplein

LEAVING THE WARM atmosphere of the de Lézardière mansion and bitten by the chill of the north wind blowing through narrow Rue de Savoie, Cécile Renault shivered. But she bravely pulled the hood of her mantle over her head.

This mantle was lilac-colored calico trimmed with a thin layer of common fur, and the wind, rushing inside it, made the flaps fly up on either side of her. She resembled a seagull struggling against a tempest, and this comparison was just as true morally as it was physically.

She reached Rue des Grands-Augustins, turned right, arrived at the quay, passed in front of the abandoned and disused Grands-Augustins Monastery, and started crossing the Pont Neuf, poorly lit by lanterns on some gallows posts which one lowered and raised with the aid of a rope. This rope, in these humanitarian and fraternal times, sometimes swapped the lantern it held for a man, a suspect condemned by popular justice.

The wind, which blew in gusts, made the pulleys screech and swung the oil lamps, projecting onto the pavement eerie, shape-shifting shadows.

Over the Seine was a thick, heavy fog that was hiding the water. In a few hours, it would lift and envelop Paris in a veil of mourning. History would refer to it as the fog of January 21.

At the far end of the bridge, three silhouettes were moving further away. And Cécile was delighted: "It's them!... Sénar is in the middle!"

23

As she had promised the baron, she wanted to approach and warn one of the two brothers without the committee police officer knowing. But how to do so? The false Sévignon was apparently not in a hurry to separate from his two companions. Cécile shuddered at the thought of him turning them over to a patrol or to some gendarmes. But two patrols having passed right by them without anything of the sort happening, the three men headed directly towards Rue de Cléry, by way of Rue des Petits-Carreaux, right to the place of the rendezvous. Cécile deduced from this that Sénar's plan, whether acting on his own or following the orders of the committees which had been informed of the plot, was more consequential than she had initially supposed, and that this plan aimed at nothing less than penetrating to the heart of the conspiracy to know its leader and arrest him, a far more significant outcome than locking up, or even putting to death, two lone conspirators like the de Lézardière brothers.

This thought seized her and so forcefully asserted itself in her mind that she said to herself: "It is the leader who must be warned, and right away! Messieurs de Lézardière are probably not in any danger for the time being. They are even useful to a spy as precious guides. And even if they are in danger, it is the leader who must be saved before them, and right away!"

And veering from her trail, she diverted left towards Rue Montmartre, aiming to get to Rue des Filles-Saint-Thomas, then to Rue de la Loi (currently Rue de Richelieu), and then finally to Rue Ménars, a section of which still exists in our modern Paris, between Rue du 4 Septembre and Rue de Richelieu.

As she advanced further towards her destination, she became increasingly aware in the rising fog of an unusual commotion all around her. All throughout the sleeping city, amidst its torpor, the rhythmic steps of marching troops resounded. Artillery batteries quickly traveled Rue des Filles-Saint-Thomas, heading for the boulevards with rumbles of thunder. The burdened wheels pounded on the uneven pavement, and she failed to hear the patrolmen proceeding towards her.

"Who goes there?" shouted the leader.

In response, the seamstress, catching sight of one of those little passages that abound in the narrow streets of old Paris, took it as fast as her legs could carry her and ended up on Rue de la Loi, which she soon exited to take Rue Louvois. Out of breath, she only stopped when she believed she had fully circumvented the patrol.

Of course, she could have given them her name and address, but it would have been difficult to explain her presence so far from home at such an hour of the night. The patrol leader could very well have decided to take her to the police station. And even if they did allow her to proceed, the encounter would have slowed her down, and her time was precious.

After she caught her breath, she went to Rue Sainte-Anne, then named Rue Helvétius, crossed Rue Saint-Augustin, took Rue de Grammont, turned right on Rue Ménars, and then found herself a few steps away from the residence she wanted to enter.

Once there, however, she stopped, stunned. Two Commune gendarmes, equivalent or somewhat close to the municipal guards of our own day (except that those of 1793 had the mentality of sans-culottes and used the informal "you" with everyone), were guarding the entrance to number seven and pacing back and forth.

They noticed her hesitation, and one of the two called out to her: "Where are you going at this hour, beautiful?"

"What's it matter to you, Citizen?" she replied.

"You look like you want to go inside here!" said the second gendarme.

"Possibly!" she answered.

"Do you have some business at the home of the has-been who lives here at number seven?" the first gendarme continued.

She fully composed herself and replied in a firm voice: "What has-been?"

"Don't play stupid, Citizeness! You know very well this house is home to a has-been, and one who is reportedly dangerous, obviously, since we've been sent to guard the front of his door."

"Do you know what you're talking about?" she exclaimed. "This house is home to Citizeness Marie Grandmaison, former actress at the Comédie-Italienne, a known patriot…"

"Yes, but the house is owned by a has-been!"

"Not at all!… This house belongs to Citizeness Grandmaison's brother, the postmaster in Beauvais!"

"My, my, you seem well-informed!… But the Commune must be even better informed than you, as it has assigned us to watch the has-been who lives here!"

"The Commune is mistaken, that's all!… Have fun!"

And concealing with a feigned gaiety the fear that gripped her soul, she boldly went and banged the knocker on the door of the home, which appeared new and spruce. She then waited.

"Why were you hesitating to knock at this door then, if this house is a patriot's, and if your conscience is clear?" asked one of the gendarmes.

"This silliness!… I saw you, and I was scared!"

"Of what?"

"Of anything!… Does one ever know, with a government that randomly arrests people, and without knowing why…"

"Oh, without knowing why!"

"First of all, who are you?" asked the other gendarme.

"I am the seamstress of Citizeness Marie Grandmaison, and I have come to do work at her home…"

"My, you sure are beginning it early, your workday today!"

"I'm a morning person!" responded the young girl.

The door opened. Cécile entered and brusquely shut the door behind her. A woman had opened it for her.

It was Marie Grandmaison, who was indeed a former actress—and presently an ardent conspirator.

She lived on the second floor of the building.

The mysterious personage at the center of the entire Counter-Revolution, whom we will soon introduce, occupied the first floor. This Rue Ménars house had belonged to him. It had been sold a few months earlier to the brother of its tenant, in order to free up his hands and to avoid an eventual confiscation; and the tenant, having gradually become one of the most active members of the conspiracy, was presently the caretaker of the residence, less and less inhabited by its former owner and more and more surveilled by the Commune.

Marie Grandmaison was then twenty-eight years old and of an exquisite and charming beauty, if one believes the documents from the time. She took care of and maintained the interior of this elegant aristocratic home with a kind of piety. This was the sanctuary of the Counter-Revolution. And in the drawing room where she silently brought Cécile, a statue of Henry IV, placed on a mahogany table, immediately drew one's attention and seemed to rally once again to his plume the friends of the dying monarchy.

Cécile knew it well, this little Rue Ménars drawing room. A little later, the Commune would order it searched, and the resulting inventory, preserved in the National Archives, reveals to us that it was hung with soft green taffeta and that, over a fireplace with girandoles, was enthroned a delightful little clock bearing the mark of Legros, the clockmaker of Marie Antoinette.

Among the paintings, engravings, and pastels, a fine portrait of a Queen's Dragoons officer with a tiger skin helmet recalled the early youth of the Counter-Revolution's creator.

Framed pictures containing faces of fashionable men and women from the time of Henry IV, Louis XIII, and Louis XIV evoked his ancestors. Beneath one of these warriors, who had a Cyrano face, was armored, helmeted, and had his neck confined in a ruff identical to that of Henry IV's, one could read these words on the old frame's gilded wood: THE REAPER, 1564-1618. Then, a little lower, were these words: *Letter from Henry IV to the Reaper: "Hardy, my great reaper!... Do not dally with the straw whilst we are in the field!"*

Marie Grandmaison, in a morning gown, with her hair rolled in curls over her shoulders, said to the young girl once the door had been carefully closed: "You, Cécile! At this hour? What is going on?"

"Where is Monsieur Baron?" said Cécile, answering the question with another question.

"God and he only know! Not here, anyhow!"

"He didn't spend the night at home?"

"He knows better than that! He hasn't slept here in a long time! His mere appearances here have been less and less!"

"Should we be glad? Or should we worry?"

"What is going on then?"

"Evidently," continued Cécile, "it's best that he didn't spend the night here, because when he stepped outside, he would have been arrested by the two gendarmes standing guard at the door... On the other hand, how do we warn him that there is a spy who has slipped in among us?"

"Just one?" said Marie Grandmaison ironically. "You would make the baron quite happy were you to prove to him that there is only one spy who has wormed his way into our ranks... He himself is convinced that there is more than one..."

"And he isn't worried about it?"

"Not at all!... The spies, he ends up making use of them!"

"When he knows who they are... He still needs to know who they are first!... The one I am talking about is Sénar, the spy from the committees, one of my father's tenants. He procured for himself a summons, and he has gained the trust of two of our friends, the de Lézardière brothers, with whom he is making his way to the Cléry terreplein."

"And what will this spy do at the Cléry terreplein?... What can he stop?" In a lower voice, she added: "Our friends there will be over five hundred in number, and I am not counting the faithful section that has specifically been designated to form a line there..."

"What incredible luck!" said Cécile Renault joyfully.

"Is it really luck?"

The smile that punctuated this question spoke so many volumes that Cécile asked, "Who then assigned the battalions their locations?"

"Santerre, at the Commune and the Executive Council's joint order!"

"But in the Executive Council, there is Minister Danton, the man who did the September massacres! There's Minister

Clavière!... It's a group after the abominable Convention's own heart!"

"Evidently!... Where are you going with this?... There are sections that are revolutionary, others that are tepid, and others that are completely good, like those of Filles-Saint-Thomas. The battalions that they supply resemble them. The worst are put around the scaffold. The best are at the end of Rue de Cléry on Boulevard Bonne-Nouvelle. Everything will be fine, and your spy will be very much surrounded—he may very well have a bad fifteen minutes and his curiosity expiated if one of our own recognizes him!"

"And these two gendarmes who are at the door, is it also the Commune that has sent them?"

"It could be, but I don't know... In any event, they are very discreet!... They haven't even tried entering to search or to ask questions."

"If they have likewise sent two of them to the doors of our other friends, that is worrying all the same!" murmured Cécile. "The baron did not spend the night here, that's good! But if he had, what would have happened?... As soon as he stepped outside, he would have been arrested..."

"They've arrested him multiple times already; he's always come back two hours later!"

"Still!"

Cécile's fears concerning the one who was venerably referred to as "Monsieur Baron" subsided before Marie Grandmaison's calmness and reassurance. But she still thought of this Sénar donning the name of Sévignon and being admitted into the heart of the conspiracy by the two de Lézardière brothers, learning secrets and perhaps signaling to Santerre to carry out a mass arrest before the arrival of the funeral procession.

She wanted to leave. Marie Grandmaison held her back.

"Where are you going?"

"To the Cléry terreplein, to warn Messieurs de Lézardière, and the baron himself if I see him."

"Poor innocent thing!... You will not make it there!... The streets are filled with soldiers and people. And how are you going to find the ones you are looking for in that crowd?... Let things be!... The baron's plans are made in a way that accounts for the unexpected and betrayals. You are exhausted; you are going to sleep a little... Then, you will help me to move!"

"Move?"

"Yes!... Before noon, I will be in Charonne, where the baron is moving his headquarters, and I am to set things up for him in the country house there, where he will be receiving many... Here, things might flare up, especially if this morning's expedition is successful. Up till now, the gendarmes have been delightful and have not caused any trouble. But will they keep up this commendable attitude much longer?"

And Marie ordered the young girl: "Go upstairs and lie down on the bed in the small bedroom. In an hour we will get ready to leave and pack the linens and the dishes..."

Cécile was so tired and enervated; her entire being yielded to such a decompression that she allowed herself to be overcome and went to sleep for one hour, without the increasing noise from outside managing to wake her.

By this time, Sénar and the two de Lézardière brothers had reached the Cléry terreplein, after having made their way through a crowd that true historians have described as dismayed and overcome with astonishment and sorrow, as if they vaguely sensed it was France herself that was to be beheaded with her king.

On this dark and awful day, these people of Paris, silent and anxious, stole along the buildings and drew behind the troops, with neither cry nor gesture. No hustling and bustling as during public festivals. The shops were closed. Few windows were open.

This Cléry terreplein still exists. All of Paris knows the tall, narrow, somewhat slanted building that forms the corner of Rue de la Lune and Rue de Cléry. In front of it would gather the men who were going to try to save the king.

One of the descendants of the organizer of this prodigious surprise attack has described the locale as it existed back then:

From the Porte Saint-Denis to here, the boulevard sloped upward and was not level as it is today. The sidewalk on the left-hand side (when one's back is to the Porte Saint-Denis), currently bordered by an iron railing, was level with the road, and the railing did not exist. It was a prime strategic location, and the procession's cannons could not even pass over this rather steep slope. From the place where Rue Beauregard meets Rue de Cléry, one looked down over the procession, and it was easy to direct operations. The terreplein that existed between Rue de la Lune, Rue de Cléry, and the boulevard was large enough to contain a great number of conspirators; moreover, as we shall explain, they had to extend just beyond Rue Sainte-Barbe (today Rue Thorel) as they lined up along the boulevard. Many people could also be positioned along the descent that ended at Rue Saint-Denis, and finally, a number of conspirators could easily position themselves in front of and behind the Porte Saint-Denis, in the open area connecting to the faubourg, and on the ascending sidewalk on the right-hand side. The horses would be pacing slowly as they climbed this slope, and one could all the better subdue and stop them.

When Paul and Sylvestre de Lézardière arrived at the terreplein with the fake Marquis de La Guiche, amidst a crowd packed behind the line of soldiers and pressing in on each other, the former asked his brother, "Do you see any of our friends?"

"No!" said Sylvestre.

"This is not normal!... Or *him*?"

"Him neither!"

Paul then addressed Sénar in a hushed voice: "You're tall, do you see *him* at all?"

"See whom?"

"*Him!*"

"Who is *him*?"

"You know we mustn't say his name, not even very quietly, especially here!"

"No, I don't see him!"

Sénar, moreover, would have had trouble spotting him. He did not even know who the person in question was. He sensed Paul was speaking of the leader of the conspiracy which he had only discovered by accident, the stages of which he was going to follow with an impassioned interest, believing it would be very profitable for him personally. But as Cécile Renault had rightly reasoned in her little head, what especially interested Sénar was the leader. He wanted to see him, to etch his features in his memory, and to arrest him if possible.

Let us say right away that Sénar was there of his own accord, without having informed any of his colleagues or commanders. He jealously kept to himself this affair he had learned of by chance, so that he could have all the resulting benefits and glory for himself. He remained vigilant, on the lookout for the least movement from the crowd, the least word said aloud, the least gesture constituting a signal of any kind.

At a certain moment, the two brothers found themselves separated from the phony Sévignon. Sylvestre said to his brother, "Perhaps if you carefully elicit the password."

Paul was behind the line of soldiers. All while giving the appearance of questioning his brother, he uttered two to three times in an indifferent tone, "Will the reaper come?"

No answer reached his ears. And a great fright assailed the two brothers. Were they therefore alone with the one whom they believed to be Sévignon? Or were there others? Where, then, was the leader? Was the plot discovered and no one able to warn them?

In a somewhat distressed voice, Paul repeated the question. But this time, he clearly heard a voice amongst the rustling and footsteps of the half-recollected, half-terrorized crowd, which murmured: "When the harvest is ripe!"

They both quickly turned around. The man who had obviously given the response, but who was impassive and looking at the road with his back turned to them, was the officer positioned behind the soldiers forming the line there, the commander of the battalion from the Filles-Saint-Thomas section (today the Bourse quarter).

His lack of military bearing gave him away as one of those bourgeois in officer's clothing, typical in this national guard created by the Revolution. The joy of the two young men was intense. The commander of the battalion forming the line at this location was for the king! By what miracle?

And with youthful oscillation, Paul and Sylvestre, who one minute before believed all lost, now believed the battle won!

This entire crowd was part of the conspiracy, no doubt, as well as all the troops amassed at this location. Was there to be then, at the leader's signal, a furious rush towards the carriage, so that the king could be taken away, hidden, and saved?

They instinctively moved closer to the corner of Rue de Cléry and Rue de la Lune, thinking the signal would have to come from there. And suddenly, a sorrowful cry of "Ah!" rose from the crowd; it was "a muffled murmur, a long moan," as the historian G. Lenotre writes. A distant rumbling of drums was coming from the direction of the Temple, and people's heads turned to look intently towards Boulevard Saint-Martin on the right, watching for the sinister procession.

The drums drew nearer. People in the crowd stood on tiptoe. Brief, crisp commands of "Attention!" followed one after another in the troops forming the line, and the front of the dismal procession appeared.

Slowly exiting first from the mist like large phantoms, the national gendarmes, expressionless and sitting upright on their horses, which were stung by the morning chill and shaking their heads, trotted forward, all while remaining aligned in formation. They spanned the entire width of the broad roadway.

The grenadiers of the national guard followed, their weapons resting on their shoulders.

Their rhythmic steps were heavy. The white straps crossing over their chests, their plumed tricorn hats, and the large cartridge pouches suspended behind their lower backs cast a little bit of color into the fog, which clouded the contours of people and things and gave this spectacle the haziness of a nightmare.

Then, there was the artillery. The cannons and ammunition wagons paraded two by two over the sandstone pavement with roars of thunder.

Finally, the drummers appeared, and, behind them, surrounded by soldiers, was the sinister, unwieldy, bottle green carriage, its windows raised and covered with condensation. With the effort of its two horses and after having passed in front of the Porte Saint-Denis, the carriage began to slowly climb the small hill of Boulevard Bonne-Nouvelle.

Suddenly, above the anguished crowd in suspense, some twelve feet from the corner building, shone the steel of a sword, while a formidable and strident voice speaking in melodious syllables—a cavalry officer's voice accustomed to commanding the charge—shouted out, over the roar of the drums: "Rise up, my friends! Now let us rise up to save the king!"

And a man rushed onto the road, his sword in one hand and his hat in the other, followed by five or six other persons, among whom were the de Lézardière brothers, who had recognized him.

With the speed of lightning, they cut through the crowd, which made way for them, broke through the line of the Filles-Saint-Thomas soldiers, who allowed them to pass out of bewilderment or complicity, and then ran up to the horses and grabbed their bridles. And they all repeated the cry of the man with the sword: "Rise up! Let us save the king!"

Some vague movements formed in the crowd. One could see some isolated persons responding to the cries and rushing towards the carriage without being able to reach it. It looked like members of a troop trying to come together. But already the soldiers surrounding the carriage, who must have been specially chosen, reasserted control and, with sabers in hand, swooped down on the daring individuals, who were forced to let go of the horses' bridles to defend themselves.

A young man, who had followed closely behind the man with the sword from the very beginning, was struggling at the hands of soldiers trying to arrest him. Paul de Lézardière freed him by slitting the throat of one of his assailants and then disappeared into the screaming, terrified crowd.

Other conspirators, pursued by soldiers, divided the attention of both the army and the crowd.

Two of these unfortunate ones rushed onto Rue de la Lune and tried to take refuge in Notre-Dame-de-Bonne-Nouvelle Church. They were unable to get inside, the order having been given the day before to lock the doors of all public buildings, and they were sabered on the steps in front of the main door.

As for the mysterious man who had given the signal, after having retraced his steps and crossed the line of soldiers for a second time, he was as though immersed in the crowd and had disappeared before the eyes of everyone.

Of everyone?... No!... For Sénar, who had not lost sight of him since the beginning of the tragic incident and had a disciplined eye, dashed onto his trail and followed him.

All of this, moreover, had taken place in a matter of seconds. The carriage had resumed its route to the place of execution.

Will it ever be known if the king, imprisoned in that somber coach where he was reciting the office for the dying with Father de Firmont, even noticed that a handful of heroes had tried to rescue him?

Both in front of and behind the procession, the spectators had suspected nothing.

It was a localized incident, and the regicides kept quiet about it. It was not in their interest to spread the news of an attempted rescue of a tyrant whose death, according to them, all the people demanded.

And the two de Lézardière brothers now found themselves on the terreplein, accompanied by the young man who had followed closely behind the signal giver. They were once again isolated in the crowd, without anyone seeming to take notice of them.

"Oh, Devaux, Devaux!" they said to the young man whom they recognized. "What happened?"

Devaux, who had tears in his eyes, responded, "The baron had summoned over five hundred of us. I know, I'm his secretary. It is not possible that out of five hundred gentlemen, four hundred eighty-five would end up being cowards!... We have been betrayed!... Even La Guiche did not show up!"

"But wait!" said Sylvestre de Lézardière. "He came with us!... Citizen Sévignon was here!"

"Where is he now?"

"Disappeared!" said Paul. "Maybe arrested, or killed!"

"Poor La Guiche!" said the young Devaux.

"And him?" asked Paul.

"He is safe and sound... Seeing that he was neither killed nor taken in front of the carriage and that he is now hidden in the crowd, I am not at all worried. I didn't leave him for a second until he crossed back over the line... Do you want to see him?"

"Certainly!... But where? When?"

"Let us go separately, please, to 95 Rue de Cléry, a stone's throw from here. We will meet there, at the Count de Marsan's."

They separated.

The crowd, still silent, was now dispersing. In the middle of the roadway, where the brief clash had left, like a sign, a pool of blood and the body of one of the soldiers guarding the carriage, a stream of sans-culottes, drunk and destined to represent "the free people applauding the death of the tyrant," followed the procession, advancing towards Revolution Square to behold the final act in the royal tragedy...

Chapter 4

The King's Hiding Place

FIVE MINUTES LATER, the two de Lézardière brothers went into the entryway for the building numbered 95 on Rue de Cléry. This building was only about eighty meters from the terreplein. Its entryway, which was paved, was very dark.

At the end of the passage, one could vaguely discern a rather wide stone stairway, thanks to a window between the first and second floors that opened onto a small, narrow courtyard and allowed a faint, gray light to filter through.

The two brothers let themselves be guided by the stairway's beautiful wrought iron railing. On the second floor, in front of the only door opening onto the landing, they saw Devaux, who was waiting for them. He had them enter inside and presented them to the lodging's owner, the Count de Marsan. The latter threw his coat and two pistols onto a sofa in a gesture of rage.

He was a man in his thirties, with strong features and a military bearing. He barely responded to the two brothers' greeting, sat on his coat, took his head in both hands, and said, "What happened?... Why were there so few of us at the rendezvous?"

And Devaux, opening a door adjoining the drawing room, revealed a tidy, carefully arranged room, with a variety of old clothes hanging in an open armoire. "It was here," he said, "that we were to take the king... This was to be the king's hiding place."

"The king's hiding place!" the two brothers said sorrowfully.

"If we had succeeded in concealing his entry into the building by surrounding him with five hundred of our friends and drawing the soldiers' attention and pursuit elsewhere, we would have kept him here for a few days. If not, we would have let ourselves be cut to pieces in front of the building and in the entryway to prevent the Convention's hired assassins from gaining access. In this small room, His Majesty was to change into these old clothes that you see. They are different disguises: the clothes of a sans-culotte, another the uniform of a national guardsman, and the third the clothing of a carter. The baron would have proposed, and the king would have decided. Then, through this window, a bridge formed by some planks was to take His Majesty over the courtyard to the facing attic room, where friends would be waiting for him. There, he would be in a home facing Rue Beauregard. He would go out by that street, go to Rue Sainte-Barbe, or Rue Barbe as it's now called, and enter my home, where another hiding place was prepared in my cellar. Additionally, we have so many friends and connecting buildings in this neighborhood that we could change plans instantly in case of unforeseen danger... Alas!... All of this is now useless!"

A profound silence followed this explanation. Then, only a sigh was heard from the Count de Marsan, seated on the couch and his head still in his hands. And he repeated, "My God, what happened?... What happened?... Our cause is accursed then!"

"Our cause is just!" a manly voice suddenly said, in melodious syllables. "But we are warring against Satan. And Satan is powerful!"

At the same time, a sinewy, supple, finely gloved hand leaned on his shoulder. Marsan sprang up. Devaux and the two Lézardières saluted. The leader had just entered.

This man was about thirty-five years old and elegantly proportioned, with a slender, albeit compact, figure. He was about five French feet tall, according to his passports, the equivalent of about one and two-thirds meters. His sweptback, tailless hair, his dark chestnut-brown eyebrows, his gray, piercing, mischievous eyes, his high forehead, his hooked and somewhat large and elongated, although not disproportionate, nose, his pointed and determined chin, and his fine, Richelieu-like mustache gave an impression of extraordinary energy. He wore a dark blue, triple-caped frock coat with large lapels. A buckled waistbelt held his sword and two pistols. His black cloak was over his arm. Top boots could be seen beneath the long, blue frock coat, whose form called to mind that of the Republic's generals. In his hand, he held a kind of felt hat that was called a Pennsylvania; it was gray with a wide, soft brim and decorated with a large steel buckle in the front. He wore gray gloves, and his narrow, frilled cuffs were of an immaculate white. Except for a tear on the right side of his blue frock coat, one would never have suspected that he had just emerged from a terrible conflict and the jostling of a very dense crowd.

"What happened," said the newcomer, "is that almost all our friends were unable to leave their homes!"

"Arrested?" asked the Count de Marsan.

"Only guarded!" He sat down, threw his hat on a table, and then explained: "Before coming here, I went by some of our friends' homes. On Rue de Tracy, where Cardinal lives, two gendarmes were standing guard. If he had gone out, they would have arrested him, or at least forced him back inside his home, keeping him prisoner there until the appointed time. Perhaps they did that. My sense is that the Commune and Council of Ministers' strategy is to arrest no one to avoid making noise, so that no one in the public knows an attempt has been made to rescue the august victim, and so that the royalists outside of Paris are not encouraged by our example. At Admiral's, on Rue Favart, two gendarmes also. In front of my door, two as well!... I did not enter."

"But this morning you luckily went out before they arrived?" asked Paul de Lézardière.

"Oh... I haven't been staying at my home for a long time!" said the baron matter-of-factly. "I stay in a place where I dare them to find me... And yet, it is the Republic itself that is giving me sanctuary."

This thought made him almost cheerful. Devaux asked, "But Monsieur Baron, how do you explain that there were no gendarmes in front of this home, or in front of the one in which I live, on Rue Sainte-Barbe?"

"I can explain that easily: These two lodgings were only rented by you the day before yesterday. They didn't know about them. And you, gentlemen," he asked, addressing the de Lézardière brothers, "you were able to leave?... There weren't any gendarmes there, on Rue de Savoie?"

"Perhaps they were placed there after our departure, since we did leave very early. Monsieur de La Guiche came to get us. Maybe he feared this measure of the Commune's."

"La Guiche was there?... I never saw him... Why didn't he join in?"

"He was separated from us at the moment we ran towards you, when you gave the signal," answered Sylvestre. "Maybe he didn't know where to meet up with you!"

"That's possible!" said Devaux, the baron's secretary. "Maybe also the unlucky one was torn to pieces. Some of our own certainly lost their lives there!"

"But who could have betrayed us?" asked Marsan, who remained crushed and dismayed.

"Who?" said the baron. "I shall investigate this matter tomorrow in Charonne. But perhaps it was only an indiscretion that reached the ear of a patient and skilled policeman who followed some of our own, and took down addresses..."

"So, all is lost!... What are we to do now?"

The baron perked up, extremely indignant.

"What are we to do, Count de Marsan!... But there is everything to do!... Temple Prison holds other victims! Is there not the Queen to save? And the Dauphin? And Madame Élisabeth? And Madame Royale?... Furthermore, was His Majesty not supposed to have given final instructions to his confessor, Father de Firmont, who is to communicate them to the senior Monsieur de Lézardière, whom I avoided dragging into this morning's fray?... And must not the King-Martyr's orders be executed even more religiously than those of the living king reigning gloriously in his Palace of Versailles?"

"Monsieur, forgive me!" said the Count de Marsan. "Forgive me for letting myself become so discouraged when the task at hand is so great and so beautiful!"

The baron became more animated: "And avenging him!" he proclaimed. "Don't you dream of it?... For the king's head, gentlemen, I myself want the heads of one hundred of these brigands!... And I will have them, or I will lose my own trying!"

He electrified them. Everyone raised their heads, and their eyes lit up.

He continued: "Certainly, the game was well underway!... And as His Majesty would have it, for a long time!... But His Majesty was not a very Christian king! He was too Christian of a king!... Scruples assailed him. He fell victim to these scruples, for fear of not being good, of not being just, of not taking pity on his people! He was made to believe that his people were those few assassins who went to demand bread at Versailles, when they were drunk on brandy, and that his people were those August 10 hirelings who attacked the palace to loot it and to rob its defenders after having killed them!"

He stood up, and as his gaze and his fist threatened, he exclaimed, "Oh, scoundrels! If you had been dealing with Louis XIV or Louis XV, heaven help you! What a bloody and well-deserved chastisement my gentle rulers would have inflicted upon you!"

He calmed down. Then, after a moment, he said, "What advantages we had, even today!... The entire Filles-Saint-Thomas battalion, which allowed us to operate!... The carriage coachman himself was on our side!"

"The actual driver?" exclaimed Paul de Lézardière.

"Yes!... His Majesty was originally to be taken to the scaffold in the mayor's carriage. It happened to be unavailable. The Minister of Finance, Étienne Clavière, offered his own... That was the one you saw passing... And I repeat, this was one more advantage for us... I'll say no more..."

"I remember," said Paul de Lézardière, "when soliciting the password around me, to know who our friends were, that a national guard officer answered me."

"Oh, yes! I'm telling you!... That was Cortey, our brave Cortey, commander of the Filles-Saint-Thomas battalion..."

He grabbed his cloak and hat, then said, "Gentlemen, it will be at my home in Charonne, from now on, that you will want to get instructions for the king's service... The king is dead! Long live the king!... We belong to Louis XVII! Prudently inform your friends that they are never again to go to Rue Ménars, and that they are to avoid saying my name as much as possible. Tell them that the fight continues, and that it continues mercilessly... From now on, we are the Avengers of the King! See you soon!"

He headed towards the door. Devaux looked as though he planned to accompany him, while Marsan said, "Allow us to escort you... If you were to be recognized..."

"Thank you!... I prefer to leave alone... I won't be recognized. I run no risk... You will always get news of me when needed. Tell yourselves and repeat to your friends that besides having the royal family to save, there is now the king to avenge, and that we have for fulfilling this mission and punishing the regicides new and powerful helpers!"

"What helpers?" asked Marsan.

The baron, crossing the lodging's threshold, laconically answered, "Their vices! Their appetites!"

Chapter 5

Shadowing

STEPS AWAY FROM the entrance to 95 Rue de Cléry, on which he kept his eyes fixed, a man equipped with a pencil jotted down the following in a small notebook:

> *Description of man who gave signal to rescue Tyrant Capet: 35-40 yrs.; height about 1 2/3 m.; hair and eyebrows near black; gray eyes; large aquiline nose; avg. mouth; pointed chin; large forehead, oval face, dark complexion; blue caped frock coat, saber with belt, officer boots, open cloak, gray hat with buckle, gloves, cuffs, loud voice. Went back to Cléry terreplein after Tyrant Capet passed. Went to Rue de Tracy, then Rue Favart, then went back via Rue Ménars, Rue Feydeau, Rue des Jeûneurs to Rue de Cléry, stopping nowhere but 95 of last street.*

Sénar, the false Sévignon, for it was he, after having reread his notes, placed his notebook in his pocket and whispered, "Now, let's wait to know the rest of the journey! I've found the conspiracy's leader, I am not going leave him, and I think I am going to learn some interesting things that are going to make the Commune and the Executive Council take notice of me... If the Convention doesn't one day decree that I deserve well of my country, it's because they are no better than tyrants!... What a brood of aristocrats I am going to uncover!"

His monologue did not last a long time, for a man exited 95 Rue de Cléry and made his way towards the boulevards.

"Devil!" exclaimed Sénar. "That's my conspirator!... Yes, that is him!... Those are his frock coat, top boots, and gray hat. He turned too soon for me to see his face, but he is recognizable enough from behind!"

And he rushed onto the trail of the one called the baron. The latter reached the boulevard, then brusquely turned his back on the Porte Saint-Denis to take Rue Saint-Denis, which he went down until arriving at Rue Tiquetonne.

There, he turned right onto Rue Tiquetonne, reached Rue Coq-Héron, then Rue du Bouloi, and passed through a tall entranceway to a transport service courtyard filled with the sounds of horses and carriages, calling and shouting, and crates banging against one another.

Sénar followed him into the congested courtyard and disappeared into the teeming of large canvas-covered carts, primitive coaches, and baskets and sacks being moved about by freight handlers. Postilions and cart drivers with whips about their necks went from the carriages to the stables, whose open doors allowed one to see the rumps of the mighty draft horses, most of which were already harnessed. Dogs barked, and fowl pecked into the gaps of the rough, uneven pavement.

At the far end, on top of the dusty rafters which were part of the large depot's ancient framework sheltering coaches and carriages for rent, pigeons cooed, cats stretched out, and dogs barked, while hostlers went up and down the length of an old, disjointed staircase leading to the fodder lofts, the rail of which, gleaming from use, dated back to at least Charles IX.

The place bore aspects of both an inn and a farm. And the stable smells mixed with the perfumes of elegant lady travelers impatiently awaiting their carriages' departures. Emigration was in full swing, and the king's execution did nothing to curb this trend.

Sénar suddenly thought, "My man is here to reserve a seat to go abroad... But he hasn't left!"

To his great surprise, he saw the cavalryman he was so intently following, instead of going to the transport office, ascend a small stairway at the right of the courtyard leading to a door on which was painted the following inscription:

OFFICE OF THE DIRECTOR GENERAL
of National Haulage of France

"Aha!" said Sénar. "It has to do with cartage!... Does he have something to send?"

And he sat on the first step of the small stairway, took out his notebook, and wrote: "Stayed half hour at 95 Rue de Cléry, took Rue Denis, Tiquetonne, Coq-Héron, Bouloi, and at 0830 entered National Haulage Office."

He then put his notebook back in his pocket and waited.

When inside, the baron walked across a small waiting room with firm steps, as if he were in his own home. He opened a door, entered a room in which a half dozen clerks were doing paperwork, and demanded in an authoritative tone, "Citizen Barbereux!"

"He isn't here!" said an old, gray-haired employee.

"For me he is here!" the baron responded. "And I am in a hurry! Come on! Let's go, Citizen!"

In response to this insistence, the employee went to open the door to the haulage director's office and had the baron enter. The latter waited till the door closed behind him. Then, addressing the director, who rose almost respectfully, he said to him in a low voice, "We lost the game!... The king died this morning!"

"I know!" said Barbereux with sincere grief, evidently shocking for the senior director of an enterprise having such close ties to the State that he could almost be considered an officer of the regime.

"You are still sure about your personnel?"

"Yes!... Wasn't it you who chose them?... All the stable grooms, hostlers, coachmen and hunting valets from Versailles Palace are here, employed in cartage and haulage. The few sans-culottes I was obligated to take in because they were recommended by Convention members or people from the Commune are watched and kept a close eye on..."

"It's not bad that we have a few of them with us. It's a certificate of civism... At what time do you have a departure for Lyon?"

"At noon—a furniture move for a senior officer changing garrisons."

"Is the driver trustworthy?"

"Very trustworthy! He's a former coachman from the Small Stable. He was nearly killed defending the queen's quarters, during the October Days."

"Perfect! I am going to write a letter that you will entrust to him and that he will deliver into the hands of the Duke de Crussol-Langeac, at his home on Place Bellecour in Lyon!"

"All right!"

The baron sat down, took from his pocket a flask of what appeared to be water—it was ink that only became visible when one put what was written with it close to the fire—and wrote:

Dear Duke, it is all over. We were unable to get the august martyr out of the clutches of those animals! It is now time to avenge him and to tend to the surviving members of the unfortunate royal family. Do as I: Disguise yourself, hide to better prepare for the future uprisings, and reach out one day to the Vendée, which is already stirring and which we are going to make the center of our massive insurrectional movement. Take on a typical name—Brutus or Gracchus—and sport a carmagnole jacket. Enter into the Jacobin milieus and make friends with the worst among them. They can be of use to us in a plan that I am contemplating and will tell you about.

See you soon and be brave!... Long live the King!

The Reaper

He could not reread this letter, its characters only to be visible to the addressee when brought near the fire. He folded it, sealed it with wax, and handed it to Barbereux, saying, "If the carter delivering this missive senses he is suspected or fears being

stopped for one reason or another, he should destroy this...
Goodbye for now, Barbereux!"

"Goodbye, Monsieur Baron!"

The baron, as he was called, left the National Haulage Office
so quickly that the toe of his boot nearly struck the lower back
of Sénar, still seated on the bottom step of the small stairway,
and who resumed his pursuit once the conspirator turned onto
Rue du Bouloi.

The police officer asked himself, "What could he have
actually done at the National Haulage Office? He wasn't even
there for fifteen minutes!... It has to do with a dispatch! But
what? And to whom?"

He walked quickly, for the baron was now leading him
towards the Palais-Royal Garden, which he only crossed at an
angle to get to Rue Neuve des Petits-Champs.

Shortly before reaching the garden, Sénar noticed that the
man he was following made a kind of gesture as if he were putting
on a pair of eyeglasses; this was just as they were about to cross
paths with a band of drunk and revolting sans-culottes who were
shouting the *Marseillaise* and the *Ça ira*, announcing the tyrant's
death in between verses.

They were returning from Revolution Square and coming to
praise the manes of Convention member Lepelletier de Saint-
Fargeau, who, as is known, was killed by the thrust of an
avenging saber on the very evening of the king's condemnation,
by the former royal bodyguard Pâris in a restaurant located just
a stone's throw away.

The baron then reached Rue Neuve des Capucines and, to the
police officer's astonishment, entered the Ministry of Public
Contributions, which was located on this street. Today we would
call it the Ministry of Finance. Its head at the time was the well-
known Étienne Clavière, a Girondist of Protestant faith and
Genevan nationality who, after having made Revolution in his
homeland, was exiled to London, then settled in Paris, where, at
the head of a financial bloc, he had fought another Huguenot
bloc, that of Necker, to take his place. The fights between

business politicians had begun even before the ancient tree of monarchy fell. These cosmopolitans temporarily ceased their own rivalries when it came time to undermine the monarchy.

But before the conspirator entered the ministry building, Sénar saw him make a gesture like that of removing eyeglasses.

At that moment, he did not attach any importance to this detail. The thought of a man, who had just tried to save the king, entering a ministry headed by a republican whose mission, like all other ministers, was to carry out the Convention's parody of a trial and ensure this same king's death, produced in him such a stupefaction that it annihilated all other accessory considerations.

He waited on the street, wanting to avoid being noticed by his target when he exited, and simply promised himself to return later, furnished with a description and time of visit, to ask the doorkeeper for the name of the mysterious visitor.

The baron crossed a courtyard, ascended a small set of steps sheltered by an awning, and met in an anteroom a doorkeeper as classy as they were five years prior. The era of rampant sans-culottism had not yet tolled, and two of the Convention's ministers had been ministers when Louis XVI was still king: Roland and Clavière. One should not then be surprised to find that the latter had a doorkeeper with a metal chain about his neck, in a formal suit, and donning the proper peruke.

"May I help you, Citizen?" asked the doorkeeper with exquisite politeness.

"I want to see Citizen Clavière!"

"This is not his audience day!"

"Are there still audience days, in an age when the ministers must take orders from the people?"

"Besides, he does not receive people so early!"

"You are not going to tell me, Citizen Doorkeeper, that the minister did not get up on the morning of the day that Tyrant Capet was executed!... Come on!... Announce me!"

"It's that..."

"My answer to you is that the minister will be here for a man who is the principal manager of big business in which Citizen Clavière has an interest!"

"If Citizen would tell me his name then!" said the doorkeeper, somewhat intimidated by the authority with which the baron spoke to him.

"Announce Citizen Manaud!"

"Citizen Manaud?"

"Himself!"

"Very well!"

And the doorkeeper went away...

He returned five to six minutes later.

"Well?" asked the one who identified himself as Citizen Manaud.

"Citizen Clavière is waiting for you... If Citizen would follow me..."

And he preceded him across a waiting room, then opened a green velvet double door, and stepped aside to let the visitor pass.

The latter was soon in the presence of Étienne Clavière, who, seated before a large Louis XVI desk of the most refined style and decorated with chiseled copper that would have sent today's collector into ecstasy, rose with an extraordinary eagerness.

"Monsieur Baron de Batz! You!" exclaimed the minister, advancing with an outstretched hand.

And his surly face, bilious, somber, wrinkled, and parched by ambition, lit up.

"How are you doing, *Monsieur* Clavière?" asked the baron as he took the republican's hand and amicably shook it.

"Well, despite all the emotions of power!... Anyhow, I think emotions are running high amongst all parties... You, I thought... I thought that you were arrested!... Imprisoned at La Force... Have a seat..."

"Arrested?... I was, in fact, fifteen days ago, after an altercation in a café at the Palais-Royal. It doesn't take much these days to be arrested on the suspicion of having a counter-revolutionary spirit... But how did you know, Clavière?" added the baron, sitting at the aforementioned desk and facing his interlocutor.

"I read in *Le Moniteur* that a Citizen Manaud had been arrested... I concluded from this that you had given to those who arrested you the name of one of your ancestors, which is a way of not lying while still disguising your identity... I did realize that was you!"

"Well done, Clavière!... And Manaud, like de Batz, is still the name of a friend of the king!... Manaud was the friend of Henry IV."

"And you the friend of Louis XVI... Now that I know you are no longer in prison, I have no doubts about your presence this morning at a certain place on the route of the procession..."

"I even saw your carriage, Clavière, in that procession."

Baron de Batz's voice, which was almost cheerful at the beginning of the conversation, suddenly became serious and moved as he spoke that last sentence. He added, "And if I come here, Clavière, it is to thank you..."

"For what?"

"For having offered your carriage, and for having put the Filles-Saint-Thomas battalion at the place where they were."

"You do not have to thank me for that. The arrangements were jointly made with the Executive Council and General Santerre. The responsibility, if the king had escaped, would have fallen on everyone and not just myself. I prudently advised Pache, the Minister of War, in such a way that the initiative appeared to come from him. I would not have insisted had it been objected to for any reason. You see then that what I did was really not heroic. I avoided compromising myself. And rather than compromising myself, I would have yielded. Between you and me, I would have been delighted had the king escaped. One does not slay a defeated man—it is vile and nonsensical... You have known me for a long time, Baron... There has not been a more committed antiroyalist than myself. Swiss and Protestant, I am not from here, and I came to France only to do business. I am a financier before all else, and my objective, when I saw the state of this country, was to become Minister of Finance, since this ambition was allowed me.

"Here or there, it was the same to me, and if England had wanted me when I took refuge there after the business in Switzerland, I would be Minister of Finance in England... As a

Protestant, I had to fight against Catholicism, against papism. As a Calvinist Swiss, it was in my nature to fight against the French monarchy."

"Yes," interrupted the baron, "your Swiss nationality naturally destined you for the approval of the 'patriots' here..."

The irony in this remark was without bitterness, in a good-humored tone which kept it within the confines of a joke incapable of offending Clavière. The baron had need of him.

Clavière continued, "To attain the goal I had set for myself, I had to discredit and undermine Necker, a compatriot and coreligionist whom I have always considered meritless and incapable..."

"I also!"

"Moreover, you, Baron, you saw in him a man who was harmful to the monarchy, a minister who was imposed on Louis XVI by his worst enemies. You helped me to take him down, without suspecting that I aimed to one day replace him."

"I beg your pardon, Clavière!... I perfectly suspected it!... But I wanted to overthrow Necker first!... One would see afterwards!... You gave me leverage... One Protestant for another, you being one as much as Necker! We have been business partners for a long enough time in our financial undertakings, and we have never betrayed each other!"

"And we remain partners, I hope!"

There was some anxiousness in Clavière's question.

"Certainly!... Why not?" answered the baron.

Clavière took a breath. He added, "A strange country you have, Baron, where I encounter, hidden beneath the exterior of a high-spirited dragoon colonel fond of adventures and partial to the most insane bouts of audacity, the prodigious financier that you are, having the prudence of an old notary, and a keenness of vision that has confounded even myself, an old hand at trade and exchange..."

"Clavière, you are making me blush!"

"Do not jest, my dear Baron, I think as I say!... Your liquidation committee reports to the Constituent Assembly were models! Right under the noses of hostile deputies, you knew how to make a reserve of a few million for the king, while they squabbled over giving him pennies and appeared to want to reduce him to begging. It was you who did the budget for that unfortunate Varennes trip. If the monarchy had continued, you would have been Chief Minister of Finance, perhaps the Colbert of Louis XVI's reign, and I would have been one of your employees... The times have chosen me to be the minister. It so happens that you contributed to my fortune. I paid back this morning, not all of my debt, but a part of it..."

The baron made no reply. He was considering whether he needed Clavière for the purpose he was envisaging. Clavière also had need of him for the big business in which they had both been involved for the past five to six years. If the baron had not been aware of it, he would have realized it at the end of the discourse of this republican minister, who seemed to want to apologize for having betrayed the Convention's regicides. Anyhow, the baron had already thanked Clavière.

"Clavière," he said, "I asked you for neither explanations nor praise."

"I thought that my explanations were necessary for our future relationship."

"This is the first time that we talk politics since we have known each other!... Let us hope that this does not get either of us into trouble!"

Clavière smiled and continued: "As financial partners, we never looked over the wall that separated us politically, probably because both of us knew quite well what the other one was doing."

"Oh, we did indeed give each other a bit of help even on political terrain, when our convictions did not suffer any harm from it... But this will be difficult in the future!" said the baron. "We are no longer two deputies of the Constituent Assembly sitting on opposing benches. We are you, a minister, and I, a conspirator, an outcast tomorrow and a suspect the day after tomorrow, although I do have papers under the name of Jean

Batz, merchant, having taken the civic oath at Dunkirk when passing through there three weeks ago on my way back from London. In any case, I want you to know, Clavière, that I will not compromise you in your position as minister any more than I did in your position as a republican deputy when I, a royalist deputy, helped you to topple Necker... In the street, I can evade being recognized by the shrewdest of policemen..."

"And how do you do this, Baron?"

"It's my secret!"

"You don't have two faces though?"

"Oh yes, Clavière, I have two faces!"

And the baron started laughing. Clavière followed suit, all the more so since he sensed a weight lifting off of him.

The instigator of that morning's bold offensive showing up at the office of him, a Convention minister, had given him a certain uneasiness. He had been delighted to receive the man who was the brains behind so many profitable financial operations that had increased both of their fortunes, but he would have rather received him elsewhere.

To readers who might be surprised at this connection of financial interests between two men of such different camps at the start of the Reign of Terror, we respond that this is the history made known to us, and that such situations are not made up. This Jean de Batz, this remarkable Queen's Dragoons officer who wore the tiger skin helmet and gallant uniform seen on so many old eighteenth-century miniatures, this hero in novels whom we showed at the Cléry terreplein, was, in fact, the one who introduced France to life and fire insurance policies. He was on the board of directors of these insurance companies as well as on that of Paris Water. He had brought in most of the capital, and Clavière, having considerable interest in these same businesses, which had branches in London, did nothing without him, especially since emigrating.

Clavière resumed, "While I have you here, Baron, I am going to ask you to give me some signatures for London and discuss with you the Paris Water business... There are difficulties..."

The baron put his hand on the minister's. "First, Clavière, I am going to tell you what brought me here."

"Ah!" said the minister with surprise. "Your visit had a motive."

"A special one, yes!... I need a lot of money, Clavière..."

"But... You are owed some first!... As the principal manager of Insurance-Life... And then, your profit shares in all our companies. You are owed over 300,000 livres!"

"I need more than that! If I could have a cash advance and then, if required, I can sell my shares."

"Not required at all! You will get your advance! Keep your shares! How much do you need? Four hundred? Five hundred thousand livres?"

Coolly, the baron dropped these words: "I need two million."

Clavière sustained the shock without batting an eye. But the baron sensed he had forced himself not to jump up... The minister then collected himself and replied, "I understand! The Revolution is turning your life upside down... You have family obligations, friends to support and to provide for..."

"To provide for!... That's it!"

"Very well! Look, Baron!... I am going to work this out... In accrued income and advances over the next four to five years, you might approach 1,300,000 livres... The Boyd and Keer firm in London will give you part of that."

"Good! And the other 700,000 livres?"

"I will personally advance it to you... If required, I will borrow..."

"Thank you, Clavière!" the baron said simply.

And he shook his hand... Clavière, thereupon giving him some documents to sign, conferred with him on certain points relating to their shared business concerns. The baron then rose to his feet.

"Where can I find you at present?" asked Clavière. "Still at 7 Rue Ménars?"

"Oh, no!"

"I might need to speak with you!"

"Every evening between eight and ten I will be at the Palais-Royal gambling house. Do you know it?"

"Absolutely!"

"You can also communicate with me through Biret-Tissot, my servant, who lives at my home in Charonne."

"All right!"

The baron was going to leave the minister through the green double door when the latter pointed him to a small door.

"Through here, my friend. You will be noticed less."

At the threshold of this open door, the baron stopped suddenly and said, "Clavière!... One good turn deserves another!... A few months from now, maybe in a few weeks, Indies Company stock is going to fall terribly..."

"Thank you for the information, Baron. I will buy some shares once they drop because they will surely go back up."

"No, Clavière!... Do not buy them!... Do not buy them!... If you value your head!"

The minister's jaw dropped.

"All right!" he said. "I won't buy them!"

And he remained standing, near the door which had just closed, listening to the former Queen's Dragoons officer's firm and self-assured steps moving away.

"What an astounding man!" he whispered, returning to his chair. "Two million!... For what? Does he want to buy off the Convention then?... Bah! He could do it for less money than that, and he knows it! But why mustn't I buy Indies Company stock?"

Meanwhile, Baron de Batz exited the Ministry of Public Contributions onto a narrow side street.

But Sénar, who was wary, had been watching at the corner of the two streets.

"Uh-oh!" he said. "Someone was trying to evade me!"

He again noticed the baron motioning as if he were putting on eyeglasses. Then he saw the conspirator rub his hands together with an air of satisfaction. But all of this intrigued him without informing him.

As closely as he had been following the man, he had been unable to hear these words which the latter whispered very softly with unspeakable joy: "One million!... Yes!... That is not too much!... I will promise one million in gold to whoever rescues the queen. The other million will be used to destroy her tormentors!"

And he made his way to Rue Saint-Honoré with such haste that the police officer had difficulty following him.

The baron led him to Les Halles.

Then, through sordid alleyways which have now disappeared, he reached Rue de la Verrerie, took Rue du Roi de Sicile, and entered an old, dilapidated building adjoining the sinister La Force Prison.

Sénar was astonished.

His curiosity was so strong that he renounced his principles of prudence this time, went in turn into the building, and ascended the five flights of steps behind the man wearing the blue frock coat. He reached the final landing just in time to see his conspirator straddle a window, boldly jump a narrow, shaft-like area over a small courtyard onto a cornice of the prison only six feet away, climb onto the prison roof at the risk of breaking his neck, and slip inside the notorious penitentiary through a roof window he then shut behind him.

Sénar did not dare follow the same route, as perilous as it was. And besides, he was utterly stunned.

Never! No, never in his time following suspects had he ever seen one go of his own accord to a place the police wanted to take him.

What was this man going to do then at La Force Prison? Maybe help a prisoner to escape! Daringness and danger seemed to be this man's reasons for existence!

Then, an idea came to the police officer.

"Oh, wait... I know Citizen Dubois, the concierge at La Force!... We shall get to the bottom of this!"

And he rushed down the stairs and made his way to the prison entrance porch.

Chapter 6

The Bullied Jailer

IN HIS BOOK *La mystérieuse affaire Donnadieu*, which is not recommended reading for everyone, Gilbert Augustin Thierry evokes amidst a colorful backdrop this La Force Prison which, in the month of the preceding September, was the scene of a portion of the "September Massacres."

It was here, we know, that the unfortunate Princess de Lamballe was beaten unconscious with cudgels and butchered, literally cut into pieces by the cannibals of equality and fraternity.

"The great La Force," he writes, "in times prior the sumptuous mansion of the Caumont La Force family, was a dreaded prison. Built in the Saint-Antoine quarter, it projected dismal walls and occupied the quadrangle formed by Rue du Roi de Sicile, Rue Pavée, Rue Culture Sainte-Catherine, and Rue des Ballets."

For the modern reader having little familiarity with the topography of old Paris, we shall simply say that Rue du Roi de Sicile runs parallel to, and fifteen to twenty meters away from, present-day Rue de Rivoli, and that Rue Pavée leads to and joins Rue de Rivoli right by the Saint-Paul metro station.

This prison at the time had as concierge a man named Dubois; and what one then called a prison concierge was in fact a prison warden.

Upon entering La Force, Sénar stopped at the front office and showed his police card to a clerk, saying, "I need to see Citizen Dubois, and right away."

Two minutes later, he was shown into a modestly furnished parlor where Dubois, seated in an old bergère with faded fabric, was warming his feet at a fire emanating from huge logs.

"Well! Sénar!" he said.

"I indeed!"

"You are all out of breath, Citizen!"

"There's good reason for it!... And just wait till I tell you why!"

"Sit down, warm up, and catch your breath!"

Sénar obeyed. Dubois anxiously stared at him.

He was a man of about forty years of age, having gray hair and appearing older than he was.

He differed from the concierges at other prisons, who were generally unrefined brutes. The Jacobin party, in fact, was beginning to secure control of all positions and was choosing the maniacal to direct the prisons, the future antechambers of the Revolutionary Tribunal.

Dubois, freshly shaven, was not exempt from a certain distinction. His face was refined, and though his hands were dirty, which in that era was the first sign of civism, they were in no way disfigured by the long-term exercise of a manual trade. To an observer, he gave the impression of one who had gone astray.

Sénar, having caught his breath, began: "You do know that Tyrant Capet was executed this morning?"

"I do know!"

"There was a plot to abduct him..."

"Are you sure?"

"I certainly am!... I have been on to it for a long time. In the building where I live, there was a has-been staying there under a fake name. I reported him. He is presently locked up... Maybe he is your boarder!"

"Who knows?... What's his name?"

"Sévignon!... But his real name is La Guiche!"

"Yes! He's here!"

"Small world!"

Sénar started laughing.

"Afterwards, I waited for anything that might arrive for him. But no letters came. However, I succeeded in passing myself off as him in an establishment at the Palais-Royal, where I met two young men, the de Lézardière brothers, two has-beens who hide under the name of Robert. I played the royalist; I pretended to be a has-been who was indignant at the Convention and I gained their trust. But they did not open themselves up to me entirely. I thought that they had to be part of a conspiracy, but I was missing the key, a gesture, a password, I didn't know what it was that evidently linked all of the conspirators together, and I was giving up on ever learning this secret, circling around it like a cat circles around a cage containing a nice plump bird, when yesterday evening, you see, yesterday evening, as luck would have it, a man with a large hat pulled down over his eyes ran into me in the hallway in the building where I live.

"This mysterious individual held numerous folded letters made of blue paper in his left hand. He came up to me and asked, 'Citizen Sévignon—on which floor is he, please?'

"'Citizen Sévignon—that's me!' I said.

"'This is for you!'... With that, he handed me one of the letters and ran off like a thief.

"I opened the letter trembling, so much did I sense that it contained the key I was looking for, the means of getting to the heart of the mystery."

"Love for your country inspired you!"

"Curiosity also..."

"And hatred for aristocrats!"

"Exactly, Citizen!... And the desire for the Committee of General Security to take notice of me... I have my ambitions, just like anyone else!"

"Fair enough, Citizen Sénar!... Continue!"

"The letter contained these simple words: *7 a.m., the Cléry terreplein.* That's explicit enough."

"Indeed!... This appointment was arranged with multiple persons—for you told me there were multiple letters identical to the one given you?"

"Yes, a thick bundle!"

"And the location of the meeting—at the top of a hill, on the route that the tyrant was to take!"

"I was ecstatic. I was nearing the goal. Quickly, I went to the place at the Palais-Royal where I was accustomed to seeing the Lézardière brothers. Only one of them, Paul, was there. I showed him my letter. He had received an identical one. His brother also. The ice was finally broken. He trusted me—the summons letter served as my password and I fully entered into the conspiracy... To be more certain that I wasn't mistaken, I suggested to Paul that I come get him and his brother very early in the morning. He gladly accepted. And all three of us went together to the Cléry terreplein..."

"Oh, this is getting interesting!" said Citizen Dubois, appearing more and more engaged in the story. "What happened there?"

"As the procession passed, a man in the crowd drew his sword and cried out, 'Rise up, my friends! Now let us rise up to save the king!' And he rushed forward. But his cry did not resonate much. Five or six followed him."

"That took extraordinary guts! So, were they all killed?"

"Some of them, maybe!... The man who gave the signal, no!... Honestly, it was only him I was paying attention to... I did not take my eyes off him for a second... The game is worth the hunt!"

"Of course!... You followed him..."

"I have been doing only that since this morning... If I told you in detail where I followed him, you would be surprised at the places this aristocrat went into, especially the last one!... But it would take too long. I have written down all the streets he took, with the times..."

"But at this point, you have had him arrested and he is behind bars..."

"Oh? Citizen, this is where my story is going to startle you!" Sénar exclaimed. "No, I have not had him arrested, but he is behind bars nevertheless!"

"How is that?"

"He put himself there all by himself!... And by taking a most dangerous aerial route, when he only had to speak to me to enter conveniently through the main entrance."

"What do you mean?"

"That he is with you, here in La Force, which he just entered through a roof window, by way of the neighboring building... This is an ending you were not expecting!... You aren't surprised?"

No, Dubois was not surprised. His face, animated by the phases of the story to which he had been listening, suddenly took on a troubled expression. He answered, "Citizen Sénar, you are speaking fantasy. I don't like these kinds of jokes."

"But no!... I swear to you!... Come!... Let's search the entire prison... I am sure that we will find him!"

Dubois could not refuse this to the police officer, but the latter could see that the concierge rose from his chair without enthusiasm.

He armed himself with a set of enormous keys and preceded Sénar through the different corridors.

"Let's go up to the top floor, right away!"

"One moment!" Dubois said.

They arrived at a landing on the fourth floor, from which they looked down over a courtyard where about a hundred prisoners were walking and being surveilled by guards. At the courtyard exits, sentries were keeping watch.

"All of the prisoners are there! We call that the lion pit. See if you can make out the man you were following."

Sénar looked for a long time, staring at them one by one.

"No!... He isn't there!" he ultimately said. "I am looking for blue frock coats; there are only two of them, and they don't have his figure..."

"I would have been surprised if he were there!"

"But in the other courtyard?"

"Those are the detained children—little thieves, little beggars..."

"Then he must be wandering the stairways and the corridors!"

"He would be arrested immediately!"

"But do you have only the prisoners who are in this courtyard?"

"I have eight others, in absolute solitary confinement."

"Where do they live?"

"On the very top floor!"

"It was perhaps to try to communicate with one of them that my conspirator came in here!"

"I will show them all to you and we will go throughout the entire floor!"

"And I will show you the window through which he entered!"

"If you like! But I would be very surprised to find the man you are looking for."

They went up. Sénar secretly thought to himself, "It is odd how indifferent Dubois is, and how he is trying to convince me that an individual I saw enter is not here."

On the top floor, below the roof, there was a wide corridor illuminated by three high windows. A dozen doors faced onto the corridor.

"We are now in the part reserved for prisoners in solitary confinement," Dubois explained. "Four of these cells are empty, eight are occupied. Let us go through here silently. You will take a look at them through the window I slide open."

But Sénar was looking up. He pointed out the high window at the far end of the corridor and exclaimed, "That's where he came in."

"Are you sure?"

"Oh, absolutely!... I've got my bearings very well... And this is the adjoining wall."

Dubois did not respond. He slid open the board covering the grilled window in the door of the first inhabited cell and said to Sénar, "Look!"

Sénar looked. "This isn't him!" he said, staring at the prisoner inside the cell.

He gave the same answer for the next six cells.

But as soon as he peered into the eighth cell, a squalid, little space having a cracked ceiling where bugs could be seen scurrying, and cracked walls decorated with nails, on one of which hung a pewter bowl, he saw, lying on a dusty, stained pallet, near which was an earthenware pitcher, a man in a blue frock coat who slept deeply, like one sleeps when exhausted by prolonged superhuman exertion. His rolled-up cloak served as his pillow.

"That's him!" Sénar exclaimed.

"Shh!... Did he hear you?"

"No! He's asleep!"

"Are you absolutely certain that this is him?" asked Dubois in an anxious voice.

"I recognize him by his clothing. But I would very much like to see his face..."

At that precise moment, the sleeper made a movement as to change sides, and his head, turning over on the rolled-up coat, almost directly faced the door.

"Well, I never!" said Sénar disappointedly.

"What is it?"

"That's not him!"

"Really?"

And the voice of La Force's head jailer betrayed the joy given him by the Committee spy's remark.

"No!" Sénar added. "That's not the face of the man who gave the signal at the Cléry terreplein!"

"Aha! You were mistaken, see!"

"No!... I can't be mistaken on this point!... I didn't let him out of my sight!... And now, how on earth, the same coat and the same boots! And that hat hanging on the nail above his head is indeed the one that he was wearing!"

"Nevertheless, it is either him or it isn't him!... Maybe in one of the places he stopped at he switched clothing with someone?"

"No!... Those are the same stocky shoulders and the same build!... But the sword!... Where's the sword?... Hidden perhaps under his pallet?... It's still him!"

"But the face?"

"That's what confuses me!... No, it's not his face!... I have it detailed so well!... I jotted down a description!"

"Well, he doesn't have two faces!"

"That's what I'm wondering!" said Sénar, genuinely embarrassed. "And if the Revolution hadn't abolished superstition, I would think this man the devil!"

"So, to sum things up, you do not recognize him," said Dubois, "and this story of a man coming to voluntarily put himself in prison by way of a most dangerous route, and opening the door to a cell to which I alone have the key so that he can put himself in solitary confinement, seems to be a figment of your tired imagination, which has been fatigued by a sleepless night and a morning full of excitement and physical overexertion."

Sénar did not respond. He made a weary and disheartened gesture. The discouragement of the police officer, who did not know what to say and had gotten himself so entangled in a false lead, was visible on his face. He asked, "What is this prisoner's name?"

"Citizen Manaud. He was arrested at the Palais-Royal and put here in solitary confinement fifteen days ago. If it interests you, I will keep you apprised of what becomes of him."

"I certainly want to be kept informed, for I sense, despite everything, that a mystery I want solved is deepening... Farewell to my hopes!"

They were now going down the prison stairs. Dubois asked Sénar, "What hopes?... A congratulations from the Committee of General Security?... A bonus?... A promotion?... You'll have future opportunities!"

"Yes, but I'm in a hurry!"

"You're young!"

"I will let you in on a secret: I am in love with a young woman who is above my condition, and I would like to distinguish myself and obtain a high position to be able, with some luck, to win her hand... before she is married to another!... Many hopes are permitted today for paupers like myself!... Everyone can aspire to a distinguished position... The dream I entertain would have been unrealizable fantasy under the tyrant. The Republic I serve, in decreeing equality, has closed distances and eliminated castes. I can therefore love with hope."

"So, you are in love with a has-been?"

"Yes!... But whose family has had misfortunes of all kinds... I can hope then, despite everything!"

Dubois smiled at the police officer's naiveté. He had lived, and there was not much in which he believed anymore, not even in the Republic.

They arrived at the prison door. Dubois kindly slapped Sénar on the shoulder and said, "All right, good luck!... Don't say a word to anyone about your chase. I am going to try to unravel the matter, which we will keep between ourselves. And I am going to keep an eye on my prisoner, who has, if not the face, at least the clothing of the one you were following."

"That's right!" said Sénar. "And begin by having bars put on the windows that are in the cell corridor. As for me, I am going to go to sleep, have dreams about the future, and then try to resume my pursuit through the two Lézardières, who can perhaps put me back on the right track."

Once Sénar left La Force, Dubois hurriedly went back up the stairs leading to the secluded cells in the attic and went straight to cell number eight at the far end of the gallery. He selected one enormous key from his bundle, had it turn inside the lock with an infernal noise, and entered the abode of Clavière's business partner.

The baron, awakening startled, sat up, rubbed his eyes, and looked at Dubois with surprise.

"Forgive me for waking you so abruptly, Citizen Manaud, but I regret to inform you that you were followed here this morning."

"From where?"

"From the Cléry terreplein!"

"Oh!" said the baron, without manifesting outwardly the fright that might secretly be upsetting him. "Was I seen at the Cléry terreplein?"

"You were seen at the Cléry terreplein!"

"And who saw me?"

"A police officer!"

"Devil!... But it wouldn't be you, Citizen Dubois, who would like having me followed?"

"Me?... And for what purpose would I do that?"

And the baron stood up, his anger causing a wrinkle to form in his forehead. "To discover my true identity, just as I knew how to discover yours, Vicomte! You doubted perhaps that I was Citizen Manaud, because you yourself hide under a false name, because you were long ago required to quit your military service, flee, and disappear after having cheated at gambling and stolen; and, because you reappeared on August 10 under the name of the sans-culotte Dubois, a supporter of the Revolution, which earned you the position of chief jailer of La Force, you have surmised that I also have crimes to hide, and so you spied on me!... You have broken all of our agreement!"

Dubois turned pale at this diatribe; his lips tightened and lost their color; his eyes emitted a sinister gleam. He had the visible temptation to leap at the baron's throat and strangle him. He then overcame himself and bowed his head. In a subdued voice, he stated, "It was not I who had you followed! I have not broken any of our agreement!... But what good would it be for me to swear to it? You don't believe me!"

"Ha, I want only to believe you!" the baron responded, his tone becoming milder. "Speak!... You have as much interest in this as I!... The police officer in question followed me all the way here, you say?"

"All the way here!... I had to show you to him through the window... Fortunately, however, he didn't recognize you!"

"Excellent!" said the prisoner, satisfied.

"He thought he recognized your clothing and your hat... But not your face."

"Well then, everything is fine!"

"For the moment, perhaps!... But for the future, I find myself obliged to put bars on the corridor's windows, take away the key you use to return to your cell in the morning, and prevent you from going out at night... If this man were to see you again in the streets when you have already been arrested, it would be too obvious that I was your abettor!"

"As you wish, Vicomte!... I will give you back this second key whose existence the guards under you are unaware of... I will no longer go out... You will be guillotined, that's all there is to it. It's you who want it this way!"

"But what would you have me do?" murmured Dubois, in a tone of genuine despair.

"Continue to abide by our agreement! Let me go out at night in exchange for my silence!"

"Our agreement!... Are you abiding by it?... You are supposed to return at daybreak... And this morning, you came back at eleven o'clock!"

"This morning I was wrong... I admit it... But the circumstances... I will return at dawn from now on... Come on, Dubois!... Pardon my anger earlier... Allow me freedom at night!"

"No, I can't!... I risk too much!"

"But you know well that if eight consecutive days pass without me going out, the Marquis de Pons' imprudent letter to you, which I have in a safe place, will be sent irrevocably to the Committee of General Security. In this letter, the marquis thanks you for having warned him in time so he could avoid arrest and for having supplied him with a passport under a false name so he could emigrate... It's not my fault, of course, if the circumstances would just so have one of your life's rare good deeds be a liable cause for your destruction!... But, by heaven, this is how you would have it! You will be arrested and condemned... The Committee of General Security does not take such matters lightly!... They will know that you are a has-been hiding under an assumed name. They will charge you for having secret ties with emigrants... That's death! Come on, think about it!"

"Yes!... You've got me!" Citizen Dubois grumbled angrily, clenching his fists.

"I would willingly accept being placed in solitary confinement for good, but even that won't save you!... The letter will be sent automatically if I am no longer seen!... And with an explanatory note... Come on, Dubois!... You still have an interest in continuing the current arrangement and not bullying me!"

"Bullying you?" said La Force's concierge bitterly. "But it's not the prisoner who is being bullied! It's the jailer!... Curses!... If I were alone in this world!... If it weren't for my daughter who risks knowing her father's infamy!"

And Dubois grabbed his head by both hands and sobbed, exhausted. Coolly, the baron looked at him, awaiting the end result of his jailer's decompression.

"Fine!" he eventually said, raising his head like one who had made up his mind. "Keep the key!... But for pity's sake, be prudent!... I am also putting myself at risk!... Spare me, and don't ever cease to do so!... And what guarantees me that you will indeed return every morning?"

"My word!" Baron de Batz answered coolly.

Dubois closed the cell door and went away. But as he descended the stairway, he grumbled, "Oh, that letter!... Get it back!... Get it back!... Yes, but how?"

As for Baron Jean de Batz, he smiled, took off his blue frock coat, and put on some white undergarments and a dressing gown which he had removed from his travel bag. He brushed off the clothing he had just taken off, stretched voluptuously, lay back down on his pallet, and fell asleep again, whispering, "Yet another all-clear!... Will I finally get some quiet now?"

Chapter 7

The Royal Letter

THE UNWIELDY, BOTTLE green carriage we saw taking Louis XVI to the scaffold had continued on its route to Revolution Square as these other events unfolded.

The king-martyr's tragic and Christian ending has been recounted a thousand times, and more eloquently than we ourselves could do. Louis XVI left for the scaffold with the same courage with which his ancestors left for war. This scrupulous and indecisive man went to his death with a serenity having as its source a trust in God and a firm belief in the afterlife.

G. Lenotre, in his *Le baron de Batz*, recounts what happened to the confessor who accompanied the king in his carriage:

When Louis XVI was brought forward by the executioner's assistants and let out his final cry, "I do not wish my blood to fall upon France," Father Edgeworth de Firmont, seized with near-lethal anguish, was kneeling at the final step of the scaffold stairs.

His strength betrayed him; he lost himself there, trying to immerse himself in prayer... Lifting his eyes, he saw the king being secured to the board: it tilted, and the top portion of the headframe swooped down. The martyr lifted his head once more and turned his eyes towards the priest; the enormous steel triangle dropped.

The youngest of the executioners plunged his hand into the basket reaching for the royal head, seized it by the hair, and, holding it with his arm outstretched, went about the

69

scaffold showing it to the people. The blood dripping from it sprayed onto the platform. Father de Firmont would have been covered in it had he not instinctively sprung back in horror when the man drew near him...

Historians have described the fit of madness of the people rushing onto the scaffold; others have followed the cart taking the executed king's body to Madeleine Cemetery; we, however, shall follow the priest, who, stunned and terrified, slipped into the crowd, whose pressing ranks instinctively made way for him.

In his memoirs, Father de Firmont described the clothing in which we saw him a few hours earlier as he was leaving the de Lézardière residence. He wrote, "I had only a poor frock coat. I was soon lost in that immense crowd."

In his pocket, he was clasping a letter the king had handed to him in the carriage. It no doubt contained those "secret orders of great importance" which Lenotre mentions in a footnote in his book.

They must have pertained to the queen and royal family's safety and were addressed to Baron de Lézardière.

The priest, with his hand in his pocket where he was keeping the precious letter, bewilderedly left Revolution Square, crossed the Seine at the bridge replaced by what is now the Pont de la Concorde, and proceeded onto the streets of the left bank, wandering about somewhat aimlessly, so much did the great tragedy in which he had just been mixed up weigh heavily upon him, haunting him and forbidding him any other preoccupation.

Finally, he managed to collect himself, get his bearings, and find the home of Monsieur de Malesherbes, who had been the king's lawyer at his trial before the Convention.

It was here that he was to take refuge if Baron de Batz's plan to save the condemned royal had succeeded. He found here the two de Lézardière brothers, who had just informed the lawyer of the foiled rescue attempt at the Cléry terreplein. Father de Firmont was in turn able to recount the ending of the doleful tragedy he had just witnessed.

Then, accompanied by the two brothers, he went back to the de Lézardière home.

All three arrived there around noon. The baron, his wife, and Mademoiselle de Sainte-Pazanne anxiously awaited that tragic morning's news. As soon as they saw the priest and two young men enter and the drawing room doors were shut behind them, no word needed to be said. They understood that if their sons had escaped the fray, it meant that the king had died. The baron silently took his sons into his arms, and the baroness, putting her hand to her heart, let out a great cry and dropped onto a sofa, becoming almost lifeless.

Adèle de Sainte-Pazanne lavishly tended to her.

Then, when the baron saw that his wife had come to, he thought to read the letter the priest had just handed him.

His hands trembled as he opened it. He brought to his lips the paper containing the royal autograph, read it a first time, and then read it several times more. Copying the essentials from the instructions contained therein, he made a second letter and said to his sons, "This letter needs to go to *him* as soon as possible. Do you know where to find him?"

"Yes!" said Paul, taking the letter. He will have it this evening if I find him, tomorrow or the day after at the latest."

"You didn't cross paths at all with Cécile Renault?" asked Adèle de Sainte-Pazanne.

"No!" answered Sylvestre. "Why would we have crossed paths with her?"

"She went running after you this morning!"

"But why?"

"To warn you about your companion. He gave you a false name and is a spy for the Committees."

"Sévignon?" exclaimed the two brothers.

"That wasn't Sévignon!"

"Have mercy!... And who told you this?"

"Cécile!... That police officer lives in her building!"

Paul and Sylvestre looked aghast. They assumed a correlation between the foiled rescue attempt and this police officer who had abused their trust and naiveté. They feared for the baron, for their mother, for their father, and for Mademoiselle de Sainte-Pazanne. And after conferring with each other, they would have advised their father that they leave their house, on which they thought the Committee of General Security would henceforth be keeping an eye, and that they choose a more hidden refuge, if it were not for Baroness de Lézardière having a second fainting spell and needing to be undressed and put to bed.

The remainder of this bleak day, for the family, was split between anxiousness over a collective arrest, which seemed to them possible, probable, then imminent, and worries about the health of the baroness, who was visibly succumbing to so many emotions and shocks, and to whom Father de Firmont had to administer the last sacraments at about four o'clock in the afternoon.

At that time, the sick one sensed a kind of great relief. Thin, pale, and her eyes shining with fever, she called everyone around her bed and said, "I feel it, I am about to die... Oh, don't cry!... We all, this morning, experienced the deepest of human sorrows... I consider it a grace from heaven to die on the day of the king's execution. It is over France, over the misfortunes awaiting her, that we must weep. From up in heaven, where I hope God will welcome me, I will be watching over all of you... I will implore the Almighty to favor all the plans of the generous man you know, and to bless the work you are going to accomplish with him... You, Paul, swear to me that you will take no one as your wife other than the one we have always considered your fiancée. The day may come, soon perhaps, when she has nothing on earth but the support of your arm. To you, Adèle, I entrust my Paul's happiness. In my absence, replace my affection for him with your own... Be to him not only a good wife, but a little mama. Watch over him!... You, my little Sylvestre..."

But she was unable to conclude her final wishes. Paul and Adèle, sobbing, took the oath the baroness wanted of them. Everyone, plunged into sorrow, scrambled to help the dying one. But Madame de Lézardière did not come to; she expired in the arms of her husband.

A few hours later, Cécile Renault appeared in the mourning home.

The family's sorrow immediately deepened due to worries over the police officer the young girl had revealed to them. Cécile, shocked at the news of the baroness's death, cried, sobbed, and prayed on her knees before the mortuary bed, repeating a thousand times, "She couldn't bear the last straw, the king's death!... The poor lady was at her limit!" The baron and his two sons took her aside and asked her if she had any news. She told them of her morning, with which we are already familiar, and reassured them. "I couldn't catch up to you," she said to the two brothers, "but I ran to Rue Ménars. *He* wasn't there at all, fortunately for him! Two gendarmes were in front of his door."

"*He* himself told us the same thing," Sylvestre corroborated.

"I only found Marie Grandmaison, with whom I shared my fears. She laughed at them. She told me that *he* eluded all spies, and that *he* thought more than one had slipped into the conspiracy. However, she advised me to warn you. I went with her today to Charonne, where *he* will have his headquarters from now on, Rue Ménars no longer being safe. And now I'm here!"

"And him?" asked Baron de Lézardière. "Where is he living?"

"No one knows! But apparently his hideout is most impenetrable."

Cécile affected such an air of assuredness that the three men were won over by her confidence.

As they went back to the deceased, Mademoiselle de Sainte-Pazanne in turn took the young seamstress aside and asked her, "Cécile!... Did you speak about me to *him*?"

"How would I have done that? I didn't see him at all... But I did speak about you to his housekeeper..."

"In what terms?"

"I said to her, 'I have discovered a spitting image of the queen.' She told me that that might interest the leader. And we, the two of us, made a plan to rescue the queen."

"A plan with me in it?"

"Of course!"

"Oh, tell it to me!"

"You will run a great risk!"

"All the better!"

"You still want to die then?"

"Less... since my poor aunt entrusted me to care for and watch over one of her sons, which I would do, even if I weren't to become his wife... I am committed to this... But I would be proud to risk my life for the queen... Let's hear this plan!"

"It's the product of two poor women's imaginations... Will it be approved by the leader? I don't know... But in any case, it can only increase the chances of escape... Marie Grandmaison tells me the queen is to be rescued from the Temple, wearing a disguise. The danger is that her flight might be discovered too soon, and that the sovereign would then be immediately captured. So, far from concealing her flight, it will be we who make it known, putting the guards and the soldiers on a false trail. They will hurry and arrest, or rather think they have arrested, the queen... It is you they will arrest, you who look so much like the queen. It is you, veiled in mourning, they will take back to the Temple. All of that will take up time, and once they realize their mistake, the queen will be far away. But what will become of you?"

"Don't concern yourself with that!... Isn't the important thing that the queen be saved?"

"And then," Cécile added, "we will find a way to get you out of trouble in turn... No one will be able to prove that you were an accomplice... You were mistaken for somebody else, it wasn't your fault!"

"That's not what worries me!... The important thing isn't drawing the police to me; the important thing is to get the queen out of the Temple."

"There is already a plan for this. They are perfecting it, I know this. They want to leave as little as possible to chance. They will take weeks to prepare it, months if necessary."

"Do you believe then, Cécile, that they would be capable of killing her like they did the king?"

"Do you doubt this, Mademoiselle?... They are animals! They will kill her if we do not get her out of their claws, the poor princess!... So, can I tell them we can count on you if the leader likes our idea?"

"You can! I am totally ready!"

"Oh, the regret I have!"

"For what?"

"For launching you on this adventure!... Your uncle and your cousins will be furious with me, maybe... Oh, I prefer it were me, but I don't look like the queen!"

"Don't worry yourself about it, my good Cécile!... What would give anyone the right to take away my own right to sacrifice myself at a time when it is everyone's duty to do so?"

"Well then, I will see you later, Mademoiselle..."

"You're leaving?"

"My father would end up worrying!"

"That is true!"

"I will keep you informed!"

"You promise?"

"I promise!"

Cécile was already opening the drawing room door to go to the main stairway when Mademoiselle de Sainte-Pazanne held her back and asked in a somewhat hesitant and awkward tone, "Tell me, Cécile."

"Mademoiselle?"

"Do you have any new information?"

"I just told you!"

"About the other matter."

"The other matter?"

Cécile appeared not to understand, and her puzzlement was not at all feigned. With a little embarrassment, Adèle de Sainte-Pazanne clarified, "That siren you spoke to me about."

"Oh, the siren!" said Cécile in a somewhat mocking tone. "The siren supposedly warring against you in the heart of your cousin. But she doesn't exist!... You know that very well!"

"I fear that she might exist!... I believe that she does exist!" sadly replied the young woman.

"I will find out!" Cécile again promised. "But I am quite sure you are spinning fiction in your head!"

And she exited. A coat-shrouded shadow descended the stairway shortly after her, but proceeded onto the street in the direction opposite that taken by the young seamstress. This shadow, which gradually vanished into the fog of January 21 that thickened over Paris, covering the city in a funeral veil, was Father de Firmont, who was getting ready to return to England, his thoughts dwelling on the grievous, heartrending sight of that tragic morning.

Chapter 8

The Siren

THE SIREN DID exist. Mademoiselle de Sainte-Pazanne had been warned of her by a presentiment, by her feminine intuition. She had read her cousin's soul more clearly than he was able to read his own.

As this siren played an important and tragic role in the history of the Revolution, she is of double interest to us. It is time to make her known to the reader.

Everyone knows that at the time of the Revolution, the stylish, intellectual, and vibrant center of Paris was the Palais-Royal Garden, surrounded by its galleries which are today so dead and deserted.

When the winter wind blows through there, it is as though the past is weeping.

Back then, however, the masses went there. Its jewelry shops, its restaurants, its political and artistic cafés, and its stores where the fashions of the day were created did not empty. In the evenings, illuminated as for an unending festival, they drew in yet heavier crowds.

It was there that people also went to enrich or ruin themselves with a throw of the dice as they exited the theatre. Gambling houses abounded, but the most famous of them was the Arcades.

In 1790, three years earlier, a certain Aucane, the owner of vast estates in Martinique and whose immense fortune the Revolution had cut into, had the idea, in order to recover his losses, to invest a portion of his funds into the Arcades gambling house, and to create there an establishment reserved not only for rich persons, but also for those distinguished by their birth, their literary, political, or artistic reputations, or their elegance and good taste.

This Aucane was the first to conceive the idea of these great Parisian circles of today, with even more exclusivity.

To have the right to go spend a fortune there, one had to be accepted by the main sponsors of the gambling house, after having been presented by two referrers who had already been granted admission.

The Arcades gambling house, furnished and decorated with the discreet and delicate luxury characterizing the end of Louis XVI's reign, when "one truly knew the sweetness of living," to use the expression of Talleyrand, achieved an unprecedented elegance. One did not at all have the sense of entering a gambling den, but rather of being welcomed into some château or elegant mansion whose owner was having his guests over for games; the supper that interrupted these games around nine or ten o'clock only contributed to the illusion.

Aucane was the brains behind this distinguished establishment, whose comfort, elegance, and ambience hid the outside storms from its pleasure-seeking frequenters. He devised completing the agreeable and intimate atmosphere of the Arcades House by giving it something better than a host: a hostess, one who was distinguished, vivacious, and held the actual title of vicomtesse.

Let us not be too surprised that a Martinican owner was able to find in Paris, in 1790, a genuinely titled woman to preside over the fate of a casino. In our own time, this vicomtesse could have been a queen and reigned over Monaco.

I very much believe it was this idea that earned Aucane, at the Palais-Royal and on the streets, this nickname illustrative of his time: "the Bayard of the Green Baize."

Nevertheless, as few vicomtesses, despite the demoralization of the time, would have accepted such a position, we must briefly recount the very authentic beginnings of Madame de Sainte-

Amaranthe, and the social and financial reversals that led to her being simply called "Sainte-Amaranthe," like one might call a dancer at the Paris Opera. Lenotre provides us details:

Madame Desmier de Sainte-Amaranthe belonged to a very old family. Daughter of Étienne-Louis Desmier d'Archiac, the Marquis de Saint-Simon and royal commander of the city of Besançon, she had married, despite her family, Monsieur de Sainte-Amaranthe, a simple lieutenant who was of rather loose morals and only recently ennobled. He was the son of a tax farmer general named Davasse, also called de Sainte-Amaranthe, and a lady named Lallemand.

Shortly after her marriage, the lieutenant became a captain. He was with the musketeers of the first company of the Royal Navarre Cavalry, but he had to resign after some ugly episode.

He moved to Paris with his wife, but this was not the way to restore the fortune of the household, already so compromised. Within a few years, they were nearly penniless, with a little girl and a little boy to take care of.

And what too often happens in such cases happened: embittered with each other, the two spouses criticized each other's faults. This mutual criticism came easily: if the husband was a gambler, the wife was a coquette and a spendthrift.

And as the family of Madame de Sainte-Amaranthe was very willing to provide for the wife and two children, but not for the husband, whom they had never accepted nor wanted to see, the couple separated.

They did so without regret. The very real affection they bore each other at the beginning of their union had fled with the money, dissipating like the latter.

Madame de Sainte-Amaranthe thus went to live in the provinces. The former musketeer, being pursued by his creditors, literally fled to Spain, where, without resources, he was reduced to setting himself up as a carriage driver to avoid starving to death. The successive stages of his decline were unknown. And a rumor of his death ended up circulating, but we shall soon see that this rumor was false.

Later, Madame de Sainte-Amaranthe lost her parents. The few years she had spent away from Paris had given her an immoderate desire to return there, where her smile, her elegance, her deportment, and her lively, engaging charm had won her so many worldly successes.

She thus returned to Paris with her two children, entertained visitors in her home there, reestablished old relationships, and consumed her paternal inheritance down to the last sou.

One wonders what lamentable existence awaited this woman lacking in foresight, who, in order to survive, had begun selling bit by bit the trappings of her luxurious life—her furniture, her jewelry, and her lace—when Aucane came to her.

Aucane had been her father's banker. He was welcomed as a savior.

His proposition was accepted with gratitude. After all, it was not at all about manning a gambling den, nor of being a café cashier. Absolutely not! But rather of assuming the role of hostess in a milieu of supreme elegance, of presiding each evening over a princely supper, of sitting at a table around which gathered Paris's most illustrious figures from the world of politics, the arts, and finance.

She would be at home, so to speak, for her private apartment would be next door. It was the gaming hall that would be her reception hall. A royal endowment would be given her from the prize pool.

In short, luck had found her!

Madame de Sainte-Amaranthe was frivolous like her times. She happily accepted this situation, which she ought to have regarded as only a stopgap. It would have been understandable for her to see in this affair, as indeed was the case, the means for feeding her children. However, what most interested her in the Arcades House was that she could shine once again and that an inexhaustible treasure was going to be within reach, in exchange for her name, her prestige, and her elegance, which she was essentially selling to a gambling house for marketing purposes.

Her daughter Émilie, who was seventeen years of age at the beginning of the Revolution, was thus going to make her societal debut in a Palais-Royal gambling den, something which singularly underscores her mother's unscrupulousness. Lenotre, in his *Le baron de Batz*, writes quite rightly:

> *It was a singular spectacle that a gambling house should have a young girl of seventeen, so perfectly beautiful and so surrounded by adulators as was Émilie de Sainte-Amaranthe, whose mother exhibited a strange casualness in making her daughter's beauty one of the elements of success of a Palais-Royal gambling den, however decent and even dignified one might want to present the place.*

For Émilie was of a stunning beauty—all the contemporaries agree on this point. She was a living pastel of which artists' pastels could never give an exact impression, and whose charm and grace no writer could describe. Madame Amandine Roland writes:

> *Never, in my long career, have I encountered such a perfect specimen. Her figure was admirable in its delicate proportions. Her medium height, her gait, and her carriage joined a charming sweetness to a gracious dignity. Her smile had a delicate allure that enchanted, and when it accompanied a certain movement of the head, one was moved by it even more than in wonder. Her dress was of the most exquisite taste.*

The Count of Tilly, a regular at the Arcades House, writes in turn:

> *She was the person in France most universally renowned for her singular beauty. She was the most beautiful person of her time; she was this completely. I have never seen anyone in any country who might remind me of her, no one so absolutely perfect.*

Louis, the boy who was called Lili, was fifteen years old at the time, and was the spoiled child of the gamblers and diners of the elegant establishment, into which one day came Baron Jean de Batz, who was basically part of what one today would call the *Tout-Paris*, or Paris high society.

The baron returned. Curiously, Émilie, who was of better stock, more traditional, and had more nobility of soul than her mother, and who had suffered in silence living in this gilded milieu whose vices shocked her delicacy, began at this time to have a seemingly less sad outlook and to take satisfaction in the existence her mother had made for her.

One would have said that the great royalist conspirator had brought with him some breaths of fresh air. He had quite simply given this child a goal in life, and the noble consolation of sacrificing herself for a great cause.

He had seen all the benefits he could reap from a neutral place like this Arcades House, whose gamblers, coming from the entire social and political spectrum, talked, opened up, and constituted, especially following the daily supper served with heady wines, a veritable source of news and information which he could exploit.

At the same time, they might make themselves easy prey for the conspirators. A ruined gambler can often be bought, and the gamblers who came to this chosen place all had considerable social and political value.

Émilie, unbeknownst to her mother, was an agent of the baron. Did her atavism not predispose her to sympathize with and serve the royal captives, and to hate their persecutors?

The baron was also in the mother's good graces, but through another means: by granting the spendthrift vicomtesse some subsidies on certain days when she had too quickly squandered the endowment, albeit enormous, which went to her from the prize pool.

He had, moreover, become a shareholder in this establishment, and was incorporating it into his big plans.

The members of the Convention more and more replaced there those of the aristocracy who were forced to emigrate. It was indeed necessary for the baron, who sought the regicides in order to fight them, to go there where he was sure to find them, and where their appetites and their vices delivered them. It was they who chose the field of battle.

A few days after the king's death, around five o'clock in the evening in a small boudoir in the Sainte-Amaranthe ladies' private apartments, a lively conversation took place between the vicomtesse and her daughter as they were finishing preparing themselves for the daily reception of their "guests."

Émilie asked, "Mother, why is it that my father does not live with us?... Why, after having the joy of finding him a few months ago, does he keep himself hidden and not come here? Why, when we live in an opulence I find at times to be excessive and ostentatious, does he seem to be poor and short of money, in a situation inferior to our own?... I have been dying to ask these questions for a long time. Forgive me if they upset you, but all these oddities pain me. If there is truly a legitimate reason for these different living arrangements, tell it to me!"

"There is one!" said Madame de Sainte-Amaranthe rather dryly. "Your father is a has-been, as they say nowadays. He lives under a false name, in a position that the Republic has procured for him. He must hide, as must his name and his past..."

This last word, which alluded to the bad conduct of which Émilie was fortunately unaware, was pronounced with such an emphasis that the young girl did not insist on knowing its precise meaning. She followed up with this question: "Why accept a position from those people?"

"To live!"

"Couldn't Monsieur Aucane find him employment if he knew he was your husband?"

"You reason like a little girl!... Your father accepted a position with the Republic because he is a republican!"

"Truly, in his heart?"

"Or out of self-interest!... He is embittered against the old regime. He has everything to hope for from the new regime... And he even has aspirations for you, Émilie!"

"For me?"

"Yes! Truly!"

This "yes" was said with a kind of mocking irony that shocked the young girl, for whom her father had always been her father.

"You aren't going to fault him, Mother, for wanting what is good for his daughter!"

"If he's thinking more of his daughter and less of himself, no, certainly not... But since you are asking me questions, you will be edified on this point. Now it's my turn to ask you a question: Do you think about having to get married some day?"

"Hardly!"

"You're wrong not to!... Too many people badger me under the pretext that I have you living in an environment inappropriate for you—as if it were so easy to choose one's way of life!—in order that I push you to marry as soon as possible... I have a candidate, you know!"

"Monsieur de Sartines?"

"Yes!... Do you not like him?"

"I neither like nor dislike him!... He's a charming cavalryman, a likeable and courteous gentleman. But I don't love him!"

The mother's voice became harsher. "Then whom do you love, my daughter?"

Émilie did not answer. She appeared engrossed in a task that consisted of running a rouge-coated hare's foot over her cheeks to give them a little more luster in the light.

Madame de Sainte-Amaranthe continued: "Might it be that young Paul de Lézardière who, when he comes here awaiting the baron's orders, is motionless and speechless before you, as though mesmerized."

Émilie was still not answering.

Her mother continued: "Let's say it is him!... He's from a good noble family, from a rich family! But his family would never consent to him marrying the daughter of Sainte-Amaranthe!"

"Mother!" Émilie distressingly cried, like a wounded bird.

But the vicomtesse let loose. Spitefully, she continued: "Your father also has a candidate. He's a man he already considers master of the Republic. A kind of dictator who would be at the same time a pontiff or high priest of a new religion! Madness!... Killing the King of France to replace him one day with some kind of sultan or Persian shah! And he's the most republican of all republicans who dreams this up, claims your father, who anticipates all kinds of wonderful things!"

"Who is this republican, Mother?" asked Émilie, less out of personal curiosity than the habit of getting information to give Baron de Batz.

"Robespierre, my daughter!"

"Robespierre!"

"Indeed!... If you want to become Citizeness Robespierre and rule France tomorrow, you need only say so... This regicide has singled you out. He loves you!... He has not yet asked for your hand... But it appears that he is going to... Your father consents so that he can most certainly become a minister, command a regiment, or head the police..."

"But I don't consent!" said Émilie, all pale, with a gesture of horror.

This spontaneous movement brought back the affection of the mother, who embraced her, saying, "That is fine!... It's just that you who love your father so much, you will cut him off from the bright future he hoped for from such a marriage!"

Émilie did not respond. Tears flowed from her beautiful eyes. At that moment, she suffered as much from her father's plans as from her mother's mockery of this same father, whom she sensed was unhappy and whom she wanted to love and respect, despite the resistance she resolved to put up against him.

Had she no role to play in Baron de Batz's conspiracy, she would have fled far from this web of base self-interest, money rackets, and scheming, in which she felt caught like a partridge in a trap, so that she could take refuge in a convent or a foreign land.

It is true that her heart had its own secret, as we shall see, but this secret was so deeply buried, like a seed that had not yet sprouted, that she herself did not know if it pertained to a vague dream of her young imagination, or whether it was a matter of the mind or of the heart.

Her mother said nothing more to her. Émilie remained immersed in her somber thoughts. Yet what a cheerful place, hardly intended to accommodate suffering, was this boudoir, owing entirely to the prodigious artists of the time.

The ceiling, completely upholstered with pleated azure silk that shimmered in the light, sheltered dainty blue and white lampas queen armchairs, casually strewn amongst heart-shaped footstools, petit point seats, and plum-colored chenille-embroidered bergères. On the walls, Fragonards in flowery frames; in a corner, a rosewood writing desk; over the fireplace, small silver candlesticks with draped styling; and beneath one's feet, a large bright rug patterned with garlands of little pink flowers signifying prosperity and the flourishing of the fine French taste that ended with the monarchy.

Into this delightful sitting room entered a tall valet with dusty shoes, in livery that would not have been out of place in Versailles in times of royal splendor. He was one of the gambling house lackeys.

"What is it?" asked Madame de Sainte-Amaranthe.

"Monsieur Paul de Lézardière!"

"Let him in."

And Paul entered, dressed and gloved in black.

"Ladies, allow me to pay my respects!" he said, with a court gentleman's bow.

He kissed the hand of Madame de Sainte-Amaranthe, and then the hand of Émilie, with a kind of trembling and hesitation that did not escape the young girl's notice.

"It's been a while since we've seen you!" exclaimed the mother.

"You're in mourning!" added Émilie.

"For my mother! Yes, Mademoiselle!" replied the young man with genuine sorrow. "She died the same day as His Majesty…"

The two ladies multiplied declarations of sympathy, compliments, and condolences.

Paul thanked them and said, "Besides the pleasure of coming to pay you a visit, ladies, I was hoping to find the baron... I have a letter to give him..."

"It's been eight days since we've seen him," said Madame de Sainte-Amaranthe.

"Do you think he will come today?"

"I don't know!"

But Émilie made a subtle gesture with her head, signaling to him that Baron de Batz would not be coming.

Paul then rose and said, "I shall return tomorrow."

"Why the rush to leave so quickly?" asked Madame de Sainte-Amaranthe.

"Stay and have supper with us!" said Émilie with her irresistible smile.

Paul stared at her, as though fascinated by the magic of her sweet gaze. He was going to accept. Then, abruptly forcing himself from his contemplation, he answered in a somewhat monotone voice, as someone in command and control of himself: "Thank you, ladies, but my recent loss requires of me a certain reserve that I know you will understand. Besides, I need to get back to my fiancée, who is rather isolated now that my mother has passed."

"You're engaged!" exclaimed Madame de Sainte-Amaranthe.

"Yes, Madame!"

"We didn't know!" said Émilie.

Her mother observed her surreptitiously. But no muscle in the young girl's face moved. The mother thought, "If it's him she loves, she certainly knows how to contain herself!"

Paul took leave of the two ladies and went away rather quickly. He passed through the game rooms, which were starting to liven up, but without seeing or recognizing anyone among the usuals, some of whom did know him. His heart was tormented, but he was proud of himself.

This young man, who possessed the courage and qualities of his race, had fought like a lion cub on a battlefield. In life, he was a timid dreamer, not given to introspection, and affected by the impressions of surrounding objects and persons, until the day when an unexpected crash of thunder woke him from his reverie. Engaged to his cousin, he, like everyone else, had been captivated by the spell of Émilie de Sainte-Amaranthe, without realizing that the siren's image had little by little eclipsed his cousin's in his heart. It had taken the penetrating intuition of Mademoiselle de Sainte-Pazanne and her cry of pain to disrupt the ecstasy of Paul, who did not himself initially believe in the reality of what had been taking place inside him.

When he realized what had happened, he had a secret, excruciating heartbreak. He regarded himself as a traitor. Never had he dreamed of making a declaration to Émilie. And now that he had stated he had a fiancée, he went up in his own esteem, he was returning to the right path, and he was fulfilling the pledge he had made to his cousin, and the one he had made to his dying mother; he was doing his duty. He was certainly suffering, but from his point of view, it was the necessary expiation for what he called his betrayal, a secret, involuntary betrayal, but a betrayal all the same for this Christian soul, having a delicate conscience his mother had helped form.

It remained to be seen whether Mademoiselle de Sainte-Pazanne would now accept this sacrifice! We shall later find out.

This absorption of Paul de Lézardière in the pain of his interior cataclysm prevented him from seeing in the gallery, upon exiting the luxurious casino, the police officer Sénar, from whom he would have certainly demanded a strict account of his conduct towards him and his brother. Even if Paul had seen him, he might not have recognized him, for Sénar was sumptuously dressed.

Certain details in his attire undoubtedly betrayed either poverty or an ignorance of fashion, but someone did recognize the man who had wanted to make himself look good.

Just as Paul was exiting, and when the ill-intentioned Sénar was about to approach him to attempt to reestablish the vital connection that might lead him once again to the mysterious Citizen Manaud, another man was on his way into the Arcades House and changed Sénar's plans.

"Sénar?" the man exclaimed.

"Burlandeux!" Sénar answered. "How are you?"

"Very well! And you?"

"Not bad!... Look at you, you've fattened up!"

"And you, you are dressed very handsomely!... Are you rich now?"

"No!... I am spending from my little bit of savings."

"To dress well?"

"Yes!"

"Why?"

"It's my secret!"

"Keep your secret, Sénar! Keep your secret!"

"And you, Burlandeux, are you still a peace officer?"

"Yes, still!"

"We don't cross paths much!"

"It's because we don't work in the same area..."

"You've been promoted?"

"No!"

"You're eating better, in any case!... Your face is like the moon!"

"One has one's supplemental side jobs!... The Republic does not pay enough!... Fortunately, there are the side jobs to help make ends meet!"

"So, you have jobs in the city?"

"Yes!"

"You would be able to help me find some as well... For whom do you work?... And what do you do?"

"That is my secret!"

"Keep your secret, Burlandeux! Keep your secret!"

And they were about to split up when they each realized that the other was entering the Arcades House.

"Wait! You're going in here?" said Burlandeux.

"Yes!"

"Me too! But how do you have access to this very exclusive building?"

"The police can go anywhere!... You must know this since you yourself have access here!"

"That is true!... So, you know then that when a gambler has money, even if he hasn't been formally admitted according to the regulations, they let him in, only to throw him out once he's been cleaned out... That's the rule for any good casino!"

They went up to the mezzanine, then to the second floor, where they found an open door through which they entered a cloakroom that resembled a hat shop.

A boy in livery took their hats and walking sticks and gave each of them in exchange a numbered iron rondel.

They then had access to the first game room, without anyone asking for their cards, which seemed to indicate that they were known. Inside the room, a crowd surrounded a long table with a green covering divided by lines into numerous squares studded with numbers and marks of two colors, onto which gamblers intermittently showered gold and silver coins and banknotes which were then automatically swept away by small rakes.

Then there was a silence, and a ball rolled about, making a little dry rattling sound in a concave plate divided into numbered squares and spinning opposite the ball.

The ball stopped and a voice announced the number, color, and winning set; a commotion and movement within the crowd followed, and the showering of gold onto the table began anew without it being known whether the cause was the losers placing new bets or the croupier paying the winners.

A gold coin in front of the fascinated Sénar yielded ten more gold coins for its fortunate owner.

"That's quite nice," he said to Burlandeux, "to put down one louis like that and then win ten of them."

"It's less nice," replied Burlandeux, "to put a louis down and see it raked up by the manager. Anyhow, I didn't come here to gamble... I'll let you be."

"But neither did I, I'm not here to gamble."

"Oh, why are you here then?"

Sénar gave no answer. He saw Burlandeux making his way to the quieter rooms, where other gamblers, some seated at small tables and others grouped around one large one, apparently preferred losing their money at cards.

He caught up with him and asked him for some names. Burlandeux willingly gave them to him. Among other fashionable persons, he identified for him the has-been Marquis de Pons, the has-been Prince of Saint-Mauris, and Citizen Barbereux, the Director of National Haulage of France.

Citizen Barbereux was playing at a small, isolated table with a thin-lipped man dressed up to the nines. This man was wearing an impeccable powdered peruke, an exquisitely cut striped silk vest, and an immaculate batiste tie, but with a coat and breeches that were somberly colored, which tempered the frivolity of the vest and tie with a touch of almost austere correction.

"Who is that dandy?" he asked.

"You don't know who that is?... Really?"

"I've seen him only once here and one other time in the corridors of the Convention... He gives me the impression of a bucolic poet..."

"He does write bucolic poetry, in fact. He's a tender-hearted fellow... He's for the abolition of the death penalty. That's Citizen Robespierre."

Burlandeux disappeared, leaving his police colleague completely flabbergasted. Sénar looked at him enviously when he saw him enter the private apartments of Citizeness de Sainte-Amaranthe.

Let us enter along with him. We shall see him there most respectfully, servilely even, hand Citizeness de Sainte-Amaranthe a very thickly stuffed envelope, pronouncing these words: "On behalf of the baron!"

He received a smile and one louis. While the has-been vicomtesse went to put in a safe place the monthly payment she had been awaiting since the day prior, Émilie remained alone with Burlandeux, asking him casually, so that her question seemed of little importance if no response came, "Will the reaper come?"

"When the harvest is ripe!" answered Burlandeux.

Joyfully, Émilie asked straightaway, "Has the baron been seen in Charonne?"

"No, Mademoiselle!"

"Do they know when he will be going there?"

"He is still invisible!"

"They aren't worried over there?"

"Not at all!... But it looks like some people are waiting for him here—I saw some friends in the game rooms."

As Émilie had no more questions, Burlandeux discreetly bowed and exited.

As he went through the door, he crossed paths with a kind of servant girl, dressed in black and wearing a lace-trimmed bib apron. He returned to Sénar, who was still in the same place and asked him, "So, you know Citizeness Sainte-Amaranthe?"

"Vaguely," said Burlandeux. "I sometimes come to say hello!"

"Could you introduce me?"

"Oh, no! I am still not on familiar enough terms!"

"Fine!" said Sénar, a little annoyed. "One other question..."

"Go ahead!"

"Do you know that servant girl who just entered?"

"She's a seamstress who works for the daughter of Citizeness Sainte-Amaranthe... She comes here often. I don't know her name, however."

"I know her... She lives in my building, and her name is Cécile Renault."

"Why are you telling me this?... What's the significance?"

And Burlandeux slipped away. Before exiting the game room, he looked to see if Sénar was following him.

Sénar had remained motionless, dreaming. He saw Robespierre get up, courteously take leave of his partner without a smile lighting up his stern, pale face, and go into the Sainte-Amaranthe ladies' apartments.

Sénar's gaze followed him with the same envious look he had had earlier for his colleague Burlandeux. He then distractedly returned to the roulette table in the first room. In his pocket, he grappled a louis, the one louis he owned. Since louis were starting to become rare in this age of banknotes, Sénar's pocket contained only one by accident, and had never contained two at the same time.

Near him, two gamblers were talking about the Sainte-Amaranthe lady and her daughter.

"She's not seventeen years old, I swear!" said one of them.

Sénar did not hear the rest. He put his louis, his only louis, on number seventeen.

And he lost.

Chapter 9

The Good Leopard

JEAN DE BATZ had judged it prudent to go five straight days without leaving the uncomfortable lodging provided him by the Republic.

In the afternoon of the fifth day after having copiously slept, as he was sitting on his pallet stretching and contemplating the resumption of his daily escapes, a key grated inside the lock, his cell door opened, and he saw before him not Citizen Dubois, the concierge of La Force, but someone he did not at all recognize.

This individual's appearance was hardly inviting. He was herculean and bestial, having red hair resembling the mane of a wild animal, a long unkempt mustache, and eyes that were a strange shade of green. He held in his hand an enormous club.

His bearing was so threatening that the baron wondered for a moment if this henchman had been sent to beat him to death, and if the horrible days of September had begun anew. The baron inched downward as though to reach for his pistols hidden beneath his pallet.

But the individual cracked a large smile, which happened to make him yet more hideous. His mouth expanded from ear to ear, revealing a toothless jaw with blackish stumps. He bowed and said, "Leopard!"

The baron did not move. The individual explained: "Leopard!... That's my name!... I was a jailer in the children's reformatory... And I am assigned here, starting today, to the prisoners in solitary confinement."

"Who assigned you here?"

"The concierge!... Citizen Dubois!"

"Oh, good!"

The prisoner seemed reassured.

Leopard added, "I would like for us to get along well..."

"That will depend on you, Citizen!"

"And that you call me the good Leopard!"

"If you deserve the name, I shall!" jestingly said the baron, whose Gascon wit perked up at the new guard's hideous drollery.

"I do deserve it! And the proof," Leopard explained, "is that the prisoner next door gave me a gold coin to communicate with you. I am giving you his letter!"

"He knows me then?"

"I don't think so!... He told me to give it to one of his neighbors, it didn't matter whom, in order to pass the time. He's tired of being in confinement. That's understandable. Needless to say, Citizen Dubois is not in the know."

The baron answered dryly, "Give me the letter if you believe it good to do so!... I ask for nothing and suffer infinitely less from solitude than the prisoner who bribed you!"

The good Leopard handed it to him. It was an unsealed, double-folded piece of paper. The baron read the following lines, written in pencil:

Citizen, whoever you are, you are in solitary confinement like I, and you are bored. Do you want to correspond with each other to ease our isolation, since the new jailer is willing to serve as a messenger? To start, I will tell you who I am. I am Citizen Sévignon, arrested on an anonymous accusation ten days ago. Who are you? Write down your response and the jailer will bring it to me. Greetings and fraternity!

The baron started laughing.

"You will tell this prisoner," he said to Leopard, "that I consider him a flat-out liar, as his name is not Sévignon. I happen to know the real Sévignon, and he was seen outside five days ago, whereas my neighbor claims to have been in prison for ten days. Go on!"

Leopard seemed a little defeated. He nevertheless went to relay the verbal response and came back to the baron with this new written message: "*I am the real Sévignon and you are a crude character!*"

On the back of this short message, the baron then wrote the following with a pencil from a small notebook: "*You are another, and I will treat you as such if I ever meet you!... I convey to you in turn my greetings, but without fraternity.*"

And he signed it, "*Citizen Manaud.*"

One hour later, the good Leopard brought back to him the following response: "*I think I know the real Citizen Manaud. He is a polite and courteous man, and thus has no connection to the ill-bred creature you apparently are. Sévignon.*"

The good Leopard was reading all these missives before delivering them. Given this latest one, he said in a discouraged tone, "I might as well cut off your communications, as profitable as they could have been for me!... I was hoping that you would become friends and get along so that you would reward my indulgence. But you have not yet met, and you are already insulting each other! So, I can see this is not going to go as planned."

The baron found this reflection comical. Moreover, it was expressed with such innocent cynicism that it proved to him that there was no police collusion inspiring his fellow prisoner's initiative. Evidently, Leopard had only his personal profit in mind.

The baron said to him, "If you were to put me face-to-face with this prisoner..."

"Never!"

"And why not?"

"You threatened to assault him!"

"I promise you not to act on my threat... Come on, let's do this!... Bring him to me and let us have five minutes together!"

And reaching into his pocket, he pulled out one gold louis which he handed to him.

"Oh! Well then!" happily said the jailer, whose large smile once again lit up his bulldog countenance.

And Leopard quickly disappeared. Shortly thereafter, he brought into the baron's cell a young, slender man who was distinguished-looking, despite his dusty clothing and four-day-old beard.

The baron choked back a cry of surprise. On the other hand, his fellow prisoner did not appear to recognize him at all.

He apologized for the slovenliness of his dress. "Ten days in a squalid cell," he explained. "You understand... I won't be getting clean linens till this evening!"

"All right," Leopard exclaimed, "the citizens are going to get along better speaking rather than writing!... I have things to do... I will leave you. If Citizen Sévignon hears any noise, it would be very kind of him to go back to his cell to avoid compromising me."

"You can count on me!" said Sévignon.

And Leopard went away whispering, "There will be more advantages here than in the youth prison... Unbelievable!... I have a confrere at the Conciergerie who makes three louis a day for some little conversations between prisoners. I don't see why I can't do as well as he!"

And he put his two louis into a leather belt underneath his clothing.

Alone to themselves, the two prisoners, in low voices, exchanged some remarks aimed at determining their respective identities.

"All right!" said Sévignon. "Let us speak quietly! You are not Citizen Manaud!"

"But I am, and I see now that you are indeed Sévignon!... You really are my friend La Guiche!"

"You know me?" said Sévignon with surprise.

"And I now give you my apologies... But I had been told that you were at the Cléry terreplein on the morning of January 21, the day of the king's death!"

"The king is dead then?"

"Alas! You didn't know?"

"I no longer know anything! I've been in solitary confinement for ten days, I tell you."

La Guiche appeared aghast. He sat down on the baron's pallet as though shattered and repeated with trembling in his voice, "The king is dead!... The king is dead!"

"My poor friend!" said the baron.

"But really, who are you then?"

"I repeat: Citizen Manaud!"

"I know him, and he's not you!... Will the reaper come?"

"He's come already!" replied de Batz, changing the response to the passphrase which the impatient Sévignon uttered to him point-blank.

And, making that gesture of removing eyeglasses which had so much intrigued Sénar, de Batz took off a thin silk string whose ends were attached to each of his ears. This string, as fine as a single hair, passed in front of and elevated the tip of his somewhat long nose, thereby modifying his appearance to such an extent that he became unrecognizable. Anyone who goes in front of a mirror and firmly raises the tip of his nose with his finger will be convinced of the prodigious change in his own face, especially if he looks at his profile.

"It's you, de Batz!" exclaimed La Guiche, dumbfounded.

"Shh!... Are you satisfied now? Yes, I have two faces!... This is what saves me! Let's sit and chat."

And the baron put back the string, which transformed his nose from aquiline to upturned and bulbous. He added, "Your idea to attempt communication with your neighbor was truly genius. I had no idea you were so close to me!"

"But who allegedly saw me at the Cléry terreplein?"

"The two young de Lézardière brothers!... They went there with you, they told me!"

"I don't know them at all!"

"But would someone else then have passed himself off as you to them?"

"A police officer, no doubt!... What a disaster!"

"The spies are beginning to slip in among us... I'll need to investigate and do a serious purge at the house in Charonne!... On January 21, we had only six people instead of five hundred at the rendezvous!... Some were arrested several days beforehand, like you; others had two gendarmes at their door to prevent them from leaving."

"And now the both of us are here, powerless, missing in action!" La Guiche angrily grumbled. After a pause, he asked, "You were arrested at the time of the fray, no doubt?"

"No!... I was here prior to that!"

"But how were you there then on His Majesty's route?"

"I was able to get out of here!" answered the baron, who did not like revealing his secrets, even to his best friends, except when it was useful... Moreover, this particular secret was not entirely his own, as he shared it with Dubois. "Don't ask me how I am able to pass through these walls... You will know one day... But believe that even here, I fight, and that I am pursuing two equally sacred objectives: rescuing the queen and punishing the regicides."

La Guiche went to see if anyone was within earshot in the corridor. He then returned and said to his fellow prisoner in a hushed voice, "You know I have an escape plan?"

"What is it?"

"Every day, like the other prisoners in solitary confinement, I am allowed thirty minutes to walk alone on a terrace located at the end of this corridor."

"I know it."

"While there, I snatched a very strong iron rod of some kind that I then sharpened for long hours on the floor of my cell. I then fitted it with a handle made from a detached piece of wood from my stool. I have thus made myself a kind of spontoon that is easy to handle and can be used as a boring tool or as a dagger to defend myself... Standing on my stool, I can reach the ceiling in my cell, and I bored into the ceiling plaster in a single place for a long time to make a hole that is barely visible. After much boring and turning, my spontoon suddenly broke into an empty space above the plaster layer supported by laths, which I noticed when poking in other places where the wood creaked upon contact with my instrument. We are here in the uppermost part of the old

La Force mansion. Above us there must be an attic or a garret. One night, in two hours, I think I can make a large enough hole in the ceiling and go into the attic, where I will certainly find an unbarred window. If it is barred, the bars can be loosened or filed off..."

"And getting down?"

"I've thought about that. This kind of escape takes weeks to prepare. We'll do like Monsieur de Latude and his companion, who spent long days braiding themselves an extremely strong rope."

"Out of their torn bed sheets?"

"Exactly! You know about this!"

"But your sheets will never suffice to give you a long enough rope."

"There are your sheets also, dear Baron!"

"True enough!... But won't they find it odd if we don't ever ask to change our sheets... And if we do ask, won't they wonder what we've done with the dirty ones?"

"I've already taken all of this into account... Today, from the place of my confinement, I was able to notify a young seamstress, the daughter of the principal tenant in my building, the young Cécile Renault."

"I know her!"

"She is one of us!"

"She's a good young soul—courageous, devoted to our cause, and willing to die for it!"

"And she understands subtle messaging... It is she who is coming this evening to bring me clean linens, sheets and shirts. She will pretend to take my dirty laundry or only take some of it. I don't even need to tell her explicitly. She will read it in my eyes. And perhaps, when she comes next time, I will find something to make a good rope, or even a rope that's already made."

The baron thought things over. Certainly, an escape plan would hardly be of interest to him when he had a key to unlock his cell from the inside. But would he always have this key?

He said to Sévignon, "Yes!... Prepare this escape in your free time, my dear La Guiche... Leave nothing to chance!... I will escape with you... But do not forget that the rope must be long! Seven stories, and they're high stories!"

"I know it!"

"I'll tear my sheets also!"

Leopard's steps could be heard. Both of them hushed. Smiling, the jailer appeared and said, "My apologies, Citizens, but all things have their limits!"

"That is too true!" said La Guiche. He shook the baron's hand and said to him, "It was a pleasure to meet you, Citizen Manaud!"

"You as well, Citizen Sévignon!"

"Very good!" the good Leopard proclaimed glowingly. "You didn't want to meet, but here you are now, a couple of chums!... Thanks to me!"

"Thanks to you! That is true!" said Sévignon.

They were soon locked in their cells. Leopard came by and successively reopened their cells to fill their bowls with a clear, steaming soup that had an extremely disagreeable taste. He then wished them a good night.

Later, after the light shining through the barred transom window above the baron's cell door, via two corridor skylights, progressively dimmed and proclaimed night, which was an interminably cold and dismal darkness that enveloped the prisoners like a shroud, the baron took his sword and pistols from under his pallet, put on his leather belt, slid his large key into the interior hole of the lock, turned it quietly with infinite care, opened the door, and locked it again with a slow, minute turning of the key. He took a stool from its familiar place at the end of the corridor, placed it beneath one of the skylights, and opened it by pushing the pommel of his sword against its iron frame. He clasped onto the edge of the opening like an acrobat onto a chinning bar, pulled himself up, and disappeared through the roof like a shadow.

The window then closed silently.

Chapter 10

The Baron's Game

CLINKING GOLD PIECES streamed onto all the brightly lit, green game tables in the Arcades House. The crowds had never been more numerous. As recorded in memoirs from the time, the death of Louis XVI had created a kind of détente that was to last for several weeks. The fury of the Convention members had been assuaged by royal blood. As for the crown's faithful, they had assumed that the Convention would not go beyond this murder and that this spilled blood would be the last.

Thus, the levity of the era reappeared, and people went to enjoy themselves at the Palais-Royal.

Present were all those in Paris then regarded as fashionable figures or great minds: Monville, the extravagant giver of parties at his forest home in Marly, the mischievous Miromesnil, the Marquis de Saint-Fargeau, who was called the Parisian Alcibiades, Tilly, Champcenetz, and the famous journalist Rivarol.

Between two spins of the roulette, they went to an intimate corner of the room to strut before the de Sainte-Amaranthe ladies, who, playing their roles as mistresses of the house, offered them a cup of tea or a glass of Madeira with exquisite manners.

At a moment when the ladies were alone with Lili, the younger brother of Mademoiselle de Sainte-Amaranthe, a man approached and had a visibly animated conversation with them.

This man turned his back to the rest of the room, to which the de Sainte-Amaranthe ladies were naturally faced as mistresses of the house, surveying their guests from this chosen corner and examining whether they needed anything.

The man, who even when viewed from behind did not fail to exhibit a certain distinction in gestures and mannerisms, was dressed decently, but without elegance. He drew the particular interest of an old acquaintance of ours at the opposite end of the room, Sénar, who, dressed in his best clothing like when we saw him here earlier, had his eyes fixed on the group formed by the de Sainte-Amaranthe family.

"There's something about him," the police officer said to himself as he observed the man. "I know that back... But where have I seen it?"

And other details captured his attention: the attitude of Madame de Sainte-Amaranthe, who seemed to be speaking volubly and holding her own with the individual; and the contrasting attitude of the beautiful Émilie, who had her head lowered and was blushing and paling in alternation. Sénar believed he saw a tear fall from one of Émilie's eyes onto her cheek. He approached. But at that instant, the has-been Marquis de Saint-Fargeau, the "Parisian Alcibiades," who had broken away from the crowd at the roulette table, went to the de Sainte-Amaranthe ladies and gave them a genuine court salute. As he kissed the mother's hand and then the daughter's, and as the daughter told a tall servant in dazzling livery to bring Citizen Saint-Fargeau's favorite refreshment, a pistachio ice cream, the ladies' mysterious interlocutor silently slipped away.

Sénar then saw the man's face.

"Dubois!" he exclaimed. "Dubois! Him! Here!... And on good terms with them!"

He advanced towards the La Force concierge, who was infinitely less surprised to see Sénar in this place.

"Well, I see!" he said. "You are *observing* someone or something here?"

"No!" Sénar answered in a serious voice.

"Would it still be my famous prisoner who, although in solitary confinement, strolls to the Cléry terreplein, according to you, on mornings when there are so many people?"

"No, I tell you!... What are you doing here?"

"And *you?*" Dubois rudely answered back.

Sénar wanted to tell him that it was none of his business, but he contained himself. "You know the de Sainte-Amaranthe ladies then?" he asked him.

"Well enough, yes!"

"You seemed to be on familiar terms speaking with them!"

"You were observing me then?"

"Yes!"

"That's your job! That's right!" uttered Dubois, who was certainly annoyed at having been "observed."

Sénar swallowed this second affront without outwardly betraying his anger, which only caused a gleam in his eyes.

"I repeat," he said, trying to subdue the trembling in his voice, "I did not come here to observe anyone, no more you than anyone else... And I am going to prove it to you," he quickly added, in order to forestall an imminent objection he perceived on Dubois's skeptical lips. "The other day I confided to you the secret of my ambitions and my desire to attain a high position in the Republic. There is a young lady I love who has no more consciousness of me than a star does of an earthworm. But now that we are all equal, all hopes are permitted... I have come here to secretly contemplate the charming face of the one who, without knowing it, is now orienting my entire life!"

"She is here then?" asked Dubois.

"You just spoke with her, Citizen! It is Émilie de Sainte-Amaranthe!"

"I was afraid to find out! It's Émilie you want to marry?"

"I hope to, yes!... It's a crazy fantasy, isn't it?"

"It is crazy! You said so!"

"However, if I attain a high position!... The era we are in now is favorable!... And the Republic is generous to those who serve her!"

"You can forget about it, my poor Sénar!" said Dubois somewhat sardonically.

But the other exclaimed, "Why? You are talking to me as if I were a commoner and you were the relative of a young noblewoman! But there are no commoners or nobles anymore, there are only equal citizens..."

"Agreed!" answered Dubois, whose face showed disquiet when his interlocutor compared him to the relative of a young noblewoman, and who then exerted more effort to take on the tone and manners of a sans-culotte. "Agreed!... But you don't know if she has already chosen someone!"

"And you? Do you know?"

"How would I know?"

"You know her. Listen, Dubois..."

"What?"

"Introduce me to Citizenesses de Sainte-Amaranthe."

"Never!"

"And why not?"

"Why not? Why not? Because I know now for what purpose you want to be introduced... It is no longer an ordinary introduction; I don't have the right. Besides, they have too high a status for you!... What gives you the right to come in here? Think about it!"

Sénar used his police card to enter. He bit his lips and blushed.

At that moment, as the has-been Marquis de Saint-Fargeau, the Parisian Alcibiades, was returning to the roulette after having enjoyed his pistachio ice cream and taken leave of the ladies, three men, including one of impeccable style, approached and greeted them, but with less formality and grace than the Marquis de Saint-Fargeau.

"Who are they?" asked Sénar in a tone of hostile jealousy.

"Convention members!... They are more arrogant than the has-beens. The first is Julien of Toulouse, the second is Delaunay of Angers... And the third..."

The three Convention members sat down. The first two each accepted a glass of Malaga and a cookie. The third one, proper, cold, his lips tight and pale, uttered in a somewhat shrill voice, "For me, divine Émilie, a glass of water! Nothing but a glass of pure water for sipping and for calming the fever that your presence provokes!"

"The third one," interrupted Sénar, "I recognize. That is Citizen Robespierre…"

"And do you know," Dubois said ironically, "what Robespierre and you have in common?"

"Well, no!"

"That you both love the same woman!"

"Devil!"

"Go ahead and present yourself to those ladies and ask for Émilie's hand… Me, my friend, I'm not getting myself involved in this, as I value my head!"

And he led Sénar into another room, laughing and telling him, "Give up your fanciful ideas!"

"It would kill me!" whispered Sénar in a tightening voice.

This revelation was like a heavy blow to him. He was very pale, and a feverish flame shone in his eyes. In one of the rooms that was quieter than the roulette room, and where the gamblers were playing cards in groups of two or four at small tables, Dubois had the unlucky man sit down, drink a glass of maraschino, and asked him, "Are you doing better?"

"Yes," Sénar said somberly, "because I still want to hope!… If I stopped hoping, I would die." Suddenly, he perked up, as though moved by an internal impulse, and exclaimed, "What on earth!"

"The police officer has resurfaced!" thought Dubois. "That's more like it!" Then, out loud, he asked him, "Do you see someone?"

"Yes!… Over there!… Look!"

And he pointed out to the La Force concierge, in a corner of the room, by a window facing out onto the Palais-Royal Garden, two men seated facing each other and playing, or at least appearing to play, for they laid down a card once every ten minutes and, with their eyes fixed on their game, they seemed to ruminate for a long time as they each soliloquized. The two soliloquies must have constituted a single important conversation. But this escaped Sénar's detection. In the gambler who was facing him, he had just recognized the baron.

"Well?" asked Dubois.

"Well! Whom do you see at that table?"

"I see the back of Citizen Barbereux, the Director of National Haulage of France. He had just been playing with Robespierre. But I don't know who the man is who replaced Robespierre as Citizen Barbereux's partner."

"I know who he is!"

"Tell me his name!"

"That is your Citizen Manaud, your prisoner in solitary confinement!"

"Come on!... I would recognize him!"

"It's true!... In his cell, wasn't it I who no longer recognized him?... Outside, it's you who no longer recognize him... Does he have two faces then?"

"You are talking nonsense! They are not the same!"

"In any case, that man is indeed the one I followed from the Cléry terreplein to La Force... That is all I need to know!"

And he got up.

"What are you going to do?" asked Dubois.

"A masterstroke!... Have Robespierre get the Committee of General Security and the Convention to take notice of me! Get promoted to higher positions by my own rival, who will congratulate me in front of the entire Convention for having saved the Republic."

Dubois, worried, also got up. "You are going to get Robespierre?"

"Yes!"

"To point out to him Citizen Manaud?"

"And to have him arrested on the spot! Yes!"

"You will be making a foolish mistake!"

"I will tell him everything about how I followed him!"

"Including this man's entering La Force through the roof?"

"Certainly!"

"You will ruin me!"

"Too bad!"

"Yet you are mistaken!... Have you been closely watching this man since the twenty-first of January?"

"Every day?"

"Did you follow him out into the street?... Did you see him leaving La Force?"

"No!"

"You see!... You are mistaken! He is not my prisoner!"

"I am going to tell Robespierre that the man who tried to rescue the tyrant is here, that is all!... What does it matter if he is not your prisoner?"

Dubois thought to himself, "Citizen Manaud will be guillotined. He has my letter; he will ruin me!"

He just so happened to notice the baron giving him repeated stealthy looks, seemingly communicating to him, "Careful!... Don't you ruin me, or I will ruin you!"

He did not know how his prisoner altered his face, but what he did know was that this prisoner was the same man Sénar followed from the Cléry terreplein. He had one means to prevent Sénar from following through with his plan. He used it.

Running after him, he grabbed him by the arm and said, "Sénar!"

"What?"

"Come sit back down! I must speak with you!"

This was said with such an urgent tone that Sénar docilely let himself be taken back to the small table where they had been served maraschino. He then sensed that Dubois was going to tell him why he must not deliver up the mysterious Citizen Manaud. He sat and waited.

Dubois began: "I lied to you!... However much Robespierre loves that young woman, he is not at all to her liking!"

Sénar looked at him, surprised. "Why," he asked, "are you reopening to me the door of hope after how hard you just slammed it shut in my face?"

"Because I have a deal to offer you..."

"A deal?"

"As you probably figured out, I know the de Sainte-Amaranthe ladies better than I wanted to let on."

"Aha!"

"I'm a relative of theirs!"

"Oh!... A cousin?"

"If you like!... And I have influence with them... Lots of influence, you understand?"

"If you don't use it to my benefit, I don't care!... Only if you agree to present me to them..."

"I will present you!"

"Really?"

"But not right away!"

"You're playing with me!" Sénar said sadly. His eyes having shone with hope and joy just a moment earlier, he made a gesture of despondency.

"I am not playing at all!" said La Force's head jailer. "But I don't want to be played with either!... I will present you, and I will even speak for you when we have succeeded in together capturing Citizen Manaud, whom you would like to deliver up by yourself..."

"We can do it right now!" exclaimed Sénar. "Let us both go to Robespierre!"

And he got up again. Dubois grabbed him by the arm and forced him to sit back down.

"No!" he said urgently. "Not right away!"

"And why not?"

"Because you would ruin me!... Do you accept the deal?... If yes, I will explain to you everything!"

The police officer was speechless. He hesitated, fearing to be lured into a web whose threads he could not perceive. But on the other hand, Dubois had just dazzled him with the unique opportunity to enter the de Sainte-Amaranthe ladies' intimate circle. As the jailer had anticipated, this prospect influenced Sénar's decision. The lover in Sénar overtook the policeman in him.

"Yes!" he said. "I accept!"

Dubois then explained everything to him: the existence of the letter by which his prisoner held power over him, and the obligation to leave this prisoner a key enabling him to open his cell from the inside and go out at night.

"Still happy," he added, "that he is willing to return in the morning and that his own safety obliges him to only go out at night! At least, in the daytime, he is there, and I am able to show him to the Committee of General Security's representatives if they show up!"

"And if you were to prevent him from leaving, what would happen then?"

"After eight days, the friend of his who keeps the letter would take it to the Committee of General Security!"

"But what if he died?"

"The same thing would happen!"

"Devil!"

"The wretch has arranged things in such a way so that I spend my life fearing for his own!"

"And how does this situation end?"

"I have no idea!"

"Obviously, this situation is an awkward one!... This man is troubling you, and you can't have him put in prison. He is there already, officially. The best thing would be to try to have him set free!... That would make things better for you... Since if anyone ever suspected you were letting him go out..."

"I would love to have him set free! But by drawing the Committee's attention to him, I risk having him condemned to death! And that's all the more to be feared because this two-faced man is evidently the head of a vast conspiracy... The best thing, for me, is that they forget about him!"

"Or that we find the letter!"

"Now, Citizen Sénar, you have come to the point to which I was leading you. You alone, the stealth observer that you are, could recover this letter... Once we have it back, my scoundrel's outings are done, finished, over! I keep him under lock and key, and the two of us denounce him. We save the Republic, we get promoted, and..."

"And you arrange for me to see Citizeness Émilie de Sainte-Amaranthe every day? And finally having a position worthy of her, I can entertain the hope of marrying her?" asked Sénar, for whom this was of the greatest importance.

"Yes!" promised Dubois.

"Good!... In that case, I am going to start my pursuit, beginning this evening! Give me some information about this letter and where you think it might be."

"It's a letter," the concierge of La Force explained, "imprudently written to me by the has-been Marquis de Pons, whose arrest I prevented and whom I provided a passport."

"Devil!"

"I owed much to the Marquis de Pons..."

"You owed him money?"

"Perhaps... Let's just say I couldn't refuse him the help that I gave him."

"Why did he need to write you also?"

"Ha!... If this letter had stayed in my hands, I might have been very happy to show it one day... One never knows how things will turn out, and it's good to have one foot in both camps. But unfortunately, I misplaced it.... It was discovered by a royalist and it has since been used to blackmail me!"

"Better that it was discovered by a royalist than by a Convention member!"

"Certainly! Better to be blackmailed than to play hot cockles in Revolution Square!... But if my prisoner disappears, if his friends go eight days without seeing him, they will blame his disappearance on me and send that sweet little valentine to the Committee of General Security..."

"What does this letter look like?"

"It's on blue-tinted, lightweight paper, with large, bold handwriting."

"Where do you think it might be?"

"In one of the places Citizen Manaud frequents at night, whether he has a domicile or goes to the home of his friends!"

"After following him enough, I'll eventually find out."

"Yes! Get me out of this, Sénar!... And each of us will reap a handsome reward for the arrest of this has-been, for he is a has-been. And I will introduce you to the de Sainte-Amaranthe family; I will plead your cause to the girl!"

"Excellent!" Sénar said simply, his face lighting up at the future he anticipated.

And they shook hands, as if to seal the pact. Then they each drank another glass of maraschino, all while observing from the corner of their eyes the baron, who was still playing with Barbereux.

And the baron was observing them also. He stared at Dubois strangely. Dubois could read his eyes, which flashed with anger. They said, "Have you been following me since I left La Force? Would you be spying on me?... If so, there will be serious consequences for you, Dubois! Serious consequences!"

And Dubois was not too comforted.

Sénar suddenly nudged him: "See that young man in mourning approaching Citizen Manaud?"

"Yes!"

"That's one of the two de Lézardière brothers..."

"He's handing him a letter!"

Indeed, Paul de Lézardière had just entered, coming from a neighboring room where likely one of the conspirators or even Émilie de Sainte-Amaranthe herself had indicated the location of their leader. For, after having looked right and left over the game tables, he caught sight of the baron and went straight to him, saying, "Monsieur, how good it is to see you!"

He looked at Barbereux distrustingly.

"Speak in front of Monsieur! He is one of us!" said the baron.

Paul then took out the letter and handed it to Monsieur de Batz, telling him, "It's from my father, who wrote on this the principal last wishes of His Majesty. They were relayed to him by Father de Firmont."

Very moved, the baron unfolded the letter and hurriedly read through its contents. He said to Barbereux and Paul, "His Majesty commissions me to save the queen, against her will if necessary, and to save only her if necessary, convinced that she will be put to death if she does not escape."

"But why against her will?" asked the Director of National Haulage. "There is nothing the queen wants more than to be rescued, I imagine!"

"She only wants to be rescued with her children! She does not want to leave them alone in the Temple! The king's intention is to try to free her, only her if necessary, if the royal children and Madame Élisabeth can't also be rescued."

He looked at the letter again and added, "His Majesty advises me, in order to communicate with the queen, to make use of a certain daring and cunning knight named Gonzze de Rougeville, who managed to communicate with His Majesty almost every day till January 21, giving him news from the outside. He evidently has a special ability, a secret way of passing letters to prisoners unbeknownst to their guards. This name is not familiar to me!" de Batz added. "Gonzze de Rougeville!... He defended the Tuileries on August 10... But where is he now?"

"I don't know!" said Barbereux.

"I don't know either!" said Paul de Lézardière.

"If we don't find him, we'll manage without him!... Is this everything you had to tell me, Monsieur de Lézardière?"

Paul did not answer. Having taken a random look around the room, he had just caught sight of Sénar speaking with a man he did not know. His heart pounded in his young chest. His face, fresh like a girl's and whose upper lip was only starting to don a fine, silky mustache, became red as anger swelled inside of him. He would have marched right over to the police officer who had fooled him, and he would have made a scene in the Arcades House, had not the baron repeated his question.

"Monsieur," the young man answered in a trembling monotone, "Monsieur, I have to speak with you about something serious, something for which I am to blame!"

"You?"

"I let myself be taken in, along with my brother, by a scoundrel... And I feel we bear some responsibility for the failure of January 21..."

"Explain!" said the baron, surprised.

"I told you earlier that the Marquis de La Guiche was with us..."

"Sévignon?"

"Yes... And well, it wasn't him!"

"I know that," said de Batz without emotion, and even with a certain good humor, for his Gascon disposition always prevailed. "Someone passed himself off for him to you..."

"You know?" exclaimed Paul surprisingly.

"Sévignon could not be at the Cléry terreplein on January 21... He was and still is in La Force Prison, where I spoke with him not three hours ago!"

"You spoke with him... You? At La Force?... But how?"

"That's my secret!"

The baron was not averse to intriguing his faithful, especially when it increased their estimation of him, for their confidence in him was thereby doubled. And he added, "Set your mind at rest, young man. The failure was not due to this incident."

"Oh, thank you!... You have removed a big weight from me and my brother's consciences!"

"But be more prudent about your relationships in the future!"

"Rest assured, Monsieur! This is a lesson!... And speaking of lessons, I am about to go teach somebody one!"

"Whom?"

"The rat who pretended to be Sévignon and who happens to be in this room right now!"

"Where?"

"Over there!"

And Paul pointed out Sénar to the baron, who was quite happy to recognize the man who had followed him.

The young man was already rushing forward. De Batz held him back by his coattail.

"Are you mad?" he asked. "A scene? An altercation in here?... I order you to play along with this individual, to continue letting him think that he is fooling you, to reach out to him as if he were Sévignon. Only the roles will be reversed. The dupe will no longer be you, but him... Do not give him any more information, but try to learn from him as much as possible. Go over to him right now and shake his hand. If he asks you my name, I am Citizen Manaud, a banker, and I have a conspiring

brother who looks a lot like me and whom I have disowned—
there you have it!"

And Paul awkwardly obeyed. He was somewhat averse to
these ruses and lies. However, they were necessary; they were an
integral part of the supreme struggle in which he was engaged.
Was it not through ruses and lies that the masonic Revolution
had been implanted and reigned in France? Was not one obliged
to breathe the air it had created?

With a little uneasiness, he extended to Sénar a hand with
which he would rather have wrung his throat, saying to him,
"How are you, Citizen Sénar?"

"Very well! Citizen Robert!... A glass of maraschino?"

"Gladly!"

And Paul sat down. He gradually settled into his role. Sénar
thought he had not been discovered and immediately remarked,
"I saw somewhere that citizen with whom you were speaking."

"Citizen Manaud? That would surprise me!... He does in fact
look a lot like his brother, who is a conspirator and has
completely disappeared since January 21. But this brother, he has
disowned him. He busies himself only with finance business. I
was just asking him for news of his brother. He has none."

Dubois and Sénar exchanged glances as if to communicate
someone was trying to fool them, but they were not fooled. They
let Paul de Lézardière go off into the adjacent room where, no
doubt, he was invisibly drawn by the desire to live a few minutes
in the presence of the "siren."

Sénar said to Dubois, "If you hadn't been here, he might have
talked, since he evidently still thinks I am the conspirator
Sévignon. In front of you, he is on guard."

"Go join him then, and try to grill him!" answered the La
Force jailer. "Me, I am going back to my prison."

"Don't do a prisoner roll call when you get back!" said Sénar
mockingly. "There might be one missing!"

Dubois made a grimace without answering. He had little taste
for jokes. He left, and Sénar remained alone, observing the baron
who was still playing with Barbereux, or rather was pretending
to play, and who at this precise minute was saying the following:

"You must always keep one carriage and three horses available. You will be given advance notice the night that the royal family is to leave the Temple, and a carter chosen from among your most trustworthy men will be waiting that evening, with a canvas-covered cart, in front of the wine shop at the corner of Rue des Gravilliers and Rue des Vertus. No one will be able to notice the cart from Temple Prison. The horses will be eating oats; the carter will be having supper as if he were about to go on a long trip..."

"You hope to save all of them?"

"I hope to, yes!... By dressing them in long, gray hoods like those worn by the soldiers who make the rounds, and having them leave in the middle of a patrol."

"And around what date would this happen?"

"I need to check with Cortey and pick one of the days he will be on guard at the Temple with the Filles-Saint-Thomas battalion. The patrol will take Her Majesty and Their Royal Highnesses to the cart. In this cart, which is well covered, they will find poor people disguises. The queen and Madame Élisabeth will be dressed as common womenfolk, like those one sees at Les Halles. They will be accepting the carter's kind offer to give them a ride back to Lagny after having just finished selling their merchandise for the day. Madame Royale might be dressed as a little boy and the little dauphin, now Louis XVII, will be dressed as a little girl. That will throw them off the trail. Once in Lagny, your carter will take his vehicle to the Soleil d'Or Inn. Her Majesty and Their Highnesses will then change into bourgeois traveling clothes. A carriage will be in the courtyard with fresh horses. And I myself will be in the carriage, with a passport Clavière will have provided me, which will be in the name of English subjects Citizen and Citizeness Atkins, their sister and mother-in-law, and their two children. Three days later, we will be in the Grand Duchy of Luxembourg."

"Did it ever occur to you," Barbereux objected, "that they will deploy cavalrymen onto all the thoroughfares as soon as the Temple is aware of the queen and royal family's escape?"

"On only one thoroughfare, my friend, the Rouen one. A carriage having someone in it who resembles Marie Antoinette will go towards Rouen, and I will see to it that it is immediately reported to the Committee of General Security, which will be busy trying to stop it. Another Drouet, like in Varennes, will perhaps try making a name for himself by arresting Marie Antoinette a second time. It will be a wild-goose chase and we will have fooled the dogs, or those monsters rather. A fake royal family consisting of a woman, a young girl, and a curly-haired child will be a half-league ahead of the fake queen's carriage in a separate vehicle."

"You have someone then who looks like the queen?"

"Émilie de Sainte-Amaranthe just informed me when I came in that her seamstress, our valiant little Cécile Renault, has discovered someone who is the spitting image of the queen."

"And ready to sacrifice herself?"

"Ready to sacrifice her very life!"

"Oh, Monsieur Baron," Barbereux exclaimed, "the age in which we live produces heinous crimes and at the same time most admirable sacrifices!"

At that moment, the two Convention members we earlier saw greeting the de Sainte-Amaranthe ladies in the company of Robespierre appeared at the room's entrance.

"Leave me, Barbereux!" said Baron de Batz. "These are delegates to the Convention, Julien of Toulouse and Delaunay of Angers. They are coming here to see me."

"Very well!"

Barbereux stood up, like a partner taking leave. In a low voice, he said to the baron, "Good luck on your game with them."

"I have many games to play!" the Gascon said laughingly. "I am playing an enormous amount today... Let's hope I win everything!... Thank you for the wish.... By the way, any news from Lyon?"

"The driver I sent to the Duke de Crussol-Langeac only left the day before yesterday... Wouldn't expect anything sooner than fifteen days..."

"See you later!"

The two Convention delegates, who seemed as though they had only been waiting for Barbereux to leave, approached the baron. They did so discreetly, to the amazement of Sénar, who was still observing from the other end of the room in front of a third glass of maraschino. They sat down, Julien of Toulouse facing the baron and Delaunay of Angers at the end of the table, almost turning his back to Sénar.

This was not a first-time encounter, for a conversation quickly ensued as if it were the continuation of an earlier meeting. Julien had one of the thickest southern accents and Delaunay spoke like a western peasant. They were both second-rate provincial lawyers promoted to the role of legislators, whom Paris life had financially strained and made needy.

"Well, did you see Citizen Robespierre?" asked the baron.

"Yes, Citizen Manaud!" answered the Toulousian. "We were just with him. He left just now, leaving his seat to some little bashful young man who seems to me to be in love with the de Sainte-Amaranthe damsel!"

"Let's get to it!" interrupted Delaunay. "We're here to do business. Let's talk about what we're here for!"

This Delaunay, with his accent and demeanor, made one think of a country bumpkin who comes to sell a cow at the fair in Cholet or Bressuire and expends all his efforts for that purpose. The baron looked hard at them both with a shrewd eye, at the back of which a fierce gleam shone. He thought to himself, "How well I have you under my control!... Oh, what useful tools you two will be for me!"

"Look," added Delaunay, "we didn't dare bring up the business to Robespierre..."

"And why not?"

"As soon as we would have mentioned money and stock shares, he would have mistrusted and arrested us... He is the 'Incorruptible One,' you see! And he is true to his nickname!"

"Incorruptible?... Up to what point?" asked the baron skeptically.

"He aspires to things higher than wealth or profiting from a stock market coup," said Julien of Toulouse. "We want nothing to do with him. Believe me!"

"What a shame!" murmured the baron.

"But we have someone who would get things started!" Delaunay quickly declared.

"Who?"

"Chabot!"

"The ex-Capuchin?"

"Yes!... And his ardent republicanism and staunch sans-culottism put him above suspicion..."

"Have you approached him?"

"We have approached him!" replied the Toulousian. "He is like us! He needs money!... Life in Paris is expensive for delegates... And if they don't raise our salary soon..."

"Let's get to the point!" Delaunay interrupted. "Chabot will give the speech needed for going after the Indies Company and sending down the prices of its stock shares, which he will buy and then we will buy. He wants to be rich. He wishes to marry the niece of Frey, the super-wealthy Austrian. When do you want to see him?"

"Chabot?"

"Yes!"

"In about two weeks, in Charonne," the baron replied overjoyed. "Citizens," he added, "I am happy that you are providing me the means to accomplish such a fine stock market coup. For, with Citizen Manaud, business is all politics!... I am only a banker and nothing but a banker. Chabot, yourselves, and your friends will all have a share in these magnificent profits. And from now on, if you are in financial difficulty, I can advance you funds and you can access my coffers in Charonne."

And he immediately signed a bill of exchange for each of them.

They each accepted with an eagerness that the most democratic, the most progressive, and the "purest" of delegates have always exhibited when taking bribes; they then withdrew with obsequious bows that would have shocked naive souls used to reading those historians in never-ending admiration of the Convention members' "flinging a king's head at Europe," a gesture that was hardly fruitful in the end.

When they were gone, the baron got up, went to the other room, and wrested Paul from his silent contemplation of Émilie, saying, "Time to go, Monsieur!... The man you pointed out to me is going to follow me. You will follow him in turn. I am going to Cortey's. Make him lose track of me as soon as possible. But you, don't lose sight of him for a second!"

The baron left. Sénar quickly followed him. And Paul, prudently bundled in his coat, followed the follower.

Chapter 11

The House in Charonne

BARON JEAN DE BATZ exited the Palais-Royal via the Perron gallery and went to Rue Vivienne. A cold, bitter wind was blowing from the north.

He lowered his head amidst the oncoming gusts and was only able to shelter himself from the wind once he turned left onto Rue Colbert.

Then, hidden behind the corner building, he peeked onto the street from which he just came. At two hundred paces he perceived a shadow, and further away one other shadow that was intuited more than seen. It oscillated over the coarse pavement, vanishing and reappearing, subject to the swaying of the streetlamps hanging by their ropes, whose pulleys the wind made creak.

He continued on his way.

At the end of Rue Colbert, he came upon Rue de la Loi (Rue de Richelieu), on which he turned right without looking back. Then, he abruptly turned left onto Rue Saint-Augustin. But this was only an artifice. He intended to throw Sénar off the trail of his nighttime excursion.

At the corner of the two streets, he looked back again and gladly saw that the further of the two shadows had reached the other, which was now only about a hundred paces from him.

He then stealthily sped back across Rue de la Loi and onto Rue des Filles-Saint-Thomas, which was and still is an extension of Rue Saint-Augustin. He stopped in front of the grocery shop at the corner.

From his pocket, he pulled out a skeleton key, slid it noiselessly into the lock, entered the shuttered shop, and silently closed the door behind him. He moved across the dark store and proceeded directly to the glass door of the faintly lit back shop.

Careful to avoid making any noise, he gently lifted the latch and pushed the door.

In the glow of an oil lamp could be seen a man sitting at a table, who appeared to be sleeping on the day's edition of *Le Moniteur*. In front of him was a classic grocer's apron, and he was wearing a red cap. He was startled by the baron's ghostlike entrance, stood up, and exclaimed, "You!... Finally!"

"Shh!... I'm being followed. Hello, Cortey," answered de Batz in a clear, lilting voice.

He shook the hand of the grocer Cortey, whose home, Lenotre explains in his *Le baron de Batz*, was situated at the exact location where the building at 68 Rue de Richelieu exists today.

Cortey folded his newspaper, went to ensure that the door was properly shut, then sat back down across from the baron.

"The things that have happened, Monsieur Baron! The things that have happened since we last saw each other!"

"Alas!... We have been betrayed, my good Cortey! God rest the king's soul. The focus now is on rescuing the queen... When will your battalion be guarding Temple Prison?"

"Not for another ten days or so."

"Could you take me in with your grenadiers? I would like to try to see Her Majesty."

"It's quite easy to enter the Temple... But what's not so easy is speaking to the prisoners. It appears that the queen, since the king's death, no longer wants to go down to the garden to get some fresh air, as it would require her to pass in front of the door of the apartment from which her husband left for the scaffold.

"She lives with Madame Élisabeth and the two children on the fourth floor of the donjon. King Louis XVI occupied the floor beneath. She only allows herself one or two hours a day on the tower terrace, and she only does that for the health of her children. If she were by herself, she would stay cooped up in her prison forever... If you knew how much weight she has lost and how pale she has become since the thirteenth of August when she went to the Temple!... Her only clothing now is a pitiful black dress that is all worn-out! But she is still noble and beautiful in the martyrdom she is suffering. She draws tears from the eyes of all her guards!"

Cortey choked up. He was a tall, stout, red-faced man, muscular and stocky, and he was tenderhearted like a child.

"The poor woman!" murmured de Batz. "This is what they've done to her who was that pretty, sixteen-year-old archduchess, the shepherdess of Trianon!... I still remember her pouring the frothy milk herself to her guests over the marble tables at her dairy... She was laughing!... She was happy!... She had no idea of the storm that was approaching!... The poor queen!"

The two remained facing each other, without speaking, immersed in their thoughts.

The baron resumed: "Why would it be difficult to speak with her? Having on a grenadier's uniform and being on guard duty, couldn't I walk around in the tower?... Being part of a detail that brings the prisoners linens or bread, for example?"

"Yes, but there's the Tison couple!"

"Oh, that's right, the two live-in guards! Who are they exactly?"

"The husband is fifty-eight years old. He's a former tax collections clerk. The swindlers dreaded him because no one was more distrusting of the agents stationed at the gates. I suspect this distrust was what made Chaumette, the commune procurator, choose him to prevent any escape attempts on behalf of the Temple prisoners."

"Could he be bought?"

"I don't think so! He's paid six thousand livres, and his wife three thousand, a fortune for them. Prudence would make him reject any offer of that kind, and he might report the bribery attempt."

"Is he harsh with the prisoners?"

"Very harsh. Hateful even."

"And his wife?"

"His wife would gladly be more lenient, but she is controlled and terrorized by her husband. She is much younger than he. Her maiden name is Victoire Baudet. She's the daughter of a master shoemaker on Rue Copeau. She still has the temperament of a kind and simple working girl, and I know that she speaks respectfully to the queen when she is alone with her. But we can have nothing to do with her on account of her husband, who is a brutal, cunning creature."

"Have you succeeded in speaking with the queen?"

"Yes, once. I was on guard duty. I acted like a sans-culotte and shouted the *Carmagnole*, and Santerre, the division general, could not refuse a good patriot the desire I expressed to see 'Madame Veto.' Maybe he even thought I would be nasty to her and insult her. He authorized me to go up to the fourth floor of the tower and to ask Tison, since Tison and his other half almost never leave their boarders.

"That day, the king was at the Convention, where he was on trial, and the jailers only had to mind the fourth floor.

"Arriving there, I pretended to have misunderstood, and I told Tison that Santerre wanted him to come down and that I would stay to look after the Austrian woman for the time being. He rushed down the steps, and I was first able to very quickly get a good look at the layout."

"Very important!" said the baron. "What did this floor consist of?"

"An antechamber and three rooms. Two of the rooms are occupied by the prisoners. The Tisons live in the third room.

"A glass door separates the Tisons' room from the antechamber, which functions as a dining room for the royal family.

"This way Her Majesty, her sister-in-law, and her children take their meals within sight of the jailers, who closely monitor their words and gestures. Furthermore, at any time of day or night, without any concern for whether the three women are fully dressed, Tison, Santerre, and the guards enter the two rooms as they please."

"Really!" de Batz lamented. "Nothing is spared them! They can't take their meals in private, and at night they can't be left in peace; they're not even given fifteen minutes of relief amidst the daily sufferings imposed on them. And these brigands dare to speak of the monarchy's prisons!"

Cortey continued: "Her Majesty and Their Royal Highnesses were at table when I entered, silent and barely touching their food. Madame Royale was peeling an apple for her brother, who then started biting into it with the carefreeness of his age. The Tison woman, who was struck by the crude and ill-mannered act I was putting on, let me go in.

"I deliberately let my saber drag continuously over the tile floor and make a loud clanking noise. And this noise prevented me from giving myself away. I might not have been able to bear the haughty silence kept by the queen, her sister-in-law, and her daughter, who did not even turn their eyes towards me. I could have thrown myself on my knees and begged forgiveness, so much was my soul burdened by the thought that I was adding a new bitterness to those already overwhelming these noble victims for whom I would give my life.

"Only the little dauphin, as he was munching his apple, smiled at me, all while playing with his cute, blond, curly hair. How moving that was!... Had the son of my king sensed a friend in this plumed, tricolor-cockaded, roughneck soldier who was advancing towards his mother?

"My temples were pounding, and you could hear my heart leaping inside my chest.

"The Tison woman stayed in her room, and I could hear her stirring her pots. I abruptly stopped. And without making a movement, without leaning towards Her Majesty, all while appearing to be indiscreetly staring at the spectacle of that sad meal, I very quickly said, 'A friend will come to see you, Madame, on a day when Commandant Cortey is on duty again...' I began walking around again, letting my saber drag, and I stopped in front of a crude drawing on the wall with a charcoal inscription which made it even worse, done by some Commune thug in charge of inspecting the Temple, or by some other of the vicious animals whose job it is to torment the poor woman. The drawing was of a guillotine with a caricature of a woman lying on the board. And the inscription said, 'The Capet woman flopping in Revolution Square.'"

"Those wretches!" the baron grumbled.

"Oh, Monsieur!" said Cortey. "The Temple tower is covered from top to bottom, inside and out, with filthy drawings and bloodthirsty inscriptions against the king and queen. The king is drawn as a pig and the queen as a she-wolf. In the stairway leading to the terrace, you can see a head on a spear and read beneath it, 'You will die like Lamballe, Antoinette!'"

"These vicious insults are not spontaneous," the baron said, "since almost all those whose duty requires them to go to the Temple end up being seized with pity at the tragic circumstances, and being outraged at the despicably vile persecution. These things are deliberate, ordered, and paid for by the masonic lodges who worked the Revolution, not only against the King of France, but against his people, at the profit of foreigners, especially of the Genevan Protestants; I know some things about that!... But continue."

"Well, Monsieur, I had the audacity to laugh loudly in front of the despicable drawing, in order to gain the trust of the Tison woman, who I sensed was watching me from behind. I didn't mind at this point. The queen now understood why I was behaving like a patriot brute.

"I turned around again.

"Oh, what gleams of joy and hope shone in those eyes of hers, wearied by sleeplessness and reddened by tears. Her poor face has wizened, but it is still so beautiful and proud when it beams. She moved her head forward to get a good look at me, as she is very nearsighted and her eyes blink a bit when she is examining something or someone. But she is only all the more graceful. I wasn't able to know the others' impressions; I only saw her. And her sweet voice echoed inside me like heavenly music. Yes, Monsieur de Batz, she spoke to me, she, the Queen of France! She said to me, 'I believe a friend has already come, Monsieur! Thank you!' And the way she looked at me told me that that friend was me!

"At that point it took real strength of soul for me not to break down, get on my knees, and kiss the bottom of her poor little black queen-martyr dress. Were it only a question of myself, I wouldn't have minded.

"For a 'thank you' and a smile from the Queen of France, one would gladly go to the guillotine, no? But I was there to rescue her, not to engage in futile heroics.

"Still, I was a little imprudent. I wanted to say too much. I said to her this: 'I am only a poor Paris shopkeeper devoted until death to Your Majesty. The friend in question is powerful, and you know him; he wants to get you out of this hell. Keep an eye out when I am on duty, and look closely that day at your bread, at your linens, and at everything that comes in here for you.' I was going to continue, but I heard steps in the stairway.

"Tison entered and began yelling at his wife, who was scrubbing her pots, and then at me. 'Santerre did not ask for me!' he shouted. I answered back, 'I thought he did!' He squinted at the queen and then at me as to insinuate I don't know what, so I grabbed the bull by the horns and shouted even louder than he, 'Hey, Citizen Tison, if I stayed here for so long with the Capet woman, it was not for my enjoyment! I was guarding the Nation's prisoners in your absence, that is all... And if ever you let escape this family which has drunk the blood of the people, you listen, Tison, I would be very capable of strangling you with my own hands!' And to really emphasize my patriotic fervor, I grabbed him by the throat and shook him like a plum tree. Oh, how much I would have liked to have finished him off right then and there!...

"But that again would have been futile heroics. I let him go, I gave him a shove, and in order to hide my emotions and my wanting to cry, I shouted at him, 'If you ever again start to question my patriotism, Citizen Tison, I will skin you alive!'

"And I rejoined my grenadiers, not without hearing Tison cry out to his wife, 'Who is that madman?'"

Cortey concluded: "So there you have it. You have been announced and are expected! What is your plan?"

Several times as the commandant of the Filles-Saint-Thomas section was giving his account, the baron's mind wandered off, leaving the sorrowful scene of Temple Prison to recall Trianon, the small apartments of Versailles, their magnificent view of lawns, flowerbeds, and hundred-year-old trees, hearkening back to the joyous and triumphant years of Maria Theresa's daughter in order to more fully taste the bitterness of this royal destiny that was ending in that small, obscure space closely shared with the Tisons, within that jail where each passing day marked a new station on the road to Calvary.

Some time passed without the baron answering. Finally, he answered: "To see the queen at all costs on your next day of guard duty. Then, the following time that it's your turn, to get her out of there, she and the other three captives, by dressing them in gray hooded overcoats, arming them with rifles, and having them leave with a patrol made up of friends. And I will be in command. I will have the required passwords and papers. I will be acting like I am from the Hôtel de Ville."

"And the Tisons?"

"Couldn't a good narcotic immobilize them for a couple of hours?"

"Maybe."

"A dagger will work, if necessary."

"The queen would refuse to have any bloodshed."

"She will not be consulted! I have my mission from the late king."

"If the escape succeeds, what then?"

"Everything is planned out!... A carriage will be waiting nearby."

"And if there's a pursuit?"

"Everything is planned for!... A false trail will be prepared!"

"Well then! May God protect us, Monsieur Baron! My life belongs to the queen!"

"I know that, Cortey!... Mine also. If you need to speak with me, come to Charonne. In my absence, you will see Biret-Tissot. If you need funds, my coffers are open to you. You were clever and courageous in your meeting with the poor queen, and I am envious of the 'thank you' and the smile she gave you!"

The baron emotionally shook Cortey's hand. Cortey went to see whether anything suspicious could be seen on Rue des Filles-Saint-Thomas or Rue de Richelieu. Upon assuring the baron he could leave without fear, the latter, throwing the flaps of his ample coat over his left shoulder, exited the shop and headed towards the Bastille, bending his shoulders beneath the gusts of wind, whose intensity had increased.

During this time, Sénar had lost the baron's trail. Just when the baron, as we know, through a clever maneuver, disappeared onto Rue Saint-Augustin by temporarily turning his back to Cortey's shop, which was his destination, the police officer felt a tap on his shoulder, and a familiar voice rang in his ear: "Passing through here, La Guiche?... What a small world!"

"Monsieur de Lézardière!" Sénar responded, very annoyed.

"You were passing this way then?"

"Yes! I gambled and I lost. It is so warm in that Arcades building, so I am taking a long detour before going back to Rue de Savoie. I need the fresh air. Which area are you heading to?"

Sénar, who was caught off guard, replied, "To Faubourg Montmartre, to a friend's home!"

"I can still go along with you a bit!"

"If you want!"

"Unless I'm bothering you!"

"No, on the contrary!"

Sénar put on a good face. Besides, his pursuit had been cut off. Showing ill humor would have been a useless imprudence, especially to the one person who could help him find Manaud again.

Paul de Lézardière accompanied him as far as the boulevards. There, he separated from Sénar, but with the intention of letting him distance himself further only to then follow him. He hid in the recess of a building's carriage entrance and saw the man proceeding on Boulevard Montmartre, then turning right onto Rue Vivienne.

"No, no, no," the young man said to himself, "that way doesn't get you to Faubourg Montmartre. I know your real objective, detective!"

And he followed closely behind Sénar. He eagerly engaged in this pursuit.

The police officer went as far as the buildings of the Filles-Saint-Thomas Convent and circled around those nuns' vast, empty enclosure. This pious place, which has since disappeared, then occupied the site of the Bourse and the buildings located behind it along Rue Notre-Dame des Victoires.

The fake Sévignon's instincts had served him well, for Paul de Lézardière suddenly saw Sénar leap back and hide behind some building construction materials.

Surprised, Paul also stopped in the shadow of a stretch of wall. In front of him, some eighty meters away, at the intersection of the street he was on and of Rue Montmartre, a massive carriage clanking noisily and harnessed with two nags had just halted; a man stiffly bundled in his coat was negotiating with the driver.

The whistling of the wind, which was beginning to carry some snowflakes into a frenzied race, and the creaking of the streetlamps swinging from their gallows posts prevented any sentence in that conversation from reaching his ears.

Finally, the man went into the rickety, old coach. The door slammed shut, and the carriage started on its way, heading east.

Paul then saw Sénar exit from his hiding place, rush towards the carriage, catch hold of it, and jump over the axle located in the far rear which supported the board meant for holding the travel trunks, night bags, and suitcases.

Most of these vehicles for hire were, at the time, old coaches, and this luggage board had previously been used by powdered lackeys who stood there, their hands clinging to the fringed straps hanging at the rear of the vehicle.

Sénar was thus only taking what would have been the footman's spot in order to travel as comfortably as possible right behind the man in the coat, who de Lézardière could not doubt was the baron himself.

Leaving Cortey's, de Batz had headed towards the Bastille, encountered this available carriage on his way, and boarded it, without noticing Sénar, who had nearly run into him, but had rushed just in time behind a pile of building stones.

And the young man was perplexed and worried. How was the pursuit to continue? No other carriage was in sight in the deserted streets. He would have been willing to pay handsomely for a good horse, but where was one to be found at this hour?... And time was of the essence. The carriage was already far-off, and de Batz was unsuspectingly guiding the Committee policeman to his retreat in Charonne, to the headquarters of the conspiracy.

Valiantly, Paul de Lézardière began running after the carriage, managing his breathing. The snow was now coming down in large flakes, stifling the distant noise of the wheels over the coarse pavement. But the creaking of the springs continued to make itself heard, and the wheel tracks and horse hooves in the snow were easy to follow.

Soon, the snow thickened, the pavement became slippery, and the pace of the horses, which had already been very restrained, slowed down. Paul was able to catch his breath multiple times by assuming a walking pace, and arrived at the Bastille without being too out of breath.

The carriage proceeded from there into the city outskirts, then turned left onto the interminable Rue de Charonne, went past the customs gate, which at the time was where the street crossed Boulevard de Charonne, and was then in the open countryside.

In place of where there are now five-story buildings erected and factories set up inside former country homes, which new industrial neighborhoods imprisoned little by little, there were vineyards and woods traversed by an encased road ascending to the village of Charonne.

The vehicle passed through the village at a walking pace. Then, once past the last houses, the carriage proceeded onto Chaussée de Bagnolet, which is now Rue de Bagnolet. There were large elm trees growing alongside it at the time, whose trunks, on that winter night, took on fantastic shapes when the moon, coming out in brief intervals from behind the storm-swept clouds, lit the whitened road and made the snow-powdered tree branches and vines sparkle like crystals and diamonds.

Suddenly, a male voice rang out: "It's here!"

And the springs stopped creaking. Paul de Lézardière, exhausted, out of breath, and his face bathed in sweat, hid behind one of the giant elm trees.

The baron got out of the stopped vehicle. Sénar was no longer on the luggage board, but while de Batz was paying the driver, the young man saw a far-off shadow hiding along a wall, behind which could be seen the barren treetops of a large park.

To the right of the road, he could make out in a kind of half-light this place he knew so well: its cart entrance covered with a slate canopy, flanked to the right by a lovely Italian-style pavilion, and to the left by a longer two-story house.

The carriage departed. A light appeared beneath the canopy, without the baron having even knocked or rung. He entered, and the door noiselessly closed behind him. All the snow seemed like quilting muffling all noise, changing men into phantoms and life's external appearances into silent dreams.

Lenotre writes: "It still exists, this mysterious house of Baron de Batz. By a truly extraordinary stroke of luck, it survived the most remarkable transformation that can occur within a hundred years to a hamlet lost amongst vineyards, such as Charonne was a century ago, having become a city of a hundred thousand souls."

We ourselves wanted to see this house. It provided us the opportunity to pass through, for the first time, one of those quarters in the east of Paris which, as they are adjacent to fortifications, are infinitely more unknown to and ignored by Parisians living and moving about in the city's central part and western quarters than are Switzerland, Italy, Nice, the English Channel, and the ocean.

By a curious coincidence, the metro line that goes from Porte de Champerret to Place Gambetta, at the top of Ménilmontant, follows, beginning at the Bourse, almost the exact same route taken by Baron de Batz's carriage. When one gets off at the Place Gambetta station and takes Rue de la Cour-des-Noues and then Rue Pelleport, which are still lined with small houses nestled beneath large trees, but overrun and disgraced by sordid hovels inhabited by ragmen and ravaged gardens occupied by demolition sites, one suddenly comes to Rue de Bagnolet and stands before a gate and large park with ancient trees.

The sight takes one by surprise. It looks like the gardens of a spa.

Is it Vichy, Luxeuil, or Aix-les-Bains suddenly looming in this corner of Paris, where one hears from behind the puffing of factories' steam engines and the ringing of iron beneath the repetitive blows of heavy hammers? Bright new buildings of yellow brick stand at the end of a central pathway, giving one the real impression of a casino or hotel. It is actually just Debrousse Hospital, built on what remains of an old manorial park.

On the right, at the corner of Rue de Bagnolet and Rue des Balkans, a pavilion of an entirely different style draws one's attention. It juts onto the sidewalk, and the railed fencing juts along with it, surrounding and protecting this work of a bygone time. The intact land is what remains of Château de Bagnolet's old park, which belonged under Louis XV to the Duke of Orléans, and this small pavilion, which dates from the *Régence* and was a hunting lodge at the corner of the estate facing Paris, is the last witness to the brilliant feasts and splendid hunts that took place here.

They called it the Hermitage. The large summer room, from which opened the vast French windows facing Rue de Bagnolet, contained frescoes depicting the life of Abraham and personages from the Bible. The groves which surrounded it had been landscaped by Desforges, the pupil and nephew of Le Nôtre, and continued along the road to the village of Bagnolet.

Since that time, the Paris fortifications would have cut the estate in two if, as early as 1770, the Duke of Orléans had not sold this magnificent property, which was immediately divided up.

The Hermitage had been the first lot to find a buyer.

Its first owner was Monsieur Morel de Joigny, a lawyer at the Parliament of Paris, who had a house constructed to the left of the pavilion, the space between this house and the lovely hunting lodge thus forming a courtyard, which was separated from the garden by a small fence.

Baron de Batz had in turn purchased this building in 1787, not suspecting the good use he might make of it one day.

The house has disappeared. The pavilion alone remains and serves to house some administrators of Paris's *Assistance publique* hospital trust.

Paul de Lézardière, once the carriage had gone away and he saw himself alone on the road, ran to the cart entrance and lifted the heavy knocker, which he let down three times, the first two times in quick succession and the third time after a pause.

He waited a rather long time. Then one side of the heavy double door partially opened. A porter holding a lantern, who did not come out or even make himself visible, asked, "Who's there?"

"Will the reaper come?" the young man said softly.

"When the harvest is ripe," the man answered, almost whispering.

Paul entered.

"The baron! Quickly!... The baron!... I need to speak with him!" he exclaimed.

"Monsieur de Lézardière!" said the man with the lantern.

"Yes, my good Biret-Tissot. It is I!"

"You are all sweaty!"

"I ran behind my master's carriage!... A policeman was on the baggage plank!"

"A policeman! Mercy!"

"Yes! He is hiding by the wall along the road. He is spying... We can catch him!... Where is the baron?"

"With his cashier! Come!"

"Biret-Tissot preceded Paul into the pavilion, led him across a circular vestibule embellished with niches which evidently still exist, then through the large living room adjacent to two studies. Monsieur de Batz's trusted servant knocked at one of these two studies.

"Come in!" said Baron de Batz.

Biret-Tissot went in alone, but was very quick to come back out. He was preceded by Jean de Batz, who ran up to Paul de Lézardière, saying, "Oh, poor boy!... You have just given us fine proof of your dedication... Why didn't you warn me from afar, with two whistles? I would have gotten out of the carriage!"

"But he would have fled!"

"You are right!... Perhaps we will catch him instead!... Come!"

They went out into the garden, followed by the cashier and the servant, who had armed themselves.

From this house, and from the far reaches of the park, which seemed silent and uninhabited when one passed by it on the road, shadows were emerging.

Paul de Lézardière was in familiar territory.

Citizeness Grandmaison, the housekeeper, appeared with Cécile Renault. Then it was the Count de Marsan and several other figures seen briefly at the Cléry terreplein and the Arcades House.

Word had evidently spread, and all had instinctively sensed the danger.

Cécile Renault went up to Paul. "A police officer followed Monsieur Baron?" she asked.

"Yes, Cécile, and I followed the police officer!"

"It's not Sénar, is it?"

"It's him indeed!... It's the fake Sévignon."

"Oh, let that snake be stomped out once and for all!" she exclaimed.

Words and sentences were exchanged in quiet voices among the twenty or so conspirators assembled in the snow-filled courtyard.

The entire property had to be circled, from the outside.

"Muzzle the dogs!... Keep them from barking!" the baron ordered.

One accomplice who had gone out exclaimed, "You can see his footprints in the snow, along the wall!"

Two large sheepdogs and four or five fox terriers on leashes were put on the trail. But a man who had followed the dogs came back running towards the baron.

"Monsieur," he said, "the footprints stop four hundred meters from here, at a place where the wall's coping has come off."

"The man scaled the wall then?"

"To get inside here, yes... The dogs also stopped at that spot, and were standing on their hind legs and scratching the wall..."

"We're getting him!... Let's go!" exclaimed the cashier, who seemed to be one of the most eager to conduct the pursuit.

Before everyone else, he hurried into the depths of the park, with a pistol in each hand.

Right against the back wall of the property, adjacent to the other lot in the Duke of Orléans' old park, upon which nothing had yet been built, this faithful servant of the baron's discovered footprints. He followed them running, and the moon came out from behind a cloud, casting a plain white light onto the completely white ground, which appeared to glitter.

And through the swirling snowfall, he saw the fugitive pushing apart some branches in a thicket to give himself cover.

"Freeze!" he exclaimed. "Or you die!"

Sénar, who was evidently seeking out a place where the wall was lower in order to escape this property he had so foolishly entered, turned around and riposted, "Not if I kill you first!... Traitor!"

And he pointed his own pistol at the cashier. But both abruptly lowered their weapons. In the light of the moon, they had just recognized each other, and two cries simultaneously escaped from their breasts.

"Sénar!"

"Burlandeux!"

But Sénar had joy painted over his face, whereas Burlandeux was pale as death.

Sénar took a gamble: "The Committee of General Security was not mistaken!... A peace officer is in the pay of a conspiracy of aristocrats!"

"It was me then you came to spy on?" asked Burlandeux.

"Perhaps!"

"If I killed you!"

"That wouldn't do you any good. You are found out! It's the Committee that sent me to *observe* this house!" he declared with a calculated impudence. "Oh, so this is what you call working for private individuals! You are a marked man!"

"You fool!... There would also be work for you if you wanted it!... But that depends on me... And this way, I would be saving you!... They are on your trail!"

"I would rather be saved differently!... Give me a boost over the wall... And I will then save you by giving a false report to the Committee. But meet me tomorrow at ten in the morning at the Palais-Royal, at Café des Aveugles!"

Burlandeux let himself be persuaded. He was caught and at the mercy of Sénar. He preferred to trust in Sénar's spirit of camaraderie. He leaned back against the wall and joined his hands together to make a foothold. Sénar was thus able to reach the top of the wall and make it to the other side. Burlandeux heard him fall with a thud into the bushes of the adjacent lot.

He quickly moved away from this place by the wall, sweeping his feet over the snow as he ran in order to hide Sénar's tracks from his pursuers, and went to meet them, crying out, "I don't see anything!... Where is he?"

The men and the dogs chaotically arrived. Burlandeux's track-covering measure was that much more effective in throwing them off the trail since the snow, falling more and more heavily, covered the older footprints.

Once the property had been thoroughly searched, however, it became clear as day that the police officer had succeeded in escaping, so the surrounding countryside was then scoured.

This time, the dogs were let loose and unmuzzled. They were free to bark, at the risk of imprudently waking the inhabitants of Charonne, Bagnolet, and the sparsely scattered country homes.

They returned empty-handed, except for one small fox terrier carrying in its mouth, like a trophy, a piece of a bottle green overcoat which Paul de Lézardière very much believed to be a scrap of Sénar's clothing. The dog was wounded. Blood was flowing out of its left flank, crimsoning its white coat with large dark stains. The wound was examined. It was the result of a dagger stab. There had been a struggle between the man and the brave little animal, and Baron de Batz declared in a lilting voice, "This fox terrier is obviously very good at hunting weasels. Let's go, Burlandeux!... This is a warning sign! Let's go work on our account books and prepare our payments for tomorrow. I've recruited new men from the Jacobin den, but they have to be paid in advance... You, gentlemen, please organize a serious guard and patrol regimen, as there is evidently some very strong curiosity about what goes on around here..."

Burlandeux worked all night with the baron, who returned to La Force at five o'clock in the morning. But at ten o'clock, his faithful cashier, the only one who was truly worried about the incidents of that night, was inside the picturesque cellar called Café des Aveugles, at the Palais-Royal.

Sénar was waiting for him there. Their meeting was brief.

"You saved me from the clutches of those conspirators you live with," Sénar said. "I will keep my promise: I will get you out of trouble if you do your part..."

"What must I do?... If it is humanly possible, I will attempt it!"

"It's in your interest!" Sénar said somewhat dryly.

"But you could have warned me of the danger I was in," said Burlandeux, consumed with fear, and in a state Sénar wanted him in for his own purpose. "Since you suspected I was working in that house, you could have informed me in time!... I wouldn't have set foot there for a few days."

"Really!" Sénar said mockingly. "You clearly no longer remember our conversation the other day at the Arcades House. Monsieur did not want to tell me where he was 'working.' Monsieur even teased me a little, I believe."

"I was wrong!"

"You're realizing that a little late!"

And Sénar doubled down on his lie: "Yesterday, I was called to the Committee of General Security. They specified a certain house in Charonne that I was to watch, in which there was a peace officer who, while conspiring with the worst enemies of liberty, was betraying the mission given him to protect the Republic. I follow the order given and I find you there... Perhaps I would have warned you if you had been more candid with me... At the present time, there is but one man who can save your head, who can come to your defense, cover for you, and affirm that you were there to spy on the aristocrats. That man is Citizen Dubois!"

"The concierge at La Force?"

"The very same!"

"What does he require in exchange for this service?"

"The leader of the aristocrats in the Charonne house possesses a letter addressed to Dubois by a has-been Marquis de Pons. This letter could get Dubois guillotined. He wants it. Find it. Bring it to me. It is your salvation!"

"I will try!"

"You mustn't try!... You must accomplish what I ask of you... What are you used for there?"

"I serve as a cashier, and I do keep custody of certain papers!... But that letter is not one of them!... If it's in a safe place!"

"Kill! Plunder!... Steal!... Burn!... Whatever it takes, you must get it!"

"I will get it!" Burlandeux promised, clenching his teeth.

He gulped down a glass of punch, paid, shook Sénar's hands effusively as he commended himself to him and thanked him, then exited.

Sénar, left alone, rubbed his hands together. He then ran to La Force to tell Dubois the good news.

Chapter 12

The Family of the "Tyrant"

W E NOW NEED to take our story to some months later. The Revolution was following its course, and the revolutionary acts of violence, little by little, were intensifying.

A decree of January 24, 1793, bestowed the honors of the Panthéon to Michel Lepelletier, a regicide killed by a saber thrust inflicted by the former royal bodyguard Pâris. In honor of this Lepelletier, the Filles-Saint-Thomas neighborhood section, which supplied the Paris Commune a battalion of which the grocer Cortey was the commander, was renamed the Lepelletier section.

The brewer Santerre, by the almighty power of Freemasonry, was still the general of the Parisian National Guard.

A little later, Monsieur, the brother of King Louis XVI, with the Army of Condé, recognized the young dauphin as King of France, under the name Louis XVII. There was thus a nine-year-old king in the Temple, a prisoner as was his father.

February saw high food prices, the famous looting of merchants, and the hanging of bakers and grocers whom the people accused of starving them, when the Revolution had promised larks falling onto people's laps perfectly roasted.

March then saw the establishment of surveillance committees in the Paris sections. Was this due to royalist sentiment penetrating certain sections of Paris, aside from the Filles-Saint-Thomas one that was renamed Lepelletier?

On the thirteenth of that same March, the younger Garat was appointed Minister of the Interior in place of Roland. Was this ministerial shuffling due to a certain plot that allegedly took place the night of March 10-11, and of which several instigators were brought before the newly created Revolutionary Tribunal? That might be so.

It is said that there was an attempt to abduct the family of the "tyrant," though specifics of this attempt were never publicized. However, Baron de Batz's name was whispered, and there was an active search for him.

A man had gotten wind of the plot, or rather suspected it, when seeing more comings and goings than normal on Rue Charlot, Rue Porte-Foin, and all the streets near Temple Prison.

He had the gates shut and called the gendarmes to reinforce the post commanded by Citizen Cortey.

This man's name was Simon.

He was a master shoemaker on Rue des Cordeliers, whom laziness, clumsiness, and perhaps also bad luck had ever reduced to lowly cobbler jobs. Having wholeheartedly embraced new ideas, he won the confidence of Citizen Chaumette, the Procurator of the Paris Commune, charged with surveillance at Temple Prison.

Chaumette made Simon president of the Temple Works Commission.

In this capacity, he had lodging in one of the lesser buildings in the vast enclosure.

The civism and clear-sightedness of which Simon gave evidence when foiling the planned escape singled him out to Chaumette when the latter, having decided to separate Louis XVI's son from the rest of his family, wanted to give the little king a republican tutor.

Chaumette, like all the pure ones of the time, was an admirer and disciple of the sensitive Jean-Jacques Rousseau, the man of nature.

And nature's man writes in his *Émile*, that book of sophisms on education, that he "honors a shoemaker much more than an emperor."

There just so happened to be a shoemaker on hand. What a perfect opportunity to test the theories of the Protestant Jean-

Jacques on that little Capet, the descendant of the most Christian kings, hailed by the Army of Condé as king of this France which had been for so long "the eldest daughter of the Church."

Not to mention that the friends of fanaticism would find it more difficult to save the queen, since she stated she would never leave the Temple alone, but only with her children.

Louis XVII was thus taken from his mother; the third-story apartment of Louis XVI was reopened, into which were relocated his son and the cobbler-tutor.

March then witnessed revolt in the Vendée, and Anjou was in insurrection. The Convention decreed the death penalty for those "agitating for monarchy," and dispatched commissioners to arrest Dumouriez on suspicion of allying himself with the royalists, but Dumouriez then arrested those commissioners. A reward of 100,000 ecus was promised to whoever handed him over, and he fled across the border. He was the only general denounced by the commissioners who was not guillotined. He was declared a traitor to the homeland.

The Committee of Public Safety was created, and the guillotine began operating on a regular basis.

The Convention relocated to Tuileries Palace on May 10, and Baron de Batz, in his asylum where he was forgotten, under the name of Citizen Manaud, was intently following all these events, and perhaps directing some of them.

But it was with grief he learned that Marie Antoinette had been separated from her son, and that, as a result, the dangers of the next rescue attempt would only be multiplied.

As he had planned, he saw the queen when Cortey was on duty, ten days after the incidents in Charonne. And he subsequently proceeded to the Temple with a patrol and papers in hand, wearing, like each of his men, two gray hooded overcoats, one over the other, when he encountered an obstinately closed gate, for which Santerre required a password to enter. This password had been changed!... Santerre ordered the false patrol to surrender. The baron was able to flee with half of his men. The other half were arrested. One hour later, the baron was prudently back at La Force.

In the Republic, the progressive parties continued to dominate and make advances, as will always be the case in France, under any Republic where outbidding on promises keeps the people spellbound and dupes them eternally. On August 1, 1793, the day broke radiantly.

De Batz prepared another escape plan for the royal family for the following night.

Let us now return to the Temple, if you like, to the same poor lodging described by Cortey, where the sordid Tison couple, to use the same expression as Lenotre, coldly listened each day to the "sobbing of the daughter of the Emperors."

In the room where the one who was Queen of France slept, two women and a young girl were seated. It was eleven in the morning.

The elder of the two women was thirty-eight years old. She was sitting in front of a small Louis XV pedestal table and reading, fully hunched over her book. She was dressed in a very simple mourning dress, which was worn-out at the elbows.

Her hair was gray, almost white, but that in no way aged Marie Antoinette, whose hair was powdered winter white from the time she was fifteen years of age.

It was only in Trianon, where she dispensed with powder at the same time as protocol, that her blonde hair could be seen beneath her bergère hat.

Her face was thinned and her eyes weary from sleepless nights and the sorrows with which she had been overwhelmed.

They had killed her husband; they were torturing her son on the floor below. The mother, the wife, and the queen in her were each being martyred one by one, without respite, and with implacable dignity.

The second woman was Madame Élisabeth, the sister of Louis XVI. She was twenty-nine years old and was silently doing some needlework very close to the queen. She was a saintly woman, and she was resigned.

Perhaps, if the monarchy had survived, Madame Élisabeth would have ended up like the sister of Louis XV, Madame Victoire, the superior of a community of Carmelite nuns.

Under the Republic, she was to attain heaven differently, through martyrdom.

As for the young girl, she was fourteen years old. She was Madame Royale, the daughter of Louis XVI.

She turned her back to her mother and aunt and looked at, in the adjacent room whose door was open, a guard inspecting the furniture and drawers, who was trying to find anything suspicious, such as traces of writing, notes, or handkerchiefs folded in a certain way. The Commune was suspicious of everything. The guard even opened books of piety, painstakingly leafing through them.

With his hat on his head, he then went into the queen's room, jostled Madame Royale, and rudely called out to the queen: "Antoinette!"

Maria Theresa's daughter, who in the French court lords did not address until after three profound bows, and the highest princesses until after three studied curtsies, did not answer the brute, and did not even appear to have heard him.

What would enrage all these guillotiners was that while the king on the one hand, more bourgeois than aristocratic, would take on a familiar tone with and try to cajole his jailers, seek to understand their grievances, and continue to regard as men these cannibals who, moreover, spoke like the future Homais, this magnificent and haughty soul that was Marie Antoinette, on the other hand, remained queen all the same, still queen amidst sufferings, amidst insults, queen all the way to the scaffold.

"Antoinette!" the guard repeated. "It's today that you're receiving your linens, which are coming back from the laundry woman. You will need to separate yours from the other prisoners."

"And why, Monsieur?" asked Madame Élisabeth, already worried by this order, which portended a new separation.

"I know nothing about it myself, Citizeness!... It's neither your business nor mine!"

And he left the room, but stayed in the adjacent one, observing the attitude of the prisoners.

Madame Royale ran to her mother and, while appearing to be hugging her, said into her ear, "Be nice with that man, dearest Mama!... He might be one of our friends!... Cortey is on duty today!... And this change with the linens might be part of some escape plan!"

Joy flashed into the queen's eyes. But she forced herself to keep it hidden; she pretended to reimmerse herself in her reading.

Madame Élisabeth understood that the princess had given her mother good news. All three of them understood each other's subtle communications via quick glances of the eyes, unbeknownst to their jailers, who only looked for lip movement.

"Monsieur!" the queen said suddenly.

The guard returned.

"What?" he asked.

"I ask your pardon for not having answered you earlier. I was absorbed in my reading!"

"It's your right to not answer me, Citizeness!"

"Might I get a little bit of fresh air today on the tower terrace?"

"It's your right!... If you refuse to make use of it every day, that's not the nation's fault!"

And with that, he withdrew. The prisoners, sensing they were alone for a moment, took advantage of this rare opportunity to exchange some words.

"You said it's Cortey who's on duty, Marie-Thérèse?" the queen asked her daughter.

"Yes, dear Mother!... I recognized him when looking through the window as his battalion entered the courtyard."

"Holy Virgin!" said Madame Élisabeth, joining her hands together. "Would it be today?"

"Pay attention cutting the bread when we are at the table!" said the queen. "We were advised to do that on the days Cortey is on duty."

"Shh!" said Madame Royale, who was watching the door.

She had just caught sight of the Tison woman, who was heading towards them, wearing a grimy apron and a dirty bonnet.

"Citizenesses," the grungy woman said, "dinner is ready!"

"I have very little appetite!" said the queen.

"You need to eat, Madame! You need to eat!" said the Tison woman, who was kinder, we know, when her husband was not there.

"I have not seen Monsieur Tison all morning. Would he be ill?" asked Madame Royale.

"The dear man is staying in bed!" said the Tison woman. "He's having dizzy spells and feeling some heaviness in his head, and he's yawning a lot... It's his fault! He smokes too much! I often tell him: 'Tison, you smoke too much! It's going to take its toll on you!' But he dismisses me. He's as stubborn as a mule!... Well, come along then!"

And she left them.

"Tison, ill!" said the queen. "Was he given a drug perhaps?"

"Oh, that's it, dearest Mama!" said Madame Royale. "Our friends are watching over us!"

The queen got up. Hope made her feel lighter. The somber prison seemed to brighten; its walls seemed less heavy.

Upon entering the antechamber that served as the captives' dining room, Marie Antoinette saw the basket containing the elements of their meal. This basket was placed on the table. She threw back the folds of the towel that covered it. Half of a loaf of bread appeared. In a certain spot, the crust was broken as if it had been struck into.

The queen quickly plunged two fingers of her right hand into the fissure, moved them around inside the bread, and felt a solid object, which she grabbed.

It was a needle case. She kept it hidden in her hand and, as she turned her back to the windowed partition separating the antechamber from the hovel where the Tisons lived, she said simply to Madame Élisabeth, "Do you want to cut the bread and serve yourself, Sister?"

All three seated, Madame Élisabeth obeyed, then took three napkins out of the basket. She stifled a cry. In one of the three napkins, there were three knots!

She showed it to the queen and exchanged a meaningful glance. She then undid the knots. At that moment, the Tison woman rushed in and asked, "What do you have?"

"Nothing!"

"It sounded like you made a little scream!"

"I accidentally nipped my foot under my chair!" said Madame Royale.

The Tison woman, reassured, went back to her husband. The princesses then ate, Madame Royale with the appetite of her age, and the queen and Madame Élisabeth with little bites.

Their meal was hardly finished when heavy steps sounded on the treads of the tower stairway. At the same time, a bark was heard.

"It's your pug, Sister," said Madame Élisabeth.

The door to the quarters opened, and the guard who had given instructions about the linens appeared at the threshold and said, "Antoinette, here is your dog, who went out at the same time as I did earlier. Though you refuse to take a walk in the enclosure's garden, it does not do the same!"

The pug ran to its mistress, yelping and licking her beautiful thin hands. She gave it some pieces of meat and responded to the guard, "Thank you, Monsieur, for having taken this little animal out for some fresh air!"

"You have nothing to thank me for!... It left all on its own, and in spite of me!... I am only bringing it back because Santerre does not want it roaming on the other floors!... He fears you might have trained it to carry letters or souvenirs of yourself to your son!"

"And what harm would there be in that, my God!" exclaimed the poor mother. "You forbid me from embracing my dear little Louis! You fear that the mere sight of this dog would remind him of his mother!... And you call yourselves men of nature!"

Tears flowed from her eyes. Madame Royale ran to her mother and hugged her, saying, "Don't cry, dear Mama, don't cry!... Don't upset this man!... This evening, tonight, we will all be reunited perhaps, and free!"

This thought quickly dried the queen's eyes.

"Monsieur," she said to the guard, "we are ready... when you want to escort us!"

With a gesture, the guard consented. The queen exited first onto the landing, followed by her sister-in-law and daughter; all three went up the spiral staircase, which ended at the top of the tower.

A watchman was standing guard there. At the sight of the prisoners, he went into a small stone sentry box and stayed inside it.

The escorting guard went to talk with the watchman, all while smoking his pipe, and this conversation absorbed him to the point that he paid hardly any attention to the prisoners.

Even with the heat of the blazing August sun beating against the mossy stone of the old donjon, the three prisoners fully breathed in the cool breeze, which on that day blew from the north. To avoid the direct sunlight, they positioned themselves over a narrow band of shadow projecting from the sentry box, thereby escaping the sight of their guard, who was positioned at the box's opposite side.

Suddenly, as if someone had been expecting them, from one of the buildings located outside the Temple's enclosure but within its field of sight, one could hear a melody from a violin.

Marie Antoinette recognized it, this tune. It was from one of her favorite operas, *Richard the Lionheart*, by Grétry.

She interiorly sang the words to it. She knew them by heart!... Certainly, it must have been a friend intentionally evoking the words by means of the song made for them:

> *In an obscure tower,*
> *A mighty king languishes.*

With her nearsighted eyes, she tried to identify the window from which this innocent, plaintive-toned ballad came. She failed to do so.

But Madame Élisabeth did identify it: "Sister," she said quietly, "there it is, over there, that window that is half-open, with a curtain fluttering outside, as if the wind is pulling on it without those living inside being aware. And the curtain is knotted with three knots!"

"With three knots!" whispered Marie Antoinette, whose heart pounded. "The signal! The signal again that Jean de Batz told us about!"

After a furtive look around her, she opened the needle case she had found in the loaf of bread. A thin piece of paper was rolled up inside, which she tremblingly removed and unrolled. It contained this laconic sentence: "Sleep fully dressed tonight."

They were speechless and overtaken by emotion. The prison and jailers around them seemed to all disappear. The breeze became more caressing; their surroundings were inhabited by friends watching over them. An atmosphere of love and respect replaced the hatred that had enveloped them, and that violin music, coming from just yonder, lulled them into their blissful reverie.

Did this day promise all happiness then?... Leaning on a crenel and looking down at the Temple's sad garden with its meager, sickly shrubs, Marie Antoinette caught sight of her son playing a little game of boules with the very large Cortey.

It was only with trembling that she looked at him at first, for one time in the past the little one had noticed his mother and blew her a kiss. But a man with a whip in his hand had immediately appeared, administering a lash to the back of the poor boy, who had screamed in pain.

The man had exclaimed: "Back this way, wolfling!... Don't you dare blow kisses at the Austrian!"

And he had the little Capet go back inside as he waved his fist at the queen. Then, at the top of his voice, he sang the insulting tune of the hired assassins of August 10:

> *Madame Veto did promise*
> *To slaughter all of Paris!...*

But now instead of the cobbler Simon, it was Cortey she saw, or discerned rather. The child let out hearty bursts of laughter, which warmed his mother's heart, afflicted by so many offenses.

Certainly, the little Capet no longer fully resembled the Louis-Charles de Bourbon, Duke of Normandy, who appeared so graceful in Madame Vigée-Lebrun's work entitled *Portraits of Marie Antoinette and Her Children.*

His blond, curly hair, the pride of his mother, had been cut very short. An ignoble carmagnole jacket covered his upper body; the red cap was on his head; baggy trousers extended down to his shoes. He was dressed as a little sans-culotte, for the term *sans-culotte*, literally "without breeches," did not refer to the indecently dressed, but to those who, rather than wearing short breeches, which was a distinguished and customary article of clothing, instead wore trousers, a clothing article that was at the time left for the abject, the distressed, and the criminal, and was part of the standard attire for convicts.

What joy!... The Duke of Normandy, whom his mother recognized more with her heart than with her eyes, as his clothing made him look so much taller and thinner, turned his gaze upwards. He noticed the queen.

He threw her kisses and, this time, no cobbler came out with a whip.

Might there perhaps be a loosening of the vise that had been clamped so tightly around the royal prisoners?

The three princesses could not contain some exclamations of joy as they signaled to the child who was presently King of France.

And the guard came out from behind the sentry box: "Hey, hey!... Capet woman! And you, Citizenesses! Don't you know it's forbidden to give signals to anyone?"

"Since when, Monsieur," Marie Antoinette gently responded, "is it forbidden a mother to answer her child's greeting?"

As she pronounced those words, the little thin piece of paper she had been keeping in her hand fell to the ground.

"What's that paper?" the guard sharply cried out.

He rushed forward and rudely pushed away the queen, who had put her foot over the paper. He went to pick it up. The prisoners, struck speechless with terror, felt as though an abyss had opened beneath them to engulf all the hopes that they had so ardently entertained.

Fortunately, the breeze swept up the thin piece of paper; it flew off like a butterfly over the crenel of the donjon.

Frantically, the guard cried out to Cortey: "The paper! The paper!"

And he rushed down the stairway hoping to retrieve it in the courtyard.

"My God!" whispered the queen, whose temples were beading with perspiration.

"Don't worry!" said Madame Élisabeth. "The paper went up in the air and whisked away; it's gone! It will get lost on the roof of some building or in some street where no one will think to pick it up. What's written on it will be meaningless anyhow!"

The guard came back up, empty-handed.

"Tell me what was on that paper, Antoinette!" he insolently demanded.

"A bookmark from the book you saw me reading!" she said.

"All right!... Go down now, all of you! That will teach you!"

And as the queen's little pug brushed up against the guard's legs, he violently kicked it.

The detainees spent the rest of their day in increasing agitation, in a sickly nervousness. The slightest sound of a footstep, or of a voice, or the least noise from outside, startled them.

When the linens returned from the launderer's, it was actually Madame Royale who helped the guard separate the laundry belonging to her mother, Madame Élisabeth, and herself, and put it in a small valise.

The guard, who was obstinate, said, "Marie-Thérèse, tell me yourself what that paper was your mother let go of."

"A blank piece of paper she used as a bookmark, I swear to you!"

"That's odd!... She didn't want to throw it to the little Capet?"

"I swear to you, no!... Doesn't she know that my brother is too closely guarded to give him the least message?"

"Well, not today at least! Didn't that idiot Simon get into a quarrel yesterday with a drunkard on the street, who struck him in the right calf with his big cane? And so now he's in bed for two days!"

This was another incident that the queen saw as a good omen when her daughter reported it back to her very quietly when going to hug her. The man who struck Simon, whether genuinely drunk or not, was undoubtedly a friend commissioned to facilitate the escape by crippling one of the most vigilant jailers!

And night fell, very late that time of year. The prisoners were lying in bed, almost completely dressed. They were unable to close their eyes. The hours passed, slowly and interminably.

At two thirty in the morning, an unusual noise echoed in the donjon stairway. The three prisoners sat up. The night was sweltering; their hearts pounded in their chests. Was that the sound of freedom? Alas, it was not!

The door opened, and the guard entered. The Temple clock tolled two o'clock in the morning.

"Antoinette!" he shouted. "Get up!"

Then, another man wearing a plumed hat unceremoniously entered the queen's room and said to her with a certain politeness, "Citizeness, I am Citizen Michonis, an officer in charge of prison inspections. I have orders to take you to the Conciergerie, your new prison."

Marie Antoinette remained speechless, as though crushed. Oh, what a terrible ending to this day that had shined with so much promise! Hope had made the poor woman's spirits soar, only so that they could fall from a loftier height!

"But us? What about us?" cried Mesdames Élisabeth and Royale, who had gotten up and rushed over.

"You, Citizenesses? You are staying here. These orders come from the Convention!... The Capet woman only has the right to take her pug with her if she likes."

The two unfortunate ones felt their legs trembling beneath them. They had to sit down. Silently, Marie Antoinette got up. She again took on the impassivity of the preceding days. Her heart had only recently opened up, like the petals of a flower unfolding in the springtime air. It closed in on itself again, contracting inside the frosty clutches of its fate.

The Conciergerie, Marie Antoinette sensed, was the antechamber to her death. But she kept this frightful thought to herself. She did not want to add to the afflictions of her already crushed sister-in-law and daughter, who were to remain alone in the horrible Temple Prison.

"Give me a hug, Marie-Thérèse," she said to her daughter, "and you too, Sister. Do not despair. We shall see each other again."

Sobbing, Madame Royale threw herself around her mother's neck.

Madame Élisabeth, pale as wax, and resigned like the saint that she was, silently embraced the queen and said in her ear, "Be brave! Let our hope now be in the justice of God!"

Michonis, the prisons inspector, who was a café owner by trade, maintained his outward insolence; he was very moved. His voice choked a little when he said to the queen, "Let's go, Citizeness! Let's go! We need to leave! The carriage is down below."

The Tison woman took the portmanteau containing Marie Antoinette's clothing and personal effects. The queen untangled herself from the arms of her daughter and sister-in-law. This was the last time she would ever see them!

She descended the barely lit stone stairway leaning upon Michonis. Her little pug followed her, joyous and carefree. She cast a sorrowful gaze at the door to the lodging on the floor below. That door, Louis XVI had passed through it a little more than six months ago, to go to his death. And behind it now, little Louis XVII was sleeping.

The queen did not even ask to embrace her child before leaving. She knew this consolation would have been refused her. Perhaps she was also scared of what she might see: Simon hurling insults at or beating the poor little one to make the mother suffer.

With both hands, she blew the sinister door a long kiss, into which she had put all the strength of her maternal love. And she proceeded away.

Down below, in the courtyard, a carriage waited. She boarded it with Michonis, who obligingly took the pug into his arms, and two other guards.

Cortey was there. The prisoner's eyes met his. She read in them terror, despair, and powerlessness.

The carriage left for the Conciergerie, rumbling as it passed over the coarse pavement of the old quarter's narrow, winding streets.

Above, in the tower, Madame Élisabeth consoled Madame Royale, who was writhing on her bed in terrible anguish.

Tison, from his hovel, cried out at the top of his voice, "I was finally going to sleep!... And now that *hussy* wakes me up!... Isn't she going to finish up her squawking?"

What had happened? What setback had caused this new rescue attempt to be aborted?

That secret was presently enclosed within the walls of another prison, that of La Force. Let us return there now to rejoin Citizen Manaud.

Chapter 13

The Escape

FOR THE ENTIRE day of August 1, Citizen Manaud himself was also restless. Around three o'clock in the afternoon, the good Leopard came to see him and brought him some food from a neighborhood vendor and a bottle of old wine.

Then, in exchange for the daily louis which he could not do without, he opened Sévignon's cell so he could go see the baron.

"Well," said La Guiche upon seeing him, "when are we going to be on our way?... I made a hole in my ceiling that's wide enough to go through. The hole is hidden by an old curtain which I nailed myself above my bed, like a canopy, on the pretext of keeping drafts away from my face while sleeping. The Leopard likes me too much to want me to get headaches. But if we delay too long, someone might discover these preparations, change my cell, and then everything will have to be started again from the beginning."

"I can't run away yet!" said the baron.

"And why not?... I have forty meters of braided cord with the sheets I have frayed..."

"I can't leave, I tell you!... I have to honor a promise to Citizen Dubois!"

"You made a promise to not escape?"

"Yes!... But you can be sure that I've had some promises made to me in return!"

Very quietly, in the ear of his fellow detainee, he revealed, "Tonight, I will be able to leave, without drawing any attention, in order to cooperate in the escape of the queen and the royal family!"

The baron did not add that he had been leaving almost every night for months, for he only ever revealed what was necessary. He explained in detail how he planned to bring a false patrol inside the Temple, throw over the prisoners one of the two gray hooded overcoats the false patrolmen would be wearing on top of each other, and then concluded: "Everything is ready... everything has now come together like the gears of a clock. I only need to turn the key to set the machine in motion. At four o'clock in the morning exactly, everything will be completed. With Barbereux's cart far-off by then, the little Cécile Renault who brings us our clean linens will go to Santerre herself and denounce the queen's flight. She will put him on a false trail to keep him from finding the real one."

La Guiche's eyes popped wide open, and he wondered if he was dreaming.

"And this little pest Cécile has been coming here every eight days without ever saying a thing to me!" he exclaimed.

"I had forbidden her!"

"And why?"

"Why! Because you would have wanted to cooperate in the escape and participate in this danger. You would have escaped, and that would have drawn the Committee of General Security's attention to La Force, and consequently to me also, and risked hampering my movement. You can escape alone, certainly, but after the event, not today!... As for me, tomorrow, and the day after tomorrow, I will remain Dubois's prisoner, as I have promised! Only if he were to violate our contract would I consider myself dispensed!"

"Fine!... But I warn you that I will never escape from here without you!... Escaping to be good for something, fine! But evading when the work is finished, what would I look like in the eyes of our friends? A coward in hiding who returned once the danger had passed?"

"The work will not be over once we free the queen, little King Louis XVII, his aunt, and his sister. And other dangers remain!"

"All the better! Because idleness is doubly abhorrent to me now that I know you are devising such important plans!"

They were at that point in the conversation when the good Leopard appeared, alarmed; his long, disheveled, red hair around his hideous face made him look like a drowning victim.

"Quickly! Quickly!" he said. "Each of you in your cells!... Dubois is coming this way with a man who has a bunch of keys!"

And without allowing any time for the two prisoners to react or to exchange goodbyes, he hurried La Guiche into his cell, used his enormous key to lock both his cell door and that of Jean de Batz's, and waited for La Force's concierge.

Dubois had not made an appearance in this section of the prison for a long time. He thought he would thereby be less suspected of connivance with his prisoner if the latter were to be caught while entering or exiting his prison.

Dubois had Leopard open the door to Baron de Batz's cell, and then, after having had Leopard and the man with the bunch of keys go away, he said to his prisoner, "Monsieur, I call upon you to give me back the key with which you open your cell door from the inside."

"Really?" said the baron gleefully, hiding his worry. "And why?"

"That is my business!"

"Sorry then that I am unable to accede to your request, Vicomte!... I have to go out this evening!... They are expecting me at the Régence to finish a game of chess. Then, I have to see Citizen Chabot, the Convention delegate. After that, I have some louis to squander at the Arcades House... You wouldn't, I imagine, in light of the agreement between us, get in the way of my business and leisurely pursuits?"

"Alas!... That is, however, my intention, Monsieur *Baron de Batz*!"

The leader of those who began calling themselves the "Avengers of the King" received like a sword thrust into his bare chest the pronunciation of his true name, which Dubois, with clenched teeth, had uttered as a challenge. The baron's true identity had been discovered. Danger hovered over him like a vulture that had skimmed his head with its outstretched wings.

He turned horribly pale, but surmounted his distress. He began joking again, like a man who laughs when he has a knife stuck in his chest: "Too bad for you, Vicomte!... You will be getting to know the public prosecutor... I know, and you know as well, there is a certain letter Citizen Fouquier-Tinville, a great champion of the guillotine as you know, will be reading with certain interest."

Dubois began laughing and, to the baron's great surprise, exited the cell. But he left the door half-open and responded, "No, Monsieur! Fouquier-Tinville will not be reading that letter at all, not him, nor anyone, because that letter, I have it in my pocket. That letter was appropriately taken from the archives of your hideout in Charonne and has just been returned to me."

And Dubois brusquely pulled the cell door towards himself, making the thickness of its oak wood like a shield between himself and the baron's fury.

He had acted wisely, for if he had remained in the cell, de Batz would have strangled him, if only to get back the letter from him.

Dubois, safe from danger, delighted in the angry roaring of his prisoner, who at that instant resembled a wildcat caught in a trap.

"The key!" he cried out through the door. "The key!"

"No!"

"As you like, Citizen Manaud! I am going to have the lock changed!... It will suffice to guard you for tonight, because, as of tomorrow, Fouquier-Tinville will know your real name, and will know where to find you, you and all of your accomplices."

"Before I die, you wretch, I will denounce you!"

"Who is going to believe the conspirator and has-been of the January 21 affair accusing a zealous patriot like myself?"

Dubois had called over the man with the bunch of keys. He was a local locksmith.

"Change this lock!" he told him.

"Very good, Citizen!"

But Jean de Batz, who walked about his cell like a tiger in its cage, had undoubtedly already taken stock of the trump cards still available to him that might free him from this impasse into which he had suddenly just been forced.

One of these trump cards likely consisted in maintaining the lock to his cell, for he cried out to Dubois, "Fine! You win!... Here is my key!"

"You give up?"

"I give up!"

"But without any surprises, no? If this is a pretense to lure me into your cave and beat me to death, I don't intend to fall for that!"

"Just partially open the door, disloyal and fearful Vicomte! Just open it enough so that I can hand you the key!... You shall see that there is no darkness in my soul and that I am resigned to my fate!... Do with me what you will!"

The door then partially opened. The prisoner surrendered the key, which really was, for him, the key to freedom. Dubois then locked the door with two turns of that same key. He went away, followed by the locksmith, singing the *Ça ira*.

Two hours later, Jean de Batz's cell door lock creaked again, but feebly, as if the key moving inside were being turned cautiously.

The prisoner smiled. He was conjecturing. And when, through the cautiously half-open door, he saw the good Leopard's frightful face, contorted by anxiousness, hope then returned to him like a beam of sunlight which, in the mornings, through the dusty, barred transom window of his cell, communicated to him a bit of melancholic cheer.

"Well, what was that then, Citizen?" exclaimed the good Leopard. "You had some words with Citizen Dubois!"

"He is a brute with whom it is impossible to reach an agreement!"

"What did you want from him then?"

This question showed that Dubois had confided nothing of their history to his underling. Jean de Batz was therefore in an advantageous position: "What did I want?... An upgrade from the stinking slop that he serves us here. Permission, at any time, to have brought in from the outside anything I might need. He refused, I became infuriated, I threatened to strangle him... And there you have it!"

"Wow! He spoke of sending you to Fouquier-Tinville."

"Whenever he wants!... Why enjoy myself here!"

The good Leopard made a sign of protestation. Seeing guillotined a prisoner who paid him a one-louis stipend each day, and had been doing so for the last six months, was something he could not imagine, despite his civism. Obviously, this prisoner would be replaced. But would his successor pay him as much?

De Batz let the jailer have a few seconds to stew in his dark thoughts. Then, he asked him point-blank: "Do you want to earn five hundred livres?"

"In assignats?"

"In gold!"

"In gold!" said the good Leopard, his eyes lighting up. "My father has been dead for a long time, but I might have killed him for such a sum."

The good Leopard had in fact been in the prison labor camp in Toulon. The future founders of the one, indivisible, and masonic Republic had freed him in the name of nature and unleashed him in Paris along with many other sans-culottes of the same origin, in order to perpetrate the Dantonist September Massacres, the Girondist August 10 insurrection, and other exploits aimed at definitively establishing the reign of virtue. These people from Toulon were described as brave Marseillais; they brought with them a hymn of blood and death that the brass bands of the Republic still blare in our own time.

The good Leopard had found refuge as a jailer in La Force.

A deal was immediately struck. In exchange for this gold, half of which was paid to the former prison slave on the spot, Jean de Batz simply asked to spend the night with his friend, the prisoner next-door. He feared he was ill, his dispute with Dubois having provoked a kind of frenzy in his veins. And, in any case, he wanted to avoid staying alone or suffering a bout of insomnia.

The good Leopard had anticipated something more significant in exchange for so much money. He therefore eagerly acceded to such a modest request.

Five minutes later, Jean de Batz was in Sévignon's cell. The latter had heard echoes of the violent scene that had unfolded between the baron and the La Force concierge.

"What was it that happened?" he asked anxiously.

"I'll tell you about it later, La Guiche. Right now, we need to get out of here."

"Both of us?"

"Both of us!... Dubois breached our contract. I am no longer bound to it... We have the night to ourselves... The time has come to employ our escape preparations..."

"Excellent!" Sévignon exclaimed, beaming. "But we have to wait until everyone here is asleep!"

"Certainly!... And until it's dark... Let's hope there is no moon!... We need to be on the roof at ten o'clock. We'll know then!'

"Then, we use the rope!"

"Yes! But we'll only know we should go down after we're up there! If it's only to lower ourselves into one of the La Force courtyards, it's not worth risking our lives!"

At ten o'clock in the evening, the drum rolled and signaled the curfew. The good Leopard came to take a final look at La Guiche's cell. He told de Batz that he would take him back to his own cell at four o'clock in the morning, said good night to both prisoners, and went away.

When the noise of the good Leopard's footsteps ceased to be heard in the cell corridor, La Guiche, without saying a word, tugged on the old curtain that hung over his pallet and removed it from the ceiling, where it was being held by nails.

A nice round hole appeared. The baron examined it as he lifted above his head a cloudy oil lamp that the good Leopard had supplied La Guiche in exchange for eight livres.

"How," asked de Batz, "were you able to dispose of the plaster pieces without arousing the suspicions of the good Leopard?"

"By collecting them in a towel I laid out on the floor right beneath where I was working, and then tossing them through the hole into the garret above us."

"The garret is directly beneath the roof?"

"Yes, directly beneath the roof!... Between the rotting beams supporting them, the roof's lead sheets are visible... You'll see!"

"Just a moment, La Guiche! We need to pack!"

"Pack?"

"Certainly!... We both need to bundle up a change of clothes. We also both need to carefully roll and strap all our rope at our shoulders."

"Right."

They quickly packed. Each of them bundled their cleanest change of clothes into a bed sheet that was knotted together at its four corners. The two bundles were tossed through the hole into the garret. They then took the rope La Guiche had prepared and strapped it around their shoulders like harnesses. De Batz ensured he had his dagger in his belt and fastened his sword behind his back similar to how a rifle is carried in a sling. La Guiche gave him a leg up and boosted him to the floor above. The baron pulled himself up and soon disappeared through the hole in the ceiling.

La Guiche himself had no need of help. He had trained himself to climb up into the garret, which he had been visiting almost daily.

From the top of his stool, he jumped up with the ease of an acrobat reaching for a high bar, grabbed on to the edge of the hole with both hands, and then pulled himself up just as his companion had done.

When he entered the garret, the baron was already striking the lighter to light the oil lamp, which he had been careful not to forget. As he was setting off sparks, he spoke aloud to himself. La Guiche could hear him saying these words: "Yes!... Certainly!... There are traitors among us!... The failure on January 21!... The letter stolen from my home!... This needs to stop!... There will be executions!"

"Let's get out of here first!" said La Guiche.

"Yes, certainly! But let's hope we arrive on time!... Monsieur de Lézardière is waiting for me with his patrol!... La Guiche, my friend, it is tonight that we will be risking our lives!... You asked for danger, and now you have it!"

The oil lamp was lit. De Batz went to the edge of the large attic to examine the roof, at the place where it formed the narrowest angle with the wall. With the tip of his dagger, he bore into the planks supporting the lead roofing sheets which, in this area, replaced the slate tiles, and he happily observed that the planks were worm-eaten and broke into pieces when attacked. La Guiche helped him with the tool he had used to bore a hole in his cell ceiling. They had soon cleared away a large space.

The baron then tried to cut open the exposed lead. But it was difficult to bore through it with his dagger.

"A better idea," said La Guiche, "would be to try lifting one of these large sheets with our shoulders."

"They are riveted over each other."

"Let's try one on the very edge bordering the gutter."

By levering the tool and the dagger between the stone gutter and one of the lead sheets on the roof's edge, they succeeded in detaching the sheet. They then used their shoulders to lift it. De Batz was soon able to raise his head into the open air. With a little more effort, his shoulders went out as well.

"The roof door is now open!" he said. "Let's grab our bundles."

They each fastened their bundles onto their backs and slung their ropes around them. De Batz went out first.

"Keep your balance by grabbing onto my belt!" he said to La Guiche. "The roof is very slippery."

"It is for you just as it is for me!" remarked La Guiche, as he exited in turn.

"Yes, but I have claws!... Whatever you do, be careful! Look up to avoid getting dizzy!"

De Batz, tugging La Guiche, did in fact seem to have claws to climb to the top of the slippery roof, where he intended to find a chimney, fasten one end of his rope to it, and let the other end drop into the chasm over the street.

He was on his knees and crawling on all fours.

Holding his dagger with his left hand, he pushed it obliquely into the joint of some lead sheets, slipping it beneath the edge of one, lifting it, and straightening it upwards. Then, with his right hand, he grabbed onto the projection thus formed and pulled himself up a little higher. His left hand, handling the dagger, reached for a yet higher sheet, and the process repeated itself slowly and arduously, yet steadily, on the slippery roof's rather steep slope.

After de Batz had thus raised about twenty sheets of roofing, the two prisoners arrived at the roof's crest and sat astride it.

"Phew!" said the baron. "Had one of those sheets given way, we would have taken quite a dive... But let's get our bearings now!"

"We went up the side of the roof that faces the courtyard."

"That's what I thought. We need to go down the opposite side then, onto Rue du Roi de Sicile."

"Let's hope we don't go down right over a guard!"

"If we could get to a certain building that is only separated from the prison by a narrow courtyard not even four meters wide, that would be much better!"

"You know of a building like that?"

"Yes!... I would go through that building almost every night... I can tell you that now, since I am no longer bound to secrecy vis-à-vis that scoundrel Dubois!"

"I didn't know any of this! How did you get to that building?"

"I went out," de Batz responded, "through a skylight above our cell corridor. No garrets to go through. Right away, I was on a kind of small terrace; I would jump across the small courtyard onto the edge of a window that lights the stairway of the other building. I would go down through that stairway."

"And when the window was closed."

"That only happened three times. The first time, I forced in the window pane with my elbow and then reached my arm inside to unlock the window. That window pane has never been replaced... Long live negligent property owners!"

"You're right then! Let's go to that building!"

"I fear it might be guarded... Dubois might have taken extra precautions!... I am going to check. Wait for me here!"

And de Batz went off to explore, keeping his dagger in hand for support in case of a dangerous slip. La Guiche saw him straddle easily over the crest of the roof, pass over the area above their deserted cells, go to the edge of the La Force building, and lean over the void.

From there, de Batz saw the small courtyard he had so often crossed with a single leap. But those times, he was at the base of the roof. As he was now on the top of the roof, he was five meters higher up. The baron was looking down on the roof of the other building.

The narrow courtyard area in between the buildings gave him the impression of a bottomless pit. Looking beneath him, into the shadow, at the window through which he normally entered the building, his attention was drawn to a speck of light which alternatingly glowed red, then seemed about to disappear, and then grew brighter. He surmised it was a lit pipe that was emitting that speck of light.

"Very well!" he said to himself. "There is a good chance that the stem of that pipe is between the teeth of a soldier who has been stationed there!"

The route on that side was cut off.

Fastening a rope to a chimney and descending to the bottom of that small courtyard also seemed unwise to him. It would require passing in front of the soldier smoking at the window, who would violently be roused from his reverie at the sight of two men descending a rope. Guards would then be waiting for them at the bottom of their perilous descent.

De Batz returned to his companion without letting himself be seen by the mysterious smoker.

"We have to go another route!" he said to La Guiche. "We'll need to follow the roof to the corner of the two streets, turn at Rue Pavée, get on a building roof along that street, and go down from there, either through a stairway or directly onto the street itself with our ropes. On this side, there is someone smoking a pipe who must have orders... The other side should be less guarded."

"Let's go!" La Guiche said docilely.

Doing an about-face, La Guiche crawled on his hands and knees, dragging his chest along the ridge of the roof's summit. De Batz followed him. This route, painfully traveled, seemed to them interminable. Four separate times, they had to make their way around groups of chimneys and cross precipices, since the prison's buildings did not smoothly connect, nor were they of the same height.

In two cases, it was necessary to use the ropes, fasten them to asperities to go down lower, throw them like a lasso, and tighten them around a chimney or cornice to climb the next obstacle. They were also forced at times to leave some of their rope behind, to the great disappointment of the baron, who said to his companion, "Let's use the rope sparingly! What are we going to do if we're forced to lower ourselves down onto the street!"

Finally, they arrived at the corner of the two streets. Midnight tolled from the clock of St. Paul's Church. Almost immediately thereafter, the moon appeared, lighting up the church's dome, towering above the buildings a little to their right.

"Curses!" the baron exclaimed. "That rascal comes out as soon as we're in plainest sight!"

"Let's hide behind a group of chimneys. There are some clouds approaching, which will dim the light."

"Is that what you're thinking, Marquis?... It's midnight. We've been out for two hours, and look how little we've accomplished!... The sun comes up a little after three o'clock this time of year. We need to be at the Temple by two thirty at the latest... Monsieur de Lézardière, the father, and his friends will be waiting for me in half an hour at Rue des Francs-Bourgeois... Let's continue on our way then... Too bad if a watchful guard shoots us!"

"Let us continue then!" La Guiche said philosophically.

They were soon alongside Rue Pavée-au-Marais, on the crest of a pitched roof. On this side, fortunately, the La Force building was more even, without gaping precipices or alternately protruding wall sections.

Then, the moon hid behind a cloud.

"Good night, and I hope to not see you again!" the baron said jokingly.

Half past midnight tolled when they reached the edge of the roof.

"Phew!" he said.

"Is this it?" asked La Guiche.

"Yes!... And it is about time. I am wet, my hands are bloody, and my breeches are tattered at the knees."

"If you think I'm in better condition, you're mistaken!... What's in front of us?"

"The abyss!... But less than six meters below us is the tile roof of another building. We need to get down there, fasten a rope to that building's chimney, and lower ourselves onto the street. It's highly unlikely they stationed guards in front of these neighboring buildings... And we won't risk putting a foot on the tip of a bayonet."

"We shall find out in any case!... I do hear the sound of steady footsteps."

La Guiche prepared a rope and fastened it at one end to a wrought iron finial on the prison roof. The baron let the other end hang down above the top of the other building and made his way down with great effort. La Guiche did the same. He found the baron straddling on the new roof and leaning over to look onto the street, since from this roof, which was less extensive than the prison's, one could peer through an indentation to see the frightful abyss of Rue Pavée.

A sentry was pacing there. In the half-light produced by the white clouds which intercepted the moon's brightness without fully obscuring it, his bayonet glistened sinisterly. The two escapees distinctively saw the man move back suddenly towards a building on the other side of the street, in order to look upwards.

Had the soldier heard some noise?... That was possible, as the baron had displaced some roof tiles with his foot.

"Devil!" exclaimed La Guiche. "He suspects something!"

"Don't move!"

They remained motionless awhile, and the soldier, neither seeing nor hearing anything, resumed walking.

His footsteps resounded on the pavement of the sleeping neighborhood, alerting de Batz and his companion that they were no longer the object of any surveillance.

The baron was concerned and reflected.

La Guiche said to him, "Let's go to the next building!"

"I have another idea: Let's get inside the building we are on right now and quietly go down the stairway."

"That's dangerous!"

"Not nearly as dangerous as lowering ourselves down onto the street with ropes!... We might be seen; the rope might break or not be long enough!... And I see a dormer window beneath us."

"You are going to go down over the loose tiles of this roof?"

"By holding on to the rope you tied to the finial, which is still long enough! Yes! Only... hold it perpendicular to the dormer so I can use it like a handrail."

And following through on his words, de Batz, with an intrepidness that made his companion tremble, sat on the roof with rope in hand and descended gently to the dormer window's small overhang. Spreading his legs apart, he then straddled atop it, with no damage incurred other than what the tiles might have done to the back of his breeches. Then holding his hands on the edges, he leaned over, cocked his head forward, and managed to see and touch with his finger a small grill, behind which there was a window whose panes were encased between thin lead strips.

Lying face down, his head leaning towards the small grill, he began using his dagger to carefully attack the plaster and stone in which it was sealed. After fifteen minutes, he succeeded in shaking it off intact. He placed it to the side of the dormer window and looked with fright as it slid over the tiles. He expected to hear it crash down onto the street, which would have given them away, but he only heard a metallic ringing sound. The grill had been stopped by the gutter that was located a little more than three meters below the window.

Then, with the aid of the rope which still hung from the prison and which Sévignon still held perpendicular to the window, Baron de Batz made his way back up to the top of the roof and rejoined his somewhat frightened companion.

The night had thickened, for the moon had disappeared behind the dome of St. Paul's, and large dark clouds were rising into the sky. A warm storm wind began to blow.

"I thought you had fallen into some precipice!" said Sévignon. "You had me so worried until I felt you pulling on the rope again."

"I did some good work, Marquis! You need to go through the window first. I removed a grill that was protecting it. The small window is made up of panes held in place by thin lead strips; it's not an obstacle. You will break one of those panes and find the latch or bolt which is locking the window."

"As you command! But if there's someone in the garret?"

"What do you want to do?... You decide!... If this someone screams, you will calm him down, or exhort or threaten him by showing him a pistol."

And de Batz handed Sévignon one of his own pistols.

Using the rope, Sévignon, who allowed de Batz to order and arrange everything, made his way down the slope of the roof to the dormer window. There, the marquis, straddling atop its overhang, leaned over, as de Batz had done, and pushed in the glass with his hand, which gave way fairly easily.

"It feels as though this is putty!" he said to de Batz.

The lead strips did in fact give way and stretch. Upon seeing this, La Guiche fastened the rope beneath his armpits, sat on the dormer overhang with his legs towards the street, and then brought his feet back in towards the window. He said to the baron, "Hold tight!... I have my legs inside the window. Slowly give me more rope."

La Guiche turned nervously, holding onto the overhang of the dormer with both hands, making his thighs, then his hips, take the path his feet had opened for him through the window. Thanks to their malleability, the lead strips holding the panes in place expanded little by little. Some pieces of glass fell inside, making a bit of noise.

But when La Guiche fully entered, the baron had to extend him a good twelve feet of rope, given how low the floor was inside.

And when he no longer felt any weight at the end of the rope, he understood that his companion had finally made it to the floor. He pulled back the improvised rope, frightened at the length he had needed to employ.

"And me," he said to himself, "what am I supposed to do?... Who is going to keep this rope taut for me? Who is going to carefully lend me more rope when I need both hands to go through the window?"

In fact, the rope, attached as we know to a finial on the prison roof, could only have been used by de Batz to lower himself to the dormer window if he had found a protrusion to which to fasten it a second time that was on the roof of this present building directly above where he wanted to end up.

No sound coming from the garret or attic into which La Guiche had entered, Jean de Batz, assured of his companion's well-being and contemplating a way to join him, crawled on his knees to a chimney, stood up in front of it, and looked all around him, seeking an inspiration.

Chapter 14

Rougeville

A LITTLE FURTHER, on the building adjoining the one on which the baron stood, there was something like scaffolding up against a chimney.

Jean de Batz made his way to that spot. He found there, on a platform made of planks, a trough filled with diluted plaster, a trowel, a set square, and a plumb line. The chimneys were evidently being repaired. A long ladder was lying on the slope of the roof, tied to the scaffolding with a rope.

The baron untied this rope. With an extreme amount of effort, he dragged the heavy, unwieldy ladder back towards the dormer window. He devised the plan to insert it into the window and use it to conveniently go down.

Sliding the ladder down with his rope until one end was flush with the dormer window and the other protruded past the gutter, he ascertained that the ladder would stay in place on the slope of the roof without sliding, thanks to the unevenness of the old tiles. Sitting on the roof, he slowly descended with infinite caution, putting down one heel, then another, then raising himself up on his hands to move his buttocks a little further down, testing the surface each time before fully resting any one of the five parts of his body that leaned on the tiles for support.

If but one tile came off, if but one of the chestnut laths, to which roofers, as is known, hung each tile with a terra-cotta hook, happened to break, there would be a terrible fifty-foot fall and a crash onto the pavement.

The baron therefore breathed a sigh of relief when, at the end of a long quarter of an hour, he had descended three meters and was sitting astride the dormer window overhang.

Grabbing hold of the ladder, he untied the rope that was attached to the first rung and retied it to the eighth. Then, letting the ladder protrude over the street, he brought back one end to the front of the dormer and pulled the ladder towards himself to make this end go inside the small window.

But it was impossible to get more than the fifth rung of the ladder inside. The end of the ladder had gotten stuck inside against the top of the dormer, and it was impossible to push it in any further. La Guiche was undoubtedly too far below and without any chair or stool available to stand on so that he could grab the end of the ladder, pull it in towards himself, and make it possible for the baron to get off the roof and step onto the rung that was level with him.

It was necessary, in any case, to raise the other end of the ladder that was hanging over the abyss.

The baron did not hesitate. He got off the window overhang and descended towards the gutter, sitting on the tiles and lifting himself up with his hands and feet alternatively. He soon had his heels in the gutter and ascertained that it was made of strong sheet metal and supported by sturdy iron clamps that did not buckle under his weight. The baron turned onto his stomach, the front of his feet leaning into the gutter.

Getting on his knees, he had the strength to raise the ladder half a foot upwards, enabling him to push forward another foot of the ladder inside the window. This reduced the weight being exerted on the roof's edge.

It was now a matter of getting at least another two feet of the ladder inside the window. Afterwards, by going back atop the dormer overhang, de Batz could, using the rope, resume getting the entire ladder inside.

To give the ladder the elevation that was required, he stood on his knees. But the force he needed to use in order to succeed caused a contraction in the back of his knees which lifted his feet from their place of support in the gutter. The tiles gave way beneath his knees and the lower part of his body up to his chest slid off the edge of the roof. He was supporting himself with only his two elbows, which he had fortunately managed to lock inside the gutter on his way down. At the same time, a shower of dislodged tiles flew about him and fell onto the street like a torrent, making a terrible racket.

This was a harrowing moment for him. He had thought himself thrown into the abyss. But the instinct for self-preservation had made him, almost unconsciously, employ all his might to support himself with his elbows. The gutter remained solidly in place, fortunately! But another man placed in this same horrible situation would have succumbed; terror and vertigo would have overcome him; he would have been hopelessly done for.

De Batz had already commended his soul to God, but God was offering him a way to safety! The ladder above him was well-positioned. In his perilous endeavor that had cost him so dearly, the baron had succeeded in getting over three additional feet of it inside the window. The ladder was almost definitively in place.

Using only the strength of his upper body, the baron gently pulled himself up enough over the gutter, which abrupt force might have ripped off or twisted, to be able to rest on his stomach. By raising his right thigh to first put his right knee in the gutter, and then doing the same with his left side, he would be able to fully get back on the roof and climb like a ladder the bare laths that had been stripped of their tiles.

The effort he exerted to achieve this result unfortunately induced a painful cramp. He felt the horrible sensation of being paralyzed. But his arms were like steel. He supported himself with them, not moving, his legs hanging over the open abyss ready to engulf him until the cramp subsided.

Two minutes later, having gradually renewed his effort, he managed to get both knees into the gutter and used the laths to climb up to the dormer window. He finished getting the rest of the ladder inside, and La Guiche, waiting, took the bottom end into his arms. The baron threw into the garret his sword, his bundle, and the remainder of his rope. He climbed down the ladder, at the base of which he collapsed into the arms of his friend, whispering, "I'm utterly exhausted! I'm dead!"

"Rest!" La Guiche said.

He helped him lie down on the hard garret floor and placed a bundle beneath his head. De Batz immediately fell asleep. His entire being was as though wiped out by the prodigious physical and moral strain he had just experienced.

While he took his indispensable rest, Sévignon had the idea to explore the place in which they were, at least to know how to access the stairway and exit the building. He struck the lighter and lit the tinder. By blowing over it, he obtained an intermittent light that enabled him to navigate a few steps at a time. He thereby realized that he and de Batz had ended up in a vast unfurnished garret. At the far end was a door with a wrought iron lock and a latch, which he lifted.

Hardly had he opened the door when a male voice cried out, "Who goes there?"

La Guiche prudently closed the door again. De Batz, woken by this disturbance, jumped to his feet and grabbed his remaining pistol.

"Are you armed?" he asked La Guiche.

"I have the pistol you gave me... What do we do?"

"Is there another door?"

"No!"

"Was the man who screamed alone?"

"I think so!... We must have woken him. In the faint glow of a small lamp, I saw him standing with a pistol, dressed only in breeches and a shirt. He's barefoot."

"Good!... Let's attack before he alerts others!"

Coolly and calmly, the baron opened the door and rushed into the other room, holding his pistol in front of him, crying out, "Surrender, Citizen!"

And he sprang at the man, who was in the middle of the room. The latter pulled the trigger of his pistol. But de Batz had

had time to grab his arm. The shot strayed; the bullet disappeared into the ceiling. Sévignon, rushing over, went behind the man, pulled his hands behind his back and bound them with a piece of his rope, while the baron kept the captured man in check and said to him, "One scream, and you die!"

"All right, all right!... I won't say anything!" the garret's inhabitant answered with resignation. "It's not the first time that I'm arrested... Where are you taking me this time?... To the Abbaye?... To Les Carmes?... To La Bourbe?... To Sainte-Pélagie?... I know all the prisons operated by your regime of liberty!"

This discourse stunned the two escapees.

"We are sorry, forgive us!" said the baron. "We are absolutely not here to arrest you!"

"We are mainly trying to avoid being arrested ourselves!" La Guiche added cheerfully.

"You mean you aren't Committee of Public Safety operatives?" asked their prisoner, who was stunned in turn.

"We were just leaving the building next door!" the baron said simply.

"By way of the roofs!" La Guiche declared. "Do you understand who we are? But you, who are you then?"

"The knight Gonzze de Rougeville, Messieurs! I risked my life for the king and queen on August 10! I am one of those whom the sans-culottes thought they would stigmatize by labeling us the 'dagger knights,' because we put our swords, and our daggers when needed, at the service of the monarchy."

"And I, Monsieur," Jean de Batz replied, "I am Baron de Batz. I am the leader of the Avengers of the King, at least this is what many of our friends refer to us as!"

"Oh-h!" exclaimed Rougeville. "I want to be one! But untie my hands that I may embrace you, Monsieur Baron de Batz!... I know your name well!"

La Guiche quickly untied the prisoner, who threw himself around the baron's neck, then did the same to La Guiche, who introduced himself in turn.

"Marquis de La Guiche!... Or Citizen Sévignon to the sans-culottes! At your service, Monsieur, and please accept my apologies for your treatment just now. It's just that we didn't know who you were."

"This is a stroke of luck! This is a true stroke of good luck that you came here, Messieurs!" Rougeville declared. "And to think that, for the last half hour, woken by the noise you made, I have been lying in wait with a pistol in hand to shoot a bullet into your head!... Thank God I missed!"

"If my name is known to you, Monsieur," the baron replied, "I have heard yours mentioned a number of times... His Majesty Louis XVI, God rest his soul, identified you to our friends as having corresponded with him in the Temple, unbeknownst to the jailers, owing to a special means known to you alone!"

"That is true!... And I am thinking about corresponding with the queen in the same way!"

"Let's hope you don't need to, Monsieur! If I have my way, the queen, His Majesty Louis XVII, and Their Royal Highnesses Madame Élisabeth and Madame Royale will be free an hour from now!"

"What are you saying?"

"I am expressing a hope!... I will explain it to you on our way, if you will do me the kindness of joining us."

"Gladly!"

"Let us leave right away then!"

During this conversation, Rougeville had lit a lamp, which allowed his two nocturnal visitors to see the poverty of the small room, containing rickety chairs and an unmade, lopsided bed with crude, torn sheets.

"Messieurs, I am getting dressed," he said.

"It wouldn't be a bad idea for us to do the same!" Sévignon declared. "Look at us, Baron!"

"True, we look like thieves!" agreed de Batz. "But our bundles contain clean clothes... One must never travel without packing some things for the journey, you see!"

De Batz's and La Guiche's clothes were torn, their faces were covered in sweat, and their hands were bloody; in this state, they would draw the suspicion of the first patrol they encountered. In ten minutes, with much fresh water and scrubbing, they were as good as new and donned their coats. All three descended the stairway. They wore red caps and kept their other hats inside their coats, which was Rougeville's idea.

Rougeville, like all tenants in apartment buildings without a concierge, which were already somewhat numerous at this time, had a master key for opening the door; they therefore did not have to draw the attention of anyone.

And in the street, they pretended to be drunk and sang in stammering voices the *Ça ira*:

> *Oh, it'll be fine, it'll be fine, it'll be fine!*
> *The aristocrats to the lamppost!*
> *Oh, it'll be fine, it'll be fine, it'll be fine!*
> *The aristocrats, we'll hang 'em!...*

This civic attitude prevented them from being questioned by the sentry whom de Batz had seen from atop the roof, and who was presently showing his corporal and three other men who had run over from the guardhouse the tiles that had rushed in a torrent onto the street, back when the baron had nearly flown off the roof with them.

Chapter 15

The Female Rivals

A HALF HOUR later, a mysterious patrol of about twenty men wearing gray hooded overcoats exited from the back of a restaurant onto Rue des Francs-Bourgeois.

The storm finally broke and burst forth in large drops onto the warm pavement.

"This is fortunate," said the patrol commander. "If it weren't raining, these hoods would have looked suspicious, since to put one on in such heat, one would really need to have a political motivation!"

The patrol headed towards the Temple. It was still about four hundred meters away from the prison when a man hurried to meet it and said to the commander, "Monsieur! Don't go any further!"

"What is it?" asked de Batz, recognizing his servant Biret-Tissot.

"The queen just changed prisons!"

"What did you say?"

Rumbles of despair and anger came forth from the twenty patrolmen in gray overcoats. Some of them struck the butts of their rifles onto the pavement in fury.

Biret-Tissot explained, "It was Cortey who sent me to warn you. I saw the carriage that took the queen to the Conciergerie pass by a half hour ago!"

"To the Conciergerie?... They're putting her on trial then?"

"Alas, Monsieur, I do fear that! As for rescuing the other prisoners, it's not the right time to think about it!... There are lots of comings and goings at the Temple right now!"

"Let us march to the Conciergerie!" said one of the patrolmen.

"And let us be killed rather than retreat!" said another.

Coolly, de Batz responded, "Messieurs, when people plan to get themselves killed, they at least need to do it in a way that is useful. Our destiny is calling!... Everything must be started over, so we shall start over!"

And he said to Biret-Tissot, "Go tell Barbereux that he is not to keep his cart parked any longer in front of that wine shop you know!"

And de Batz commanded his men, "About turn!"

Inasmuch as the patrol had been cheerful and light-hearted on its march to the Temple, it appeared heavy and downcast as it retreated. The rain was raging. All the men bowed their heads beneath the heavy downpour. The weather was in unison with the events at hand, and several of the men were crying. De Batz himself was clenching his fists!

But all the clockwork set in motion by him to save the queen had not stopped moving instantaneously. Cécile Renault, who was not forewarned, played her part.

Assuming the tone and mannerisms of a so-called *tricoteuse*, or "knitwoman," one of those females of the Revolution who relished watching the guillotine in action, she ran to the Tuileries asking to disclose a grave matter to the Committee of Public Safety.

For this Committee of Public Safety was always open for business; it was headquartered in the palace's "Two Columns Hall," which in times past had been, so ironically, the queen's chamber. That very night, several of the members remained there on duty, and Fouquier-Tinville, the public prosecutor, who had been dropping heads all day long, came to reach an agreement with them regarding the next day's batch of victims. This Committee of Public Safety was the great provider of that human slaughterhouse called the Revolutionary Tribunal. And naturally, Freemasonry had veiled this savage enterprise with a patriotic name.

Cécile Renault's written denunciation caused a commotion among the Committee members.

Fouquier-Tinville, who had been getting ready to leave, tried to reassure them, saying, "That's impossible! The Capet woman is at the Conciergerie!"

"What if she was captured on her way there?"

They sent gendarmes on horseback to the Temple, the Conciergerie, and the Rouen thoroughfare as additional security measures.

Those gendarmes sent to the Rouen thoroughfare brought back a carriage containing a young woman who resembled the queen. It was suspected that she was an accomplice in an enterprise that had perhaps been attempted. And they put her in jail.

But the next day, Citizen Robespierre received this letter:

Dear Citizen Robespierre,

A young maid who recently entered my service and was sent by me to Meulan via stagecoach to get news of a dangerously ill friend from school, was just arrested by order of the Committee of Public Safety and imprisoned in the Old English Convent.

I would be infinitely grateful to you, dear Citizen Robespierre, if you would return to me as soon as possible this girl whom I very much need and who is the victim of an unequivocal mistake. I shall thank you verbally when I have the pleasure of seeing you.

Your affectionately devoted
Émilie de Sainte-Amaranthe

Robespierre was the absolute and unchecked master of the Revolutionary Tribunal, of Fouquier-Tinville, of the Committee of Public Safety, of the Convention, and of all the "no God, no master" types of that moment.

That very evening, Adèle de Sainte-Pazanne was with Émilie de Sainte-Amaranthe, who tearfully embraced her and said to her, "Mademoiselle, I very much like and admire you!... I bless heaven for being able to meet you!... Will you be my friend?"

"Gladly!" the young woman said. "Thanks to you, I did not run a great risk!"

"Only the risk of your head!... And your head is lovely! It would have been a pity!"

Cécile was beaming. A little later she said to Mademoiselle de Sainte-Pazanne, "I kept my promise. You now know the siren."

"Good heavens!" the young woman exclaimed. "It's her?"

"Yes!... Luck has even made it so that you are competing with her face-to-face!"

"Alas!... I am done for!... She is too beautiful!"

"Fight all the same!" Cécile said smilingly.

Part Two:

The Red Harvest

Chapter 1

A Convention Meeting

SINCE MAY 10, the Convention had relocated from the Salle du Manège, where Louis XVI's farce of a trial had taken place.

It was now headquartered at the Tuileries Palace, in a vast hall adapted for its use, having on hand the Committee of Public Safety, which was tasked with executing its bloody orders. It was the beginning of October, and in this palace's garden, at the end of which the guillotine stood permanently, the sun beat down its last rays on the foliage, which was starting to russet; it was like a smile from nature tinged with autumnal sadness.

Three young women walked slowly into the garden. Two were elegantly attired in bright, striped dresses. Ribbons in national colors decorated their hair and their bodices, ribbons that one could say were obligatory, and even ended up being imposed by decree, as is fitting in a time of liberty. Even before the decree, they were tantamount to a civic card.

The third young woman was dressed more somberly. An imperceptible cockade emerged from her luxuriant blonde hair gathered beneath her bonnet *à l'indépendante*.

All three became the focus of those strolling in the garden, the majority of whom looked sinister.

With the Reign of Terror well underway, elegance was suspect, and good manners were regarded as completely contrary to the civic spirit. The elegant therefore stayed at home, at least when they were not in prison.

The only decently dressed persons one saw in the garden were Convention deputies stepping outside for some fresh air before returning to their meetings. They did still often wear the hideous red cap. One had to be Robespierre to have the right to show off silk stockings, an embroidered vest, and a beaver hat without drawing an angry mob of sans-culottes and knitwomen. These ruffians kept watch near the palace for the next cart of condemned to appear on the so-called *Rue Honoré* on its way to Revolution Square, in order to jeer and heap insults at the unfortunate ones in their final agony.

In the meantime, they stared maliciously at the three young women, but without accosting them. For them so boldly to parade the dresses of has-beens a mere stone's throw from the guillotine, there must have been a very powerful Jacobin they felt was protecting them: Robespierre perhaps, or Fouquier-Tinville, or Chabot, the renegade Capuchin.

The reader has perhaps already identified the three young women: Marie Grandmaison, a half hour earlier, had gone to the Arcades House to get Émilie de Sainte-Amaranthe and her lady-in-waiting, Adèle de Sainte-Pazanne, who had not left Émilie since the famous day of the aborted attempt to rescue the queen.

It had long been planned for Marie to pick them up to attend a meeting of the Convention. It was an amusement to which one could treat oneself at the time, just like Chamber of Deputies meetings today.

Waiting for the moment to enter, they were enticed by the warm sun and clear skies. While conversing, they strolled the paths between the Terrasse du Bord de l'Eau and the Terrasse des Feuillants.

"Many of our friends are here!" Marie said.

"Is this supposed to be a tumultuous meeting?" asked Émilie.

"No, not in theory!"

"Too bad!... I was so hoping to see one!"

"Don't worry!... It could become one. A spark is all one needs to cause an explosion in a milieu that is always overheated!... At any rate, the baron told me that during the discussions there would be some serious things prepared for our enemies!"

"What is to be discussed?"

"The question of abolishing the Indies Company!"

"That's not very interesting!" said Émilie, making a cute pouting expression.

"True, but you will hear Chabot, the former Capuchin, speaking, one of our most zealous regicides! And what will interest you, I think, is that he is going to pronounce his own death sentence when he talks!"

"And how is that?"

"It's the baron's secret!"

"A defrocked Capuchin!" Mademoiselle de Sainte-Pazanne murmured. "It was not a long time ago that my parents took me to a mission in the Vendée that was preached by a Capuchin!... And this renegade I am going to hear will perhaps use the same eloquence to condemn what he glorified in times past!... The same gift for speaking that God gave him, he uses against God!... It seems I am going to witness a betrayal similar to that of a fiancé who would pledge his loyalty to me and then to another using the same words and eloquence!"

And she looked at Émilie de Sainte-Amaranthe as she said this. But the young woman's look remained innocent. Only a little bit of surprise manifested itself in her gaze.

Mademoiselle de Sainte-Pazanne did not read any hidden thoughts or emotions in the facial expression of the one whom Cécile had denounced to her as the formidable "siren."

Marie and Émilie observed their companion. The emotional tone with which she uttered her comparison betrayed a deep secret of hers that they respected. They changed the subject and entered the palace.

In the past two months that they had been living together, Adèle and Émilie had ended up becoming friends. Émilie, in the shady environment in which her mother had her live, was grateful for the circumstances that led under her roof a young woman of her age, condition, and aristocratic education, like her in manners and outlook. With the new arrival, it seemed to her she was now living in a more familial atmosphere.

So that the fable of gendarmes mistakenly arresting on the road to Rouen a young woman in Citizeness Émilie de Sainte-Amaranthe's service could be substantiated, Robespierre himself had to be able to attest that this young woman did not leave the Sainte-Amaranthe ladies' residence and that she indeed dressed according to her inferior status.

To the outside world, therefore, Mademoiselle de Sainte-Pazanne was at Émilie's command, something like a reader or a stewardess. In private, she was a friend who was valued more and more each day, although sometimes Émilie found in Adèle an unexplained coldness or instinctive hostility, which prevented her from opening herself up to the young Vendée woman as much as she would have wished.

Mademoiselle de Sainte-Pazanne, for her part, rejoiced at being in the heart of enemy territory, and was grateful to Cécile and the luck that had allowed her to observe and fight to save her happiness, which she believed was under threat.

At the onset, she tried hard, out of a very feminine instinct which overcomes the best of women, to seek out imperfections in the one who was her rival without knowing it.

But Émilie's beauty was like an impeccable marble in which she had to quickly give up on finding any flaws. She looked for a moral weakness in her, setting traps for her ego, her vanity, and her pride. She was soon angry with herself for experiencing the attraction that Émilie exerted on all her entourage, and for feeling sorry for some wounds of the soul that the other had ingenuously revealed to her, as if she had wanted them to be healed.

Of the two, it was Émilie who envied the other!... She complained about the atmosphere in which she lived, about the daily impure throng of gamblers who came to the Arcades House to satisfy their unrestrained passions like drinkers who go to the tavern to satiate their need for drunkenness. She suffered so acutely from this disgrace to her mother, to her brother, a young child whom bad example could corrupt, and to herself, that Mademoiselle Adèle de Sainte-Pazanne one day took pity on her and tenderly hugged her.

This was a spontaneous movement, that of one sister instinctively rushing to console another. But almost immediately, jealousy took over and tried to exploit her own heart's generous gesture: "What do you have to be afraid of?" she asked. "You are beautiful and well-born enough, and your soul is noble and pure enough, that a young man you love one day, or that you perhaps love now, will overlook this bad environment in which he finds you and marry you just as if you had always lived in the most austere provincial château."

And she listened, eagerly, for her response.

Émilie de Sainte-Amaranthe replied, "Monsieur de Sartines would marry me if I wanted!"

"And why don't you want to?"

"I don't love him!"

"You will love him!"

"No!... Because I love someone else!"

Adèle turned frightfully pale, but Émilie, fully preoccupied with herself, did not at all notice her emotion and asked, "And you, Adèle, do you love someone?... Since we are now starting to share confidences, you can certainly tell me!"

"Yes!" answered Mademoiselle de Sainte-Pazanne, her throat tightening a little.

Émilie, in turn, joyfully hugged her, saying, "Oh, how happy I am!... You yourself will understand me better when I tell you everything!... But tell me first, my dear Adèle, does the one you love, love you?"

"Does one ever know those things?" she asked seriously.

"You are right!" Émilie responded. "Do I know him?"

"You have seen him, and often!"

"I see so many people here!... You know that I am only able to pick out a few of the friendly faces in the regular crowd... If you told me his name, I would realize..."

"His name?"

"Yes!... Unless..."

"His name?... Oh, never!"

This cry escaped Adèle, despite herself, as she simultaneously crossed her arms over her breast as if to keep inside the secret it contained. Saying his name, in fact, would risk, in this unspoken struggle, putting Émilie on her guard if she did love Paul de Lézardière; it would precipitate matters and weaken the means on which she depended to learn that which could potentially kill her.

The sharpness of her response and gesture surprised Émilie. But the charming girl did not at all take offense; on the contrary, she found it amusing.

"Fine, my dear!... Keep your secret!... But to punish you, I will tell you only half of mine, to intrigue you. You will still know more than Mama, who would very much like to know my secret herself! Now, you must admit that it is unfortunate for me to have two suitors, neither of whom I love, and to have given my heart to a third who has never spoken to me except with his eyes!"

"With only his eyes?" asked Adèle.

"Yes!... And you are already intrigued now!... Your punishment now begins!... Have I told you the name of my second suitor?"

"No!"

"Robespierre!"

"Oh! Heavens!"

Mademoiselle de Sainte-Pazanne let out a cry of terror and said to Émilie in a sincere tone, "How sorry I am for you! And you are indebted to him! Because of me!... Oh, I feel horrible!"

"I am not yet his wife!... And perhaps my handsome knight will save me from that monster, like in the fairy tales! But will he be able to do it in time?... I feel like I'm playing with a tiger that is ultimately going to devour me!"

"Her handsome knight!" Adèle thought to herself. "Oh, how much I would want her to be rescued if I were certain it wasn't my handsome knight doing the rescuing!"

But given that during these two months she had not once seen at the Arcades House Paul de Lézardière, whom Baron de Batz employed for distant missions, she ended up recovering her serenity. Jealousy no longer took hold of her, other than in occasional fits.

As all three ascended the Tuileries stairway leading to the boxes reserved for distinguished guests—for even at the apex of this regime of equality, the sans-culottes and shrews who heckled the representatives of the people were as though corralled into separate areas—Émilie, full of joy, said to Mademoiselle de Sainte-Pazanne, "I am happy, because I think *he* will be here!"

"Did *he* then know you would be coming here?"

"He seems to sense everything I'm doing, and he's everywhere I go!"

In the vast Convention meeting hall, barely two thirds of the deputies were at their seats.

Once Émilie and Marie Grandmaison appeared in the hall, many of them turned their heads and eyed the two as if in the theatre, a sign that the meeting did not fascinate them much. Robespierre also showed his crabbed and otherwise expressionless face, which lit up with a faint smile when he recognized Émilie.

Mademoiselle de Sainte-Pazanne modestly sat down in a second-row seat, as was appropriate for an inferior. And there, in a semi-obscurity favoring her desire to see without being seen, she scanned all the corners and recesses of the immense hall, especially those reserved for the public, fearing to discover there Paul de Lézardière's young face with a nascent mustache. For if he was there, her misfortune was certain, she thought, and it must be he who went everywhere that the "siren" went.

Down below, before the famous bar placed in front of the president's desk, various delegations marched in, as was customary at the beginning of the session: soldiers bringing the representatives flags of conquered "slave peoples"; sans-culottes coming to file complaints or make denunciations; drunk murderers and plunderers paying the Convention homage with treasures from churches and abbeys, crossing the hall mockingly dressed in church vestments and wearing bishops' miters. These impious masquerades were so frequent that they no longer provoked anything beyond a relative curiosity.

Still, there was a moment of solemn silence when a man in a carmagnole jacket and red cap then came forward to the bar, presented a box to an usher, and cried out, "Representative citizens of the people, I come from Reims, sent to you by the patriot Rühl. He has commissioned me to put into your hands the pieces of what was the Holy Ampulla that contained the oil for consecrating the tyrants. He himself crushed with his heel this shameful fetish of abolished superstition and reason-depriving tyranny in the presence of the liberated people, who expressed their joy by dancing in circles in the old basilica."

Robespierre gave the signal for applause. The president embraced Citizen Rühl's emissary, and the sans-culottes in the tribunes sang the *Ça ira*.

Adèle de Sainte-Pazanne, who felt like she was attending a Satanic sabbath, heard something like a muffled rumbling of anger next to her. In the dim light of the box, she made out, sitting to her right, a man whose eyes blazed, and who muttered, "Horrible sacrilege! The very day they begin the queen's trial!"

In front of her, Marie and Émilie, still eyed intermittently by the representatives, who seemed to them much more preoccupied with elegant women in the boxes than with government matters, feigned laughs and indifferent remarks. A single gesture contrary to the civic spirit, or any sign of anti-republican emotion, and one was very quickly deemed suspect!

The procession of delegations had ended. A representative was getting ready to deliver a speech.

"Is that Chabot?" Émilie asked.

"I don't know!" Marie said.

The man with the blazing eyes in the second row responded in a hushed voice, very courteously, without moving his head forward, as though he wanted to avoid moving his features out of the semidarkness that enveloped him: "No, Citizeness! That is only a friend of Chabot's; that is Delaunay of Angers."

"Thank you, Citizen," Marie said.

"But I recognize him!" Émilie said. "I saw him one day, at the house, sitting at a table with…"

"Shh!" whispered the mysterious spectator who intrigued Mademoiselle de Sainte-Pazanne. "He was at a table with another deputy named Julien of Toulouse, a defrocked Protestant pastor. As for the third person with them, do not speak of him here, Citizeness Émilie de Sainte-Amaranthe."

The young woman blushed from ear to ear, while Adèle leaned towards her two companions and whispered, "You were right to say that we would find friends here!"

"They even keep our lips from loosening too much!" Émilie added playfully, so as to be heard by the mysterious individual.

Delaunay of Angers had begun his speech. His western peasant accent imbued his discourse with a vulgar, even comical, tone. No charisma and nothing lofty. He argued like a merchant promoting his wares at a fairground.

"Representative citizens," he said, "I come to denounce the schemes of the Indies Company, a carryover of the old regime's banditry, which ought to be abolished like that regime itself was. The directors of this company just circumvented the law to steal 2,249,786 livres in registration fees from the Republic, and I will prove it. The laws of August 27 and November 28, 1792, as you know, made the shares subject to registration fees with each transfer of ownership. What did the Company do? It substituted its stocks with an acknowledgment similar to those that were created for the State's debt. Under this new form, the stock no longer belongs to the holder, the name of the owner is inscribed in a register, and the transfer is executed by a simple mention in the company's books. The law is circumvented! More than 128,000 transfers have taken place in 1793. You see then, Citizens..."

But the Convention was hardly listening. A good number of deputies were yawning; others were dozing off.

Émilie said to Marie, "Oh, how boring this is!"

"Chabot might have been more interesting!" whispered Marie Grandmaison, laughing. "This Delaunay has the accent of the old comic opera gardeners! Don't you think so?" she added, turning towards Mademoiselle de Sainte-Pazanne. "You expect him to say, '*Jarnigné!*'"

Mademoiselle de Sainte-Pazanne gave no answer. Pale, and her heart beating heavily in her breast, she had just noticed Paul de Lézardière in a public gallery at the end of the hall, among the sans-culottes and the knitwomen. He himself was dressed like a man of the people and was looking in their direction. And Adèle thought to herself, "Him! It is him!... No more doubts!... He has come for her! And it really is he who goes wherever she goes!"

Then she tried to be reasonable: "Why am I here torturing myself? He is dressed in a carmagnole; he is playing a role then, so he can spy, and he is here on the leader's orders!... This hall is full of friends!"

But she nevertheless remained in doubt, and this doubt was perhaps more dreadful than being certain of her misfortune.

She was distracted from her painful thoughts by the voice of her mysterious neighbor, who said to Marie, "You want to hear Chabot?... Why didn't you say something sooner, Citizeness Grandmaison?"

And standing up, he made a sign. A man seated not far from there in his same row got up and approached him.

"Devaux," Adèle's neighbor said to the beckoned man, "arrange to go down and have an usher ask for Citizen Chabot. You will ask him, on behalf of Citizen Manaud, who has his reasons for not showing himself down below, to replace Delaunay and to deliver a short and thunderous speech. I know that he already has one ready; it was I who wrote it. Do it quickly! This has gone on long enough!"

Marie and Émilie were jolted with surprise.

"Him! Him!" they whispered.

And Émilie, turning to Adèle, said to her, "Don't ask your neighbor if the reaper will come. It's him sitting next to you!"

"Oh, Monsieur," Mademoiselle de Sainte-Pazanne said very softly to the baron, trembling with surprise, emotion, and respect, "let me thank you for having allowed me to risk my life for the queen, and I implore you to take my life if it is possible to still save her at this cost!"

De Batz took her hand, kissed it, and replied, "I am pleased, Mademoiselle, to make your acquaintance, and to tell you how much I have admired your dedication. For the time being, the best thing you can do is to pray for the poor queen. I hope to distract the Revolutionary Tribunal's attention away from her by giving them the heads of some bandits down below to chop off... That would give us some more time... I fear we are too late!... In any case, to risk mowing down a life in full bloom, such as yours, without an urgent reason or hope of success, would burden me with needless regret!"

"What a shame!" Mademoiselle de Sainte-Pazanne said sweetly.

Delaunay was now quiet, and the president gave the floor to Chabot, the deputy from Loir-et-Cher, who had sanctions to propose. The three young women understood that it was Baron de Batz, from his obscure place, who was in reality directing the debate like a magician with his wand, and that the leader of the Counter-Revolution was perhaps, at this moment, more the master of the Convention than Robespierre himself. Chabot was under his control!

Despite their ignorance of parliamentary procedure, they listened to the Jacobin's discourse with a kind of keen nervousness.

Émilie de Sainte-Amaranthe, through the lenses of her tortoiseshell lorgnette, curiously examined this renegade Capuchin who at the king's trial had been, with Robespierre, among the most implacable and cruel judges.

She saw a short, squat man with a stocky, muscular body, having fiery eyes like those of a wild beast in search of prey, thick lips, and shaped for battle. His bearing was vulgar, and he awkwardly sported new clothes of the latest fashion.

This was no longer the legendary Chabot from the Convention's beginnings, when he used to wear a sloppy shirt, had his legs half-bare, sported the red cap, and strove to embody, both morally and physically, the ideal sans-culotte.

Was he now trying to imitate the elegant Robespierre? No! He aspired to marry into wealth and to enter the ranks of the Revolution's "profiteers." He had not left the cloister and tossed his habit out the window so that he could continue a life of austerity!

He had met some very wealthy Austrian Jews, the Freys, who were bankers on Rue d'Anjou, and he had been smitten by the eastern charm of their young sister Léopoldine. He had asked for her hand in marriage. However, the bankers, despite all their patriotism—for the Jews in France, newly arrived from Frankfurt and Vienna, were beginning to acquire a monopoly on patriotism—refused to let him wed their sister until he first became rich himself.

"How do I become rich?" Chabot wondered, when three Convention member friends of his identified to him a sure way he could procure the comfortable and luxurious future he dreamed of for himself.

These three Convention members were our two old acquaintances Delaunay of Angers and Julien of Toulouse, as well as a certain Bazire, a staunch republican who had no more of a penchant for austerity than the Third Republic's founders or the socialists who continue their work.

If Lenotre's curious book *Le baron de Batz* is to be believed, they took Chabot to Charonne, where Citizen Manaud presented himself as a man free of any political prejudices and only concerned with bank business. He told the Jacobin about the stock market coup that would reap him a fortune overnight.

This proposition had been made at the end of a fine and lavish meal, something that Chabot always appreciated. It was between two wines when the baron formally began tackling the Indies Company.

"It's so simple!" repeated Delaunay, who was Chabot's tempting demon in this circumstance. "Just one speech at the rostrum is all that's needed to make the value of a company's stocks drop. You take advantage of the price reduction and buy. Afterwards, you provoke an increase in the value and sell!"

"You still need funding!" objected Bazire, who was at the feast. "Since to be able to buy when the shares are low, the money has to be available right away!"

"Don't worry about that!" exclaimed the baron sardonically. "I am here to advance the money. My coffers are open to you!"

The baron had received the two million promised by Clavière a long time ago. He had plenty of gold on hand.

The next day, Chabot, who had sobered up, went to ask the Frey bankers for advice. They would not have been Jews had they advised against such a stock market coup. They encouraged Chabot, decided to buy shares in bulk when the price dropped, agreed to give him the hand of their sister Léopoldine once he had made his fortune, which they were now certain was imminent, and invited him to take up residence with them.

Chabot accepted. But he could not live in one of the most luxurious mansions on Rue d'Anjou Saint-Honoré dressed as a sans-culotte. That is why he now wore new clothes and decently clad himself. But the baron would have been surprised, perhaps, had he known that one of the most immediate results of his great counter-revolutionary schemes was to be the edifying marriage of a defrocked Capuchin to an Austrian Jewess! Did not this marriage essentially epitomize this epoch's "regeneration of humanity"?

Chabot's discourse delighted the baron, and Mademoiselle de Sainte-Pazanne could hear the latter rubbing his hands with satisfaction.

The ex-Capuchin further amplified the text he had been given. He spewed diatribes against corruption and the monarchy's thievery, spoke of the monster of financial speculation with tremors of indignation, and denounced Louis XV's "crimes" and Calonne's scandalous speculative trading.

Jean de Batz truly must have enjoyed hearing this depraved man accuse the old regime of corruption.

People were listening to Chabot attentively. He had there, in the Convention, more than a hundred accomplices who planned to profit from the stock market coup.

Those who contrast the venality of our present parliamentarians with the alleged incorruptibility of their great ancestors forget too easily that this "list of one hundred four" within the Convention could already be made back on this early October of 1793.

The draft decree promoted by Chabot and Delaunay in their speeches was welcomed with thunderous applause. It consisted of ordering a liquidation of the Indies Company, *all while putting the company's current directors in charge of this liquidation.*

The decree itself had also been drafted by Baron de Batz. If Chabot's fierce discourse had the certain effect of lowering stock prices, keeping the company's directors allowed the company, in actuality, to continue; the company could win back trust, and its stocks could regain their value little by little.

"This is in the bag!" the baron whispered. "I finally got them!"

But a discussion ensued about the text of this decree, and the president suddenly gave the floor to Citizen Fabre d'Églantine, a curious bohemian who, after having been an actor, a journalist, a painter of poor-quality miniatures, a playwright, and a dishonest military supplier, was to become a Convention deputy, get swallowed up in this present venture, and be known to posterity as the writer of the innocent pastoral song *Il pleut, il pleut, bergère.*

He was not part of Chabot's group and spoke logically, unaware of the hidden motives behind the two previous speeches: "If the directors of the Indies Company are such great criminals," he exclaimed, "why leave them in charge of liquidating their business? I propose that the Government confiscate and sell all of the company's assets, and that the directors' papers be secured in order to uncover further evidence of their mischief!"

There was applause, and Robespierre supported this motion. Chabot was aghast.

In the back of his dark box, the baron stamped his feet with rage: "The idiot! The idiot!" he grumbled. "He is ruining all my plans! There will be no more company then! And a rise in stock prices won't be possible! The scoundrels will get away. The bait all these sharks were already biting is being taken from me!"

During this time, a confused discussion ensued. Chabot, initially disheartened, bustled about and had his accomplices take action. The matter ended up being entrusted to a commission which was tasked with completing a report. This commission consisted of five members: Delaunay, Chabot, Ramel, Cambon, and Fabre d'Églantine.

The baron reflected, "I don't have Ramel or Cambon, but I have the first two. By buying Fabre, with a hundred thousand francs if necessary, I will have the majority in this commission!... But what an unfortunate delay!... Will they kill the queen before I have time to busy the Revolutionary Tribunal with all these brigands?"

And he very swiftly departed, without saying goodbye to the three young women.

"Let's go! He has left!" said Mademoiselle de Sainte-Pazanne. "There is nothing else of interest to learn here!"

That last utterance had a double meaning!

The tribunes for the public emptied slowly, but methodically, as if an order had been given.

Marie Grandmaison said to them, "Almost everyone from Charonne is here... The policeman who wanted to arrest the baron in the garden would have had his hands full!"

Paul de Lézardière, who had been among a group of sans-culottes, exited with them. Adèle therefore made this new deduction: "He came with the ones from Charonne, on orders, and not for her, since he didn't even greet her!"

Then her mind soon thought of a contrary motive: "He couldn't come to greet her since he was in disguise. It would have caused a sensation. Besides, I am here with her!... And that would have made it awkward for him."

As all three were going down to the terrace that opened to the garden, they crossed paths with a young man of distinguished bearing. His chin was freshly shaven and ensconced in a triple-layered cravat; his torso was fitted into a puce-colored silk suit with large lapels which left visible the lower part of a white waistcoat; and he wore pale green gloves. He acknowledged them as they reached the bottom of the steps, removing his beaver hat decorated with a black silk band.

"Good afternoon, Elleviou!" said Marie Grandmaison with a small familiar gesture.

"Good afternoon!" the young man replied in a serious voice.

But of the three pretty Parisian women, it was only Émilie he looked at.

"Elleviou?" Adèle asked. "Is that the singer from the Favart Theatre whom all of Paris is obsessed with?"

"Yes!" said Marie. "I sang with him when he was just beginning. He has progressed nicely in just a few years!"

"What do you think of him?" Émilie asked, blushing a little.

"He has a gallant bearing," answered Mademoiselle de Sainte-Pazanne. "One would think he was a man of court rather than a comic opera singer!"

"That's because he is well-born," Émilie explained with a kind of vivacity. "His father was a well-respected physician; his mother was a Kervalan!"

"How is he at the theatre?"

"He's an accomplished show singer. It's gotten to his head. Citizen Monvel has written plays for him. Who would act and sing *Philippe and Georgette* if he were no longer there?... We will go see the show one of these evenings. Do you want to?"

"Certainly," Adèle replied, without enthusiasm.

"It will be more fun than a Convention meeting!" Marie affirmed, smiling.

As they returned to the Arcades House, they strolled leisurely across the Palais-Royal Garden, and Adèle, seeking to turn the conversation to what preoccupied her, asked Émilie, "By the way, did you see him?"

"See whom?"

"The one who goes everywhere you go."

"Yes!... I did see him!... Have you figured out who it is now?"

"I have!" answered Mademoiselle de Sainte-Pazanne, who felt as though a dagger had just entered her heart.

With less reticence, Adèle might have learned everything and then jumped for joy, for while she was assuming Paul, Émilie was referring to Elleviou, that handsome, well-born man who had become a singer!

Chapter 2

The Barber Gracchus's Envoy

O N THE MORNING following the escape of Baron de Batz and Marquis de La Guiche, a report from the post's commanding sub-officer was brought to the concierge of La Force Prison, who was still in bed.

This report stated that the soldier on duty on Rue Pavée-aux-Marais, between midnight and two in the morning, had heard noise from the upper stories of the building adjacent to the prison, and that tiles had fallen from the roof onto the street. But he was unable to see anything on account of the darkness, and silence followed. He thought to inform his command when he saw three drunk patriots exiting the building who he assumed were the cause of the disturbance, and who were evidently just out reveling.

Dubois was shaken by a kind of presentiment and got up quickly. He had barely finished getting dressed when Sénar familiarly entered, looking happy and in the handsome suit he wore when going to the Arcades House to contemplate his idol.

"I didn't sleep at all last night, I've been so excited," he said, "and now I've come to get you!"

"To go where?"

"To the Tuileries, to the Committee of Public Safety!"

"To do what?"

"To hand over the infamous de Batz and collect our reward for the service we are rendering the Republic! I could have gone there all by myself, but we agreed, did we not, that this was to be a joint venture!... I don't suppose you already denounced your prisoner to keep the reward all for yourself?"

"Calm down!... Before going to the Committee, come upstairs with me to check on the prisoners in solitary confinement... I'm worried!"

"About what?"

"I will tell you later!"

They went up, Dubois leading Sénar with a swiftness that troubled the latter. In the corridor for the prisoners in solitary confinement, they saw the good Leopard. He was very pale, his eyes were frenzied, and his unkempt hair hung down like a weeping willow tree. He was pacing back and forth like a wolf in a cage. Seeing his boss, he could only utter the following words in a choked voice, "Oh, Citizen!... Oh, Citizen!... What an ordeal!"

Without stopping to respond to him, and sensing disaster, Dubois grabbed the bunch of keys from his hands and opened the baron's cell.

"Empty!" he cried.

"Empty!" repeated Sénar, who rushed to also look inside. He added, "He had a key then?"

"No!" Dubois said to him whispering. "He no longer had it!"

"Well, how did he get out?... There's no sign of a hole!... Nothing is broken!"

"Yes, how?" said Dubois, clenching his teeth.

And suddenly, he grabbed the good Leopard by his throat and yelled at him, staring into his eyes: "You know, you miserable wretch!... Come now!... Tell me everything!... Confess!... You let this conspirator escape for money!"

"I swear to you, no!" the jailer insisted. "What good would that do me?... They gave me generous tips, and I wanted nothing more than to keep them! Their escape costs me more than it does you!"

"*Their* escape?" Dubois asked.

"Yes!" Sénar added. "You said *their* escape! But there's only one escaped prisoner!"

"You don't know everything!" said the prison guard in unparalleled desolation. "The other one also left!"

And he opened the door to La Guiche's cell. Inside, there was an enormous hole visible in the ceiling, directly above a pile of torn curtains.

Sénar cried out, "They escaped through there! But who put the two prisoners together?"

"I did!... But I didn't know about the hole!" groaned the good Leopard. "Curtains were hiding it... And to think that it was I who forced them, so to speak, to get to know each other and to become friends so that I could get generous tips from them, and they end up playing this trick on me!... Oh, if I ever catch them!"

"Then run and catch them now!... Idiot!" Dubois exclaimed. "Too bad for you! I am going to write up my report, and you will be guillotined!"

"Me!" objected the good Leopard, in a tone of incredulity. "Me? A good Marseillais, and a Lamballe Septembrist? Guillotined?... You'll be guillotined before I am!... You are higher up than I... and more guilty... And it is I who am going to denounce you first!"

He was already walking away to make good on his threat, which fell on Dubois's fury like an ice-cold shower. Sénar sensed the danger; he ran to the jailer, stopped him, and led him back to Dubois.

"Listen, Citizen," Sénar said to the good Leopard, "we are arguing, we are angry, and it would be better we all get along with each other. We are in much danger, all of us, despite who we are!... The two of you, especially!... You will not say anything to anyone, and Dubois will not say anything either. These two prisoners were forgotten here for months and months... Given how much the papers of the Committees and the Revolutionary Tribunal are in disarray, they don't even know anymore which prison they are in, and it sometimes takes Fouquier-Tinville half a month to find a choice accused he wants to sacrifice to the guillotine. Meanwhile, he randomly goes through the prisons picking out prisoners with whom to restock his pantry.

Therefore, there is no danger if none of us says anything!... We risk our heads, however, if the secret comes to light!... Patch up this hole yourself so that no worker finds out there was an escape here. Then, we will try to find our escaped birds; we will in-process them as new captures and earn a bonus payment that we will divide among ourselves!... I know where to apprehend them!"

Dubois made no reply, but acquiesced by his silence.

"Fine!" the good Leopard conceded. "But before they are sent to the Revolutionary Tribunal, I want them to stay here for half a month, so that I can fleece them and get compensation for the loss they're causing me, those scoundrels!... You won't refuse that to a patriot, eh?"

"Agreed!" said Sénar.

And leaving the good Leopard to inspect the damage done by La Guiche and to make the needed repairs with a good application of plaster, the police officer led the La Force concierge to the modest office where we saw them first meet.

When they were alone, Dubois said to his accomplice, "Let's speak little, but let's speak honestly! You told that rascal upstairs you knew where to catch the baron and his escape companion. Was that empty bluster or the truth?"

"That's the truth!"

"Where then do you believe they are taking refuge?"

"At the house in Charonne!"

"You poor soul!... They know better than to get themselves into a trap!"

"And why would they think that's a trap?... The day I tried to get inside and had the unthinkable good fortune of encountering Burlandeux and forcing him to meet me and hand me over the famous letter, I sowed panic in that house, I won't deny it!... The following day, all the birds had fled the cage. But after a few days, they came back little by little. Through Burlandeux, I knew that they were worried at first, that they were initially more on guard than before, but that they later felt safe again. They now believe they are forgotten and are perfectly calm. It would be a huge mistake to unsettle them now, since we have Burlandeux in place and know everything that happens there. We need to let a few days go by and make them believe that no one is thinking of them. And then, the net is cast!"

"How exactly? By whom?"

"By Burlandeux, whom I still threaten to denounce. He needs to give me a list of all the conspirators, and we ourselves will take the list to the Committee of General Security. The Committee will order a full-scale raid, surround the house, and we will have saved the Republic! Are you with me?... And it matters little if the baron should escape them again. We denounced him, we were vigilant, and no one will have any objections. Here, it was Citizen Manaud who was detained. And we are still the only ones who know that Manaud and the infamous de Batz are one and the same person!"

"Go find Burlandeux," Dubois said approvingly, "and make him comply!"

"Oh, he will comply!... Whether willingly or by force!... But you will keep your promises?"

"Yes!" said Dubois with effort.

"You will use all your influence so that I can marry Citizeness Émilie?"

"Yes!"

"You don't seem committed!" observed Sénar.

"Make Burlandeux comply!... And you shall see!"

"Yes, we shall see!" Sénar added, with a hint of threat in his voice.

Dubois's attitude irritated Sénar, but what could he do? The police officer saw the means for making his way up in the world; it was supremely important to him to not let the opportunity escape him. Upon leaving Dubois, he immediately made his way to Charonne.

The baron had preceded him there, along with all his associates comprising the false patrol, following the unfortunate setback in the attempt to rescue the queen. The baron's first concern when he arrived was to go to a secret room for which he alone had the key and which contained a Louis XV writing desk with a storage compartment.

He opened this room without difficulty and examined the lock; it had not been forced. But he saw that the flap of the desk had been pried open and that the famous letter he used against Dubois had disappeared.

He then went to find Burlandeux, the cashier, and had him give money to some associates who were leaving for England that same day and resupplying themselves from his counter-revolutionary war chest.

The baron said to Burlandeux in the most natural tone, "Give me a thousand livres."

Burlandeux gave him the requested amount. As he counted the louis, the baron, looking into the police officer's eyes, abruptly said to him, "There is a traitor here, Monsieur Burlandeux."

Burlandeux bore the shock without betraying his internal agitation. With a remarkable outward calm, he even had the courage to respond, "If you know who he is, Monsieur, he must be executed without delay."

Anxiously, he sought to read in the baron's eyes the effect this bold utterance had on him.

Coolly, de Batz ordered him, "Will you empty your pockets in front of me, Monsieur?"

"But, what for?... I don't quite see what... Am I a thief?"

"I hope you are not something worse than that!... Let's go!... Empty your pockets!"

And the baron conspicuously played with his pistol, which he had removed from his belt.

Without saying a word, Burlandeux took from his pockets various bundles of keys, some letters, his purse containing some louis, his handkerchief, and an eyeglasses case. Then, he pulled the insides of his pockets out to show that he had nothing else.

But the baron was only interested in the keys; he examined them one by one. He sought to embarrass Burlandeux by trying to find on him a key to the secret room with the writing desk containing his papers.

Only one key to this room existed, and it was in the baron's possession. If Burlandeux possessed a second one, it was because he had it manufactured after making a wax imprint of the lock. His treason would be manifest. There would be nothing left to do but slaughter him like a rabid dog after having revealed his crime to the others in the Charonne house.

But no key to the secret room was found in the cashier's possession. Had he prudently placed it somewhere known to him alone? Was he innocent of treason? The baron remained in uncertainty. He coolly said to Burlandeux, but in a tone in which the latter relievedly detected some affability, "Take back all of this, Monsieur Burlandeux. I suspected you, but it's your own fault. You have custody of my secret archives. I put you on guard at their door, and you are the bad watchman who fell asleep. You know what happens in wartime to the watchman who falls asleep! He wakes up one morning chained to a post blindfolded, with twelve of his comrades firing on him at a sub-officer's signal. I would summon our friends, explain your case to them, and ask them to judge it, and do you want me to tell you what would happen to you, Monsieur?"

Burlandeux responded, very moved: "You are right, Monsieur! I am at fault! But spare me, and I will do the impossible and find the culprit, for if I am understanding you correctly," he added with a cynical poise, "someone went into your archives and took a document?"

"Yes!... A letter!... And this theft is the cause for my arriving too late at the Temple to rescue the queen!... An hour earlier, and I would have succeeded!... But I was required to escape from a prison myself!"

"Monsieur! I swear to you, I am utterly shocked!"

"Fine!... Redeem your culpable negligence with an untiring zeal!... Or otherwise..."

The baron made a menacing gesture and exited. He nevertheless warned his main associates to keep an eye on Burlandeux, and the latter, now alone, thought to himself, "Burlandeux, my friend!... You got yourself out of that pickle nicely! That was a fine inspiration you had to never keep on you that key to the secret room!... But from now on, avoid Sénar and no longer provide him any services like you did with that infamous letter!... You must choose once and for all between the Revolution and the monarchy. This little game would end up being too dangerous."

One hour after this scene, the baron returned to Burlandeux's office, accompanied by a young man whom the cashier did not remember ever seeing before. It was just La Guiche, Jean de Batz's escape companion, who had returned with him to Charonne that same morning, after the foiled endeavor to save the queen.

Burlandeux felt the need to ask: "I hope, Monsieur, that I at least have not gone down in your esteem or trust?"

"Not at all! And the proof is that you are immediately leaving for Paris to pay a bill to Citizen Cortey, my grocery supplier. If he asks for more as a deposit for future provisions, give him what he wants. The same for Citizeness Sainte-Amaranthe. These are gambling debts. She will tell you herself the exact amount to give her. The same for Citizens Dufourny, Montaut, Hébert, and Renaudin, staunch members of the Jacobin Club, to whom I have obligations. We are political enemies, but that is no reason for not paying what is owed! As you can see, my trust in you is still unchanged. My friend Monsieur de La Guiche needs to go to Paris, and I ask you to accompany him, to lend him a hand in case he is attacked. His situation with the authorities is unclear."

Burlandeux grimaced. He believed, on the contrary, that La Guiche was accompanying him to watch him.

Thus, perspiration nervously dripped down the sides of his temples when, after having gone down the small winding road through the vineyards and come to the first houses in the village of Charonne with his companion, he heard a familiar voice call him by name.

He recognized Sénar, who was sitting at an outdoor restaurant table beneath a pergola, and had been watching for him since leaving his earlier meeting with Dubois.

"One of your friends is calling you!" La Guiche remarked to Burlandeux.

"Oh, one of my friends?... Hardly!" said the police-conspirator. "Besides, I don't have the time..."

"You can take the time to answer him... I don't want to stop you from speaking to a friend. I don't foresee any immediate danger, and I can continue on my way by myself."

And he forced Burlandeux to stop. Sénar, for his part, cried out to La Guiche: "You too, Citizen, you're invited also!... The friends of our friends are our friends!"

"Thank you!' said La Guiche. "I'm hurrying to Paris to punish a devil who was and perhaps still is walking around using my name, something that singularly risks compromising my reputation!... Farewell, and drink to my health!"

After La Guiche's long months in La Grande Force, he was drunk on freedom.

He went away after having forced Burlandeux to stop.

Burlandeux was uneasy and wondered if this was a trap or a simple kindness on the part of his traveling companion; but he could no longer, at present, refuse to sit with Sénar, and to drink some of the local white wine of Charonne, which was acidic like that of Suresne, if the tradition is to be believed, but completely thirst-quenching in the August heat.

"Who is that?" asked Sénar, after the routine handshake and standard "how are you."

"A certain La Guiche!"

"Oh, by thunder!"

"What's the matter?"

Half laughing and half concerned, Sénar explained that the man walking around impersonating La Guiche was none other than himself, and that this was even how he had first learned of the conspiracy that his friend Burlandeux, incidentally, was going to help him denounce.

This conversation's beginning boded poorly for Burlandeux, who thought to himself, "If only I had known earlier it was you for whom La Guiche was looking! He would have destroyed you on the spot and I would have been freed of you! So, you have come to see me again in order to set me off on a new adventure?"

Sénar interrupted the course of Burlandeux's thoughts and remarked, "You don't look enthused about what I am proposing!"

"I am just astounded by your bad faith," replied Burlandeux somewhat dryly. "I am suspected for that blasted letter's disappearance! I just now escaped a certain death against the greatest of odds. Since I have a boss who does not take treason lightly!... And you come here asking me to risk my life a second time, I who saved your life in the gardens of the Charonne villa?... And this, despite your formal promises to not ask me for anything else of this kind!"

"What do you expect!... There are some unforeseen circumstances!... Besides, what do you risk by denouncing this conspiracy? Losing the position your conspirator friends have given you? You will find it much nicer being a savior of the Republic, since Dubois and I plan to include you in the reward for the operation."

"How is it you want me to denounce the conspiracy?"

"Give us as complete a list as possible of all the people who frequent the house in Charonne and of those conspiring with Baron de Batz, since it is Baron de Batz, is it not, the man of January 21, the man who, from his headquarters in Charonne, corresponds with Condé, with the federalist cities, with the émigrés and has-been princes, and tries, he and his army of conspirators, to overthrow the Republic by inciting Lyon, the Vendée, and Normandy against the Convention."

Burlandeux made no response.

Sénar ordered a pitcher of white wine, filled Burlandeux's glass to the brim, and continued: "It was in fact Baron de Batz who escaped from La Force Prison last night!"

"I didn't know that he was in prison!... I've always seen him as free as a bird!"

"Because he had a way to get out!... He had a good luck charm that I destroyed!"

"That proves he is more powerful than all of you... Some people say he is craftier than the devil himself!"

"The Convention will outsmart him, like others..."

"Or he will outsmart the Convention!"

"Don't believe that!... No one will outsmart the Convention... And it is the Convention, believe me, that it is in your interest to serve."

"Unfortunately, it is too late!... Since the incident with the letter, I can tell I'm being watched... And if I put myself in the Convention's service, they'll have my head, or rather they'll kill me by firing squad against that very wall I helped you climb over to save your life... I'm telling you, the group I am in does not play around! Almost all of them are former officers of the late king!"

"And me, I'm telling you, Burlandeux, you will be ruined if you stay with them!... They will be captured one day or another, like rats in their hole! That house will be raided one day, and..."

"And since you are so concerned about me, my dear Sénar, you will see that I am warned ahead of time so that I can avoid being caught!"

"Who is to tell me that you won't warn them in turn?"

"If I promised you that I wouldn't?"

"There is something better you can do: Give us a complete list of the conspirators!"

"What would you need it for? If you're raiding the house, you will have them all, and as for me, I won't have to fear their vengeance."

"We will take all those who are there, but not the ones who are absent! I want to take the whole lot of them!... The list first!... Since we will be operating in multiple cities at the same time!... I want to have a significant document to present to substantiate my claims and to obtain sufficient forces to raid this hideout... Got it?... And since you want to save your head, give me a list!... It's the best way to do so!... Do you understand?"

"Very well!... If I don't give it to you, you will have me guillotined?"

"I am not saying that!... I am not the sole master of your life or your ruin!"

"In other words, I have to choose between the firing squad in Charonne or the guillotine in Paris…"

"That's not my fault!"

"It might as well be, Sénar!… You are exploiting my initial favor to you!… At least, allow me to choose!… What would you prefer yourself, death by firing squad or death by guillotine?"

"Neither will happen to you if, after giving me the list, you stop going back to those people!"

"You don't know them!… They even have agents in the Jacobin Club!… Even in the Convention!"

"Denounce them!"

"I don't know them all!… If someone told me Robespierre was on their side, that would surprise me, but I wouldn't think it impossible!… Do you yourself understand?… I am telling you: They are more powerful than you think!"

Sénar became pensive.

Burlandeux resumed, "What if you entered their service yourself?"

"You are mad!"

"What is it you're ultimately after by denouncing them? Do you want money?… They will give you more of it than the government will ever give you, even for a service as extraordinary as this!"

"The difficulty, my friend, is that I am not only after money!… I am ambitious! I aspire to become someone in the Republic, because it is the only way for me to obtain the hand of a young woman I love! That is why, Burlandeux, you must give me this list!"

"Oh, I see!… I'm required to risk my life so that you can marry for love!… You think that's completely normal!"

And Burlandeux burst into laughter. But this laughter was so forced, so metallic, and sounded so inauthentic and threatening, that Sénar appeared worried.

Burlandeux added, "Very well!… It's agreed!… I will compile this list of conspirators!… But I will be the first one to profit from it!"

"How so?"

"I will take it myself to a proven and well-known patriot! A patriot of my choosing!"

"If you wish!" responded Sénar, a little disconcerted. "But I will point out that by giving it to Dubois and myself, you would also keep the reward, since we would be the first to attest to your civism. Who is to say that you aren't trying to fool us right now? To which proven patriot then do you want to deliver it?"

"To Chabot!... You wouldn't doubt his civism, not his!"

"Why not Robespierre then?"

"I've seen him at the Sainte-Amaranthes and have reservations about him!... I am not sure about the people who frequent the Arcades House!"

"There are two camps there, that's all!"

"Exactly! But I've never seen Chabot there!"

"And on what date will he have this list?"

"At the beginning of October!"

"We shall see!"

"And on that note... Goodbye!"

"No! Until next time!"

Burlandeux left Sénar abruptly, and in very ill humor.

He checked whether La Guiche was still in the vicinity and had stayed to spy on him, but he saw nothing suspicious and went to Paris, where he promptly and faithfully ran his errands and made payments on behalf of the baron. He reflected on his situation, which was not a pleasant one, and compared himself to hot iron placed between a hammer and an anvil. He felt anger towards Sénar and Dubois. He headed back towards Charonne with the following resolution: "Yes! I will confess everything to the baron, and I will thwart those two scoundrels! After that, I will be at peace!"

However, the moment he entered, he thought, "If I confess, the baron will know that it was I who stole the letter and was the cause for the queen not being rescued! Will he really believe in my profession of loyalty for the future?"

And Burlandeux did not dare confess. This courageous candor would have perhaps saved him. Lacking certainty, he continued to play a double game, resigning himself to all that entailed.

This digression, which we now conclude, is helpful to the reader's understanding of why, two months later in the beginning of October, on the evening of the very day when Delaunay and Chabot succeeded in having the Convention appoint a commission to handle the Indies Company matter, Burlandeux stealthily made his way to Chabot's residence, crumpling a paper his hand clutched inside his coat, so much did he fear misplacing it.

At the exact time this two-faced traitor, no longer fully responsible for his actions since he was caught between two fires, was running to the Jacobin he believed—oh, police naiveté—a pure one among the pure, the baron, still feeling the emotions of the Convention meeting but pursuing his wondrously crafted plan, the workings of which were proceeding without effort or noise, with a serene and unrelenting power, entered Barbereux's cartage office on Rue du Bouloi.

Barbereux was waiting for him.

"Well, my dear baron?" he asked.

"The game is on!... And with a vengeance!... Chabot and his gang are on their way to the guillotine... Biret-Tissot told me you received some news from Lyon?"

"A man is here, sent by the Duke de Crussol-Langeac."

"Have him enter!"

Barbereux opened a door connecting to his office and a dark, hideous sans-culotte appeared, with a short-stemmed pipe in his lips and a club in his hand, and his bare feet in sabots, from which a little bit of straw was sticking out. Without removing his red wool cap, he insolently asked Barbereux, "Who is this citizen?"

"Baron de Batz!"

"Oh, pardon!" the sans-culotte said, suddenly assuming more respectful manners. "I did not know! I am sent to you, Citizen, by Citizen Gracchus, of the Jacobin Club in Lyon, a barber friend of the people who pays well those he employs... He told me that you had some work to give me and that you are not stingy with your payments. Here I am!... What is it that needs to be done?... Oh, one minute, I forgot!... Here is a letter from the barber Gracchus, who vouches for me... You need to know with whom you are doing business! That is only appropriate!"

And removing his filthy, greasy cap, he felt around inside as in a purse and took out a scrap of paper. He handed it to de Batz, who was looking at and listening to him without saying a word.

The baron unfolded the disgusting piece of paper and read the following:

Gracchus to Manaud, greetings and fraternity!... I am sending you one of our hatchet men who is rock-solid, Citizen Cassecœur. He knows the clubs, speaks well and for a long time, and with a voice of thunder!... You can count on him. Long live the one and indivisible Republic!

Gracchus

This note was written in heavy, irregular characters, with a glaring abundance of spelling mistakes.

Going to Barbereux's fireplace, in which a bright woodfire was burning, Jean de Batz held the letter close to the flames. Between the crude lines, other lines suddenly appeared, which were in neat, exquisite handwriting.

This letter, invisible to the carrier, was brief and simply said the following:

Lyon, 15 September 1793

Dear Baron,

I hereby attest to the visible note signed Gracchus. Cassecœur is a scoundrel capable of anything. With money, he will do whatever you want. He is my most active agent at the Jacobin Club in Lyon, and I know, through him, everything happening on the enemy side. I have him under my control for his own crimes against his party; he will not betray you. He is a dog you need only unmuzzle and unleash on the devils you want to destroy. Here, we have executed Chalier and Riard, two ferocious animals whose deaths finally allow us to breathe more easily. But the Convention is besieging us. We are holding up well with Précy at our helm.

May God further our cause and save the queen. May He keep you. I embrace you.

Duke de Crussol-Langeac

The baron threw the letter into the fire and turned towards the sans-culotte.

"Citizen Cassecœur," he said, "you will go tomorrow evening to the Jacobin Club and tell them, on behalf of the Jacobins in Lyon, a secret that must not appear to have originated in Paris, namely that the Revolution and its virtuous principles are being betrayed by Chabot and a certain number of Convention members."

"Which ones?" Cassecœur asked.

"You will find them on this paper, as well as the speech that you are going to deliver!"

And he handed him a bundle of documents.

"Good, good!" said Cassecœur. "I am going to study this all evening, and tomorrow, I will be in the corridors of the Convention, where I will start grumbling and insinuating things about the representatives in question."

"That is a very good idea!... Anyhow, to put it briefly, this is the situation: Chabot and Delaunay went after the Indies Company this afternoon. Was it out of republican virtue? No! They want to lower the stock value, and tomorrow during the day they will purchase all the shares, they and their friends. They want to get rich while the people are dying of hunger. A member of the commission, Fabre d'Églantine, is to receive one hundred thousand livres this evening to support the draft decree liquidating the company!"

"A hundred thousand livres!" thundered Cassecœur, who demonstrated at that moment that the barber Gracchus, in his letter, had not exaggerated the power of his voice. "A hundred thousand livres!"

His white eyes rolled about in his dark, bestial face. He was undoubtedly sincere at that moment and again repeated, indignantly, "A hundred thousand livres!... A deputy receiving a hundred thousand livres when poor patriotic wretches like me..."

"The poor patriotic wretches like you will have their revenge, especially if they serve me well!" de Batz said in a low voice.

And taking a handful of louis out of a purse, he presented them to the sans-culotte, who put out both of his hands to receive them like a handful of grain.

The baron added, "This is just a small beginning!"

"And you will be served well!" exclaimed Cassecœur, drunk with joy, as he pocketed the godsend. "They are going to see what I am made of, the Chabots, the Fabres, and all those Convention Judases!... Goodbye for now!... You will be happy with me!"

And he exited like he was in a rage.

"That man is on fire! He is going to do some good work!" said Barbereux.

"Yes! The machine is well-oiled. You will see it in operation!"

"But how the devil do you know Fabre is going to take a hundred thousand livres?"

"You are sharp, Barbereux! I am on my way now to give Chabot the money so that he can give it to Fabre!"

"You don't say!"

The baron shook hands with Barbereux and left.

Chapter 3

The Traitor Unmasked

THE EX-CAPUCHIN CHABOT, as we said earlier, lived with the Frey brothers, Jewish bankers who had recently come from Austria and whose sister Léopoldine he was to marry.

The Frey brothers' mansion, located on Rue d'Anjou, was one of the most beautiful in Paris. Lenotre, who knew old Paris better than most Parisians know the new one, wrote this interesting passage on the Convention member's relocation to the Frey residence:

> The Freys had relinquished the mezzanine level between the first and second floors; it was accessed via a large and solemn stairway. The anteroom, only, was arranged in such a way as to insinuate the fervent and austere patriot who lived there; it constituted a sign. One saw there the bust of Brutus on a pedestal and engravings depicting the Tennis Court Oath and the tombs of Marat and Lepelletier; even, hanging on the hat pegs, were a bearskin cap, which was a favorite emblem of the Jacobins, and a red knitted cap decorated with four tassels of fake gold.
>
> The furniture in the large drawing room was upholstered with green and white lampas; thick checkered taffeta curtains in the same colors filtered the light pouring through the windows, which were also fitted with twill blinds striped in soft hues. On the mantelpiece was a pretty blue and white marble clock, serving as a pedestal for a Sèvres bisque porcelain cupid. In the adjacent bedroom, yellow and white damask curtains lined with white taffeta draped a large,

218

gilded wooden bed, whose four columns supported the canopy. Two sofas, four armchairs, two armless chairs, one mahogany washstand, one large mirror, and one chiffonnière table with a blue marble top, surmounted by a bust of Cicero, completed the furnishings.

Certainly, one could live here, and no doubt if Chabot had been free to do so, he would have forever renounced political struggles, to devote himself entirely to the peaceful joys of homelife.

It cannot be denied that Chabot, this Convention member with an austere facade, who as a representative of the people now gloried in all this voluptuous luxury, had come a long way from the humble Capuchin cell he used to occupy. And this would suggest that he abandoned the religious state in order to live better, to taste the delights of luxury and good food, and not for a higher purpose based on reason and wisdom—that he did so to liberate his passions, not, as the Protestants claim in their humanitarian jargon, to "liberate his conscience."

Moreover, one must admit that the job of a deputy, of a friend of the people, of a progressive democrat, has always fed its holder, but has never enriched the people, though the office was misleadingly created to defend the people's rights and to improve their circumstances.

In the large drawing room of green and white lampas, the pudgy Chabot, collapsed onto a sofa and wrapped in a soft dressing gown with a silk belt tied around his waist, was resting after the tiring meeting.

Léopoldine Frey, a pretty creature of exotic eastern charm, with catlike gestures, and fingers ringed to excess in diamonds, was adding sugar to Chabot's cup of hot milk. Junius Frey, the elder of Léopoldine's two brothers, was heaping congratulations on Chabot, in an accent that would make some believe he was still speaking the Jewish patois of the Galician ghettos.

"It's a success! A great success!... You are going to become rich!... We are all becoming richer!... I am buying ten thousand shares tomorrow!... And you?"

"Oh, me?" said Chabot. "That will depend on the amount of money I am disbursed... I will then report it to you... I have prepared the soil, and it's up to you to make it bear fruit!"

"Drink!" said Léopoldine, holding the tray on which the cup of milk was.

Chabot, with a smile of gratitude and adoration, took a sip of the beverage.

"Is it good?... Is that enough sugar?"

"Yes, thank you!... You are the most delicious of women!"

But Junius interrupted the conversation of the charming engaged couple to bring the discussion back to business.

"And the commission?"

"It is meeting this evening at the Palais National..."

"Oh!... If it rejects the draft decree..."

"Impossible! We will have the majority!"

"Are you sure?"

"Out of five members, there are two favorable, including myself, and a third who is unsure, Fabre d'Églantine, but he will be favorable once I give him a small sum!"

"That you have?"

"That I don't have yet!"

The Jewish man's face darkened. He feared Chabot was asking him for the money. But the Convention member immediately reassured him and said, "Someone will be bringing it to me shortly, the small sum."

"Oh!... Bravo!... Starting tomorrow, the stock price will fall!"

"It certainly will!... The Convention meeting this afternoon and the commission vote this evening—a company can't withstand two blows like that back-to-back!"

"This affair is beautifully hidden!"

"Well then," said Léopoldine, her eyes sparkling and her face beaming, "as a wedding gift, could you get me one of those carriages of the late king that they will be putting up for sale?"

"Certainly!" promised Chabot, who was himself euphoric. "The has-been queen will be condemned, but it will still be a queen riding in the royal coach!"

"Come on, come on!" said Junius. "We are talking business!... What the devil!... You're going off-topic!"

Then, speaking directly to Chabot, he asked, "And how much is this little bit of money you are being given to give Fabre d'Églantine?"

"One hundred thousand livres!"

"What!... That is too much!" exclaimed Junius, both shocked and dazzled by all this gold which was suddenly circling around his brother-in-law, who until recently had not been so gilded. "At least keep some of it as a nice little commission!"

"I wouldn't refuse it!"

At that moment, two bell rings sounded in the ground level's large vestibule, announcing a visitor.

"It is perhaps the money they are bringing you!" said Junius.

"That is likely!"

"Come, Léopoldine!... Let us leave your fiancé to his business... We will come back later."

And Junius led his sister out and disappeared with her, while a tall servant in livery entered the drawing room and said to Chabot, "Someone is asking for the people's representative Chabot!"

"Who?"

"A citizen who does not want to identify himself..."

"It is the good Citizen Manaud!" whispered Chabot. "Let the citizen enter!"

But it was not at all Manaud who entered. It was Burlandeux, who was very pale. He stammered, "Representative citizen, I went to Rue Saint-Honoré, to your old address, and they redirected me here... If you will excuse me... I have come to see you for a very serious matter..."

"Relating to the Indies Company?"

Chabot had only the Indies Company business on his mind. He was therefore surprised when Burlandeux responded, "Not at all, Citizen, it has to do with a conspiracy against the Republic..."

"Who are you then?"

"Burlandeux, a peace officer. You know me, in fact!... We have met rather frequently at the Committee of General Security!"

"Oh, Burlandeux!... I remember now!... Yes!... What is this conspiracy?"

"People are meeting in Charonne, in an isolated house. Here is the list of all the conspirators. The house is the hideout and refuge of all the aristocrats who go back and forth between Paris and the has-been princes."

He handed the list to Chabot, who asked, "This is a denunciation, in other words?"

"Yes, Citizen!"

"Why aren't you taking this directly to the Committee of Public Safety?"

"I am embedded with the conspirators in order to better learn their secrets. They have spies everywhere. I was concerned they might see me entering the Tuileries."

Chabot read the list out loud, saying the names written by Burlandeux: "De Batz, Marsan, Lézardière the father, Paul and Sylvestre de Lézardière, Admiral, Biret-Tissot, Devaux, the actress Grandmaison, the has-been Marquis de La Guiche, also known as Sévignon, Pottier of Lille, Balthazar Roussel, Hyde of Neuville, Cortey..."

Chabot stopped at this last name.

"Cortey?... The grocer?... The commander of the Lepelletier Battalion?"

"The very same!"

"That is remarkable!... It was a day when he was on duty that there was an attempt to rescue the Capet woman!"

He resumed reading.

"And this de Batz," he asked, "is this the famous de Batz people speak about so much?... The man that they say is the head of the great conspiracy from abroad?"

"The same one!... The great counter-revolutionary leader!"

"Devil! This is serious!"

"Very serious!"

"And this is happening in Charonne?"

"In a house located on Chaussée de Bagnolet, on the right-hand side as you're going to Bagnolet, once you've passed through Charonne, in a corner of the park of the former Duke of Orléans. You will do what you want with this list; as for me, I have done my patriotic duty. You will attest to this!"

Chabot shuddered. This description had enlightened him. Was not this the house to which Julien of Toulouse and Delaunay of Angers had taken him, the one belonging to Citizen Manaud, who had hosted such an exquisite dinner for them? Did he suspect the trap? Did he want to throw Burlandeux off the trail? Proceeding into redundancies as if he were speaking formally from a podium, he declared, "I thank you, Citizen Burlandeux, for the service you have just rendered the Republic. The Committee of Public Safety will be apprised of these underground intrigues of the enemy within, and your name will be showered with praises, publicly."

"I am a modest man!" objected the police officer. "I am not hankering for people to talk about me, as long as I am not destroyed with the traitors whom I swore to exterminate!"

He had barely finished his sentence when the bell rang again in the echoing vestibule of the beautiful mansion, announcing a new visitor.

Burlandeux had something of a presentiment and instinctively sought out a dark corner of the room in which to hide himself. Chabot, for his part, not at all eager that Burlandeux see entering in his home the mysterious man who had invited him for dinner at that yet more mysterious house in Charonne, went into the anteroom after having shut the door to the drawing room, and almost immediately met there with de Batz, who was escorted in by a liveried servant.

"Leave us!" Chabot said to the servant.

With a gesture, he invited de Batz to sit down. It was thus in front of the bust of Brutus and between the engravings of Marat's tomb and the Tennis Court Oath that this scene unfolded, in which the comical stubbornly inserted itself among the tragic.

"Citizen," said de Batz, whom that imperceptible string we know about gave the features more generally associated with Citizen Manaud, "I have brought the money: the one hundred thousand livres to give to Fabre d'Églantine, and two hundred thousand livres for you, so you can buy shares when the price drops..."

Chabot felt his heart softening in front of so many wads and louis which the baron removed from his moneybag with a calculated slowness. It seemed inexhaustible, this moneybag. It was like the horn of plenty dispensing all delights. How could one confront the owner of a moneybag that was so bounteous and corpulent!

Thus, Chabot did not dare get confrontational with Baron de Batz. Once he had taken the money, Chabot contented himself to voice some thoughts Burlandeux's visit had inspired, but in a polite and roundabout way.

"Citizen Manaud," he began, "who is it that owns the house in Charonne where you had me over for dinner?"

"I do!"

"But you don't live there alone, do you?"

"Why are you asking these questions?" asked the baron, knitting his brows.

"Because people claim it is a headquarters for the Counter-Revolution."

"That's news to me!... Me, I'm only involved in financial business!"

"These same people claim that your house shelters the most dangerous counter-revolutionaries, and in particular that mysterious de Batz whom people are starting to talk about way too much... I would not at all want to do you any harm, but I am now obligated, under penalty of being suspected myself, to present the Committee of Public Safety a list of conspirators that I have just been given..."

"Oh really?... I would be interested in seeing it!"

"Here it is!"

And Chabot handed him the paper, which the baron eagerly pored over.

"The man who gave you this list, has he left already?"

"He is still here!"

"Good!" said the baron, with a joy that was almost savage. "You feel, Citizen Chabot, that you must take this list to the Committee because the man who brought it to you might denounce you, correct?"

"Yes, of course!... Also, because it's my civic duty to..."

"Leave your civic duty out of this, will you?... But if you're taking this list, it should at least be complete. Let me add something to it."

Without waiting for Chabot's authorization, he added in pencil, in front of the words "de Batz," the following note: "known also under the name Manaud, which belonged to his great ancestor Manaud the Reaper, a companion of the tyrant Henry IV."

And he returned the list to Chabot, who jumped in surprise as he read this bold addition.

"What is this?" cried the renegade Capuchin. "You are de Batz?"

"I am de Batz!... And you are my associate, Citizen Chabot!"

"What kind of infernal trap have I fallen into?... You want to ruin me!" said the Convention member, wringing his hands and turning very pale.

"I want to make you rich!... That is not the same thing!... Is that wanting your ruin?"

"They said they were taking me to a financier... And they took me to a conspirator!... A dirty plot!"

"Whether I'm conspiring or not, what does it matter to you, if you're rich one day?"

"But my connection with you will be denounced!"

"By whom?"

"The man who is here!"

"The man who is here will not be alive in two hours. Let me take care of him!"

And he went into the drawing room, removed the mysterious string fastened to his ears, marched over to Burlandeux, and shouted, "I knew I would unmask you one day or another, you wretch!"

Stunned and terrified, the police officer became white as a sheet. His teeth chattered and his lips quivered in deathly anguish. He stammered, "You are the devil!... I had said so myself... And I was wrong to have agreed to work against you!... I have lost, and I will pay!"

"We will settle everything in one go, you scoundrel!"

And the baron, having put back on the silk string that made him unrecognizable, reappeared in the anteroom, his hand pressed heavily on the back of Burlandeux's neck, gripping it like a vise.

He found Chabot stunned and worriedly dumbfounded, and said to him, "Be on time to the commission meeting this evening, Citizen!... And let the text of the decree be voted on tomorrow by the Convention!"

Chabot made no answer. De Batz exited, taking his prisoner with him.

A carriage was in front of the home. A man waiting out front opened the vehicle's door. The baron pushed his prisoner inside, went in after him, and said to the man, "Get in with us, Admiral, and if this traitor screams or moves, shoot him in the head with your pistol."

At the same time, he gave two shrill whistles. Two other men seemed to come out of nowhere and ran to the call. "Biret-Tissot, and you, Devaux," the baron ordered, "take a carriage and follow us. When we get to Charonne, assemble everyone together. I discovered the traitor, and he must be judged."

The carriage took off in the direction of the Porte Saint-Honoré.

Chabot, still in the anteroom beneath the stern gaze of the bust of Brutus, remained crushed. His future brother-in-law found him in the same place, immersed in a kind of lethargy. He had to shake him to bring him back to reality.

"Well, the money?"

"I have it!"

"How much is for you?"

"I don't know anymore!... I'm ruined!... I won't go to the commission meeting..."

Junius Frey passed from a state of most profound surprise to one of most heated anger.

"What! What!... You are going to make us miss out on this extraordinary venture?"

And he lambasted him with perfidious insinuations and insults!... Chabot had deceived them and gotten himself housed, fed, and pampered in all this luxury by promising them mountains and miracles. But this situation would not continue!... He would be thrown out! He would not be marrying Léopoldine!... He would reimburse them the costs for his stay at the Frey mansion... Really! He had just promised a royal coach to his fiancée, and now he was behaving like this! Oh, revenge would be exacted!... The Convention would be told that the Indies Company paid him to delay and prevent the liquidation decree...

Chabot, upon hearing this last threat, felt as Burlandeux had, that he was caught between two fires. Whether he took part in the corrupt scheme or kept his hands clean, he was under threat. Perhaps the risk was less if he actually did continue with the money scheme. After all, the clouds which had just amassed over his head were going to dissipate; de Batz was only a financier who had need of a deputy to launch a business venture, a scenario which was frequent enough in one parliamentary country—one needed only to look at England! France would gradually become accustomed to these practices... It was going to be made impossible for that man with the list to do any harm, according to what de Batz had told him. Two hours later, Chabot was forcing himself to laugh about the future and the good things it held for him, as he made his way to the commission meeting to rule on the Indies Company's fate.

The three Frey siblings rubbed their hands together in anticipation. Putting their spirit of lucre aside, who knew whether they themselves might not be agents of that terrible leader of the Avengers of the King, and being paid to ruin Chabot the renegade, Chabot the regicide?

Chapter 4

Burlandeux's Last Card

THE NEXT DAY, early in the morning, a tragic scene was being readied in the park of the Charonne house, where about sixty conspirators were assembled.

The Avengers had tried Burlandeux during the night, very scrupulously and very justly. Monsieur de Lézardière, the father, had presided over the debates in the large summer room with the frescoes. Baron de Batz, playing the role of prosecutor, had recalled the theft of the letter, then showed as an exhibit the list of Charonne conspirators delivered to Chabot by Burlandeux, which had been recovered just in time.

The effect was instant.

"Death! Death!" all the conspirators unanimously cried.

Burlandeux sensed he was irrevocably lost. He had confessed to everything, even the theft of the letter, but he thought to soften the hearts of those he nearly sent to death by recounting to them his past as a police officer, his encounter with Sénar and the obligation he was under to obey him, and his regret for not having confessed his situation earlier to the baron, who might have forgiven him, which would have perhaps saved him. But this long and interminable confession, interspersed with sobs, appeals to mercy, and pledges to forever break with his old ways, only moved the youngest of the Avengers to pity.

Tender souls like Paul de Lézardière allowed themselves to be swayed by tears, but the old-timers were merciless. They had experienced, prior to the Revolution, the rigor of military regulations in times of war, and they considered themselves to be at war. Furthermore, the scaffold had decimated their betrayed families, denounced by men similar to Burlandeux, and they demanded death. Not the glorious death of a soldier, but an ignominious hanging from a tree branch.

Admiral, who had one of the fiercest, boldest, and most threatening appearances of the counter-revolutionaries, asked to be the executioner.

Supplied with a rope, he stood near the condemned man underneath an oak tree. A tall step ladder was there, and he waited for the moment to hang the traitor high and short.

Burlandeux had requested a priest, and one had been sought out. Waiting for the priest to arrive, the miserable Burlandeux tried one last time to save himself.

"If I managed to rescue the queen," he said to de Batz, "would you spare my life?"

The proposition was too interesting to not at least welcome it with some skepticism.

"Certainly!" replied the baron. "But if you had a serious escape plan, Monsieur Burlandeux, I think you would have proposed it to us earlier!"

"I thought to move you to pity with the true account of the terrible situation in which I found myself and which led me to betray you, against my will, yes, I swear, against my will!... I saved my own skin to your own detriment, I acknowledge that! But if it hadn't been for Dubois and Sénar's scheme that I revealed to you, I would have sooner or later proposed what I am proposing to you now!"

"The condemned man is playing games with us!" said one of the Avengers awaiting the execution.

"You do not play games with anyone when you are about to die!" Burlandeux articulated passionately, as if mustering all his strength to expend one last effort and hang on to his life. "You won't believe in my sincerity, my loyalty, or my disinterestedness, fine!... That is your right!... But you will believe in my love for money, I imagine!... You no longer look on me with any noble sentiments, but that necessarily leaves you to look on me with only base ones... Monsieur Baron, you promised one million to whoever would rescue the queen... I would rescue her tomorrow; the day after tomorrow, would you give me the million?"

"Certainly!" said the baron.

"Tomorrow and the day after tomorrow, you will be dead!" uttered Admiral implacably.

"Of course!... And even if you were sure that I could rescue the queen tomorrow, you would kill me beforehand, no doubt?" he added with a certain irony. "Let the queen perish rather than your vengeance!"

"No, no!" protested several voices in the crowd of Avengers. "That would be blasphemy!"

"The scoundrel is trying to beguile us!" said an old officer with a white mustache.

"Monsieur," de Batz said to him very courteously, "the heart of the royalist must always give exceptional consideration to any prospects for the queen's escape, and I want this man to follow through on his word."

Addressing Burlandeux, de Batz continued, "Would you like a deferment in order to try to get the million, Monsieur Burlandeux?... Do you have some heirs to leave it to then?"

"I have no heir, Monsieur Baron. I am alone in life, and I am eager to hold on to this life. If I save the queen, you will keep your million and let me keep my life... It is worth more to me than a million, under these present circumstances!"

"You still need to tell us about this plan that you have, and this plan must be serious!"

A murmur of approval welcomed these words from the leader.

Burlandeux then explained: "Gentlemen, the queen is guarded at the Conciergerie by two gendarmes, Gilbert and Dufresne. I can go to replace one of them. Once in place, I can get the other one drunk and escort the queen out as if I were the gendarme in charge of taking her to her hearing. I will have a proper requisition that gives me access to Her Majesty's prison."

They were all listening to him now, as though hanging on his every word. Encouraged, Burlandeux made his plea to them on an infinitely more solid basis: "Gentlemen," he said, "you will not deny that I am gambling with my life, but I have no merit in doing so since I have a one-in-two chance of winning and am already no better than a corpse if you uphold your present decision. If I die guillotined, your vengeance is satisfied. If I live, it is because I have succeeded in rescuing the queen. In either case, you will be happy..."

"But what guarantees us that once you leave here you will seriously try to save the queen and not be making your list again and taking it where I have no chance of running in to you, to the Committee of Public Safety, for example!"

Burlandeux was at a loss and could not argue with this objection: "Obviously," he said, "you don't trust me; you can't trust me!... I should have known better!... This was inevitable!"

"However," the baron responded, "if at least one of our friends was willing to help with this attempt, to vouch for your goodwill, and to be able to monitor you and prevent any unpleasant possibility of another betrayal on your part..."

Burlandeux cast his suppliant eyes on the crowd of those who had condemned him to death. But no one moved. A deathly silence hovered. In the large trees pierced by the pale rays of the October sun, the birds sang, and the wind rustled the russet foliage. The condemned man experienced a foretaste of the cemetery that this garden would henceforth be to him. In a corner, close to the wall, his grave had already been dug.

"Gentlemen," the baron repeated, "is none of you of the opinion that Burlandeux is of goodwill and has the means to rescue the queen?"

"Yes! I am!" a voice replied.

And Rougeville came out from the group, with a riding whip in his hand and his boots on. He had just arrived in Charonne and been apprised of the night's events.

Burlandeux threw himself on his knees and embraced Rougeville's boots, crying. He said, "Oh, Monsieur!... I will be your slave, your dog! Give the orders, and I will obey!... It is more than my life you are giving me back; you are giving me the means to rehabilitate myself."

"We shall see!" said Rougeville to de Batz. "I must see the queen soon at the Conciergerie, and this scoundrel seems to be speaking the truth. If one of the gendarmes was on our side, we could do some good work. I'll have an update for you soon, Baron!"

Rougeville left the house, taking Burlandeux, to whom de Batz addressed the following goodbye: "I am warning you, Monsieur Burlandeux, this is your last card that you are playing! Try to win the game!"

Chapter 5

Citizen Cassecœur's Speech

ON THE PRESENT site of the Saint-Honoré market, formerly stood the beautiful friary of the Jacobins, perhaps better known to the reader as the Dominicans. When the Revolution had emptied it of its friars, these vast buildings accommodated various purposes, but its Gothic refectory became a meeting hall for a club composed of the most progressive republicans.

This club was called the Jacobin Club, and the word "Jacobin" has since been used to this day to designate the strictest, most sectarian, and most tyrannical demagogues.

It was from here that came forth the most heinous and criminal motions, docilely voted for by the Convention, which trembled before this club that was completely dedicated to Robespierre's ideas.

Beneath its high sculpted arches which for centuries had sheltered the peace of the cloister, howls from wild beasts now reverberated every evening. One found there, gathered around the rostrum and the table of the "regulator" (the name given to the club's temporary president), the Convention's most exalted deputies, mixed in with the sans-culottes and knitwomen in the tribunes, mutually goading each other to murder, pillage, and massacre the best of the citizenry.

The evening of that same day when Burlandeux had come so close to dying, the club was very restless.

Citizen Hébert, author of the ignominious pamphlet *Old Man Duchesne*, requested the floor to alert the vigilant friends of the people who constituted the Jacobin Club that a betrayal was being readied against the Republic.

"Citizen," he cried out in that style which made his sordid periodical successful, the vivid images of which so greatly delighted good sans-culottes, "it is utterly baffling that the Convention and the Revolutionary Tribunal do not want to walk a straighter line and that we are unceasingly obliged to remind them here of their civic duty.

"Without us, my dear sans-culotte brethren, oh, the aristocratic monsters would have a long time ago recommenced crushing the people's heads and drinking their blood!... Without *Old Man Duchesne*, who is obligated in each edition to go into a terrible rage, the Temple swine, Louis Capet, would perhaps not yet be beheaded. It was you and I who protested the Convention's delays and who sent the tyrant to 'try on his neckpiece' in Revolution Square. And well? Now we are starting all over again!... The rumor circulating today is that the Capet widow, who is going on trial in a few days, will be deported and not guillotined!... These are the games they want to play with us. Very well! If the moderates in the Convention and the Girondins in the Revolutionary Tribunal want, in turn, 'a date with the national razor,' they need only follow through with their lovely plans! I am telling you, if justice is to be rendered to the Austrian tigress, she must be chopped like mincemeat for all the blood she has shed. I promised the people the head of Antoinette, and I will go cut it off myself if they delay in giving it to us! Today, in my capacity as deputy prosecutor of the Paris Commune, I myself questioned the little Capet, son of the guillotined Louis, and he revealed to me shocking things about his horrible mother!"

Hébert's discourse continued in this tone for a long time, interspersed with applause and crude, approving remarks from the ignoble crowd, two thirds of whom had come out of the prison camps of the defunct kingdom. The Jacobin repeatedly returned to his brilliant idea of having had the queen accused by her son, who, incidentally, had been intoxicated with alcohol beforehand and forced to answer "yes" to the most foul and deceitful questions.

Hébert was given an ovation when he stepped down from the rostrum.

A club member was already requesting the floor to propose they vote on sending a delegation to the Convention regarding the strange leniency the Revolutionary Tribunal was suspected of showing the infamous Antoinette, when a giant man in a carmagnole cried out, "First, citizens, I ask you to listen to Citizen Cassecœur, a fine fellow who has come from Lyon and has some revelations to make known to you!"

The giant man was a certain Dufourny, one of those whom Burlandeux, one will remember, went to give a sum of money on behalf of the baron some days earlier.

Dufourny was one of the most heeded loudmouths in the Jacobin Club, a jolly man who ate enough for four people and drank enough for eight; he had an infectious jocularity, and his motions were often imbued with a novel and sensational character. He was the idol of the demagogues there, and the knitwomen praised him to the skies.

Thus, it was especially the female voices that responded to his proposition: "Yes, yes!... Dufourny is right!... Let us listen to this Cassecœur first... Go on, Dufourny!... Bring up your protégé!... Show yourself, citizen from Lyon!"

"Here I am!" replied a voice of thunder, which filled the vast Gothic hall with smoke and shook the old stained-glass windows hidden in the shadows, at a height that could not be reached by the light of the Jacobin lamps.

It was like a scene from the old court of miracles. Cassecœur's dark face, hideous beneath the red cap and ascending to the rostrum, evoked some underworld king climbing onto a barrel to harangue his subjects.

There was silence in the vast hall; the roar of the Lyonnais Jacobin's voice had impressed those vile, savage creatures, who only respected power.

"Citizens!" thundered Cassecœur, whose eyes were flashing. "We others, the friends of the people, we have been raised, in Lyon, in the school of adversity. If the guillotine has been set up there, it is against us... Patience!... The wheel is turning. And tomorrow, Lyon will be called 'Liberated Commune'!... But adversity has made us distrustful and clear-sighted!... I wouldn't want you to say that a Lyonnais has come to Paris to teach you Parisians a lesson, but over there, for a long time, we have been hearing bad reports about certain Convention members, and precisely about those in whom you place the greatest trust! About those whom you welcome here, who are registered at this club, and who pretend to be of one mind with you, only in order to more easily betray you in the corridors surrounding the meeting hall of the Palais National!"

Some grumbles could be heard in the audience. They unmistakably came from the Convention members affiliated with the Jacobin Club, who found that their sensitive feelings were not sufficiently spared.

"I haven't named anyone!" shouted Cassecœur, his thunderous voice intensifying. "I will be giving names shortly!... What a shame that there are traitors and suspects among those who are grumbling!"

The deputies became silent and were careful not to relapse. The single word "suspect" had a unique magic to it; it was a special curse, a civic excommunication against which no argument could prevail.

Moreover, Dufourny voiced and gestured his encouragement to Citizen Cassecœur, and elegantly shouted to the interrupters, "Let those who feel snotty blow their noses!"

This utterance provoked much laughter from the audience, and one knitwoman, a sordid witch with disheveled hair, dressed in tatters, started yelping, "Blown are the snot-noses! Blown are the snot-noses!" This set off a new wave of hilarity.

Cassecœur continued: "It was folly to have the national representation headquartered in that old lair of the tyranny, still oozing with secret schemes and crimes against liberty. Too bad for those whose civic spirit has not been strong enough to resist the poisoned atmosphere in that palace of the tyrants!

"Having come to Paris to communicate with our republican brethren, I thought about denouncing to them certain schemes that had been reported to me in Lyon by persons too timid to enlighten you about what they had uncovered here, when yesterday evening I learned what had happened during the day at the Convention: the appointment of a commission to liquidate the Indies Company.

"Oh, pure hearts, fed with the virtuous lessons of the divine Jean-Jacques, you believed it was about toppling a rotten institution from the infamous monarchy!... That was the pretext!... But the goal being pursued was a terrible money-trafficking scheme!... The Indies Company's stock has plummeted. There are fifty, a hundred deputies who purchased shares this morning and hope to make a fortune from this shameful speculation, worthy of the times of the Regent and of Law, while the French people are dying of hunger, after having been beaten for the liberty of the world!"

The audience broke out in curses. The words "traitors," "sellouts," and "exploiters" clashed beneath the vaults of the old friary, while other more attentive and upset club members, better understanding the mechanics of the stock market coup denounced by Cassecœur, or rather by de Batz, whose discourse the orator was repeating like a parrot, demanded at the top of their voices, "The names, the names! Give us their names!"

"You want names?" replied Cassecœur. "Start then by looking at those deputies who make up the commission that met yesterday evening, and who decided to liquidate the company, but while keeping as liquidators the condemned company's very own directors, which is in order to reassure investors after having frightened them, so that the stock value can go back up after having gone down, so that the corrupt Convention members can buy for nothing and resell high... in a word, get rich from this ghastly stock market coup!... Am I making myself clear, citizens?"

A man in a carmagnole armed with a knotted club, who was gradually getting closer to the rostrum and was followed by some people who appeared to be under his command, then began acclaiming the orator and crying out, "He is right!... This is shameful for the Republic… Death to the sellouts! Death to the corrupt! Death to the traitors!"

His friends joined in chorus, and the hall, shaken with indignation, repeated over and over, "Death to the sellouts! Death! Death!"

For a quarter of an hour, a tumultuous uproar ensued, during which the club members belonging to the Convention were threatened with shaking fists and had to feign even greater indignation than the others.

Among them, there were some who had participated in the lucrative stock market coup, and who felt caught in the trap the Machiavellian baron had laid for them using their love for money. Beneath the appearance of feigned indignation, they hid their mortal anguish, which a hundred years later, towards the end of 1892, would seize other representatives of the people during the tragic time of the Panama scandals.

The audience then began again to cry out, "The names, the names!… Give us the names of the commission members!"

Then the man with the carmagnole, who had just made his way through the crowd with his friends, handed a paper to the orator, who needed only to read it: "The names? They are Chabot, Delaunay, Ramel, Cambon, and Fabre d'Églantine!"

This denunciation was met with jeering, but a voice penetrated through this storm of cries, screaming, "I object!"

"There are other corrupt ones!" shouted Cassecœur, dominating the tumult. "But it is for the Convention to seek them out and to cut off those within it who are rotten, if it has the courage to do so!… I'm not here to do its work!"

The enthralled audience, hanging on every word of this sans-culotte, who performed like a highly skilled public prosecutor capable of equaling Fouquier-Tinville himself, was now applauding him after each of his sentences. But the same penetrating voice made itself heard again amidst this spellbinding dialogue between the orator and the exasperated crowd, and its desperate, unceasingly renewed protestation was eventually noticed.

In the group of club members belonging to the Convention, a tall, slender man of harmonious proportions and gestures thrashed about as if he were acting in an ancient tragedy. In fact, he truly had been an actor, as he had worked all kinds of jobs, and he could have provided Beaumarchais the inspiration for his immortal Figaro, a type of caustic, denigrating bohemian whose schemes wreak havoc in the society around him.

For, when the regulator finally noticed his protestation and asked him what he wanted, he replied, "I ask to speak!... As I have been unjustly calumniated! I am the Convention member Fabre d'Églantine!"

A new wave of jeers broke out, but this time addressed to him alone. Clenched fists waved at him; tooth-gapped, black-gummed mouths spewed the worst insults against him: "Sellout! Exploiter of the people! Corrupt! Has-been! Speculator! String him up! Death!"

This was the hatred of the skinny dog for the sumptuously well-fed dog, like what is happening in our own day between the socialist on the street and the socialist in parliament. The battle around the dog bowl had begun with the dawn of the new revolutionary era, and in this delirious crowd opposed to Fabre d'Églantine, there was less virtuous indignation than base envy and insatiable appetites.

Thus, to what a feverish pitch did Jacobin anger rise when Citizen Cassecœur began laughing loudly and said, "Oh! You are Fabre d'Églantine?... Delighted to see you, Citizen, and to be able to charge you to your treacherous face for your crime against the people! Will you deny that you received one hundred thousand livres yesterday evening?"

"I do deny it!" Fabre shouted.

"To support Chabot and Delaunay in the commission and to vote for a decree that will allow stock shares to go up?" the ranter continued.

"I deny it!" Fabre repeated indignantly.

This time, the audience became quiet. A harrowing silence hovered in the air, as heavy as lead. It felt like one was watching a mortal duel. The mysterious man in the carmagnole at the foot of the rostrum, where Cassecœur was now perspiring heavily, was feeding the Jacobin his retorts, and handing him papers.

Fabre d'Églantine suddenly appeared to have the upper hand: "Citizens," he said with an outward calm, regardless of what he might have felt internally, "if I had received a hundred thousand livres, it would have been very poorly earned, since what I signed yesterday at the commission meeting was a draft for a decree, and not a decree itself. For this to become a binding decree, there must first be a public discussion at the Convention, and then the Convention will vote and decide on whether to adopt the commission's draft. Where then is the betrayal? Where then is the horrible trafficking that was just denounced? That is not all! Nowhere in this draft does it say that the Indies Company's current directors will liquidate the company themselves, which would actually perpetuate the company we were supposedly eliminating. Did my own hand write the opposite?"

"You lie!" countered Cassecœur, brandishing a paper that had just been handed to him by the sans-culotte who was giving him his cues. "You are lying! Here is a copy of the decree. It is abundantly clear that the company will be liquidated *according to its statutes and regulations*, which gives it back its right to liquidate itself and to continue its operations, once the sold-out Convention members have in hand all those stock certificates that will bounce back to their original value! I know that right now, in fact, they are quietly passing around the decree for signatures, in order to avoid any public discussion!"

"How do you know this?" asked Fabre.

"I know it! That's all!... I have exposed a scandal! It is for you, citizens, to punish it!"

"This copy is a fake!" protested the Convention member.

At the mysterious sans-culotte's signal, Cassecœur came down from the rostrum.

The audience was now split, divided by various currents of thought.

But another Jacobin went up and took Cassecœur's place. He rallied the pure ones who hungered for justice.

"Citizens! No more words! It is time for action! I propose sending the Convention a formal delegation to inquire whether the revolutionary French can still count on the integrity and disinterested patriotism of their representatives!"

The entire assembly approved this measure with frenzied cheers. Bloodthirsty proposals were blurted out here and there.

"Let the entire Jacobin Society go en masse to the Convention and demand an investigation into the conduct of Chabot, Delaunay, Fabre, and their one hundred accomplices!"

"I will be the first to demand it tomorrow!" Fabre stated.

"Let them be guillotined first!" proposed a drunken voice. "They will examine their conduct afterwards, if they have the time!"

And it was with this proposal, which had many supporters, that this stormy discussion ended.

They then resumed the debate on the deplorable leniency of the Revolutionary Tribunal, which was sending no more than fifteen or sixteen suspects to death daily.

Outside, the mysterious sans-culotte and his friends led Cassecœur towards Rue du Bouloi.

The Lyon man, pouring with sweat, said, "That blasted Fabre gave me trouble!"

"You achieved the desired effect!" replied the sans-culotte. "But now, Citizen Cassecœur, you mustn't be seen here anymore!"

"I'm not eager to be!"

"You are heading back to Lyon this very evening!"

And he handed him an already prepared wad of money, which the other nimbly pocketed.

"Biret-Tissot!" the sans-culotte then said to one of his friends, "take Cassecœur to Barbereux, so that he can have him clear out immediately. There's a departure for Lyon this evening."

"Count on me, Monsieur Baron!"

The baron hailed a carriage, climbed inside, and said to those accompanying him, "Tomorrow, it's to the Convention we're going, isn't it, gentlemen? It will be interesting!"

The carriage left for Charonne.

Chapter 6

The Tiger Hunt

FABRE HAD SPOKEN the truth. He had never received the one hundred thousand livres. Chabot had kept the money for himself!

This, succinctly and precisely, is what had happened in the famous commission.

Chabot, as we had seen, when going the prior evening to the Tuileries, had put aside the painful episode of Burlandeux and de Batz's encounter in the Rue d'Anjou mansion. He had ended up convincing himself—so much do we end up believing what is most convenient for us—that the baron was only a financier who, to do business, was forced to conceal his has-been name. He had envisioned a rosy future, with dazzling millions. Then, he had thought about the bribe he was to give Fabre, and he had realized that his future brother-in-law had been right to advise him to keep a nice percentage of it. This nice percentage grew by the minute, so much so that when he had arrived at the Tuileries, in the vestibule leading to the room where the commission was to meet, and which was called the Liberty Antechamber, this good percentage had absorbed the entire amount. Chabot was allotting himself one hundred percent. He was born to enter a family of usurers.

"I will try," Chabot said to himself, "to get Fabre to vote like us, and I will say nothing to him. Why buy a vote when you can get it for free? Who will ever know that I didn't give him anything?"

He just so happened to cross paths with Fabre in the antechamber and approached him. He presented him the draft of the decree that he intended to propose at the commission meeting and said to him, "Read this draft and sign it. The other commissioners will be signing it in turn! We agree in principle on liquidating the company!"

Fabre read the draft Chabot handed him and objected: "I'm sorry... I cannot accept that we keep the directors for the liquidation of their own company. This was the point I made at the Convention meeting! And Robespierre agreed!"

"So what? One day people say one thing, and another day another!"

"No! Absolutely not!"

Fabre d'Églantine took a pencil out of his pocket and edited in the proposal he had made at the Convention. He then signed and went off to bed, since he was ill.

At that moment, Chabot had the idea to take out a wad of bills representing the hundred thousand livres and to offer them to Fabre in exchange for his consent to revert to the original text.

A fear held him back: "And if he refuses!... I'll be compromised..."

Another idea occurred to him: "Come on, Chabot!" he said to himself. "You're making yourself an excuse!... Fabre would not refuse a hundred thousand livres!... And you know it well! What you really want is to trick your colleague and to keep the hundred thousand livres for yourself!"

The time for these reflections was over, and Fabre had already left. Chabot entered the commission's meeting room. He found there Delaunay of Angers with his old accomplice Julien of Toulouse, the Protestant pastor, who had no right to be there since he had not been appointed a commissioner, but who, in the absence of Ramel and Cambon, impatiently awaited Chabot's arrival.

"Well?" Delaunay asked the former Capuchin anxiously.

"I just ran into Fabre; he insisted on his proposal from earlier!"

"You didn't offer him the money then?"

"I did!"

"And he refused a hundred thousand livres?"

"No!"

"It would have surprised me if he had!"

"It's just that he insisted on his proposal!"

"That wretch!... He certainly knows how to steal his money!"

"The stock coup has failed!" lamented Julien. "It was such a beautiful opportunity!"

"Why has it failed?" asked Chabot.

Delaunay replied, surprised, "Because if the directors do not stay to liquidate and, in reality, to continue operating the Indies Company, the shares will remain low. We will be able to purchase them, but what good will it do us to resell them?"

"Are you naive?" Chabot exclaimed. "We are going to copy this decree again without the text added by Fabre. Delaunay will sign it, I will sign it, and I will take it to Fabre this very evening. He will be in bed, in the dark. He will sign it in turn without reading it, on my word that it is an exact copy of what he already signed before!... Once I have these three signatures, the decree is good. We are the majority, and Ramel and Cambon, who have not even shown up, cannot undo our work. They are in the minority!"

Everything was done as Chabot stated. The decree, copied and signed by Chabot and Delaunay, was taken to Fabre, who, half-asleep, signed it in turn. And Chabot brought it back triumphantly. The document was slipped in among those bills the president reads aloud quickly and indistinctly at the beginning of every parliamentary meeting and which are respected. No one listens to them, and they are voted for mechanically. The decree's ratification was certain. Chabot returned radiant to have tea with his Léopoldine and his two brothers-in-law, and Delaunay reported the news to Citizen Manaud, who used the incident, as we saw earlier, to supply Citizen Cassecœur with one of the greatest successes he had ever achieved at the rostrum, even in Lyon.

But the day following the tumultuous Jacobin meeting, you can imagine how angry Fabre was when he approached Chabot at the Convention, just five minutes before the start of the meeting!

"Are you not aware of what happened yesterday at the Jacobins?" he asked him.

"Something happened?" asked Chabot, a little concerned.

"They will be coming as a delegation in just a few minutes to demand explanations for the Indies Company decree. Do you understand? You wretch!"

Chabot turned horribly pale. He felt the same dread as when Citizen Manaud had told him, "De Batz! That's me!" He sensed the terrible trap.

"Our conscience is clear!" he stammered.

"Mine is, yes!... But yours?... Where is the draft of the decree?"

"On the president's desk."

"I want to see it!"

"Fabre!" said Chabot. "You signed it... No one will believe you if you say your proposal was withdrawn without your consent! Let things be for now. We'll see how things go!"

Fabre d'Églantine saw red. He seized Chabot by the throat and cried, "But I told the Jacobins that my proposal was kept!... It would look like I had lied!... Oh, you scoundrel! You traitor!... You are destroying me!... My one consolation, you see, is that my head will not be going down without yours!"

"Instead of devouring us, defend us!" said Chabot. He then added, "I have fifty thousand livres for you!"

"To the devil with that!... What good is that now?"

And Fabre stormed off towards the meeting hall.

In the garden, a wild rumor was breaking out. The Jacobin Club's delegation was on its way to call certain Convention members to account for exploiting their positions for financial gain.

The virtuous Dufourny, so abundantly well-paid by de Batz, was in command of these dispensers of justice, and de Batz, in the second row of the obscure box where we saw him once before, waited, like a casual observer getting ready for a rare spectacle, surrounded by his ordinary phalanx of conspirators. These latter, in their disguises, very much intended to take part in this new tragedy over which the curtain was about to rise.

The delegation's arrival was the prologue. Dufourny, in a red cap and carmagnole, preceded his band composed of hideous-faced men wearing sabots, armed with pikes, their arms and legs bare, and sabers hanging from the baldrics placed over their dirty shirts. They shouted at the Convention members with cries of: "Shame on the corrupt!... Death to the exploiters!"

The knitwomen in the tribunes joined in chorus. Dufourny then called for silence and spoke: "Citizen President, revelations were made to us yesterday, at the club, concerning money racketeering related to the liquidation of the Indies Company. We come to inquire, according to the club's vow, whether the revolutionary French can still count on the integrity and disinterested patriotism of their representatives!"

"I ask for the floor!" a voice said.

It was the Convention member Philippeaux. Chabot, sitting in his seat, got a bad impression when he saw this man rise to go to the rostrum. He knew that Philippeaux was not one of those who had purchased shares. But why was Philippeaux getting himself mixed up in this business? How would he know anything about it? And he suddenly sensed he was surrounded by mysterious enemies, each waiting his turn to make himself known.

Philippeaux employed the romantic, theatrical phraseology of the time: "Let the masks fall!" he declaimed. "Let virtue show itself completely naked! Let the people know whether all those who claim to be their friends truly work for their happiness; but let us begin by being strict with ourselves. I call for each Convention member to be required to report, for the space of the last decade, the state of his fortune before the start of the Revolution; and, if he has increased it since, to specify by what means he has done so. For every law, there is a penalty. I call for those Convention members who will not fulfill the provisions of our decree to be declared traitors to the homeland and to be prosecuted as such."

Despite the applause which welcomed this proposition, one could detect a certain uneasiness. The Convention members who had dipped their hands into the stock coup business sensed a kind of secret power that was hell-bent on their destruction. The others suffered from the offensive suspicion that was cast on all the deputies, guilty or not.

Chabot did not know what attitude to adopt to deflect an assault that impacted him more directly than the others, when one of his accomplices, Bazire, asked for the floor, suddenly opening for him new horizons.

"I rise to speak against Philippeaux's proposal!" said Bazire.

As derisive "ahs" and "ahas" came from the tribunes filled with Charonne confederates, intermixed with Dufourny and his Jacobins, Bazire angrily objected: "It is not for myself that I speak against this proposal. I am the poorest man in the Convention! With this plan, you will not be able to find the scoundrels. Crime thinks up all kinds of trickery. Scoundrels find frontmen to hide their fortunes, while honest men, on the other hand, display the fruit of their savings in the open. Do not be so quick to take the bait dangled in front of you by villains, lest we all tear each other to pieces. It is not out of patriotism that there are these denunciations and calumnies; there are counter-revolutionary intentions behind them!"

"Bravo! Bravo!" cried Chabot, who felt that the ideas bubbling in his own head were being expressed. He was the only one of the conniving money schemers who could provide evidence that the Counter-Revolution was behind this. But how could he name de Batz without confessing to the stock coup? It did not matter! He now had the material for a rebuttal and asked for the floor.

From his obscure box, the baron said to Devaux, his secretary, "What could this regicide possibly say to his accomplices?... Things are heating up... I feel like we are on a tiger hunt, and this is a dangerous hunt!"

"Yes! But instead of dogs, you have wolves!" replied Devaux, indicating Dufourny and his Septembrists, who, with their eyes blazing and their mouths convulsing, were already baying against Chabot, yelling at him, "Go put back on your sans-culotte clothes!... You're dressed like a has-been! Traitor to the people! Sellout!"

Very pale, Chabot, without responding to these insults, began in the calmest manner, as though fearing an indignant protestation would be perceived as personally defensive. He said, "I call for deputies to enjoy the same right as individuals, that is to say, that they not be indicted until after they have been heard. If you do not adopt this measure, what virtuous man will want to tend to the interests of the Republic if he can be struck down the very instant he devotes himself to her! Death cannot frighten me; if my head is useful for the preservation of the Republic, then let it fall! But be very wary of hidden forces behind this discussion. What makes you think, citizen representatives of the people, that the counter-revolutionaries do not intend to send our heads to the scaffold? One of our colleagues heard someone say, 'Today is this one's turn, tomorrow is Danton's turn, the day after tomorrow is Billaud-Varennes's turn; we will eventually get to Robespierre!'"

"And that colleague is well-informed!" whispered Baron de Batz in Devaux's ear.

"Shh!" said Devaux. "Robespierre is now getting up to speak!"

Indeed, the elegant Robespierre, who during Chabot's discourse appeared busy penciling some notes on a writing pad, jumped up from his seat, and in his sharp, curt voice, with his right hand pointed towards Chabot, proclaimed, "By what right, Chabot, do you dare pronounce here the name of him who is called the Incorruptible One, in a debate that is focused only on corruption? I, also, will die for the Republic if necessary, but I will die with clean hands and a clear conscience! Would that all could say the same!"

And he looked at Danton as he finished his sentence.

It was indeed Danton he was targeting, Danton whose popularity and talent he resented, Danton whom he suspected might one day vie with him for the dictatorship of which he dreamed, Danton whom our rulers immortalized in statues as a popular hero when they ought to have proclaimed him for what he truly was: the father of parliamentarian money schemers. Robespierre slyly attacked Danton's weak point in this way each time he saw an opportunity, but his attack was never anything more direct than looking into his eyes as he just did while condemning corruption. Danton contented himself to shrug his shoulders imperceptibly and disdainfully while Robespierre sat back down and reread the notes on his small writing pad. This was a private duel between two of the Convention's great personalities which went unnoticed by the others in the hall. Everyone assumed it was just Chabot who was the object of Robespierre's anger, and Chabot himself hunched his shoulders beneath the weight of it, but the anger was entirely for Danton.

When the applause that followed the Incorruptible One's interruption was over, Chabot continued: "I was not implying any connection! I was putting forward a hypothesis! I was warning the Convention and the Society of the Jacobins against the Counter-Revolution's insidious attacks, by which they could very well be fooled!"

And as the people in the tribunes were interrupting him, Chabot, rather than loudly and firmly retorting as he had done in times past, back when he was a sans-culotte and demanded heads, instead made himself smooth, paid homage to the Society of the Jacobins' patriotism, even called for the Convention to award this society a commendation, and concluded with this supplication which betrayed his inward panic: "Imagine then that one might come, on the basis of a forged letter, to solicit charges against the best patriots. Do not tolerate the indictment of a deputy without first allowing him to be heard!"

He then stepped down from the rostrum, and there was zero applause!

A man in the Convention who was seething out of feeling himself muzzled was Fabre d'Églantine, whose imprudent signature bound him to the fate of Chabot and the speculating deputies. Thus, he sensed a genuine relief in being able to utter this apostrophe: "Chabot is right, Citizen! He knows what he is saying when he exhorts you to beware of forged papers!"

Bourdon of Oise then got up. "So, Chabot," he said, "today you don't want us to condemn a deputy rashly. But the Girondins you helped throw onto the chopping block, were they heard?"

"Those," retorted Bazire, to save Chabot, "those, public opinion had condemned them already! I support Chabot's motion!"

"Fine!" Bourdon said approvingly. "But at least let it be understood that a deputy who seeks to elude an indictment will be outside the law!"

Julien of Toulouse, one of the sellouts, protested: "Marat hid when he was charged! He was never faulted for it by you!"

The corrupt ones very carefully regained their courage and supported one other. Within the Convention, a movement visibly formed against an indictment.

But then a voice rang from the boxes. Dufourny, who had risen, proclaimed in a loud voice, "The Society of the Jacobins will judge this evening whether the Convention is against the sellouts or with them!"

"Yes, yes!" furiously screamed the knitwomen and the tatterdemalions brandishing their pikes.

Chabot was singled out for attack. They shouted, "He is marrying an Austrian woman like Antoinette! His brother-in-law is an Austrian agent!"

The Convention was scared. This supposed "Assembly of Giants" was in fact always scared, ever cowardly, and always voted on command from the noisy crowd shouting at its doors or in its tribunes. In a republic, is it not always the forces of demagoguery that dominate the assemblies?

The Convention therefore rendered an indictment against the corrupt officials. It was now only a matter of making a list of names, and Chabot's name would of course be at the top.

Panicking, Chabot left the meeting and ran to the Frey mansion where he had an attack of despair. He blew up at Julius

Frey, who had encouraged him to do the Indies Company stock coup, and was then rebuffed by the Jew, who called him a klutz.

Then, an idea suddenly taking hold of Chabot, he cried out, "Just one man can get me out of this!"

"Who?" asked Léopoldine, who was terrorized by these events.

"Robespierre!"

"You must go see him!... And right away!"

Chabot ran to the Incorruptible One's home. On Rue Saint-Honoré, he passed a band of sans-culottes who were coming from the Convention and chanting one of those chants which functions as a kind of slogan and is shouted in the streets of the capital for any political event:

> *Lo, the lowest of the low:*
> *Julien, Bazire, and Chabot!*
> *Foulest vermin in our sphere:*
> *Julien, Chabot, and Bazire!*
> *No worse scoundrels than these men:*
> *Chabot, Bazire, and Julien!*

This chant bore the signature of Baron de Batz, for it corresponded too much to the movement he had created.

Chabot sensed it. "De Batz, you wretch!" he muttered. "You made a bad move driving me into this corner! When I go down, I'm taking you down with me!"

Chapter 7

At the Home of the "Incorruptible One"

LENOTRE TELLS US in his *Vieilles maisons, vieux papiers* that Robespierre "then resided at the house of the carpenter Duplay, on Rue Saint-Honoré, where Danton said he lived 'amidst fools and gossips.' Given lodging by Duplay and his wife and daughters, who surrounded him with attentions and showered him with adulation, he had found there a new family."

Between the Anjou mansion where Chabot lived with the Jewish Freys, and the Rue Saint-Honoré house currently numbered 398, there is not, I think, three hundred meters.

Citizeness Léopoldine's fiancé arrived in little time at the entranceway leading to a courtyard where Duplay was stacking planks he needed to plane. The courtyard was surrounded by old convent gardens, whose visible treetops the early autumn had already rusted.

Duplay was at the entrance of his workshop, at the far end of the courtyard, when Chabot appeared.

"Is Citizen Robespierre here?" he asked. "I am Chabot, his friend. I need to see him about an urgent matter…"

"I believe he is back from the session," Duplay answered, "but he strongly advised me not to let anyone go up. He is working."

"Those instructions could not be meant for me, Chabot!… I've come to speak with him about an extremely serious matter!"

"Go up then, Citizen. Go up at your own risk and peril. The stairway is over there."

Chabot did not have to be told twice. He headed to the building facing the street and went up to the floor where Robespierre's room was.

The great man was in fact working in his room, which had a spartan simplicity and could have passed for the cell of a monk if a crucifix and pious pictures had replaced the portraits of Jean-Jacques and the hideous caricatures of Louis XVI and Marie Antoinette.

He was transcribing in ink onto a blank sheet of paper the notes he had written at the meeting on his small writing pad.

Beside him was a letter he had just written, which read as follows:

24 Vendémiaire, Year II

Your invitation to supper, divine Émilie, fills me with happiness. You have left it to me to choose the day, but I think it best to leave this choice to your convenience, only too glad to sacrifice for you the occupation that would aspire to compete with you for my attention, and to prove to you that at your beckoning, no matter the hour, I will always run to cast myself at your feet.

Deign to accept these flowers and these verses which I bring you through my messenger.

I kiss your hands and those of your citizeness mother.

Robespierre

And what he was transcribing were the verses he composed during the Convention session, to the great fright of those who feared he was making a new list of victims. On those lists of proscription, how many had seen their names written for a forgotten greeting, for a sharp word spoken in session, or for a wrongly interpreted glance!

These verses, he reread while copying them:

O, my dear and tender Émilie!
Object of the most ardent love,
In my humble sojourn,

When will you come to guide my life?
Everywhere I see only darkness!
I fear the assaults of injustice...
Hanging over a precipice,
The depth of which I fear less
Than I abhor the artifice
That hollowed it beneath my steps,
My thoughts turn to you;
And suddenly my soul, wearied
From tumultuous battles,
Reposes in your remembrance.
Whilst the present overwhelms me
And the past makes me tremble,
With pure, inviolable happiness,
I compose my future.
Worshipper of my homeland,
Ardent defender of her rights,
I have long sought the honor
To sacrifice for her my life.
But envy, alas, is everywhere,
Among the Jacobins, at the rostrum;
Of the glory that importunes it,
Its breath does in the end
Sully the brilliant image.
Against my enemies, against their rage,
I can oppose your suffrage.
I am loved, I can die...

The great guillotiner who unleashed over France an immense river of blood and tears would have long continued writing to Émilie his poem of petty political annoyances intermingled with sugary declarations if there had not been three knocks at his door.

"Come in!" he cried, no longer pressing his goose quill to the paper.

And he saw Chabot enter. He was pale, downcast, his forehead wrinkled, and his cheeks hollowed by anguish.

"Robespierre," Chabot said, "I have come to reiterate that when I mentioned your name at the rostrum earlier, there were not at all any ill intentions behind it."

"I didn't think so!"

"No hard feelings then?"

"Not at all!"

"So... you will rescue me then!"

"From what?"

Robespierre, after letting a look of surprise appear on his face, put back on his cold and impenetrable mask of stone.

"Sit down!" he said sternly.

Timidly, Chabot sat down. He took notice for a minute of the modest room, the white wooden table, the bed, and the two armless straw chairs, which contrasted with the silk, the draperies, the padded, sculpted seating, and the chiseled bronze furniture of the Frey mansion, and he regretted coming. No help would come to him from the Cato who lived here.

However, he attempted to play his one last card.

"Robespierre," he said, "I have come to urge you to save the homeland. I am privy to the most dangerous conspiracy ever to be plotted against liberty."

"Well, you must expose it!"

"I penetrated this awful network by associating with the conspirators and pretending to accept their proposals."

Then, taking out the notorious wad of money he was supposed to give to Fabre d'Églantine, he placed it on the table of the Incorruptible One, telling him, "Here is the money they gave and that I pretended to accept to gain their confidence and to learn what they were ultimately planning. I will tell you their names; you will have them arrested and attest to my civism!"

"Take this money and your revelations to the Committee of General Security!" Robespierre replied coldly. "They will eagerly receive you!"

"Agreed!... But I fear that my associating with the conspirators, although it was only for the purpose of unmasking them and delivering them to the sword of the law, will be misconstrued by the Committee of General Security!"

"And why do you think that if your case gives the Committee of General Security reasons for suspicion, that it will not also do the same for me?"

"Because you know me! Because you are my friend! Because we have always defended the Republic together, and you have no interest in letting your friends and faithful be suspected and accused, but on the contrary, you want to defend them!"

"The interest I have, I who am called the Incorruptible One, is not to let myself be suspected by saving those of my friends who are suspected of corruption! Go!"

And with a curt gesture, he showed him the door.

Chabot, his head lowered, was getting up to exit when Robespierre suddenly asked him in a kinder tone, "Who then are these conspirators?"

"De Batz! Delaunay of Angers! Julien of Toulouse! Fabre d'Églantine! Bazire!"

The wretch threw his accomplices into the water to save himself!

"Isn't Fabre d'Églantine a good friend of Danton?" asked Robespierre.

"Yes, of course!... But why this question?"

"He was his secretary, I believe?"

"Yes! When Danton took him with him to the Ministry of Justice, as well as Camille Desmoulins!"

"Camille Desmoulins as well, that's right!"

A strange grin materialized on Robespierre's face. It seemed the grin of a wild beast scenting the tracks of its prey.

"That suffices!" he said. "Go to the Committee!"

And he dismissed him for good. Chabot left, despairing. Now alone, a ferocious smile lit Robespierre's bilious face. His thin lips spread out. He whispered, "Rescue these corrupt men?... Compromise myself when I can instead use them to destroy Danton and his pirates?... Never!... What fine carts to offer up as holocausts to Virtue!"

And he resumed his *Epistle to Émilie*:

> *Yes, my young and sensitive beloved,*
> *Armed with my cause and your heart,*
> *Scorning enemy fortune,*
> *I can brave the scaffolds...*

There was another knock at the door. He had a moment of impatience, then cried out, "Come in!"

It was our old acquaintance Sénar. His face was red, his eyes were animated, and he was muddy up to his waist. He wore a triple-caped frock coat which was unbuttoned, thereby making visible its interior pockets stuffed with papers.

"Citizen Representative," he said, out of breath, "pardon me for forcing myself in and taking up moments of the precious time you use for the defense of the Republic, but this precisely concerns the preservation of the homeland!"

"Who are you?" asked Robespierre, looking over him sternly.

"Sénar!... An observer of public sentiment! An agent of the Committees!... You have seen me many times at the Committee of General Security. I have often denounced conspirators who, thanks to Fouquier-Tinville, have been brought to revolutionary justice!... But never has there been a conspiracy such as the one I have come now to denounce to you..."

"Oh?" interrupted Robespierre with annoyance. "Yet another conspiracy? This is the day for them!"

"It is tied to the infamous de Batz!"

"Him again?... But why aren't you going to the Committee of General Security to denounce this conspiracy?"

"Why, Citizen?" Sénar moved his head forward and said in a low voice, "Because I distrust some of the Committee of General Security... De Batz has agents everywhere!"

"I was told this before, not a long time ago," said Robespierre with great calm. "Sit down and continue!"

"I will begin with what is the most urgent, Citizen Representative. Yesterday, at a restaurant on Rue de l'Oseille, in the Marais district, two men were dining, around noon. One was the café owner Michonis, who was elected a member of the municipality, and whom the municipality then thrust into the position of prisons director."

"I know!"

"It was this Michonis who oversaw the Capet woman's transfer from the Temple to the Conciergerie."

"And the other man? The one who was dining with him?"

"The other was a certain Rougeville, who defended the lair of the tyrants on August 10 and shed the blood of the people. He is an agent of the has-been Baron de Batz. Rougeville was paying for the dinner, and that imbecile Michonis ended up getting drunk. The conversation then turned to the female prisoner in the Conciergerie. It's a subject which Michonis never shuts up about, because it gives him importance. Every day, he breaks from tending his café to visit the has-been queen and to check whether she is still there."

"That is proof of his civic zeal!"

"Certainly! But he also does it to feed his vanity. Michonis is so puffed up by his mission, and so proud to be in contact with the Capet widow, that he would like the entire world to see him speaking to her with his hat on his head and his hands in his pockets. Rougeville said to him—this was overheard—that he was so lucky to be able to treat himself each day to the philosophical spectacle of a fallen queen. Michonis agreed. He offered to let Rougeville enjoy this spectacle for himself. And he immediately took him to the Conciergerie.

"The Capet woman, Robespierre, is guarded in a cell divided into two sections by a partition. She lives in one section of this cell, which is lit by a barred window that faces out onto the women's courtyard.

"The other section of the cell is reserved for the two gendarmes who closely watch her night and day, Gilbert and Dufresne.

"These two soldiers let Michonis and his companion enter the Austrian woman's cell, and they very clearly noticed the Capet widow's face light up upon seeing Rougeville. She therefore knew him.

"Rougeville had more self-control, but he had a carnation boutonniere that he removed and nonchalantly threw behind the small stove that heats the has-been queen's cell. Michonis, who was drunk, saw nothing, and the two guards did not at all alarm themselves about this gallantry..."

"They were wrong not to!" interrupted Robespierre violently. "Any token of sympathy for that tigress is suspect, and they should have arrested this Rougeville..."

"Certainly, Citizen, if Michonis had not been there!... But Michonis was there! Michonis who is responsible for overseeing the prisons! Michonis to whom they owe obedience, whose zeal they had never doubted, Michonis who might have retaliated had they arrested a man who very much appeared to be his friend!"

"You are right, Citizen Sénar!... It is Michonis who deserves to be handed over to the Revolutionary Tribunal. Has he been arrested?"

"I don't believe so!"

"He will be... Continue."

"Rougeville then went back to the part of the cell reserved for the gendarmes and offered them drinks, with Michonis's consent. A bottle of wine and two glasses were brought from the refreshment bar that serves the Revolutionary Tribunal jurors, by a servant girl who seemed only to be waiting for this order, which I find suspicious, since Citizeness Richard, the wife of the concierge, told me when I was investigating these events, that this girl was very solicitous for the Austrian woman.

"Gilbert, one of the gendarmes, pretended to drink, and contented himself to dip his lips into the glass. The other, Dufresne, less distrustful, drank to the health of the Nation and downed his glass all at once. During this time, Gilbert was watching the Austrian woman from the corner of his eye through the partition door, which remained half-open. He saw her bend down, pick up the carnation, happily smell it, and then, to his surprise, feel around inside and remove its petals. She removed a small roll of paper from the inside of the flower and unrolled it. She read this paper and hid it inside her dress.

"Michonis and Rougeville then left. And when Gilbert pulled on Dufresne's sleeve to tell him what he saw, he noticed that his comrade was not responding.

"Dufresne had his forehead down on the table at which he and his comrade normally played cards. He was sleeping, out cold, perhaps poisoned. This is at least what Gilbert thought at the time.

"He got up to ask for help when two other gendarmes entered. Gilbert did not know them and had never seen them before.

"The arrivals looked stunned when they saw Gilbert standing there in front of them. Those two conspirators dressed as gendarmes no doubt counted on Gilbert being knocked out, which would have happened had this soldier, like his companion, imprudently drunk his glass, into which the infamous Rougeville had deftly slipped a narcotic.

"Both of them blocked the door to the corridor to prevent Gilbert from leaving. He bravely demanded, 'Who are you? What do you want?'

"'We have come to take the prisoner to her hearing. Citizen Fouquier-Tinville is waiting to question her, as well as Citizen Herman, the president of the Revolutionary Tribunal. Here are our orders!' And they boldly presented some papers.

"'No one but my comrade and I have the right to guard and escort the prisoner to the tribunal!' Gilbert cried. And he put his hand on the grip of his pistol.

"At that moment, Antoinette fully gave away the plot by crying out, with hope in her eyes, 'Monsieur, I beg you!... I will make you rich!'

"The two traitors then dropped their masks. They said to Gilbert, 'Your fortune is made! One million for you, one million if you let her leave with us!... And we will also save you from the clutches of Fouquier-Tinville!'

"'Get out of here!' Gilbert cried. 'Or I'll blow your brains out!'

"One of the traitors drew his sword and attempted to stab this soldier faithful to his civic duty. Gilbert fired, and the bandit went down. Richard and Gilbert rushed at and grabbed hold of the accomplice, who was resisting and trying to clear a way for himself with his sword. Meanwhile, the Capet woman fainted onto her bed—so shaken was she by this drama in which perished her last hope of escaping the sword of the law, that it took a good hour for her to come to!

"The paper found on her informed her that two friends would be arriving disguised as gendarmes."

"And the man that was arrested?" asked Robespierre.

"He will be handed over to the Revolutionary Tribunal. His name is Burlandeux!"

"And Rougeville?"

"He was able to flee in a carriage drawn by two strong horses. He was waiting by it, on Rue de la Barillerie, for the Capet woman and the two fake gendarmes!"

Robespierre got up and walked about agitatedly.

"And the man that was killed?" he asked. "Did you figure out his identity?"

"His name was Leblanc. He was affiliated with the Committee of Public Safety and was betraying the Republic, like Burlandeux, in exchange for money from the conspirators... It was, Citizen Robespierre, owing solely to Burlandeux's participation in the Capet woman's escape attempt that I was able to piece back together the entire scheme!"

Robespierre sat back down, and Sénar, so taken with his subject, continued without even giving himself the time to catch his breath.

"Burlandeux, Citizen Robespierre, had already been caught red-handed by me once before in the act of conspiring against the Republic. I had threatened to denounce him if he did not supply me a full list of the conspirators with whom he lived. He promised me he would make this list, but on the condition that he give it to a republican whose allegiance was beyond suspicion: Chabot!"

"Chabot?... Well, well!" said Robespierre. "So did this Burlandeux give Chabot this list?"

"I believe so..."

"Why then didn't Chabot ever mention it?"

"I don't know!"

"I'm afraid I do know! Continue!"

"In any case, this Burlandeux, whom I had essentially given the means to repair his offenses against the Republic and to resume his patriotic obligations, very quickly went back to the traitors and hastened to conspire with them to free the tyrant's wife, that cruel enemy of the people."

At that moment, someone knocked. Before even receiving authorization from Robespierre, the younger of the carpenter Duplay's two daughters peeked her blonde head through the door.

"Citizen Robespierre," she said, "your friend, the painter David, is down below."

"What does he want?"

"He would really like to see the Austrian woman's cart passing by when she goes to the guillotine, to sketch a portrait of her from your window facing the street."

"That's no problem at all!"

"But what time can he come without bothering you?"

"What time?"

Robespierre reflected: "Antoinette, presently, is at the tribunal. The sentence will be pronounced tonight, tomorrow morning at the latest. The execution will take place immediately. Tell David he should be here by seven o'clock in the morning to not miss the cart going by."

"Very well, Citizen!"

And the blonde head disappeared.

Sénar, without being invited to do so, continued his narration: "Now, Citizen Robespierre, who then are these conspirators with whom Burlandeux so criminally associated himself? They are the has-been Baron de Batz and his henchmen!"

"De Batz!" exclaimed Robespierre. "Oh, him! I don't want to hear this man spoken of anymore! Chabot has also had dealings with him!"

"I did not know that! But nothing would surprise me from the leader of a conspiracy who is like an octopus, his tentacles slipping little by little into all the organs of the revolutionary government! You don't want to hear the has-been de Batz spoken of anymore, Citizen Robespierre? Be very convinced that you will hear him spoken of more and more unless you order a raid on his hideout and arrest all his recruited miscreants!"

"And where is this hideout?"

"In Charonne!"

"Well, Citizen Sénar, you need to make a formal denunciation to the Committee of General Security!"

"No, Citizen Robespierre! I distrust the Committee of General Security!"

"Have they been bought by de Batz?"

"Yes! Not all of them, but a portion of them! And how can one distinguish between the pure and the corrupt?"

"You are right!"

Danton's enemy got up and again began walking around like a tiger in its cage. He spoke to himself, and bits of sentences reached Sénar's ears: "All these rotten institutions need to be purged!... Too bad if the Convention is decimated! I'll govern with the Commune and the Society of the Jacobins! Woe to all!"

He woke from this somnambular state and said to Sénar, "Citizen, I will have that hideout raided. Continue observing and reporting to me what you know, and keep all this a secret, since we are surrounded by traitors!... If you serve me well, I will repay your civic zeal, for it is indeed your civic zeal that is driving you..."

"Yes, Citizen! And the desire to distinguish myself in the defense of the homeland, to conquer a heart that is dear to me!"

"Serve me well, and I will make you a partner in my designs!... And I will see to it that you marry the one you love, whoever she might be!"

"Citizen," replied Sénar glowingly, "I am yours, body and soul!"

Oh, if he had only known to whom Robespierre addressed those verses he was transcribing!

But he was inebriated with joy, seeing himself, thanks to the patronage of Robespierre, on track to ascend to the highest posts, while passing over the carcass of that poor Burlandeux, who, as we see, had lost his last card.

Robespierre continued: "You must go to the Committee of General Security and demand in my name the arrest of Michonis, the concierge Richard, and his wife, who, whether complicit or negligent, nearly let the Austrian tigress's escape succeed. I also want arrested that servant girl who you told me was suspect. They wouldn't dare refuse me that, would they? For the Charonne business, we will see to that later! Go!"

And Sénar, obeying the order, left and took Rue Saint-Honoré towards the Tuileries. He carried his head high, and his footsteps proudly resounded on the pavement—he was officially transmitting the orders of Citizen Robespierre!

At that moment, in the garden of the Tuileries, on the Terrasse des Feuillants, a man, wrapped up to his eyes in a long coat whose flap was pushed back over his left shoulder, was walking slowly. Sometimes he stopped. His right foot impatiently striking the ground contradicted the calm with which he resumed his walk. This man was waiting for someone.

Another individual, coming from the Tuileries, went to meet him.

"Is that you, Biret-Tissot?" asked the impatient stroller.

"It is I, Monsieur Baron. Head towards the Tuileries. A member of the Committee of General Security will come and speak to you without looking at you, while he throws bread to the garden sparrows and appears to be doing only that."

Biret-Tissot went off towards Revolution Square.

De Batz proceeded to walk calmly towards the palace. A man came towards him, holding a piece of bread, crumbs of which he from time to time tossed over the railing. One by one, the sparrows came, chirping, and growing bolder. They soon became a swarm.

The man, having drawn level to the baron, spoke as though monologuing: "Chabot is filing a deposition before our committee. He proposes handing you over to us tomorrow evening, in Charonne or at Rue d'Anjou. Beware of an ambush! Hide!"

"Have Chabot arrested tomorrow morning then, with the Freys... That will create a diversion, and you will have the Jacobin Club's approval. At Rue d'Anjou, you will find all the evidence of Indies Company trading."

The mysterious Committee of General Security member, leaning over the terrace railing, was still throwing bread to the sparrows. They drew nearer to him and flew around him; a few landed on his shoulder.

De Batz, behind him, appeared to be a passer-by enjoying this spectacle, which is still frequent today in Parisian parks.

It was in this manner that the two interlocutors decided the fate of Chabot, who was arrested the following morning. Ten deputies were arrested in turn during the day, among whom were Bazire, Fabre d'Églantine, Delaunay, and Julien of Toulouse. This was only the beginning of the hecatomb.

All these corrupt officials were locked up in Luxembourg Prison.

The Jacobin Club, on Dufourny's recommendation, congratulated the Convention for having cauterized the gangrene that was invading it.

De Batz returned to Charonne satisfied. The reaper was beginning to work, and the red harvest promised plenty.

Alone in his austere room following Sénar's departure, Robespierre had imperturbably resumed his *Epistle to Émilie*:

> *We will make use of the goods*
> *That the one nature gives...*
> *Within this pure spring*
> *Never poisoned by*
> *Remorse, regrets,*
> *Plots, or imposture...*

Chapter 8

The Arcades House Supper

SEVERAL WEEKS LATER in the de Sainte-Amaranthe ladies' private apartments, steps away from where gold still poured onto green game tables with the same frenzy, although the well-bred gamblers more and more gave way to slovenly dressed proto-profiteers of the Revolution, preparations for a great feast were underway.

Émilie, in response to Robespierre's epistle, had invited him to come for supper that evening. It was her mother who had chosen the date.

"Daughter," she had said to her a few days earlier, "your father insists we give the Incorruptible One a magnificent reception, and that your engagement to him be officially celebrated."

In response to Émilie's gesture of horror, Madame de Sainte-Amaranthe added, "I said 'engagement,' my dear Émilie!... It is a concession we can make to your father, who must need some influence with Robespierre, and will find none better than his daughter. Besides, I am starting to fear for you..."

"Fear?"

"Yes," Madame de Sainte-Amaranthe continued, "I am scared... Since the queen's execution, the beheadings have accelerated and become more numerous; every day the carts are fuller and fuller!... You do notice here sometimes that friends, regulars, go missing. People will ask around about someone and learn that he has been arrested. A couple of days later, the public criers tell us of his death along with ten others, or twenty others: men, women, elderly, young girls, adolescents!... This blade chopping around me nonstop terrifies me. We need to deal carefully with Robespierre and buy us some time. But I promise you that we will not take this any further than an engagement!"

"But will we be able to get away with this?" said Émilie sadly.

"If necessary, we will flee, we will go hide in our little cottage in Sucy-en-Brie. Then, from there, we'll disguise ourselves and make our way to the border."

"Poor Mama!... I have told you often: You are making me play with a tiger; I will end up getting eaten!"

But there was no sting of reproach in this bitter reflection of the young girl. Émilie was by no means a rebel, and her contact with Mademoiselle de Sainte-Pazanne, who preached by example, as we shall see, had rather brought out in her the spirit of sacrifice. She thought the risk of danger was well worth her father's future and her mother's security.

She had written to Robespierre:

You will pardon me for having delayed so long in thanking you for your lovely flowers and for your so gallantly crafted verses which betray such somber worries. Come then and forget them for one evening at the house, having supper among some friends who are not at all corrupted with ambition. Here you will find no rival or anyone envious of your glory. My mother and I invite you.

Since you leave it to me to choose this blessed day, I set it for the day after tomorrow, 2 Frimaire, at ten o'clock in the evening.

After the letter was sent, she fell into a somber reverie. Placing her burning forehead against a window that faced the Palais-Royal Garden, she looked, without seeing, the crowd of people who were brushing against each other in the galleries. She then whispered, "I will end up having to marry him!"

A voice answered back, very near her, as though an inspiration: "No! You will never marry him!"

She turned around, stunned. Adèle de Sainte-Pazanne was close to her, very pale, her face imprinted with a kind of sorrowful pity, telling her without even giving her time to express her surprise, "You! You!... Bound to the destiny of that monster you do not at all love?... No! No!... Your mother is right. You will flee if necessary, and I will help you to do it... Besides, it is not just you that this concerns... There is him!"

Adèle blushed. Émilie did also. Émilie thought Adèle meant Elleviou when she really meant Paul de Lézardière. This misunderstanding persisted, and it was impossible for it not to continue between these two souls who were keeping their secret, neither of them daring to pronounce the different name that burned on their lips.

"Was I speaking that loudly?" Émilie asked.

"Yes, and since I heard your conversation with your mother, I understood what you were speaking about... I would have understood it just by the expression of despair with which you said, 'I will end up marrying him!'"

With an exaltation produced by the greatness of her sacrifice and the legitimate pride that was already its painful reward, she continued: "And him? Do you consider his despair?... But I will speak to him!... You deserve to be happy, Émilie, and him also. And since you love each other..."

A bit of surprise appeared in the eyes of Mademoiselle de Sainte-Amaranthe. She only saw in this gesture a proof of sincere and deep affection. Spontaneously, she spiritedly embraced Mademoiselle de Sainte-Pazanne and kissed her on both cheeks.

"You are the dearest of friends!" she said to her.

Mademoiselle de Sainte-Pazanne turned around so that her tears could not be seen. Directing her thoughts towards her aunt, she spoke to the dead woman as though she were present there and said to her, "Are you happy? I am fulfilling the mission you entrusted to me before you left for the abode of the blessed. I am taking your place for him and seeing to his happiness, to the point of no longer loving him except as you yourself loved him!"

Émilie sensed nothing of what was taking place in the wounded soul of Mademoiselle de Sainte-Pazanne. Moreover, she was happy! Thus, she was selfish. The other had consoled her by crucifying herself, and Émilie only experienced the joy of this consolation.

"Shall we go to the Favart this evening?"

"Oh, no, not this evening! Do you want to?"

And Mademoiselle de Sainte-Pazanne retired to her room, awaiting the moment, as she had promised, as she believed she had promised, to have a serious talk with her cousin. Afterwards, everything would be over!

Émilie had appeared stunned. Why had Adèle refused? The young brother of Émilie, who as we know was named Lili, had entered precisely when his sister was speaking of going to the Favart Theatre.

"But I want to go there myself," he said. "What's playing?"

"*Philippe and Georgette*, by Citizen Monvel."

"Again?"

"It's a show I love seeing over and over!" said Émilie.

"That's obvious, sister dear! It's nice once, twice, or three times, but more than that, no!"

"The music is so beautiful!"

"You only see that show!... But there are other fine shows they have at the Favart! I don't know why they offer that one so often!"

Émilie herself did know! Lenotre writes:

All Paris was wild about a one-act comic opera, Philippe and Georgette, in which the singer Elleviou played the main role. The entire hall became enraptured when, in his tender voice, he sang:

> *Oh, my Georgette,*
> *You alone brighten this sojourn!*

One evening, as Elleviou came on stage and approached the footlights, while the orchestra played the ritornello for the anticipated couplet, his gaze landed on the box of the de Sainte-Amaranthe ladies. Upon seeing Émilie, the artist's mouth went agape, and he missed his cue... then, immediately recovering, he placed his hand on his heart and, looking directly at the young woman, sang with even more emotion and passion than ordinary:

Oh, my Georgette...

And this was the first declaration of love that he addressed to her.

At the following performance of *Philippe and Georgette*, Émilie was again there, and the aria was again addressed to her. From then on, Elleviou performed it every two days, the show being in vogue, and this was a rendezvous of sorts which Émilie never missed. Her presence was a response, an encouragement. They wondered in Paris why *Philippe and Georgette* was so often performed at the Favart Theatre. Creators of other shows complained that their works were being performed less and less. The elegant Elleviou gave no answer and continued to signal his predilection for this short comic opera.

Such was the romantic intrigue that enchanted Émilie de Sainte-Amaranthe: a duet in which she remained silent, during a secret meeting before a thousand people, occurring on both sides of the footlights!

Through the same door Mademoiselle de Sainte-Pazanne had exited, Cécile Renault then entered, saying to Émilie, "If Mademoiselle wants to come and try her dress?"

"Is it finished? Will I be able to wear it this evening?"

"Certainly!"

"Oh, yes then!... Right away!"

Skipping with joy and clapping her hands, she preceded the young seamstress into a small neighboring room where the fitting commenced. As she did alterations, inserting pins and making a stitch here and a stitch there, Cécile, kneeling on the floor, could not help remarking, "How happy Mademoiselle is!"

"There's good reason to be!" Émilie said ironically. "In a few days, I'll be engaged to Robespierre!"

"The horror!"

Cécile stopped the fitting and stood up, ashen.

"But don't worry," Émilie added in a hushed voice, frightened by the effect Robespierre's name had on Cécile. "Things will be sorted out so that I don't marry that monster!"

"He will be dead first!" Cécile said in a muffled voice.

"How you said that!... How strange you have been for some time, Cécile! You are not your cheerful self anymore. You no longer joke! You no longer tease! You no longer laugh!"

"Not since October 16! No, Mademoiselle. You did not see her yourself, on the cart, the Queen-Martyr, seated with her hands behind her back, on a board, her back to the horse. She was so pale, so deathly white! Spent! Killed by miseries and affronts. She held her head high, but how much she was suffering! Her fichu came undone; she was shivering in the cold wind. I followed her Calvary to Revolution Square. I saw Robespierre, at his window, watching her pass by with an evil joy in his eyes. A man, next to him, was sketching the martyr's portrait. I thought they were going to stop the cart to allow him to finish his sketch more easily... That would have allowed her to suffer longer, no?... At the square, the murderers had the cart make a big circle so that as many as possible drunk Jacobins and knitwomen smelling of brandy could see her and insult her, and also to prolong her agony, so that she might suffer more slowly and better taste her own death. I thought they were going to graze her neck with the blade a long time before chopping her head. But they were scared she would die beforehand. They then took her onto the scaffold. Sanson quickly removed her bonnet, and you could see her white hair. They brutally threw her forward, and the blade dropped. I saw the flow of blood! Oh!"

Cécile let out a cry and put her hands over her eyes as though to hide from them the sight they had already seen.

"Cécile! Cécile!" said Émilie. "Pull yourself together!"

"On my way back," the young seamstress continued, "I passed again in front of that vicious animal's window. I grabbed my knife in my small bag and I understood Charlotte Corday... No! No! You will not be marrying that executioner of our queen!... Trust me!"

Cécile looked implacable and determined. A writer of her time would have called her an Erinys. She frightened Émilie, who said to her, "I beg you!... Don't do what you are saying you are going to do! Don't think of it anymore!... Think of yourself, of your father, of your brothers! Of those who love you!"

"It's all thought out! I am waiting for the right moment. We have friends who are avenging the king. Some of the murderers are in prison now; others will be tomorrow; they are going to get their turn to try the guillotine. Isn't it for a woman to avenge the queen, or must we leave all the work to our baron?"

Cécile was overcome by a fit of tears and went back home.

The fitting had not been finished. Émilie put on another dress and dragged along to the Favart Theatre her mother, who commented to her, to no avail, "I am like Lili! I would also like to see a different show from time to time!"

When Elleviou was on stage that evening, Émilie appeared to him worried and troubled. But she was there! Was that not the important thing?

As Émilie was exiting in the dense crowd, a crowd that was mixed but elegant, into which had already slipped some of those parvenus, still Jacobins, who would constitute the aristocracy in the era of the Directory, a male voice whispered into the young girl's ear, "Will the reaper come?"

"When the harvest is ripe!" she answered softly.

She saw a man in a blue coat with very long tails, wearing a round hat of gray beaver fur decorated with a simple band having a steel buckle. Gloved and elegant, he carried no sword and wielded a large, twisted cane of the sort that would later be called a Directory cane. Émilie gave him a hard look, but without recognizing him. He appeared very satisfied with that. It was the baron.

His famous string was on, pushing his long nose upwards. But his fine Richelieu mustache was shaved off. His face, owing to some fake sideburns, was broadened, and some blue pencil lines gave the impression of wrinkles. De Batz had made his naturally long face rounder and fuller, like a financier of the newly emerging social classes. Very suddenly, the young girl recognized him.

The baron then said, "This famous supper you are always telling me about, when will it be?"

"The day after tomorrow!... It will be my engagement celebration!"

"Good!... Give your ordinary headwaiter that day off... I will be sending you one of my own."

"Anything else?"

"Nothing else!"

He disappeared into the crowd. Madame de Sainte-Amaranthe, who was walking in front of her daughter, had heard nothing. She boarded a carriage and Émilie got in with her.

The baron headed towards Boulevard Bonne-Nouvelle. He entered a café located at the corner of the boulevard and Rue Poissonnière and sat near a man who was devouring cookies drenched in Bordeaux.

"Knight!" he said.

"Oh! It's you, Baron!" said Rougeville with his mouth full. "What's new at the Convention?"

"There will be news the day after tomorrow. The deputy Goupilleau will avenge Chabot and the arrested Convention members by in turn denouncing Dufourny, Montaut, and a few other champions of justice... The friends of Robespierre are going to destroy each other this way..."

"What will Goupilleau say?"

"That Dufourny received money from the Counter-Revolution to plunge the Republic into scandal. It's the normal spiel!"

"He will provide proof of this?"

"Of course, I gave it to him! He will also accuse Renaudin. This is a new batch that's being prepared! Especially since the Cordeliers Club is going to back Goupilleau's motion and demand the arrest of all the sellouts in the Jacobin Club!... The sellouts in the Cordeliers Club will then have their turn a little later! We will have them attacked by the survivors of the Jacobin Club!"

"Are there sellouts at the Cordeliers Club also?"

"Of course, I bought them myself, just to make sure of it!"

"You know what, Baron?"

"What, Knight?"

"Robespierre will end up being stripped of his troops if, under the pretext of purging the Republic, he starts having his best soldiers slaughtered! He will soon be ripe to take out!"

"I intend to take him out the day after tomorrow, at the Arcades House. I am even counting on you to get twenty solid men in Charonne to come down the same evening, around ten o'clock, to the Palais-Royal. You will want to watch for them at the base of the house and let me know when they arrive. We will take him in the building or once he leaves cover. He will offer little resistance; I will have been pouring him drinks the entire evening. Have a carriage waiting at the top of Passage du Perron, on the Rue Vivienne side. We will take him to a safe place."

Rougeville seemed so interested by these details that he forgot to eat his cookies.

"How did you manage to set this trap?"

"It's the classic wild animal hunt, isn't it?... A friend in the regiment, Monsieur de Faverolles, who served in the Indies, told me long ago how they catch tigers. They get a small goat kid and tie it to a post. Lured by this bait, the wild beast approaches. Men waiting in ambush shoot it with a musket, unless a pit covered with branches has been dug and he falls inside. In that case, you have it alive!"

"But the poor little baby goat?"

"It risks nothing! Unless... well, what do you expect! A tiger hunt is dangerous for everyone, including the hunters!... Can I count on you for the day after tomorrow?"

"I would hate to miss this hunting party! The republican Goupilleau taking shots at the Jacobin Club in the Convention, and we at the same time lying in wait for the biggest beast in the demagogic jungle... All of this, the same evening!... Only a fool would abstain from such festivities!"

"I will see you the day after tomorrow, Knight!"

"See you then, Baron!"

And the baron left the knight to devour his cookies and finish his bottle of Bordeaux.

Two days later, at six o'clock in the evening, his face disguised in the same manner, de Batz was wearing the proper uniform for a headwaiter at the home of the de Sainte-Amaranthe ladies.

Émilie had given the evening off to the headwaiter who ordinarily served them, to the great astonishment of her mother.

The preparations for the feast were completed by the time Robespierre, with more refined elegance than ever, made his entrance into the great game hall and was received there in somewhat the same manner one would have received the French king a few years earlier.

These homages delighted him. More and more, he revealed his ambitions through his clothing, his bearing, and his speech. The worst leaders of demagoguery stoked in his favor a popularity he believed was unshakable and eternal, and he already viewed himself as a dictator.

The principal regulars of the gambling house had been invited to supper at Émilie's request. But it was de Batz who had composed the guest list. Included was Barbereux, one of Robespierre's regular game partners. Robespierre considered Barbereux someone of exalted civism and intense conviction.

At the beginning of the meal, Danton's enemy appeared worried and preoccupied. He successively cast a suspicious glance at each of the guests. It was only when his gaze met the pure and sweet face of Émilie that his surly countenance lit up and his thin lips drew apart to form a faint smile.

"Citizen Robespierre!" said Madame de Sainte-Amaranthe. "Are those worries, intrigues, and threats of plots to which you alluded in those beautiful verses you wrote my daughter still preoccupying you?"

"Anyhow," Émilie declared, with a smile she forced to be inviting, "Citizen Robespierre is required to leave those things at the door for this evening!"

"Oh, Citizenesses," Robespierre declared in a very gentle voice, "why is it that establishing in the Nation that pure and simple life sung by the divine Jean-Jacques requires of me such a tormented existence? Tyranny has been uprooted, but its spirit still hovers and poisons everything!... If I abandon the struggle, the homeland is lost!... Otherwise, my desire would be to live in a cottage and enjoy simple, happy days woven with friendship and love."

"Friendship, you have that here, Citizen!" said Madame de Sainte-Amaranthe.

"And love is not far away!" added Barbereux.

"A simple soup!" continued Robespierre, who saw Émilie blushing, and thanked her by means of a glance for what he believed to be an admission. "Spring water flowing from the neighboring mountain to quench our thirst, would that not be happiness?"

A respectful male voice sang in his ear at that moment: "Moulin-à-Vent, 1785?"

A discreet, courteous, perfectly trained headwaiter was behind the disciple of Jean-Jacques, with a dusty bottle in hand, making his offers.

While Robespierre waited for the soup and spring water of future ages, he held out his glass, which the headwaiter filled to the brim. Robespierre dipped his lips and smelled the aroma, despite its date evoking the era of tyranny.

Dishes came one after another. After all other French traditions had been overthrown, one remained intact: French cuisine and its wise configuration. The country's new masters preached much about Spartan soup, but they in no wise practiced it; moreover, not one of them could have given the recipe to his cook or his chef. The national dish of Lacedaemon thus existed only in Jacobin discourse, where it was served with other republican nonsense.

After the crayfish soup, the four starters adorning the four corners of the centerpiece were brought out: pigeon pie, chicken à la "citizeness" (to avoid the old name of chicken à la queen), veal breast fricassee, and a piece of beef. Then came roasted partridges and a duckling. This was followed by a pâté and champagne truffles. Robespierre, in this warm and kind atmosphere, his eyes charmed by the grace and beauty of Émilie, surrounded by guests who listened to him and flattered him like a Caesar, satisfied by the good meal, and somewhat inebriated by the exquisite wines, ceased to be suspicious and worried, and felt his democratic rigorism softening. He even sensed a friend, supporter, and political admirer in the very respectful headwaiter, who approached him only to whisper in his ear the name of some celebrated wine.

His temples turned pink, he opened up, and a need to share confidences took hold of him.

At various instances, Barbereux pursued the following line of thought, upon which each guest in turn elaborated: "What the Republic needs is a man capable of shedding his blood for her, but who is also fit to embody her, to govern her in a way conducive to the people's happiness, to protect her against the intrigues of the counter-revolutionaries and deceitful men who exist in all parties, even in yours, Citizen Robespierre!"

This reflection tickled the proud rhetorician too much for it not to trigger, in this more relaxed state he was in, an admission of what was burning on his lips.

"Patience!" he said. "Patience!... I have been thinking like you for a long time, Citizen Barbereux!... It's just that I must be prudent! Breaking one by one the thousand chains my enemies tie around me! Since I do have enemies everywhere!" he added somberly.

De Batz sensed that the great man was launching into interesting confidences. He approached him with a bottle in his hand and whispered, "Chilled champagne! Cuvée Royale, 1788!"

Hating the old regime did not consist in banning wines specially produced for Versailles. Robespierre dipped his lips into the sparkling froth of the fine gold-trimmed Bohemian crystal flute, filled by the headwaiter; he then continued more cheerfully:

"To steer the ship of the Republic in the lanes of public interest, these lanes must be cleared of all obstructing impediments. The guillotine sees to that!"

"Oh!" started Émilie, with a sad smile and a pretty gesture of supplication. "Is the death of so many people absolutely necessary for the happiness of the Nation?"

"It is absolutely necessary, Citizeness!... And you can all the more trust my opinion since I am not, in principle, a supporter of the death penalty... I am even for the abolition of this punishment!"

"I would have thought the contrary!" said carelessly Madame de Sainte-Amaranthe, who was a ditz, as we know, and intended no malice in this sentence that came across as a witticism.

Had he been sober, Robespierre might have taken this remark very badly. But his dulled mind no longer grasped irony; he addressed this objection with the greatest seriousness: "How so, Citizeness? The first speech against the death penalty ever given in France was by me at the Constituent Assembly, on May 30, 1791!

"I said, 'News having been brought to Athens that citizens had been condemned to death in the city of Argos, people ran into the temples and begged the gods to turn away from the Athenians such cruel and baneful thoughts; I come imploring, not the gods, but the legislators, who must be the organs and interpreters of the eternal laws the divinity has dictated to man, to efface from the French code the laws of blood that command juridical murders and which are repulsive to their new mores and constitution. I mean to prove to them first that the death penalty is essentially unjust, and second, that it is not the most reprimanding of punishments, that it multiplies crimes much more than it prevents them...'"

Robespierre was animated and ranted his discourse like an old, hamming, third-rate actor reciting a monologue from a play in which he had once been applauded. Vain show-off that he was, he added, "That was one of my first successes at the rostrum!"

The indulgent headwaiter approached and refilled his flute with chilled champagne. Robespierre emptied it in one swig and very animatedly exclaimed, "Today, it is not a matter of punishment! It is a matter of giving life to a people who have languished for twelve hundred years in the stagnant swamp of tyranny! In the field of despotism which produced only slaves, we want to raise free men!... The wheat of liberty would be choked by the weeds of tyranny if the Republic did not keep a gardener at Revolution Square to uproot the weeds relentlessly, without respite, every day!"

He was inflamed and excited in his state of intoxication, like an ancient sibyl presaging and prophesying. Addressing Émilie, he cried out in a lyrical outburst, "I shall have my reward, and it will be my joy to make you a partner with me, to see you at my side, above all women, united to my destiny as Great Ruler of the One and Indivisible Republic and High Pontiff of the Supreme Being! For over the fanaticism of the past, I shall establish the worship of Reason and the Supreme Being, alone worthy of a great, regenerated people!... It is coming, this feast of the Supreme Being! You will be present at the procession I am preparing for it, Divine Citizeness Émilie!... I shall appear in the eyes of this French people, who have ascended from the degradation of bondage to the summit of glory and liberty, as a guardian protector of their institutions and their decadal cult, while the blood of those who sought to forge them new chains will redden Revolution Square."

Everyone listened in silence to this manifestation of madness and pride. Behind him, de Batz remained quiet and impassive, and to those who were in on the secret of the surprise ending and waiting for it, it seemed that the hand of the counter-revolutionary leader was already opening itself wide to crush this redundant lawyer, this indisputable ancestor of Joseph Prudhomme and Homais.

After this oratorial outburst, Robespierre succumbed to a kind of depression and considered realities. He then continued somewhat melancholically: "But the weeds are there!... Growing back as quickly as one uproots them!... Contaminating the wheat!... Many parts of the field of liberty had to be sacrificed!...

Chabot, Lacroix, Fabre d'Églantine, Bazire, Ronsin, Julien of Toulouse, and twenty others are on the eve of being guillotined!... Brissot, Hébert, and the execrable Danton will in turn be delivered to the executioner! It must be done!... The conspiracy from abroad will be struck also, it as well!... It has corrupted everyone!... The infamous de Batz is being sought out!... We will apprehend him this evening!... Where does his gold come from, if not from abroad?... Yes! Yes!... This evening!... He is done for!... He has no idea!... But the sword of the law is raised against him!"

Robespierre held out his glass to the headwaiter, who filled it with champagne. Émilie was white as a sheet, and Barbereux felt the hair on his head standing on end. But the neck of the bottle did not at all shake; it barely touched Robespierre's glass, so much did the hand pouring the champagne remain calm and in control.

"Émilie, my child, are you ill?" asked Madame de Sainte-Amaranthe, who did not at all recognize the new headwaiter as de Batz or suspect the cause of her daughter's paleness.

"Not at all, Mother!" answered the young girl in an anguished voice.

"Citizeness could take a little champagne, that would make her feel better!" very quietly advised the obliging headwaiter as he filled Émilie's flute.

Robespierre, already fired up, continued, as if the ideas that had been bubbling for so long in his head had found an outlet, and as if he felt relieved unburdening himself of such heavy secrets: "There is no doubt!... This foreign conspiracy has decimated my troops by corrupting them. I had to sacrifice many of my old friends to not be compromised with them... But the Jacobin Club remains intact; with it, I fear nothing. That is where my true bodyguards are. My citadel, that is the Paris Commune! Then, with de Batz taken down, I will finally see clearly; I will be able to crush my last enemies: Tallien, Barras, Bourdon of Oise, and Merlin of Thionville, who have already sharpened their knives against me!... That foul brood would tremble and be struck with terror if they knew what was in the drawer of my humble, little table; their files are already prepared for Fouquier-Tinville and the Revolutionary Tribunal!"

He made a gesture of triumph, became silent, and smiled at the thought of this future hecatomb. Barbereux proposed a toast to the glory of Robespierre, first citizen of the Republic, and to the death of the monsters seeking to obscure this glory. Robespierre accepted. As with any good parliamentarian, past, present, or future, the least pretext was enough for him to imagine himself at the rostrum, transform an engagement meal into an extraordinary session, cough up a political speech, and assume old-fashioned posturing.

"Thank you," he said to Barbereux, "for not having called me a dictator! I do, in fact, only want to be the first citizen, in other words the first servant of the Republic! Dictator!... What horrible use the Republic's enemies have made of this one name of a Roman magistrate! And how disastrous their erudition has already been for me!... Dictator! This word is starting to be hurled at me from everywhere! All the hatred and all the knives directed at fanaticism and aristocracy are thus aimed at me now! I am and only want to be, I repeat, the first servant of the Republic, the first one ready to sacrifice life itself for her!"

Turning towards Émilie, he raised his glass and said, "May I be excused, Citizeness, if preoccupation with public affairs has followed me to a gathering where a sweeter sentiment has called me. I drink to your virtues, the radiance of which shines upon your face... I drink to..."

But a commotion interrupted the new rant of the inexhaustibly loquacious orator.

A servant from the game hall, in fine livery, appeared, saying, "Citizen Duplay asks to see Citizen Robespierre about a very urgent matter."

"What could it possibly be?"

"The Convention, he told me, is holding a night session. Citizen Goupilleau is calling for the indictment of the Society of the Jacobins' leading members!"

Robespierre jolted. "What infernal hand is behind this vile ploy of my enemies, at the Convention, and precisely on the day I am absent from it!"

He hurried into the game hall to see Duplay, his carpenter landlord, whom a friend of Robespierre's had warned.

During the short space of time that the Jacobin was absent from the banquet room, Barbereux leaned towards the headwaiter and asked him, "Are they waiting for him down below?"

"No!... Rougeville is still by himself, stamping his feet in the gallery walkway to keep warm."

"What are they doing then? What are they doing?"

"I am starting to worry!"

At that moment, Cécile Renault gestured to the headwaiter from the half-open door. The latter hurried over, suspecting there was news.

"Monsieur Paul de Lézardière just arrived," she said. "He is out of breath and very pale! I fear disaster!"

The baron, worried, was taken by Cécile to the anteroom of the de Sainte-Amaranthe ladies' private apartments. There he found Paul, very emotional, in conference with Mademoiselle de Sainte-Pazanne, who had not been present at the supper and stayed in the servants' area to play her role as a maid. Émilie had also told her to keep her eye on Cécile, who had appeared agitated by Robespierre's presence, and who, behind a door, had not stopped listening to the Jacobin elaborating his ideas and revealing his proud designs.

"Finally," the baron said to Paul, "you are here! The others are down below, I imagine... Robespierre will be leaving to go to the Convention. Duplay will be with him."

"Alas, Monsieur!... He will be able to go very peacefully! No one will be coming!... Everyone has been arrested!"

"What are you saying?" asked de Batz, thinking he had misheard.

"The truth!... The house in Charonne was raided by two hundred fifty gendarmes!... We were surrounded like a net...

Marie Grandmaison has been taken prisoner. Also arrested were my father, my brother, Devaux, Biret-Tissot, and La Guiche! Everyone! Everyone!... They will be going to the scaffold! Only two were able to escape, Admiral and myself. I hurried here to warn you!"

"Curses!" said Cécile in a choked voice. "Our friends will be avenged, however!... And this very night!"

Paul sat down, exhausted and weighed down by a dark despair. With his face in his hands, he wept, in a decompression of his entire being before the work's collapse. His cousin consoled him. But the baron had already recomposed himself. Returning to the supper, where the guests were in confusion, he himself helped Robespierre put on his coat and escorted him down, at which point the great man hastily left with Duplay, to run to the aid of his last troops.

Madame de Sainte-Amaranthe and her guests went to the game rooms. Émilie remained alone with the baron.

"Everything is lost for us now, isn't it?" she asked, her voice trembling. "Poor Marie! They are going to guillotine her! As for me, I will have to marry that man, who has obviously prevailed!"

"Who has prevailed? When I am dismantling his Jacobin Club at this very moment! No, Mademoiselle!... Calm down! The fight is becoming bloodier than ever, but it isn't lost!... Leave tomorrow for Sucy-en-Brie and relax with your mother in the nice country house she has there. Robespierre will seek you there. Let him come! And allow me to do my work!"

"Oh! Anything you say! As long as I am freed of that man!"

"You will not marry him. I give you my word!"

The baron said goodbye to her, went back to the anteroom, shook Paul de Lézardière's hand, and said to him, "Be brave! We shall save them perhaps! If we do not save them, we will avenge them!"

"Oh! Yes!" said Paul, energetically straightening up. "We will avenge them!"

"See you tomorrow, in the boxes of the Convention, and be disguised! And don't spend the night at Rue de Savoie; they will be conducting a search there tonight."

He said goodbye to Mademoiselle de Sainte-Pazanne, who was still by her cousin, and left the Arcades House. In the gallery surrounding the Palais-Royal Garden, he found Rougeville conversing with a fierce-looking, wild-gestured colossus. It was Admiral, the very one who nearly served as executioner for the unfortunate Burlandeux. When the baron approached, Admiral did not recognize him and started moving away. The baron kept him: "Well, Admiral!... You escaped with Monsieur de Lézardière, the son, from the ambush?"

"You?" said Admiral, recognizing his voice. "You!... Monsieur Baron, the devil if I would have recognized you!"

"He was telling me what happened in Charonne," explained Rougeville. "An unfortunate setback, Baron!"

"Oh my," said the baron, "in fencing parlance or in a duel, this is what is called the double widow play. The two opponents thrust each other at the same time, leaving two widows... if they're married... We are wounded, certainly!... But Robespierre also has a sword in his chest. The Convention, which the Jacobin Club discredited, is now discrediting the Jacobin Club. The Revolution is now disgraced in its leaders. We will behead it by getting our hands on Robespierre, for we will get our hands on him!"

"But where?" asked Admiral.

"In Sucy-en-Brie. Leave it to me, Knight, to set a new trap for this tiger; the young goat is still here!... We have men out on assignment; they will return; not everyone was at Charonne. If Charonne is now in enemy hands, and if Marie Grandmaison, the good hostess of the Counter-Revolution, is now a prisoner, tell our friends to lodge here and there... I will pay for it!... As for our meeting places, they are the Convention, around the guillotine during executions, and here at the Arcades House when the game rooms are open..."

"Monsieur," said Admiral, "count on me for all of this and for the expedition in Sucy-en-Brie, but you won't stop me from thinking that now is the time for us all to each track down one of these monsters and knife him. We can purge them from the land!... See you soon, Messieurs!"

And he departed.

"That man is going to do something foolish!" said Rougeville.

"I think so also. What can I do about it?... He's already gotten himself out of lots of trouble. He's a former servant, he was also an office boy at the lottery. He has unfailing loyalty, herculean strength, indomitable energy, and is very clever, with his papers always in order: his certificate of civism, his security card, his rent receipt, and his patriotic contributions receipt. He often asks me for money—he gets the gendarmes drunk and extracts interesting information from them."

"He ought to have inebriated those who went to Charonne!"

"He didn't see them beforehand; otherwise, he would have!... Just so you understand better who he is, it would be useless to try to dissuade him once he has planned something. If he wants to do something foolish tonight, no human power can stop him!"

"Incidentally," exclaimed Rougeville, "I forgot to tell you about a news item that the newspaper criers were shouting an hour ago."

"What?"

"The suicide of Clavière, the former minister!"

"Devil!"

"He was your business partner."

"I know it!... Why did he kill himself?... Might his association with me be suspect? Did he fear the scaffold?... It was he who advanced me huge sums of money!... And although he was Swiss, it wasn't foreign money, despite what Robespierre says!"

After reflecting for a moment, he said, "Bah!... Clavière was a sad Huguenot whose only joy in life was climbing the next step on the ladder... In Geneva, he would have stayed a bank clerk. In France, he became a minister... There was no hope of him ascending any higher and he killed himself, no longer enjoying his time on earth. I knew him well. The richer he became, the more bored he became! Oh, Calvin did not teach his followers the art of being happy!"

Both arrived at the top of the Perron gallery. They boarded the carriage that was supposed to take Robespierre to Charonne as prisoner, and took it instead to Vaugirard, where Rougeville was living, across from the small St. Lambert Church, now destroyed, that stood at the corner of Rue Saint-Lambert and Rue de Vaugirard.

This home of Rougeville's still exists, I believe, as a part of the one belonging to Baron de Batz. Flowerbeds planted with carnations surrounded it. It was here that was cut the carnation offered to the queen and that brought her, in its stem, the illusory hope of freedom.

Chapter 9

Like Charlotte Corday

IN THE ARCADES House, where Émilie had given a room to him, since his family's mansion had become too dangerous, Paul de Lézardière, drawn by his cousin into a small, discreet room, far from the hall of the interrupted supper and from the comings and goings of the servants, gently repeated, "My poor father and poor brother are done for!... And I can do nothing for them!... The only one I have left in the world is you, Adèle!"

"Yes, my dear Paul!" Mademoiselle de Sainte-Pazanne replied with an infinite sweetness and deep, serene tenderness. "And I will not fail in the mission your dying mother entrusted to me. I will not abuse it any longer!"

"What do you mean by that?... And how could you abuse this mission?"

"By imposing on you actions incompatible with your happiness!... Paul, my grown-up child!... Your happiness will be my own... But I don't want mine to come at the expense of yours... No, no! Don't respond!" she said, as she placed her pretty hand over the young man's mouth. "I read you better than you read yourself, and I am certain now that you are loved..."

She was going to continue and elaborate on this misunderstanding with which she had ended up coming to terms, and in which she even tasted the savory bitterness of sacrifice, when Émilie entered, worried. Adèle became quiet upon seeing her.

Mademoiselle de Sainte-Amaranthe asked, "Have you seen Cécile at all?"

"Good heavens!... I lost sight of her amidst everything that has happened... Is she no longer here?"

"No one can tell me what's become of her!"

"Hopefully, nothing unfortunate happens to her!"

"That's what I was just telling myself!... Adèle, I have sad forebodings!... Don't leave me alone this evening. I sense that I am going to be crushed in this terrible battle that is continuing."

"Let's go!" said Mademoiselle de Sainte-Pazanne with the sweetest of smiles. "I must console both of you this evening!"

And she looked at her cousin and Émilie alternatively.

"Go to sleep, Paul!" she said.

She thought to herself: "And who will console me?... No one! With whom then can I confide what I am suffering?"

And she stayed with Émilie, who confided to her her intention to leave Paris and stay in Sucy-en-Brie, to facilitate a certain plan of the baron's.

"Will you come with us?" she asked.

"Certainly!... The house on Rue de Savoie is off limits to me, just as for my cousin..."

"You will often accompany me to Paris. The trip is not that long. One can go back and forth in the same day. Sucy is in the forest, south of the Marne bend, and there is nothing I find so beautiful as the forest in winter, when the dry leaves form a carpet!"

They chatted long into the night, forgetting young Cécile, who was at this moment the heroine of the most tragic adventure.

Cécile Renault, as though impelled by a will other than her own, had followed Robespierre when he left the Arcades House. Her head covered with the hood of her mantle and gripping the handle of a long knife purchased the same day as the queen's death, she shadowed the Jacobin as he walked to his domicile accompanied by the carpenter Duplay.

She saw them enter the building on Rue Saint-Honoré through the carriage entrance, which they left open. This detail did not surprise Cécile, who knew that the deputy would be going to the Convention. He had certainly stopped here to fetch some papers.

She entered the courtyard, which was poorly lit by a small candle in a glass lantern hanging on the back wall.

"What do you want?" asked Éléonore, one of the carpenter's daughters, who was coming out of her father's house.

"To speak to Citizen Robespierre. To speak to him in private!"

"At this hour?"

"Why not, if what I have to say to him is serious?"

"He's gone out!"

"I just saw him come back with Citizen Duplay."

"You won't be seeing him!"

"Why not? Being a public servant, he is meant to receive all those who come to him!"

Didier and Boulanger, two friends of Robespierre who had arrived from the Convention a minute earlier to bring news to their friend, intervened and addressed Cécile.

"You are very irreverent, Citizeness!"

"We ought to take you to the Committee of General Security!"

"In the old regime," Cécile proclaimed, "when you went to see the king, you entered right away!"

"So, you miss the time of the kings, do you?"

"Oh, I would shed my blood to have one... In my opinion, you are nothing but tyrants!"

"Arrest her!" said Didier. "She's a conspirator!"

"No, she's a lunatic!... Since she talks as if she were trying to get herself guillotined!... Get out of here!"

"All right!" said Cécile. "I am leaving, but I will be back!"

And she began going back towards the street. But this was a ruse. She hid in the thick shadow of the entryway, grazed the wall, went back into the courtyard, and, without being seen, slipped into the stairway from which Didier and Boulanger had exited, and which she assumed to be the stairway leading to where Robespierre lived.

The two men, during this time, had entered Duplay's home, and the courtyard was empty.

Cécile quietly snuck up the stairway. She stopped in front of a door through which she heard the voices of Robespierre and Duplay, then went up some more steps towards the floor above.

She saw Robespierre and Duplay exit. Robespierre had a bundle of papers under his arm and went down alone. Leaning over the banister, Duplay lit the stairway with a lamp. The door to the room remained open. As bold as any creature that was sacrificing its own life, Cécile slipped into the future dictator's room as quietly as a mouse and crouched behind the bed.

Duplay, having lit the way for his tenant, returned to the door, locked it with two turns of his key without entering, and went away with the lamp. Cécile was in darkness.

Feeling her way around, she searched for a chair and sat down. Coolly, she devised her plan.

She would position herself close to the door, and when the Convention member returned, she would strike him, without even giving him time to realize that she was there. She would then remain without fleeing; she would calmly explain to those who came to arrest her the act of justice she had just performed. If she fled, one might think Robespierre had been the victim of a private enemy, or of a madwoman. That, she did not at all want. She wanted to be arrested red-handed like Charlotte Corday, state the justification for the murder, and ascend the scaffold with her head held high, just like Charlotte Corday.

The crowds had marveled at that young Girondin woman's deed and courageous death. At that time, plenty were dying, and people attached a kind of pride to dying well, to dying beautifully, as they would say today. More than others, Cécile had succumbed to this allure of the scaffold, to this need to kill her own monster and to "live in history." The Roman attitude existed only at the Convention, and the glorious pedestal to which the executioner had elevated Charlotte Corday tempted, at the time, many female imaginations among whom antiquity's virtues momentarily prevailed over Christianity's. Who was it, moreover, who had created this ancient atmosphere, if not the Robespierres and the Desmoulins, admirers of Brutus?

Was it possible for a royalist woman to do what a Girondin woman had done? Cécile Renault proved it was. If it was a glorious thing to avenge Vergniaud and Barnave, was it any less glorious to avenge the king and queen? Fate seemed to be thwarting Baron de Batz's plans. Cécile would oppose fate and override its dictates. And if striking down Robespierre was to kill the Revolution, she would kill the Revolution. Was there any work more beautiful for which she could offer up her life?

Cécile pondered these thoughts in her mind, delighting in them. She wanted everything to be finished already; her work being accomplished, she would then only need to appear before the Revolutionary Tribunal, in front of those official massacrers. With what complete calm and peace of soul she would fulfill that last formality!

Then, a fear came to her.

"I am going to strike, yes! But what if it's not Robespierre who enters first?"

Cécile decided to hide behind the window curtains, and to only jump out and attack once she was certain it was the vicious animal that she wanted to purge from the land.

She acclimated to the darkness. A streetlamp that was swinging from its rope on Rue Saint-Honoré cast some light into the room, whose shutters were fortunately open. She made out the small table and suddenly remembered its drawer's touted dossiers on Barras, Tallien, Bourdon of Oise, and Merlin of Thionville. Robespierre had spoken of these files when he was drunk.

By some strange divination, did she deem these files might one day be useful for the cause whose triumph she wanted to die for?

She went to the small table and tried to open the drawer. It was locked. She forced it open with the powerful blade of her knife, took all the papers inside, without even trying to read them in the vacillating glimmer of the streetlamp, and hid them in an inside pocket of her hooded mantle.

Then, she sat back down on her chair.

How long did she stay there like that? She did not know. She was dozing, physically exhausted, when the clock of the nearby Assumption Church tolled three o'clock.

Men's voices in the street made her get back up. As she had decided earlier, she hid behind one of the window curtains. The noise of a heavy door closing, then of steps in the stairway, reached her ears. Robespierre was not returning alone. He seemed exasperated and was yelping in a falsetto voice.

"Dufourny under indictment! Renaudin under indictment! All of this is aimed at me!... But the Revolutionary Tribunal is mine!... Fouquier-Tinville belongs to me!... I will take down this Convention through terror. I will decimate it through the scaffold."

"Don't worry, Citizen!" said a voice Cécile knew. "Your worst enemies are in prison now, and this was just them spewing out the last of their venom!"

"No, because de Batz has escaped me!"

"I will deliver him to you, Citizen! I will take care of it!"

"Sénar!" whispered Cécile, recognizing his voice. "Sénar, here!"

Other voices and footsteps made themselves heard. Curses were exchanged, and Robespierre, in his falsetto voice, dominated all the cries with his threats: "I need an immense holocaust that will make all Europe tremble!... I intend to slay this foreign conspiracy as if it had but a single head!"

"You will have this holocaust, Citizen!" answered Sénar, who had become the Convention member's docile agent.

A key grated inside the lock, and Robespierre appeared, red and a little disheveled, as if he had endured a frenzied struggle at the Convention meeting.

Fast as lightning, Cécile darted forth, knife raised.

"Die, you drinker of blood!" she cried in a strident voice.

Robespierre let out a cry and brusquely moved to the side. The knife struck into the air, ripping only a sleeve of the orator's coat. Sénar rushed forward and grabbed the young girl's wrist. The citizens who followed in assisted him; they removed Cécile, exclaiming, "Where did this viper come from?... She needs to be crushed!"

"Daggers lie in wait for me everywhere!" shouted Robespierre, after his shock had subsided. "This must end!"

Sénar and the Convention member's companions, after having made Cécile descend the stairway, brought the young seamstress's face up to the hazy light that lit the back of the courtyard. A saber was already poised to strike her; a paving stone was going to crush her head. But Sénar recognized her and held back the assailants, saying, "She belongs to the sword of the law! And the Revolutionary Tribunal might discover her accomplices when they question her! Back away!"

They yielded to these reasons and contented themselves with insulting her. One of them took the young girl by one arm, and Sénar took her by the other; both removed her from the property. The others went back up to Robespierre, whose apoplectic clamoring echoed onto the streets: "Blood! Rivers of blood! To exterminate all these assassins!"

Now crammed in the back of a carriage between Sénar and the citizen assisting him, Cécile was riding to the Conciergerie.

Sénar said to her, "You unfortunate girl, it's not just your own death sentence you signed with the tip of your dagger. You signed your father's and your brother's!"

"How is that? They didn't commit any crime!"

"They committed the crime of having you as a daughter and a sister!"

Beneath the young girl's mantle, the police officer could feel the papers she had taken out of Robespierre's drawer.

"Uh-oh! What do we have here, Citizeness? Papers? Maybe conspiracy secrets? I will take these!"

And he confiscated them! Cécile cracked a small, nervous smile.

At the front office where she was taken upon her arrival, she came face-to-face with Admiral, who was guarded by four gendarmes.

"No luck!" Cécile said to him. "Everything is slipping away from us! I failed to get Robespierre."

In a hushed voice, Admiral replied, "And I failed to get Collot d'Herbois. We are going to die, Cécile! But we will be avenged! He won't escape what's awaiting him in Sucy-en-Brie."

He was going to speak about it more, but Sénar was listening. Admiral became silent.

"I have brought in a young fanatic of the tyranny who tried to assassinate Robespierre!" Sénar said to the concierge, who was seated in front of his prison registry book.

"Her name?"

"Cécile Renault!" said Cécile in a clear voice. "And add, Monsieur, that I wanted to avenge our king and poor queen, and that my only regret is not having succeeded in stabbing to death their executioner."

"Well!" said one of the gendarmes who was guarding Admiral. "This one tried this evening to kill Collot d'Herbois as he was returning from the Convention. He wounded him with a pistol shot; he was waiting for him at the top of his stairway on Rue Favart."

"This one," said Sénar, "was waiting for Robespierre in his room! How did she even get in there?"

"I will explain it to the gentlemen in the Revolutionary Tribunal!" answered Cécile. "It was very easy!"

A jailer took Cécile to the women's section. She said to him, "Monsieur!... Would you point out to me the queen's cell?"

As the man was taking her across a courtyard, he pointed to a foreboding window on the ground floor that was heavily barred.

"That's it!" he said.

"Thank you, Monsieur!" she said. "I am happy to be a prisoner like she, and to suffer so close to the place where she herself suffered so much."

And she looked at that window until she passed through the door of the women's prison.

Admiral, restrained in handcuffs, was in turn incarcerated in the men's section. He was resisting, kicking, biting, and howling!

It required eight men to subdue him.

The concierge, now alone with Sénar, said to him, "This similarity between the two assassination attempts is extraordinary! Might there have been a conspiracy?"

"I think so!... There was a raid and mass arrest in Charonne tonight, but some of the poison was away at the time!"

In the light of the office lamp, Sénar examined the papers he had seized from Cécile. His face suddenly assumed an expression of surprise and terror: "Devil!" he whispered. "This is serious... She took these from Robespierre!... Was she there to steal these?"

He asked himself, "Should I return these to Robespierre?"

He then said to himself: "No!... In fact, one never knows!... It might be good to hold on to these."

And he tucked the papers into an inside pocket of his large overcoat.

Chapter 10

The Chess Game

FOR WEEKS AND months, it was like one big chess game between Jean de Batz and Maximilien Robespierre, a bloody game in which each piece was a life, in which the opponents took heads like pawns, in which each of them was a king at either end of a chessboard seeking to checkmate the other, by delivering him to the executioner or by catching him in an ambush.

Danton, Chabot, Lacroix, and the Jewish Freys had been guillotined. Fabre d'Églantine had followed them soon thereafter. In the carts that followed, there were as many counter-revolutionaries as revolutionaries, and one might say that the two great adversaries were tied.

Arrests and denunciations occurred with increasing fury; the Cordeliers Club, thanks to the baron's mysterious hand, had joined the dance, accusing sometimes the Jacobin Club and sometimes the Convention, until the Cordeliers themselves were accused.

Robespierre decimated France, but de Batz, with his dagger, had ripped open the bowels of the Revolution. He had not beheaded it, but he had already disgraced it. He purchased its sons, then had them tirelessly accuse and denounce one another. The "purer" a republican was, the quicker that republican sold himself. That million no one had earned by rescuing the queen, the baron spread it widely, and it was as if he had sown pestilence and death into the enemy ranks. He would have eventually bought Robespierre himself, if the "Incorruptible One" had not had the higher and more consuming ambition of a dictatorship which would give him absolute power and the wealth of the entire country.

But fear sometimes tormented the master of the Convention upon contemplating his own massacres. If he was slaughtering the old France, he was also shedding torrents of blood in the new one, as if compelled by a power superior to him, and he had the feeling he would one day be all alone, without friends, before the implacable and uncatchable adversary. He had to purge, always purge, for de Batz had agents everywhere, and "suspects" even existed in the progressive parties.

Robespierre's destructive and vengeful rage was even targeting things. And after the deaths of Camille Desmoulins and Hérault de Séchelles in early spring, it is to this state of mind that one must attribute early Floréal's (late April's) imbecilic Convention decree ordering the "dismantling of the coronation carriage."

Fouquier-Tinville, the public prosecutor, was extremely busy. To please his master, each day he had to bring the Revolutionary Tribunal a copious batch of victims. He called the prisons his "reservoirs" and the Conciergerie his "pantry."

Beginning on Floréal 19 (May 8, 1794), there was no longer more than one revolutionary tribunal for all of France, the one in Paris, so that the scaffold would be most directly attuned to the will of none other than Robespierre.

His friend Saint-Just, backing his designs, had prepared this decision by declaring at the Convention's rostrum that "the weakness of judges emboldened the conspiracies."

The daily juridical massacres terrorized the Convention, maintained the republicans in passive obedience, and answered the assaults of the Counter-Revolution, provoking and threatening it.

But not one of Jean de Batz's confederates captured in Charonne had yet ascended the scaffold. Long weeks having passed since their arrests, Cécile Renault and Admiral were still in prison. The Robespierrist party was keeping them for a show trial and wanted to round out this lot of choice defendants by capturing other accomplices, notably the knight Rougeville and Baron Jean de Batz.

The holocaust that day would be colossal and make Europe tremble. It needed to coincide with the feast of the Supreme Being that would mark Robespierre's triumph as dictator of the Republic and supreme pontiff of the new state religion. Everywhere, the impact of this celebration needed to paralyze the Counter-Revolution, this octopus whose tentacles enveloped provincial France but had its head in Paris.

Meanwhile, the bloody chess game continued. Amidst the randomness of the carts ushered to the scaffold, royal blood spilled once again on Floréal 21, the day of Madame Élisabeth's execution.

The baron was plotting a decisive blow, and Robespierre, at the beginning of Prairial (late May), provoked him at the Convention rostrum without daring to name him, when alluding to the assassination attempts of Admiral and young Cécile Renault.

The anger and violence of the situation made Robespierre poetic; it was not a speech but stanzas he proclaimed to rally the French people against the Avengers of the King. He exaggerated everything, distorted everything, labeled a "poisoning attempt" the case of the gendarme who was put to sleep to save the queen, and laid blame for the Republic's bankruptcy and the famine on the conspirators.

"What remains for the friends of tyranny?" he cried out.

"Assassination!

"They thought to overcome us through the efforts of their sacrilegious alliances, and especially through treason. The traitors tremble and perish, their artillery falls into our power, their satellites flee before us, but they still have assassination!

"They sought to dissolve the National Convention through degradation and corruption; the Convention punished their accomplices and rose triumphant over the ruins of factions and with the support of the French people; but they still have assassination!

"They tried to deprave public morals and extinguish those noble sentiments comprising love for liberty and the homeland, by banishing from the Republic common sense, virtue, and humanity. We have commanded virtue in the name of the Republic. They still have assassination!

"Calumnies, treasons, fires, poisonings, corruption, famine, and murders—they have propagated all these crimes! They still have assassination, assassination, yet again assassination!

"Let us then rejoice and give thanks to heaven, since we have served our homeland well enough to have been judged worthy of the daggers of tyranny!"

Poor little Cécile Renault! How happy she would have been to hear this discourse!... Was this not the sound of her "entering into history"? Or better yet, as they said in the mythological language of the time, her "inscription in the temple of remembrance"?

The evening of the day this speech was delivered, Sénar went to La Force Prison to visit his old friend Dubois, of whom we have not spoken in some time.

He was now quite busy, Citizen Dubois; he was no longer the happily idle concierge we earlier saw spending entire hours in front of his fire.

Sénar had to wait for him in his office. When Dubois appeared, he gave the impression of a man who was drained and exhausted.

"Are you tired?" Sénar asked him.

"Who wouldn't be?" Dubois replied. "I just sent a batch of forty aristocrats to the Conciergerie for their hearing tomorrow. They are now being replaced by sixty-six whom I am supposed to lodge. I don't know where to cram my prisoners. La Force is packed to bursting point. Since having just one revolutionary tribunal, they have been sending us prisoners from every corner of France. I have here Bretons, Auvergnats, Flemings, and Marseillais, bewildered and exhausted by several weeks of travel, horribly ill and dying of hunger. Every morning I find some dead. For tomorrow, I've been told to expect a bunch of Carmelite nuns from Saint-Flour and some refractory priests from Orléans! Where am I going to put them?"

He sat in his armchair and put his feet up to the fire.

"Sending so many people to death and knowing that de Batz is not among them, de Batz whom I had at my mercy and who escaped me, this is what troubles me most!"

Sénar cracked a small, triumphant smile and, amicably patting the shoulder of his old accomplice, confided to him, "De Batz!... I came here precisely to speak to you about him! I intend to bring him back tonight!"

"You?"

"Me!"

"And how?"

"It's quite a story. I was just at Duplay's home chatting with him and waiting for Robespierre to receive me, since I am now his personal observer and confidant. He has unlimited trust in me, and I even think he trusts only me. A messenger entered and asked in a nasal voice for Robespierre, saying he had a letter to give him and that an immediate response was needed. Duplay asked me to accompany this messenger. He did not like the look of him; neither did I, in fact. Ever since the incident with that little reprobate Cécile Renault, they are distrustful at the Duplays..."

"Is she still in prison, this Cécile?" asked Dubois.

"Still! And her father, her brother, and an aunt of hers who is a nun have gone to join her. Anyone closely related to an assassin must be suspected. One never knows! And at the Renault father's home, they found a picture of the tyrant and his wife. So, I went upstairs with the messenger, whom Robespierre appeared to recognize, which reassured me. He received him right away and dismissed him a few moments later.

"The messenger came out with a letter in his hand, evidently the response to the one he had brought. He descended the stairs and went away. I did not follow him, especially since Robespierre asked me then to come into his room and confided to me, very happily, 'Serious business will wait until tomorrow, Sénar! I am worn out by all these battles I am fighting for the homeland; an opportunity for some rest has been offered me, and I am taking it. I am leaving in a half hour for Sucy, where I have been invited for supper, and I won't be returning until tomorrow morning.'"

Dubois abruptly got up and interrupted Sénar, exclaiming, "In Sucy?"

"Yes, he said in Sucy."

"In Sucy-en-Brie?"

"Yes!... But why this alarm, Citizen Dubois?"

"Continue!... And don't omit a thing!"

And Dubois appeared feverish.

Sénar, surprised, continued, "The name Sucy struck me as it did you, Citizen Dubois. Where then had I heard it?... I tried to remember, and I couldn't. I knew though that my mind had a reason for associating this name with a mysterious danger. Then, suddenly, it came to me. I thought back to the Conciergerie, to the night when I took Cécile Renault there after her parricide attempt..."

"Parricide?"

"I said that right!... Doesn't the new law liken the murder or attempted murder of a representative of the people to the crime of parricide? Doesn't it punish it as such?"

"That is true!"

"Admiral was there!"

"The one who wounded Collot d'Herbois?"

"Exactly. Cécile said to him, 'I failed to get Robespierre.' Admiral responded to her something like, 'They won't fail to get him in Sucy-en-Brie' or 'They'll take him in Sucy.' There is no doubt a trap was being set for Robespierre in Sucy-en-Brie! And who is behind it, if not the infamous de Batz? And the messenger was one of his confederates."

"Or himself!" exclaimed Dubois, who became pale and anxious.

"He only has two faces, and I know them both!"

"Who is to say he doesn't have a third? That man is the devil."

"That poor Burlandeux said the same thing... It is possible after all that that messenger was de Batz himself... His face did not sit well with me... Come to think of it, some of his features struck me as..."

"Get on with it! Continue with the story!" ordered Dubois, stamping his foot.

Sénar continued: "Robespierre was already calling one of the Duplay daughters for some clean laundry and formal attire. I said to him, 'Citizen, are you sure about that messenger who brought you the letter?'

"'He's the headwaiter for a family I know!' he said to me. 'A trustworthy man who I believe is loyal to me personally!'

"'Beware!' I said to him. And I recounted to him the scene at the Conciergerie.

"Instead of jumping at this, he seemed disheartened. I heard him whisper, 'Betrayed!... I would be betrayed then! And by her?'"

"Mercy!" groaned Dubois, who had sweat dripping down his face and wiped it with his handkerchief. "Go on! Continue then!"

"'Citizen,' I said to him. 'I have every reason to believe that instead of going to Sucy, it would be better for you to order a raid of the house you are supposed to be visiting. De Batz must be waiting there for you with his confederates. He wants to take you; it would be you taking him... The tables would be turned!'"

"You said that?" exclaimed Dubois, his face convulsing with terror and anger.

"Yes!... But what's the matter?... Why are you making that face?"

"You wretch!... Do you have any idea what you've done?... I myself see it very clearly!"

"But..."

"You have killed my daughter!... To put it simply!"

"Your daughter?... You have a daughter?"

"And you know her!... You miserable man!... Only you don't know that her mother and she left the Arcades House, whose aristocratic clientele are almost all behind bars!"

He advanced towards Sénar and, blinded by rage, grabbed him by his collar and shook him, crying out, "Because it is my daughter whom you love, it is Émilie de Sainte-Amaranthe!"

"Good heavens!"

"You have killed her!... Sucy is the location of her mother's country house!"

Sénar went down as though collapsing; he fell to his knees and, without defending himself, declared, "What have I done? Avenge yourself! Yes, kill me!... Greater punishment has already been given me, and death will taste sweet to me now. But how did she get involved in this infernal plot?"

Dubois let go of the police officer. He banged his own forehead with his fists, like a man who was hopeless and had gone mad. He let out some sparing phrases: "I didn't know myself... But now, I understand everything!... You did see de Batz at the gambling house!"

"Everyone was going there!"

"I ought to have suspected something!... He had an objective! He coaxed my wife and my child!... Robespierre loved Émilie!... He wanted to marry her... De Batz gambled with the life of my child!... Do you now understand?"

"Robespierre wanted to marry her?... You knew this?" exclaimed Sénar. "But then... you were deceiving me! You scoundrel!"

His passion for Émilie now prevailed over everything. He wanted to know more. Now was his turn to seize the jailer by the throat: "Did she love Robespierre?" he asked.

"No!"

"And you accepted the idea of this marriage? You forced her then, as a despicable and unfeeling father!... To benefit from Robespierre's power, you peddled him your child! But if you are Émilie's father, then that makes you the has-been Vicomte de Sainte-Amaranthe, the disgraced officer who cheated at gambling... You would exchange anything for money then!... You wretch!... Your honor as an officer and the happiness of your daughter!"

Dubois lowered his head, ashamed and trembling.

"De Batz knew my secret! Do you understand?" he stammered. "For a long time, I had to be careful how I treated him."

"I understand that you are vile and despicable through and through!" In a muffled voice, Sénar added, "Well! As for me, I love your daughter more than you have ever loved her! And I am going to prove it to you!... Your daughter, she is the star to whom I constantly lift my eyes, the enchantress for whom I would commit the worst crimes and the most virtuous deeds. One word from her would enrapture and transform me... She does not know me, does not love me, does not know who I am or even if I exist... Perhaps she loves someone... Today, that matters little... The scaffold threatens her. I want to save her from the scaffold!... A single smile from her, I will accept that as my only reward... She will marry whomever she wants! It does not matter whom, so long as she is happy! I want nothing more... Time is running out... Come with me!... Let us get two horses... Guide me to Sucy, and we will try to get there before Robespierre's henchmen!... I will forget everything! I will forget that you played me, that you exploited my love for your daughter to recover that infamous letter, I will forget everything!... But let us save her!... Come with me!... Let us go!"

Sénar was sublime; Sénar was eloquent. The La Force concierge obeyed.

Dubois threw his coat over his shoulders and grabbed his hat. Both left the prison, hired two saddle horses at a postmaster's in Faubourg Antoine, mounted them, and set off at a gallop in the direction of the Bastille.

They were excellent horsemen. Dubois, as we know, was a former officer. Sénar had served in the dragoons under the "tyrant." In the blink of an eye, they reached Charenton, then Créteil. One of the horses, out of breath, then made such heavy wheezing sounds that Sénar feared being unable to finish the journey.

"Is it far?" he asked anxiously.

"We are halfway there."

"Let's stop at this inn and let the animals breathe a bit. My horse is about to collapse."

Dubois agreed. He had the horses given some oats, asked for a bottle and two glasses, and poured Sénar and himself a drink. He emptied his glass in one go. Although not having uttered a word to his companion throughout the trip, he then asked him as though responding to an objection, "If you love her this much and Robespierre agrees to save her on condition that she marry him, what would you do?"

"I would thank Robespierre!... Her life comes first!... Before all else!... The thought of seeing her beautiful head roll beneath Sanson's blade breaks my heart and devastates me!"

"Then, yes!... Truly!... You will have loved her better than I... However, I never realized, until now, how much I do love her! I remember her so little, when my wife and I were still happy and carefree, and before I committed my unfortunate deed!... I remember her with her curly hair, climbing on my knees, being fascinated with my sword, already so pretty, a bit of an attention getter, with such adorable gestures and such a beautiful laugh!... I wanted to see her great, wealthy, married to the master of the new France, and reintegrating into the military or civil hierarchy her father who had been banished from the old society... I didn't reflect enough on whether it was her happiness I was seeking, or my own... She, throughout this time, not having fallen like myself, remained in her caste and was fighting for the old cause."

"And I, a triple imbecile, was fighting against her!"

"But if Robespierre captures de Batz, shouldn't he be so happy that he would perhaps pardon my wife and daughter for having been mixed up in this business?"

"Robespierre, pardon them?" murmured Sénar, shrugging his shoulders. "Believe me, it's best not to count on a pardon from Robespierre... It would be better to save de Batz when saving your daughter than to have both of them taken... Let's go! Onto our horses! Mine is rested."

They resaddled, and the fantastic ride continued on the great paved road of Brie-Comte-Robert. Shortly before Bonneuil,

Sénar's horse, overworked and wheezing, stumbled and fell. Sénar rolled onto the road.

"Ah, this cursed beast that postmaster gave me!" the police officer furiously exclaimed, getting back on his feet. He was covered in mud.

He prompted the horse back up with his riding crop. A country woman passing by cried out, "You have time!... You'll catch up with them... They aren't far!"

"Who?" asked Dubois.

"The troop you're running after, I assume..."

"There is a troop ahead of us?"

"A troop of gendarmes, yes!... There are over a hundred of them, and they are trotting at a steady pace... But you'll catch up with them!"

"Curses!" murmured Dubois, white as a sheet.

"She is lost!" groaned Sénar. "Ah, Robespierre issued his orders very quickly. It doesn't matter!... We will still try..."

He remounted his horse, and both headed towards Sucy, which they could see in the sunset on the wooded slope of a scenic hill, with its château whose tower soared above the houses.

"The property is isolated, in the direction of Notre Dame Forest!" Dubois indicated. "Let's bear right."

They entered some underbrush on their right. After five minutes, they heard in front of them some isolated gunfire, then a full-scale shoot-out.

"They're fighting!" exclaimed Sénar.

"They are besieging the house, which is being defended by de Batz and the men he stationed there to take Robespierre... That is the only explanation for this gunfire! What are we going to do?"

"What are we going to do?... You are asking?... We are going to throw ourselves into the melee and either save your daughter or die with her!"

"Let's go!"

They did not go far. They soon encountered a troop of gendarmes on galloping horses, surrounding a coach with lowered blinds that was heading towards Paris. Two sub-officers with sabers in hand did caracoles at the doors.

The procession passed before them like a whirlwind. Dubois and Sénar stopped their horses and looked at each other without speaking. But their terrified looks spoke volumes. The coach contained two female prisoners, at the very least. For Dubois and Sénar to attack the impressive forces escorting them would be folly.

However, the gunfight continued. They proceeded.

In the night that had completely fallen, Dubois recognized the property. Both flaps of its gate had been left wide open.

"Let's go in!" he said.

They crossed a small park and found the house deserted, empty from top to bottom. Like the gate, its door had been left open. In one room, a lamp was still lit. A harpsichord had its keyboard uncovered, and its music stand was holding the love song from *Philippe and Georgette*. Further away, an embroidery frame held a wool canvas in which a needle was stuck. On the floor lay a small handkerchief embroidered with the letter 'E.'

Sénar picked it up and hid it in his breast.

"They were arrested!... That is certain!" said Dubois, his voice choking. "Let's get out of here!... This is heartbreaking!"

The gunfighting continued in Notre Dame Forest, but became more distant.

As they left the park and wandered on their way, they discovered three corpses, two of them gendarmes and a little further away that of a man wearing top boots with a rifle next to him.

"If this was de Batz!" said Dubois. "No! It's not him! But he might be arrested as well!"

"Oh, what does it matter to me!" sobbed Sénar, as he inhaled the fine perfume emanating from the small cambric handkerchief.

The gunfire stopped completely. Galloping could be heard. Horsemen came out of the woods. They were again gendarmes.

"Who goes there?" cried a corporal upon seeing them.

They showed their civic and police cards.

"What happened here?" asked Dubois.

The corporal explained: "This was a has-been hideout that we raided. We arrested two women and a young boy without any resistance; that went fine!... A third woman, a maid of some kind, ran off while making awful screams. We pursued her. She went into the woods along this road and led us into a full-scale ambush, since we were welcomed with the gunfire of thirty rifles!... We fought back. The battle was fierce. They had horses. We killed two of them and wounded four or five... But it was impossible to arrest a single one!... They cleared out with that blasted spy woman!... We are rejoining our comrades."

And the gendarmes sprinted from the two, rushing to catch up with the coach and its entourage.

"They even took Lili!" said the La Force jailer bitterly.

Dubois and Sénar mounted their horses and returned alone to Paris in darkness.

"How do you explain what happened?" asked Dubois.

"It couldn't be simpler!... De Batz and his men were lying in wait outside. They were only waiting for Robespierre. Once he had gone inside, they would have raided the house and taken him... Oh, would to heaven that had happened!... And to think that it was my foolish denunciation!"

"Instead of Robespierre," continued Dubois, "it was gendarmes who came!... And the young woman who was able to escape took refuge where she knew she would find help! Everything is clear now!... Listen, Sénar, I have an idea!"

"Tell me!"

"Since you know Robespierre, could you beg him for my daughter?"

"I told you that I would be doing the impossible to save her. Yes, I will go find Robespierre!"

"Do you think you can convince him, and move him to take pity?"

"If he loves her enough, yes!... But a man like Robespierre only loves himself, his glory, and his ambition. And woe to anyone who stands in his way... It doesn't matter!... We must try everything!"

They returned to Paris in darkness. Sénar, upon arrival, ran to Robespierre.

Chapter 11

The Mines of Montmartre

THERE WAS GREAT commotion that night at the home of Robespierre. Letters were exchanged between his domicile and the Committees of General Security and Public Safety at the Tuileries. A certain Élie Lacoste, a member of the first of these committees, had been designated, at the inspiration of Robespierre, to draft a report that would be read at the Convention on Prairial 26.

This report would pertain to the "conspiracy from abroad" and "the accomplices of the infamous de Batz." The day after, Prairial 27, the victims would be handed over to Fouquier-Tinville. It was necessary to capture the public imagination and deliver the Revolution from its nightmare.

Fifteen minutes prior to Sénar's arrival, a gendarmerie officer came to recount to Robespierre the happenings of the Sucy-en-Brie expedition. Upon learning of de Batz's escape, the despot's anger was frightening, so frightening that the officer feared for his own head and prudently made a quick retreat on the pretext of having another work obligation to fulfill.

Élie Lacoste was also troubled by the setback: "How does one present the Convention a report on the de Batz conspiracy and admit our inability to punish de Batz himself?" he asked. "We would have to wait!"

"Wait for what?" cried Robespierre. "We have already waited too long!... We have sixty accomplices behind bars! Are they not a suitable and presentable batch to show the patriots that the conspiracy was active?"

"Certainly!"

"Make the list then…"

And he dictated to the reporter the names of the defendants: "Cortey! Biret-Tissot! Devaux! Roussel! The Lézardière father! Sylvestre Lézardière! Citizeness Marie Grandmaison! Nicole Bouchard, her domestic!"

"She's only sixteen years old!" objected Lacoste.

"She was at Charonne, in the hideout of the friends of the tyranny."

"Maybe she didn't know!"

"She ought to have known… Besides, she will add to the holocaust!"

And he continued: "The has-been Count de Marsan! The has-been Marquis de La Guiche! Michonis! The has-been Prince of Saint-Mauris! The has-been Marquis de Sombreuil! Montmorency! Pons! Du Hardaz d'Hauteville! Baussancourt! The Grinois woman! The d'Eprémesnil woman! The Renault father! The Renault son! Cécile Renault! The Renault woman, a has-been nun! Admiral!"

The names followed one another as if struck with death sentences, and Lacoste docilely wrote them.

Suddenly, someone knocked at the door. Sénar entered. He acted as if he knew nothing: "Well," he asked, "was my information good?"

"Very good! But de Batz escaped. We think he is wounded. The gendarmes only brought back his two accomplices, the Sainte-Amaranthes!"

"The Sainte-Amaranthes, his accomplices?" exclaimed Sénar. "His dupes perhaps, but not his accomplices! They are solid republicans, I can assure you of that!"

"Everything is against them!"

"One mustn't trust appearances!"

"You defend them well!"

"Because I swore to deliver you de Batz and I counted on those women to lure him…"

"If you operate in de Batz's circle, you automatically lose!… Besides, these women know secrets I divulged in their presence. They must die…"

"The Sainte-Amaranthe woman! Émilie Sainte-Amaranthe! The has-been Count de Sartines! The Lamartinière woman! Lafosse and Ozanne, peace officers who betrayed the Republic."

Sénar sensed that if he insisted while Robespierre was in his current state of mind, his name risked being added to those of his two colleagues just mentioned. He hardly cared to go on living, but he did not yet want to abandon the hope of saving the one he loved. He exited. But before going, what a hate-filled look he cast at that cutthroat!

Robespierre, in a cold-blooded rage, continued dictating, while annotating the charge before each defendant's name.

"Cardinal! Barbereux! Saintenac! Citizeness Lemoine!"

Lacoste interrupted him: "I don't recall that last name."

"Citizeness Lemoine-Crécy was denounced by another tenant in her building who overheard her shouting for joy upon learning of Cécile Renault's attempt on my life. I had her arrested in addition to her servant, a man named Portebœuf who said, 'Well, good for her!' You will also find on the list the name of Paindevoine, a porter at the old lottery building."

"What did he do?"

"He knew Admiral and met him on Rue Vivienne the day before his assassination attempt on Collot d'Herbois."

"But that doesn't prove he was part of the conspiracy!"

"That suffices to make him part of the batch. Lump all of them together, Citizen, and link them to their respective charges. Help yourself to my notes and prepare your report for the session on Prairial 26."

And he dismissed him.

At that moment, Sénar arrived at La Force, where Dubois was anxiously awaiting him.

"Well?" he asked.

"Well, I came up against a rock... He wants both of them to die!"

"We have only one hope left: that they forget them in their prison. I made inquiries; they were just imprisoned in the Old English Convent. There are some who are never talked about again and whose files get misplaced. Perhaps, with the help of some friends…"

And he questioned Sénar via the look on his face. There was something pleading about this look.

"Perhaps!" said Sénar approvingly. "We will try what we must. But if that doesn't succeed, there is only one thing left to do!"

"What is that?"

"Avenge her!"

Sénar left abruptly. He aimlessly wandered the streets, split between various conflicting ideas. At times he wanted to run to the Committee of General Security and try to convince them of the de Sainte-Amaranthe ladies' innocence, to mislead them and destroy their files; then he considered the futility of such bold action, the Revolutionary Tribunal having no problem issuing verdicts without prior hearings, without files, and without defendants even having lawyers. Then, sentiments of anger and vengeance crowded his mind. He had a vague inspiration to run to de Batz and say to him, "I killed Burlandeux for you. Let me take his place; I, too, thirst for the blood of Robespierre. I have come to help you destroy that murderer of women."

But where was de Batz now?… Oh, if he had known how near to him he was!

When Rougeville and the baron were lying in ambush in Notre Dame Forest, with thirty horsemen who were fortunate enough not to be in Charonne the night of the Arcades House supper, Mademoiselle de Sainte-Pazanne, dressed as a lady's maid, appeared to them, panicking and out of breath, crying out, "We have been betrayed!… The house has been raided by gendarmes… The de Sainte-Amaranthe ladies have been arrested… I was able to escape, but the gendarmes are right behind me…"

The small troop went into defense mode. Paul de Lézardière took his cousin behind him on his horse. Everyone fired and drove back the assailants. Only one was killed. But the wounded were numerous, and a final shot struck de Batz in the thigh and unsaddled him.

Rougeville dismounted and rushed to him: "My friend, my master!" he cried. "What is the trouble?"

"A broken thigh, I think!" answered de Batz. "The pain is horrible... Leave me and clear out of here! Rougeville, from now on you will command the Avengers of the King, at least what is left of them!"

"Abandon you like a dog? What do you take us for?"

Everyone jumped down from their horses and surrounded de Batz. Mademoiselle de Sainte-Pazanne, aided by a young man who had some knowledge of medicine, made a dressing with her lace-trimmed apron, which she tore in two. With an abundance of caution, the baron was raised onto one of the troop's gentlest horses, and they began the journey to Paris in darkness.

Rougeville led the way. He explained: "I lived for several weeks in the mines of Montmartre; it is a refuge inaccessible to the police, an asylum safer than emigrating. Outcasts and refractory priests have made it their home, and they worship there like in the Roman catacombs."

They skirted the Marne by way of Champigny, Joinville, and Vincennes, passed not far from Bagnolet and the Charonne house—that hostel of the Counter-Revolution whose hospitable hostess was in Abbaye Prison—and reached Montmartre by way of Saint-Ouen.

At daybreak, guided by Rougeville, they disappeared into one of the underground passageways which then haphazardly pierced and burrowed through the hill like a molehill, and which today are still the cause of so many landslides. The Mount of Martyrs was as though hollowed out through the centuries by sand and rock extractors, and we know that the Basilica of Sacré-Cœur stands on ashlar pillars supported by the deep floor of these ancient mines.

There, passages wound about, leading to vaulted excavations. They left the horses at the entrance to an underground passageway, with two men to guard them. They disappeared into the mines on foot. Rougeville, with the light of a torch, had a bed of straw and moss made for the baron, in a niche where he himself had lodged in times past. Coats completed the field soldier bedding. De Batz was settled there, and then someone left to find a surgeon.

Adèle de Sainte-Pazanne, seeing the Avengers leader stretched out, well covered and beginning to sleep, went to her cousin, who was seated not far from there on a rock, with his elbows on his knees and his face in his hands.

"Paul!" she said. "You are suffering!"

"Yes, I am suffering!... But I still consider myself fortunate," he said, "knowing that you are here... If you had been captured in Sucy, I would have felt my guardian angel was abandoning me... You are the only good that makes me feel I am still alive..."

"Right now?" she asked.

"Certainly!... Right now!... For everything is over for all those we love and who are in the clutches of Robespierre. If we had been able to capture him, he would have made a valuable hostage, we could have hoped to rescue almost everyone, we could have begun negotiations with his enemies, who are numerous inside the Convention itself!... But who warned him? Who told him to put his guard up?... My poor father! My poor brother!"

"They are the ones you miss most? It is for me then to say, 'Poor little Cécile Renault!... Poor Émilie!'"

"Yes! You are right!... Poor Émilie!" With a sad smile, he added, "You don't have much longer to be jealous of her... if you still are jealous of her!"

"No!" she said. "I am no longer jealous of her... I am being reasonable, finally!"

"I am happy to hear that... It pained me so much that you were able to doubt me for a time!"

"But you, have you ever doubted my deep affection for you?"

"Never!"

"Thank you, Paul, my grown-up child!... I shall perhaps prove to you, one day, that this affection was yet deeper than you ever imagined!"

She looked so serious that Paul de Lézardière looked at her with surprise, a little worried.

"Adèle," he said, "we have rarely had the opportunity to talk to each other. I was always traveling out and about, and you had your share of cares and excitement. For over the past year, we have almost always been separated. But why is it each time we speak with each other I sense a certain reserve, a serious and somewhat sorrowful tone that resounds in your soul and that in turn troubles my own?"

"Your mother commissioned me to be her replacement for you, and it is this role that is serious!... I must ensure your happiness, and I tremble at the thought of not succeeding..."

"You are such a child!" he said teasingly. "From the moment you loved me and I loved you, was not your happiness my own? Must settling our destiny be so complicated?"

She gave no answer. She had her idea, her plan. And Paul would not have the opportunity to question her further, since one of their friends had brought the surgeon, a reliable man who, upon examining the baron's wound, judged it less serious than had been assumed from the pain it caused. No bone had been broken, and no muscle had been injured. With some dressings and a few days of rest, the baron would be able to walk with the support of a cane.

While waiting for this recovery, the Avengers remained around their leader. It was from inside the mines of Montmartre that they followed the bloody tragedy Robespierre had prepared.

Chapter 12

The Day of the Sixty

THE REVOLUTIONARY TRIBUNAL was seated in the former Great Hall of Parliament, the one in which the *lits de justice* and solemn audiences had been held. The gold fleurs-de-lis painted on a blue background had been whitewashed, the beautiful velvet drapes emblazoned with fleurs-de-lis had been removed, and the impressive oak ceiling, a marvel of carpentry and sculpture, had been covered with canvas.

The public entrance to the Revolutionary Tribunal was in the large gallery known as the Salle des Pas Perdus, exactly at the location of the entrance to what is presently the First Hall of the Civil Court, to the left of the statue of Berryer, at the far end of the wall.

At about ten o'clock in the morning on Prairial 29, Year II (June 17, 1794), an immense and noisy throng crowded into the enclosure reserved for the public at the Revolutionary Tribunal. The ordinary defendant bench was replaced with large bleachers able to accommodate the batch for the day, the sixty accused in the de Batz conspiracy. This show trial had made all the populace come rushing.

A terrible "Ah!" filled the old Great Hall when a door opened and the accused entered one by one, each escorted by one gendarme, which made a total of one hundred twenty persons sitting on the defendant benches!

The first who entered was Admiral, a gloomy, withdrawn, and threatening colossus, who did not even look at the crowd.

The gendarme who preceded him had him sit in the stand beneath the bleachers, directly facing the tribunal. The others were seated on the bleachers as they came in. There was an extraordinary uproar. The public observers, who were clearly hand-picked, booed the defendants, chanted, whistled, and laughed. Biret-Tissot fiercely shouted back at this mob, and La Guiche hurled at them some bitter invectives. But silence came at the entrance of Émilie, whose beauty was proverbial. People jostled to look at her.

Once the defendants were seated and each separated by a gendarme, the Tribunal entered, feather-hatted and booted. First was President Dumas, who would mock defendants after they were condemned to death. He was followed by his assistant judges Bravet and Garnier-Launay. Fouquier-Tinville appeared at his table, wearing a Henry IV hat. His dark black and very thick hair and eyebrows combined with his small round eyes gave the impression of a sinister bird of prey. He had a low forehead, a full face, a short, pockmarked nose, thin, shaved lips, square shoulders, and bulky legs.

Near him was seated his deputy Lieudon. The court clerk was named Wolff… so appropriate!

Dumas, wearing on his collar a tricolor ribbon and on his head a hat with black feathers, ordered silence, told the clerk to read the charges, and proceeded with the questioning.

"Admiral, rise!"

Admiral stood up.

"Do you acknowledge making an attempt on the life of representative of the people Collot d'Herbois?"

"Yes!" the colossus grumbled. "And my only regret is that I failed to kill that scoundrel!"

"Sit down! Cécile Renault, rise! Do you acknowledge making an attempt on the life of representative of the people Robespierre?"

Without fancy speech, and even with a kind of sweetness, Cécile answered, "Yes! To avenge the queen! I consider Robespierre one of the most despicable tyrants in my country!"

To the others, the same question was asked. All responded, "No!"

The same question was even asked of sixteen-year-old Lili, whose young age had by no means disarmed the hatred of Robespierre!

Of these sixty defendants, about thirty-five were genuinely part of the de Batz conspiracy. The others did not know why they were there. They were therefore rather quiet. This one question asked of everyone constituted the entire questioning for the trial. The Revolutionary Tribunal simplified things. The Revolution, however, had promised more substantial safeguards for defendants than they had under the old regime!

"The floor is yielded to the public prosecutor!" said Dumas.

Fouquier-Tinville rose. And this was his address in full: "Citizen jurors, you have just heard the responses of the accused, and it is now up to you to give them your due consideration. I simply ask you to be mindful that this is the most important case yet submitted to the judgment of the Tribunal. I therefore commend this decision to your patriotism, and to your common sense."

This was incitement to kill, pure and simple, for these murderers, in their parody of justice, understood each other's insinuations.

Dumas thought it good to insist: "Citizen jurors," he said, "the defendants who are before you are foreign agents. The National Convention has delivered them to the Tribunal so that you will rule on their fate. Their denials will not deceive you. I think it unnecessary to remind you that the people demand vengeance of the monsters who sought to deprive them of two representatives they cherish. You will fulfill their expectations by deciding on the questions I am about to submit to you."

They were thus all accused of trying to assassinate Robespierre and Collot d'Herbois! The absurdity of the insinuation reassured most of these defendants, who were unaware of the cruelty and heinousness of the recent law of Prairial 22. It deprived the defendants of an attorney and empowered the jurors, a collection of scoundrels selected from lists of Robespierre's making, to judge according to their "love for the homeland," thereby giving them complete liberty.

Many of the defendants wanted to explain themselves and argue. But Dumas, in a curt voice, said to the gendarmes, "Take them away!"

They disappeared one by one through the small door.

The public recommenced laughing, chanting, and enjoying themselves.

The jurors had withdrawn. After a half hour, a bell announced their return. Dumas ordered the defendants to be brought back in. All, as they entered, looked at the president as though trying to read his face. But Dumas was joking with his assistant judges. They were very merry in the Revolutionary Tribunal, especially on days when heads were "falling like shingles," to use the expression of Fouquier-Tinville.

When the defendants were again seated, the president took from his desk the paper that the jury foreman, upon returning, had placed there, and read it amidst a deathly silence: "The declaration of the jurors is affirmative for *all* the questions with respect to *all* the accused; therefore..."

No one seemed able to hear the rest of the statement. Boos, sobs, and despairing and angry cries issued from throughout the defendants' bleachers.

Admiral bellowed: "We have not been tried! It is you who are the murderers!"

He waved his fist at Dumas, provoked Fouqier-Tinville, and would have lunged at him if the gendarmes had not kept him in place.

Dumas sneered; Fouquier-Tinville launched sarcastic remarks at the defendants; the entire Tribunal was gleeful.

Finally, the president resumed reading the death sentence amidst the tumult. He then gave the gendarmes a signal and brusquely exited, followed by his assistant judges. The trial had not lasted one hour! Not even one minute per defendant condemned to death!

The gendarmes brutally removed the condemned from the courtroom. The vile populace applauded. They in turn evacuated the Tribunal; the knitwomen and sans-culottes went into the Palais courtyard, ensuring themselves a place on the steps to watch the departure of the eight carts containing the sixty condemned.

These latter were already taken to the registry where the executioner was waiting for them, to prepare them for their beheadings. Some were morose and resigned, and others were bantering. Lili was weeping profusely. Émilie, expressionless and marmoreal, with her left hand resting on Cécile Renault's shoulder, was supporting with her right hand her faltering mother, who was terrified half to death.

Chapter 13

The Red Veils

A T THIS TIME, Sénar, alone in the Committee of General Security offices in the Tuileries, was consulting files, examining documents, and editing certain papers.

He nourished the insane hope of proving Émilie's innocence to Fouquier-Tinville by producing favorable documents and files attesting to her civism.

He was deep into his work when someone knocked discreetly at the door.

"Come in!" he said, as he hurriedly closed the files.

A young blonde girl entered, dressed like a laborer. It was Mademoiselle de Sainte-Pazanne.

"Citizeness! What do you want?" asked Sénar, rather harshly.

"Citizen, I was told one had to come here to obtain a card granting access to the Conciergerie."

"Who told you that?"

"A Convention gendarme stationed in the courtyard."

"He assumed you had the right to possess such a card! Since it is quite bold of you to present yourself here without a letter of recommendation! Additionally, there is no commissioner here, and I can't take it upon myself... Besides, you need to have a reason to enter the Conciergerie!"

"I have one!"

"What is it?"

"I would like to say goodbye to a friend who will go before the Revolutionary Tribunal today and who will, I fear, be condemned to death... unless the judges are lenient..."

"Oh, the Revolutionary Tribunal judges lenient!" murmured Sénar, not forgetting he also had someone dear to him whose head Fouquier-Tinville wanted. "And who is this friend?"

"Émilie de Sainte-Amaranthe!"

Sénar painfully shuddered.

"Who are you then?" he asked, with benevolent courtesy.

"I am a loyal maid of Citizeness Émilie de Sainte-Amaranthe!" she said, blushing. "My name is simply Catherine."

Sénar could clearly see she was lying. He responded, "So, you are not her friend!... Why didn't you originally tell me you were her maid?"

"But Monsieur... I thought I would more easily get..." She stammered and could not finish her thought.

This word "Monsieur," which was hardly civic, aggravated the suspicions of Sénar, whose brain was tirelessly working and drawing conclusions.

"Child," he said, "I am going to give you a card!"

"Oh, thank you!"

"Do not thank me!... I am only too glad that Citizeness Émilie de Sainte-Amaranthe can see a friendly face before leaving for the scaffold. But do me the favor of telling her that there is someone she does not know who would give his own life to save hers, and that her death will, in any case, be his own!"

Adèle looked at him, surprised. She had been expecting to be scolded, suspected, and harshly interrogated, but now she was facing this very sweet and tender man. Sénar himself, as he looked at her, called to mind a host of memories. Yes, this young blonde girl, who was a youthful image of the late queen, was she not the same one who had led the police on a false trail the day of a certain escape attempt? Émilie had reclaimed her as her servant girl and gotten her out of prison... What powerful motive was it this young royalist had for visiting Émilie today, at the risk of getting herself arrested? Did she have a mission? And from whom? The idea of a mysterious, unknown man loved by Émilie crossed the mind of the police officer, and it revolted him. But he reflected on how this visit might be one last consolation for the condemned one, and he did not have it within himself to deprive her of it.

Mademoiselle de Sainte-Pazanne, very moved and very confused, said to him at that very moment, "Certainly, Citizen, I will convey your message!"

Sénar scribbled some words on a printed card, put the stamp of the Committee of General Security on it, and handed it to the young girl. She left immediately, abundantly grateful. Sénar then reopened his files. But his thoughts were elsewhere. Eleven o'clock tolled. Then, flinging the papers away from him, he made a gesture of discouragement and murmured, "What good is it?... She has been sentenced!... Everything is over!"

He thought again about the strange young girl and her extraordinary daringness. He wanted to know what she was going to do at the Conciergerie. He rushed onto her trail and saw her in the distance, heading towards the Pont Neuf. She was moving quickly.

Fifteen minutes later, she had arrived at the Palais courtyard. Sénar struggled to follow her. She cut through the dense crowd, inquired about where to go, and paled with fright upon seeing the eight carts waiting. She showed her card to a guard, who let her inside the narrow courtyard, and came to the door of the Conciergerie's registry, which consisted of two rooms.

One, rather large, served as the office of Richard, the prison concierge, who had been able to keep his position despite Rougeville and Burlandeux's plot to save the queen. The other room was ordinarily reserved for holding the daily batch of condemned until their departure for the guillotine.

It was in this latter room that the executioner and his assistants came to cut hair, slice off shirt collars, and bind the hands—in other words, to dress up the future guillotined.

On that day, Sanson, whom Fouquier had warned well ahead of the trial, had arrived earlier in the morning with eleven assistants and the necessary materials.

Mademoiselle de Sainte-Pazanne saw these assistants enter with large baskets and ropes still stained with the blood of victims from the day prior.

Her courage failed her. She experienced a kind of disgust; she felt as though she had entered a slaughterhouse. She stiffened and attempted to pass between two of the basket carriers.

"What do you want?" she was bluntly asked by one of the two, a bestial-faced young man with no facial hair, between twenty and twenty-two years of age, his arms bare and holding large scissors.

Her teeth were too clenched and her throat too constricted from fear to say a word. She contented herself with showing her card. Another assistant with graying hair confirmed the existence of the Committee's stamp on the card and said, "It's in order!... Come in!"

But he held her back by her shoulder, and this contact made her shudder.

"You have a sweet, pretty face!" said the man, whose kind appearance contrasted with his sinister work. "I would hate for something unfortunate to happen to you. If I may give you some advice, don't lose your card, since you wouldn't be able to leave! You'd be getting on a cart with the others... It's happened. In this place, they don't check for a surplus of travelers!... It's not like at the stagecoach depot!"

And he went in laughing.

The young girl followed him, holding tightly the card in her hand.

She took a few steps and stopped; her legs could no longer carry her. Before her was a vision of hell.

She was surrounded by cries, wails of agony, groanings, and distressing sobs.

The condemned men and women were seated next to each other on benches, guarded by fifty gendarmes. Sanson was going back and forth, directing his assistants, who were cutting the top portions of shirts and dresses so that shoulders were bare, throwing helter-skelter into baskets clumps of hair, collars, and lace extracted with large scissor cuts from each of the victims, without distinction for age or sex.

Then, brutishly, they took the hands, drew them behind their backs, and tied them together with thick, red rope.

They acted with the indifference of cooks trussing a bird for the spit, or of butchers tying up an animal before the fatal blow.

Suddenly, she noticed, at the end of one of the wooden benches, Émilie de Sainte-Amaranthe, who was waiting her turn to be readied for execution. Mademoiselle de Sainte-Pazanne let out a cry, ran to her, hugged her, covered her with kisses, and said to her, sobbing, "I came to see you!"

The ravishing young girl maintained complete calm.

"Not wise!" she whispered. "What are you doing here?... And why, when God wanted to preserve your life, are you descending among the dead?"

"I've come to rescue you!" Adèle whispered in her ear.

"Rescue me? How?"

"I have a card from the Committee of General Security. Take it! You will leave... there is such chaos here that no one will notice a thing!... They will have their number—I am going to take your place!"

"Why?" asked Émilie, surprised. "This is bad!... I have gotten so used to the idea of death!... Why come here to call me back to life?"

"Because he loves you, and you will marry him!... His happiness before all else!... I promised his dying mother that... As for me, don't be sorry for me at all! I will die happy when I would have lived so unhappy! I can admit this to you now!... You can see it is for the best that I take your place!"

Émilie looked with surprise, not understanding.

"Adèle!... My dear child!... This is a bout of fever that has taken hold of you!... I don't understand what you are trying to tell me!... I must not profit from such a sacrifice!"

"It is for him that I am sacrificing myself!... I want to give you back to him!"

"To him?... To whom exactly?"

"To the one you love!... To the man who was at the Convention meeting!"

"To Elleviou?"

"To Elleviou?" repeated Mademoiselle de Sainte-Pazanne automatically. "Did you say Elleviou? Did I hear that right?... So, it is Elleviou you love!"

"I thought you implied it often enough!... Don't you remember that I refused to tell you his name to tease you, to punish you one day when you did not want to share a confidence with me?"

"Oh, good heavens!... And I was thinking..."

"Thinking I loved someone else, weren't you?" said Émilie de Sainte-Amaranthe with a faint smile, a smile which resembled the perfume of a rose ready to lose its petals.

"Don't make me say his name!... Oh, miserable fool, what a miserable fool I am!"

"What a miserable fool you *were*!" said Émilie de Sainte-Amaranthe, in a tone of ineffable kindness. "Oh, I understand now, your times of sudden hostility and your sad moods!... And yet, you loved me!... You were torturing yourself!... And all for lack of pronouncing two names dear to us! Yes, a miserable fool you were!... But how happy you are going to be!... My wonderful friend! My dear sister!"

"Oh, forgive me!... Forgive me!" said Mademoiselle de Sainte-Pazanne, kneeling down sobbing. "Forgive me the hate that I bore you, despite my efforts to overcome myself... I was suffering so much!... Oh, yes!... I was suffering..."

"Let's go! It's your turn!" suddenly said a harsh voice near the two girls.

An assistant had approached, with his rope and his basket full of blond, brown, white, and auburn hair, and women's braids randomly mixed with knots of men's hair still tied with velvet ribbons, some still powdered frosty white, others chestnut brown or jet-black.

Mademoiselle de Sainte-Pazanne stood up, scared and trembling, her eyes suddenly dry and fiery, while tears still flowed down her flushed cheeks.

Émilie, smiling and calm, although deathly pale, evoked at this moment the image of a virgin martyr leaving for the arena where the wild beasts awaited her.

"Goodbye!" she said. "It is my turn now to ask you something: to pray for Mama, for my little brother, and for me!"

Then, pushing away the assistant's hand which had swooped down heavily on her delicate head, she said, "I beg you, Monsieur, give me your scissors!... It's not to kill myself! Don't worry!"

She took the scissors from the hands of Sanson's associate, twisted into a thick braid her splendid hair, the admiration of so many Parisian women, and cut it with a firm hand, close to the nape of her neck.

Then, handing it to Adèle, she said to her softly, her voice noticeably altered by emotion, "You will give this to 'Philippe,' on behalf of 'Georgette.' This is my testament. My earthly affairs are now taken care of. From here to the scaffold, I will put myself right with God!"

"I'm sorry, Citizeness!" objected the assistant. "This braid belongs to us!... All the personal effects of the condemned go to the executioner."

"Oh, Monsieur!" said Adèle, taking a purse out of her pocket, through whose mesh three gold coins were visible. "Let me have this relic... Here is this in exchange!"

Sanson's assistant grabbed the purse.

"Fast pay makes fast friends!" he said. "Keep the braid, Citizeness!"

Then, he gently said to Émilie, "Citizeness, put your hands behind your back."

"This is horrible!" gasped Mademoiselle de Sainte-Pazanne, biting her lips to avoid bursting into sobs.

She then remembered she still had a task to fulfill: "The man who gave me this card," she said, "asked me to tell you that your death would be his own, and that he would have given his own life to save you!"

"That is the ultimate declaration of love!" said Émilie, with a melancholic smile.

She now had her hands tied behind her back. The executioner was cutting around the neckline of her clothing with hefty scissor cuts. There was a dreadful scream: "My daughter, my daughter!... Have mercy on my daughter!"

Behind Émilie, the frivolous and charming Madame de Sainte-Amaranthe, already groomed for the guillotine, annihilated, prostrate, and silent, had just then experienced a shock in seeing those large scissors come near the white, round neck of her daughter. She fell unconscious onto the shoulder of Admiral, who kept her up.

The Count de Sartines, himself tied up, and kept in place by gendarmes, tried to free himself and yelled at the man preparing Émilie: "Murderer!... Mercenary!... Get your filthy hands away from her!"

Lili, his hands behind him and seated on the ground with his back against his mother's knees, was crying like the child that he was, and Admiral was bellowing insults and threats against Fouquier-Tinville and Collot d'Herbois.

Mademoiselle de Sainte-Pazanne could not bear this any longer. She moved away like a madwoman. As she went further, she ran into Cécile Renault, whom she embraced crying.

"Don't feel sorry for me!" said Cécile. "I am dying like the queen. This is what I always wanted!"

Mademoiselle de Saint-Pazanne then heard her name called. Monsieur de Lézardière, the father, and his son Sylvestre, who were also tied up, were imploring her to come say goodbye to them.

Was it thus her entire life and all her past, with all her bonds of affection and friendship, that were assembled in this dungeon of death?

She ran to them and covered them with kisses.

"Oh!" she cried. "I feel I am being deserted! I long to leave with you, to flee this world where virtue, beauty, and everything that is good and decent is insulted, condemned, and put to death!... It's as if God judged me unworthy to die like you and with you!"

She was succumbing now, as Cécile had succumbed when seeing the queen's cart, to what Lenotre calls the "contagion of the masses," an illness particular to this bloody era consisting of an attraction to the scaffold, a feverish hankering to be executed.

"And Paul?" asked Sylvestre in her ear.

"Live for him!" added Baron de Lézardière. "Marry my son Paul! Teach your children how we died, for God and for the king... And now, my dear one, one last kiss, and then begone with you! Get out of here!... God wanted you to live! Do not tempt death!"

She fled, distraught and stunned by this spectacle of horror. And outside, in the courtyard, in the open air, this mental prayer sprang from her heart towards God: "My God!... Why must it be precisely on a day such as this that you return to me my desire to live?"

Émilie's confession had delivered her from the evil that had been eating away at her for eighteen months!

Despite everything, and although she reproached herself for this sentiment, she was happy that she was destined to go on living when so many of those she loved were on their way to death!

"Citizeness, dry your tears!" suddenly said a voice next to her. "People are already looking at you, and tears, in this place, are not civic!"

She recognized Sénar and instinctively put herself under his protection.

"Who are you?" she asked him.

"A miserable man weighed down by his own crimes, who is expiating them at this moment by a thousand sufferings." In a quieter voice, he added, "Did you see her?"

"Yes!... And I told her what you asked me to tell her. She smiled sadly and said, 'That is the ultimate declaration of love!' She is a brave and courageous soul!"

"And it was I who lost her!" Sénar said in a muttered whisper. "I will be getting on the cart with her!... Yes, I will be getting on it!... And it will be a joy for me!"

The crowd increased in size. The condemned had not yet appeared, and people were growing impatient. Rue de la Barillerie, on which the Palais's entrance gate was located at the time (not to be accessed via Boulevard du Palais until seventy years later), was a lively and turbulent ocean of heads.

It was June, and the blazing sun had brought out the bright clothes and parasols.

In front of disused St. Bartholomew's Church, which one can see on old Paris maps at the present location of Rue de Lutèce and Boulevard du Palais, was stationed the squadron of gendarmes on horseback who would be escorting the carts. The horsemen, with their feet on the ground and one arm through their horse's bridle, were smoking as they merrily conversed with passers-by. The street urchins were singing, whistling, and shouting. Licorice water vendors, which the crowds attracted, were walking to and fro, ringing their bells. Dust rose into the fresh air with the people's high spirits. One would have thought it was a feast day.

Deprived of their former Sundays which had been replaced by the short-lived republican calendar's "Decadays," and numbed by the solemn stupidity and off-putting Huguenot aspect of official ceremonies in honor of the Supreme Being and of Reason, the carefree Parisian people, who have a need to enjoy themselves, had scarcely anything else left to them, under the one and indivisible Republic, other than celebrations of the guillotine.

In the registry, which Mademoiselle de Sainte-Pazanne had just left, the concierge Richard was now signing the bill of transfer of the condemned to Sanson, which signaled their departure.

"Women first!" he ordered.

"Lean on me, Mama!" said Émilie to her mother. "And you, Lili, stay close to me!"

Several of the women were virtually lifeless. The brutal hands of the assistants seized them, forcing them to get up from the benches. There was already a gathering at the exit when Sanson, to whom a gendarme had just brought a letter, cried out, after having unsealed and read it: "We have a counter-order!"

The prisoners sat back down, surprised. In the small courtyard, one could hear a discussion and some swearing, and some of the condemned recognized the voice of Fouquier-Tinville.

A glimmer of hope shone in the eyes of the victims. Marie Grandmaison whispered in Devaux's ear: "Might this be a last-minute surprise from the baron?"

"With him, anything is possible!" Devaux replied. "But let's not get our hopes up!"

They were unaware that de Batz was bedridden, wounded, and powerless in the mines of Montmartre, under the watch of the last of his faithful.

The prolongation of their agony had been caused by an oversight of Sanson. Dumas had just reminded him of some legislative text. Fouquier-Tinville, for his part, was vehemently scolding the executioner and his eleven assistants.

Condemned as assassins of representatives of the people "cherished by the nation," the sixty were to be punished as parricides, meaning their shoulders ought to be covered with red veils. Bailiffs from the Tribunal and employees of the Conciergerie were thus scouring shops all over the city center to find some red muslin or cloth. They brought back bundles from which conscripted seamstresses began cutting out and stitching together various kinds of capes, shawls, and shirts destined to cover the busts of the condemned. Respect for the law is such a beautiful thing! That day, it meant inflicting an unprecedented several hours of moral torture on women and two children, the young Nicole and Lili.

It was not until four o'clock that they boarded the unfortunate ones onto the carts, which began their route to the Gate of the Throne.

They had no longer been guillotining at Revolution Square since Madame Dubarry had been dragged there on Frimaire 18, Year II (December 8, 1793) and filled Rue Saint-Honoré with her terrifying screams and desperate cries. So long as the sinister cart had only been transporting those who scoffed at death, made a show of courage, or were just stoics disdainful of their executioners, the neighborhood's inhabitants said nothing. But they started fussing the day a condemned woman began protesting, sobbing, and pleading. How true it is that touching man's heart often requires first getting on his nerves.

The Convention and its Revolutionary Tribunal, which rarely heeded movements of opinion, were concerned about this one. They changed the location of the guillotine. They thought that the brethren and friends of Faubourg Antoine, through which the carts would from then on pass, would be more easily accepting than Rue Saint-Honoré's more doubtful republicans of the daily patriotic spectacle of Fouquier-Tinville's batches. That was not at all the case. And the frightful holocaust of this Prairial 29, in particular, would provoke a general disgust.

Already, on Rue de la Barillerie, the festive and noisy crowd became glum and silent upon the passing of the first cart, which contained six women, including Cécile Renault, her nun aunt, Marie Grandmaison, and Citizeness Lamartinière. This last one was only there because she was on the stairway when Admiral shot at Collot d'Herbois, and she had fled terrified instead of helping to stop the assassin.

Cécile was calm and serene, as though liberated from all cares. She even seemed happy. Marie Grandmaison seemed to miss life; she was sad, and large tears formed on her long eyelashes.

Five other women were seated on the benches of the second cart, among whom were Émilie and her mother. Lili, in virtue of his young age, and due to an explicit favor of Fouquier-Tinville, who, we see, did have his moments of tenderness, occupied the sixth seat in this cart for the women.

Émilie was the focal point of all gazes. Confused murmuring, of both admiration and pity, circulated through the crowd: "Sainte-Amaranthe's daughter! Sainte-Amaranthe's daughter!"

From certain windows, lorgnettes were focused on her, as if at the theatre. The vivid red of her veil made stand out the pale white of her shoulders and the back of her neck which had been cleared for the chopper. Never had she been so beautiful. She shored the courage of her mother who was weakening by the second, going from one fainting episode to the next. And people have quoted this utterance of hers, heroic and charming for having been pronounced during such a Calvary: "Look, Mama, aren't these pretty, all these red mantles? We look like cardinals!"

Fouquier-Tinville himself, at Émilie's departure, had admired her strength of soul from one of the windows of Richard's apartment facing the Palais courtyard. He had with him there some members of the Committees of General Security and Public Safety, notably a certain Voulland, and he exclaimed, "Hell! I want to see if that wench doesn't break down before the end. I want to see her neck chopped, even if I do miss my dinner."

"Let's go out to meet them," replied Voulland. "*Let us go now, to the foot of the high altar, to assist at the Red Mass.*"

And they left for the Gate of the Throne, or, as they said at the time, Gate of the *Toppled* Throne. The spectacle would be worth the trouble. It would be the first time so many were killed in a single day.

The other carts were filled with men, the first holding the eldest and the last holding the youngest, who were, it seemed, extremely cheerful. They were being playful and shouting at the crowd, as if they were on a carnival float.

Only one of the condemned men there was shedding copious tears. It was Portebœuf, who was there for speaking some unfortunate words he did not think to be of significance. He still did not understand of what he had been accused or why he had been condemned to death.

Behind the squadron, beneath the burning sun, the carts slowly followed Rue de la Vieille-Draperie and turned onto Rue de la Lanterne.

Cécile Renault found herself in her neighborhood. She smilingly greeted some familiar faces on which tears were flowing. The sinister procession then crossed the Seine via Notre Dame Bridge and reached Rue Saint-Antoine, where the crowd became more and more packed. The windows were still filled with spectators. Silence fell as the carts approached. Men uncovered their heads.

Mademoiselle de Sainte-Pazanne and Sénar were following Émilie's cart, as though prompted by an invisible power. Both had a plan they were unable to communicate to the other. They did not take their eyes off Émilie's face, upon which there was now fixed this faint, sad smile which struck the crowd.

All of a sudden, Adèle saw this countenance become serious; those adorable eyes moistened with tears as her head gestured a farewell to someone in the crowd.

Adèle followed the direction of her gaze and recognized Elleviou, the handsome singer, who, with his face contorted, his fixed eyes beaming with a glimmer of madness, and his arms as though agitated by convulsions, had his hands joined in a gesture of commiseration.

Mademoiselle de Sainte-Pazanne rushed to him and handed him the braid of hair, which she had rolled and tied with a ribbon.

"This is Georgette's bequest to Philippe! I am relaying it to you!"

And she went away. Émilie had seen the short scene; she thanked Adèle with a nod of her head. Then, she lowered that charming head onto her breast and wept. Elleviou, faltering, had to sit down on a post, no longer able to bear the sight of this harrowing Calvary.

That was the end of their ethereal romance. Between them, there had always been the footlights of the stage. Between them now, there was death.

Near the Bastille, a powerful voice suddenly rose from the silence of the crowd. This voice cried out, "This many victims to avenge Robespierre?... Would the number have been greater if he were king?"

It was Sénar. Still escorting Émilie's cart and panicking seeing the destination nearing, he sought to get himself arrested. A little further, pointing to the two carts of women, he cried out, "These women are going to die because they know Robespierre's secrets!... Is this just?... No! Robespierre is a monster!... A despicable beast of prey!... A murderer!... Humanity expels him from its bowels!... Down with Robespierre!... Down with the dictator!"

He was waiting to be taken, arrested, and thrown onto a cart... And nothing!... Cries rose from the midst of the crowd, repeating his own, endorsing what he was saying: "Yes! Yes!... Down with Robespierre!"

And there was applause.

"Uh-oh!" he thought. "The great slaughterer is losing ground!... People are disgusted!"

For a long time, he continued shouting insults at the man of nature who, to regenerate a people according to Jean-Jacques Rousseau's own heart, had simply brought back human sacrifice. Then, weary from shouting and realizing he would not be arrested, he raised his hat, slowly and respectfully saluted Émilie, and kept his hat provocatively raised before the other carts, until they had all passed in front of him.

Sénar then looked all around him for Mademoiselle de Sainte-Pazanne. She had followed the carts to the entrance of Faubourg Saint-Antoine. But she had now become scared of the looming spectacle of executions and reversed course.

Sénar gestured like a man who had just made a firm resolution and rushed onto her trail, but without allowing himself to be seen by her.

"My last pursuit!" he whispered. "I do not know to what place she is taking me, but I do know to whom she will lead me!"

It was not until seven o'clock in the evening, at Throne Square, that the victims, having come off the carts, lined up in front of the wooden benches that were permanently installed at this place, given the numerous batches.

Nearby, one could see the already begun construction of a masonry gutter destined to directly carry into the Seine the flow of blood that was daily shed at this place to cement the foundations of the nascent Republic.

It was the time for farewells and final sobs. Cécile Renault was already ascending the steps of the scaffold with a firm step.

Barely had she made it to the platform when the assistants flipped her downward on the tilting board. It took two seconds, which seemed like a century, to adjust the headframe, and then the blade dropped. Someone let out a scream in the group of the condemned, as if all of them had had their heads chopped off at that moment. In a way, were not those waiting their turn dying multiple times?

The young Lili followed Cécile. One could not hear his cries at all; they were covered up by those of his mother, who was literally screaming to death, like an animal from whom its baby was being stolen. Madame de Sainte-Amaranthe fainted one last time when the executioners came to take her. It is possible Sanson dropped the chopper on a woman who was already dead.

It was then Émilie's turn. When the red veil covering her shoulders had been pulled off by the executioner, she appeared so imposing and so beautiful that the knitwomen and fawners of the guillotine, paid to insult the victims and cheer the Republic with each falling head, forgot their work. She was thrust into the blood of her mother and brother, and the same basket collected all three of their heads.

For more than an hour, without interruption, the blade rose to drop back down onto a neck. The blood went everywhere. It spurted from afar and flowed into streams, onto the ground and over the steps. The executioners on the platform walked in it, and their feet left red footprints.

The last one executed was Admiral.

But there had been, they say, one other death: a robust man, built like an athlete, had bet he could watch all the executions up close, in such a way as to take in absolutely everything of the horror they emitted.

He bore everything without batting an eye, except for one detail.

Marie Grandmaison's young servant girl Nicole, aged fifteen, with the name and little face of a comic opera soubrette, had manifested since morning only an astonishment and stupor out of which nothing could pull her. She could not get herself to admit that she would be killed. Why? When it was her turn, she moved forward, politely greeted the executioner, went to the board on her own, and asked very innocently, with little emotion, "Monsieur Executioner, am I on here right?"

The man who had borne everything spun around and crashed to the ground like a ton of bricks. He had to be carried to his home.

During this time, at this very hour, the Convention, which had ordered this festive day of revived cannibalism, was taking refuge in the realm of pure abstraction.

It was listening with heartfelt emotion to the humanitarian bleating of Roger Ducos, the future Directory member and future consul, who was speaking at length about philanthropy.

Lenotre underscores this contrast with his usual irony.

He also underscores that on the following day, Prairial 30, all the Parisian women were wearing red shawls and scarves *à la Sainte-Amaranthe*. Poor Émilie had launched a fashion trend which perpetuated the memory of her cruel Calvary. Her ghost haunted the streets, the Convention, the theatre, everywhere, much to the horror of Robespierre.

Chapter 14

Cécile Renault's Victory

BARON DE BATZ, on the night following this tragedy, was alone in his small niche in the mines of Montmartre, where he was finishing his recovery. His faithful were sleeping not far from there, grouped like encamped soldiers.

Mademoiselle de Sainte-Pazanne had recounted to him all the details of the horrible hecatomb. She was now taking some rest in a nearby niche she had arranged for herself, and where she had assembled a little pharmacy to care for the wounded one.

Illuminated by a poor candle forced into the neck of a bottle, the sad, desolate, and discouraged Jean de Batz ruminated, weeping over his dead and blaming himself for living.

The reaper had reaped, and severely within the revolutionary ranks, certainly!... But the enemy had also executed a red harvest in the royalist fields, and what a harvest it was!

The revolutionary hydra was still alive. All the slain heads appeared to have grown back. Jean de Batz had not destroyed the right one, the one in which the monster's life force resided.

A light noise drew him out of his reverie. He sat up straight, stunned. Sénar was in front of him!

De Batz was already putting a whistle to his lips. With a calm gesture, the observer from the Committees stopped him from calling, saying, "What good is it?"

"You are right!" said de Batz. "What good is it? Your mere presence here tells me that we are surrounded and that you have conducted a search of the mines to find the has-been Robespierre is looking for!... What good is it?... Your search has been fruitful!... Robespierre has won this bloody chess game!"

"He has lost it, Monsieur Baron!" replied Sénar in a serious voice. "The Sénar who is before you now is not the Sénar you saw one evening speaking with Dubois at the Arcades House."

"With Dubois?"

"With the Vicomte de Sainte-Amaranthe!... Your former jailer!"

"Oh! You know!"

"I know!... Yes!... The Sénar who is before you is no longer the one who is Robespierre's henchman. This is the Sénar who comes to deliver you that infernal monster of the Convention!"

And, unbuttoning his coat, he threw onto the baron's bed the files he had confiscated from Cécile Renault.

He explained: "Cécile Renault found them in the drawer of Duplay's tenant. Perhaps she was intending to hand them over to you... She is dead... They have nevertheless reached their destination."

"The files!" the baron whispered. "Oh! Yes!... At that supper at the Arcades House, she was listening behind a door... She was listening intently, with hate in her eyes!"

And he opened the files, skimmed them over, and gleefully tapped on them.

"How much?" he asked.

"I don't understand!"

"Ten thousand livres? Twenty thousand?"

"How much? Only the happiness of seeing Robespierre's head chopped off will suffice for me! And it will suffice amply!"

"What did he do to you then?"

"He killed a woman I loved!"

The baron, in the face of this game-changing development, recovered all his cheerfulness and loquaciousness.

"Obviously," he said, "this man is killing too many people. He troubles the living and does not sufficiently trouble himself about the survivors... Help me get up!"

Sénar lifted him and set him on his feet.

"I am standing all by myself!" said the baron joyfully. "This is the first time!... And with my cane, I will not walk, I will run!"

"Where are you planning to go?"

"You are asking?... To Tallien, Barras, Merlin, and Bourdon..."

"You don't waste any time!"

"Are you not eager to see Robespierre slaughtered?"

"Oh, yes!"

"Well then!"

The baron, holding his candle with one hand, and with his other a small mirror which he had owned since fighting in the Queen's Dragoons, looked at himself meticulously. "I have grayed," he said. "I have a fifteen-day-old beard. Leaning on this cane and limping, I'll look like an old dodderer. No one will recognize me, and it's unnecessary to disguise myself. Let's go!"

In the carriage he boarded with Sénar, at the bottom of the slopes of Montmartre, he had the account of the day's executions repeated to him. He said softly, "I had told each of them, 'Your life is but one mesh in the net I am casting.' Brave gentlemen! Valiant men of the people!... Heroic women!... Forgive me if the net tore up too quickly!... Perhaps I handled it roughly... But the sharks were terrible!"

At Blanche Gate, Sénar showed his security card; they entered Paris. By early morning, Barras, Tallien, Bourdon of Oise, and Merlin of Thionville were each in possession of the respective dossiers Robespierre had compiled on them, and they now knew the unenviable fate he had reserved for them. They did not know which carts they would be in, but they knew their carts had been prepared.

These four strapping fellows valued their lives; they evidently had already prepared themselves for a future brighter than the one Fouquier-Tinville had waiting for them at Throne Square.

All four met and in turn compiled files of their own. They were not taking little notes anymore but already using them. They capitalized on Robespierre's arrogant and already dictatorial attitude on the feast of the Supreme Being and prepared a parliamentary campaign which succeeded on the ninth of Thermidor.

Tallien was, on that day, the most zealous. It was known he had saved from the guillotine a charming woman with whom he was in love. Imprisoned again, this woman wrote Tallien this simple note on the eighth of Thermidor: "They are killing me tomorrow. Would you be nothing but a coward?"

Tallien was the one who, on Thermidor 9, at the Convention rostrum, dared to grab Robespierre by the throat and touch the idol. Many of the Convention members were perhaps surprised that he was not struck by lightning on the spot, and the "Incorruptible One," on that day, lost his prestige.

Defeated by a Convention vote and indicted, Robespierre took refuge in the Hôtel de Ville, his fortress, in the company of his brother, Couthon, and Saint-Just. The gendarme Merda, ordered to arrest him, broke his jaw with a pistol shot to avoid any resistance. Robespierre had forgotten "respect for the law." One gendarme reminded him of it. It is unclear why certain historians have pitied him so much.

On the following day, judged and condemned in fifteen minutes by his own creatures in the Revolutionary Tribunal, he was taken to the scaffold with his accomplices, lying at the back of the cart, his jaw wrapped in bloody cloths.

A furious, unleashed crowd booed him. Sénar stoked the crowd's hatred and amplified it tenfold.

The baron, leaning on his cane, saw Robespierre pass by, shook his head, and said, "Checkmate! Game over!"

Then, he addressed Rougeville, who was giving him an arm: "But it's thanks to little Cécile Renault that we won the game! This is her victory! I always thought, moreover, that the French woman would one day kill the French Revolution."

"She is equal to Charlotte Corday," Rougeville said approvingly. "She, too, killed her monster... She paid beforehand. The other paid afterwards. That's all."

Rougeville and the baron boarded a carriage and were taken to Rue de Savoie, to the de Lézardière mansion.

Paul de Lézardière and Mademoiselle de Sainte-Pazanne, both now orphans, had returned to the family nest.

The Reign of Terror was over, and the prisons were opened; the outcasts began to venture onto the streets and return to their homes. The expatriates, as well, pricked up their ears upon hearing the thunderbolt that struck Robespierre dead.

"Paul," Adèle said to conclude a long conversation, "do you know now who it was Mademoiselle de Sainte-Amaranthe loved?"

"Monsieur de Sartines?"

"No, Elleviou!"

"She loved Elleviou!" said Paul very slowly, his mind suddenly drifting.

"Now it's your turn to be jealous!" she said, smiling.

Then, extending her hand, as if to apologize for this bit of naughtiness, she said, "I will never resent you for thinking of her, and I will never be jealous of her remembrance. She was a great soul who never had on earth the happiness to which she was entitled. In fact, we mush cherish her memory! We must remember her courageous death, and the Calvary that she climbed!"

The baron appeared, supported by Rougeville.

"My work is finished!" he said. "But Lord have mercy, at what a price!... I have come here, children, to take in a less sorrowful and less somber sight of this Paris that I am about to leave.

"Here in this great family mansion, missing so many loved ones, you are the survivors of a diabolical catastrophe.

"Out of death, God draws life, and I see your young, pure love as a flower growing over graves!

"Graves, graves!... I see them as far as the eye can see... Were it not for you, I would carry with me through Europe a taste of blood and death. Thanks to you, I'll have a happier outlook for the future. When I return, an ancient stock will have reflourished here, an extinguished hearth will be rekindled, and I will be able to come here and warm my limbs, chilled by old age. I know I will find here friends with whom I can recall the terrible emotions of these bloody days. To their children, who will listen with wide-eyed amazement, I will tell this story, seeming to them legendary and distant, of the Avengers of the King!"

He embraced Paul, kissed the hand of Adèle de Sainte-Pazanne, and disappeared, still leaning on Rougeville's arm.

Eight days later, Paul married his cousin.

* * *

The contemporaries of this bloody drama only knew the spectacular and tragic outcome of a mass march to the scaffold.

Our own contemporaries are still unaware of the backstories of their own history. It required more than a century to pass over the events for Lenotre to write *Le baron de Batz*, and for a descendant of the baron himself, retired in his château in Mirepoix, in Gers, consulting his old family papers, to reveal so many unknown details in the fascinating books *Histoire de la contre-révolution: l'agonie de la royauté* and *La vie et les conspirations de Jean, baron de Batz*.

Putting those things aside, the Paris of 1794, carefree and frivolous as the Paris of today, was content to celebrate such heroism and suffering with the passing fashion of red scarves *à la Sainte-Amaranthe*. For eight days, it also lost itself in conjecture about the reasons for Elleviou no longer singing *Philippe and Georgette*, and never knew why this comic opera, which had continuously been featured with such stubborn persistence, suddenly ceased to be part of the Favart Theatre's repertoire.